D0085594

The Collected Works of

Langston Hughes

Volume 4

The Novels: *Not without Laughter* and *Tambourines to Glory*

Projected Volumes in the Collected Works

The Poems: 1921–1940

The Poems: 1941–1950

The Poems: 1951–1967

The Novels: *Not without Laughter* and *Tambourines to Glory*

The Plays to 1942: *Mulatto* to *The Sun Do Move*

The Gospel Plays, Operas, and Other Late Dramatic Work

The Early Simple Stories

The Later Simple Stories

Essays on Art, Race, Politics, and World Affairs

Fight for Freedom and Other Writings on Civil Rights

Works for Children and Young Adults: Poetry, Fiction, and Other Writing

Works for Children and Young Adults: Biographies

Autobiography: *The Big Sea*

Autobiography: *I Wonder As I Wander*

The Short Stories

The Translations: Federico García Lorca, Nicolás Guillén, and Jacques Roumain

An Annotated Bibliography of the Works of Langston Hughes

Publication of

The Collected Works of Langston Hughes

has been generously assisted by

Landon and Sarah Rowland

and

Morton and Estelle Sosland

The Collected Works of

Langston Hughes

Volume 4

The Novels: *Not without Laughter* and *Tambourines to Glory*

Edited with an Introduction by Dolan Hubbard

University of Missouri Press
Columbia and London

University of Missouri Press, Columbia, Missouri 65201
Printed and bound in the United States of America

5 4 3 2 05 04 03 02

Library of Congress Cataloging-in-Publication Data

Hughes, Langston, 1902–1967.
[Works. 2001]
The collected works of Langston Hughes / edited with an introduction by Dolan Hubbard.
p. cm.
Includes bibliographical references and indexes.
ISBN 0-8262-1339-1 (v. 1 : alk. paper)—ISBN 0-8262-1340-5 (v. 2 : alk. paper)—ISBN 0-8262-1341-3 (v. 3: alk. paper)—ISBN 0-8262-1342-1 (v. 4: alk. paper)
1. African Americans—Literary collections. I. Hubbard, Dolan. II. Title.
PS3515.U274 2001
818'.5209—dc21 00-066601

⊗ This paper meets the requirements of the American National Standard for Permanence of Paper for Printed Library Materials, Z39.48, 1984.

Designer: Kristie Lee
Typesetter: BOOKCOMP, Inc.
Printer and binder: Thomson-Shore, Inc.
Typefaces: Galliard, Optima

Contents

Acknowledgments

The University of Missouri Press is grateful for assistance from the following individuals and institutions in locating and making available copies of the original editions used in the preparation of this edition: Anne Barker and June DeWeese, Ellis Library, University of Missouri–Columbia; Teresa Gipson, Miller Nichols Library, University of Missouri–Kansas City; Ruth Carruth and Patricia C. Willis, Beinecke Rare Book and Manuscript Library, Yale University; Ann Pathega, Washington University.

The *Collected Works* would not have been possible without the support and assistance of Patricia Powell, Chris Byrne, and Wendy Schmalz of Harold Ober Associates, representing the estate of Langston Hughes, and of Arnold Rampersad and Ramona Bass, co-executors of the estate of Langston Hughes.

The editor would like to thank Morgan State colleagues Wendall Jackson and Caroline Maun, who read and commented on a draft of the introduction; Scott West; and Ruth, Aisha, and Desmond.

Chronology

1902 James Langston Hughes is born February 1 in Joplin, Missouri, to James Nathaniel Hughes, a stenographer for a mining company, and Carrie Mercer Langston Hughes, a former government clerk.

1903 After his father immigrates to Mexico, Langston's mother takes him to Lawrence, Kansas, the home of Mary Langston, her twice-widowed mother. Mary Langston's first husband, Lewis Sheridan Leary, died fighting alongside John Brown at Harpers Ferry. Her second, Hughes's grandfather, was Charles Langston, a former abolitionist, Republican politician, and businessman.

1907 After a failed attempt at a reconciliation in Mexico, Langston and his mother return to Lawrence.

1909 Langston starts school in Topeka, Kansas, where he lives for a while with his mother before returning to his grandmother's home in Lawrence.

1915 Following Mary Langston's death, Hughes leaves Lawrence for Lincoln, Illinois, where his mother lives with her second husband, Homer Clark, and Homer Clark's young son by another union, Gwyn "Kit" Clark.

1916 Langston, elected class poet, graduates from the eighth grade. Moves to Cleveland, Ohio, and starts at Central High School there.

1918 Publishes early poems and short stories in his school's monthly magazine.

1919 Spends the summer in Toluca, Mexico, with his father.

1920 Graduates from Central High as class poet and editor of the school annual. Returns to Mexico to live with his father.

1921 In June, Hughes publishes "The Negro Speaks of Rivers" in *Crisis* magazine. In September, sponsored by his father, he enrolls at Columbia University in New York. Meets W. E. B. Du Bois, Jessie Fauset, and Countee Cullen.

1922 Unhappy at Columbia, Hughes withdraws from school and breaks with his father.

1923 Sailing in June to western Africa on the crew of a freighter, he visits Senegal, the Gold Coast, Nigeria, the Congo, and other countries.

1924 Spends several months in Paris working in the kitchen of a nightclub.

1925 Lives in Washington for a year with his mother. His poem "The Weary Blues" wins first prize in a contest sponsored by *Opportunity* magazine, which leads to a book contract with Knopf through Carl Van Vechten. Becomes friends with several other young artists of the Harlem Renaissance, including Zora Neale Hurston, Wallace Thurman, and Arna Bontemps.

1926 In January his first book, *The Weary Blues,* appears. He enrolls at historically black Lincoln University, Pennsylvania. In June, the *Nation* weekly magazine publishes his landmark essay "The Negro Artist and the Racial Mountain."

1927 Knopf publishes his second book of verse, *Fine Clothes to the Jew,* which is condemned in the black press. Hughes meets his powerful patron Mrs. Charlotte Osgood Mason. Travels in the South with Hurston, who is also taken up by Mrs. Mason.

1929 Hughes graduates from Lincoln University.

1930 Publishes his first novel, *Not without Laughter* (Knopf). Visits Cuba and meets fellow poet Nicolás Guillén. Hughes is dismissed by Mrs. Mason in a painful break made worse by false charges of dishonesty leveled by Hurston over their play *Mule Bone.*

1931 Demoralized, he travels to Haiti. Publishes work in the communist magazine *New Masses.* Supported by the Rosenwald Foundation, he tours the South taking his poetry to the people. In Alabama, he visits some of the Scottsboro Boys in prison. His brief collection of poems *Dear Lovely Death* is privately printed in Amenia, New York. Hughes and the illustrator Prentiss Taylor publish a verse pamphlet, *The Negro Mother.*

1932 With Taylor, he publishes *Scottsboro Limited,* a short play and four poems. From Knopf comes *The Dream Keeper,* a book of previously published poems selected for young people. Later, Macmillan brings out *Popo and Fifina,* a children's story about Haiti written with Arna Bontemps, his closest friend. In June, Hughes sails to Russia in a band of twenty-two young African Americans to make a film about race relations in the United States. After the project collapses, he lives for a year in the

Soviet Union. Publishes his most radical verse, including "Good Morning Revolution" and "Goodbye Christ."

1933 Returns home at midyear via China and Japan. Supported by a patron, Noël Sullivan of San Francisco, Hughes spends a year in Carmel writing short stories.

1934 Knopf publishes his first short story collection, *The Ways of White Folks.* After labor unrest in California threatens his safety, he leaves for Mexico following news of his father's death.

1935 Spends several months in Mexico, mainly translating short stories by local leftist writers. Lives for some time with the photographer Henri Cartier-Bresson. Returning almost destitute to the United States, he joins his mother in Oberlin, Ohio. Visits New York for the Broadway production of his play *Mulatto* and clashes with its producer over changes in the script. Unhappy, he writes the poem "Let America Be America Again."

1936 Wins a Guggenheim Foundation fellowship for work on a novel but soon turns mainly to writing plays in association with the Karamu Theater in Cleveland. Karamu stages his farce *Little Ham* and his historical drama about Haiti, *Troubled Island.*

1937 Karamu stages *Joy to My Soul,* another comedy. In July, he visits Paris for the League of American Writers. He then travels to Spain, where he spends the rest of the year reporting on the civil war for the *Baltimore Afro-American.*

1938 In New York, Hughes founds the radical Harlem Suitcase Theater, which stages his agitprop play *Don't You Want to Be Free?* The leftist International Workers Order publishes *A New Song,* a pamphlet of radical verse. Karamu stages his play *Front Porch.* His mother dies.

1939 In Hollywood he writes the script for the movie *Way Down South,* which is criticized for stereotyping black life. Hughes goes for an extended stay in Carmel, California, again as the guest of Noël Sullivan.

1940 His autobiography *The Big Sea* appears (Knopf). He is picketed by a religious group for his poem "Goodbye Christ," which he publicly renounces.

1941 With a Rosenwald Fund fellowship for playwriting, he leaves California for Chicago, where he founds the Skyloft Players. Moves on to New York in December.

1942 Knopf publishes his book of verse *Shakespeare in Harlem.* The

Skyloft Players stage his play *The Sun Do Move.* In the summer he resides at the Yaddo writers' and artists' colony, New York. Hughes also works as a writer in support of the war effort. In November he starts "Here to Yonder," a weekly column in the Chicago *Defender* newspaper.

1943 "Here to Yonder" introduces Jesse B. Semple, or Simple, a comic Harlem character who quickly becomes its most popular feature. Hughes publishes *Jim Crow's Last Stand* (Negro Publication Society of America), a pamphlet of verse about the struggle for civil rights.

1944 Comes under surveillance by the FBI because of his former radicalism.

1945 With Mercer Cook, translates and later publishes *Masters of the Dew* (Reynal and Hitchcock), a novel by Jacques Roumain of Haiti.

1947 His work as librettist with Kurt Weill and Elmer Rice on the Broadway musical play *Street Scene* brings Hughes a financial windfall. He vacations in Jamaica. Knopf publishes *Fields of Wonder,* his only book composed mainly of lyric poems on non-racial topics.

1948 Hughes is denounced (erroneously) as a communist in the U.S. Senate. He buys a townhouse in Harlem and moves in with his longtime friends Toy and Emerson Harper.

1949 Doubleday publishes *Poetry of the Negro, 1746–1949,* an anthology edited with Arna Bontemps. Also published are *One-Way Ticket* (Knopf), a book of poems, and *Cuba Libre: Poems of Nicolás Guillén* (Anderson and Ritchie), translated by Hughes and Ben Frederic Carruthers. Hughes teaches for three months at the University of Chicago Lab School for children. His opera about Haiti with William Grant Still, *Troubled Island,* is presented in New York.

1950 Another opera, *The Barrier,* with music by Jan Meyerowitz, is hailed in New York but later fails on Broadway. Simon and Schuster publishes *Simple Speaks His Mind,* the first of five books based on his newspaper columns.

1951 Hughes's book of poems about life in Harlem, *Montage of a Dream Deferred,* appears (Henry Holt).

1952 His second collection of short stories, *Laughing to Keep from Crying,* is published by Henry Holt. In its "First Book" series for children, Franklin Watts publishes Hughes's *The First Book of Negroes.*

1953 In March, forced to testify before Senator Joseph McCarthy's subcommittee on subversive activities, Hughes is exonerated after repudiating his past radicalism. *Simple Takes a Wife* appears.

1954 Mainly for young readers, he publishes *Famous Negro Americans* (Dodd, Mead) and *The First Book of Rhythms.*

1955 Publishes *The First Book of Jazz* and finishes *Famous Negro Music Makers* (Dodd, Mead). In November, Simon and Schuster publishes *The Sweet Flypaper of Life,* a narrative of Harlem with photographs by Roy DeCarava.

1956 Hughes's second volume of autobiography, *I Wonder As I Wander* (Rinehart), appears, as well as *A Pictorial History of the Negro* (Crown), coedited with Milton Meltzer, and *The First Book of the West Indies.*

1957 *Esther,* an opera with composer Jan Meyerowitz, has its premiere in Illinois. Rinehart publishes *Simple Stakes a Claim* as a novel. Hughes's musical play *Simply Heavenly,* based on his Simple character, runs for several weeks off and then on Broadway. Hughes translates and publishes *Selected Poems of Gabriela Mistral* (Indiana University Press).

1958 *The Langston Hughes Reader* (George Braziller) also appears, as well as *The Book of Negro Folklore* (Dodd, Mead), coedited with Arna Bontemps, and another juvenile, *Famous Negro Heroes of America* (Dodd, Mead). John Day publishes a short novel, *Tambourines to Glory,* based on a Hughes gospel musical play.

1959 Hughes's *Selected Poems* published (Knopf).

1960 *The First Book of Africa* appears, along with *An African Treasury: Articles, Essays, Stories, Poems by Black Africans,* edited by Hughes (Crown).

1961 Inducted into the National Institute of Arts and Letters. Knopf publishes his book-length poem *Ask Your Mama: 12 Moods for Jazz. The Best of Simple,* drawn from the columns, appears (Hill and Wang). Hughes writes his gospel musical plays *Black Nativity* and *The Prodigal Son.* He visits Africa again.

1962 Begins a weekly column for the *New York Post.* Attends a writers' conference in Uganda. Publishes *Fight for Freedom: The Story of the NAACP,* commissioned by the organization.

1963 His third collection of short stories, *Something in Common,* appears from Hill and Wang. Indiana University Press publishes *Five Plays by Langston Hughes,* edited by Webster Smalley, as well as Hughes's anthology *Poems from Black Africa, Ethiopia, and Other Countries.*

1964 His musical play *Jericho–Jim Crow,* a tribute to the civil rights movement, is staged in Greenwich Village. Indiana University Press brings out his anthology *New Negro Poets: U.S.A.,* with a foreword by Gwendolyn Brooks.

1965 With novelists Paule Marshall and William Melvin Kelley, Hughes visits Europe for the U.S. State Department. His gospel play *The Prodigal Son* and his cantata with music by David Amram, *Let Us Remember,* are staged.

1966 After twenty-three years, Hughes ends his depiction of Simple in his Chicago *Defender* column. Publishes *The Book of Negro Humor* (Dodd, Mead). In a visit sponsored by the U.S. government, he is honored in Dakar, Senegal, at the First World Festival of Negro Arts.

1967 His *The Best Short Stories by Negro Writers: An Anthology from 1899 to the Present* (Little, Brown) includes the first published story by Alice Walker. On May 22, Hughes dies at New York Polyclinic Hospital in Manhattan from complications following prostate surgery. Later that year, two books appear: *The Panther and the Lash: Poems of Our Times* (Knopf) and, with Milton Meltzer, *Black Magic: A Pictorial History of the Negro in American Entertainment* (Prentice Hall).

The Collected Works of

Langston Hughes

Volume 4

The Novels: *Not without Laughter*
and *Tambourines to Glory*

Introduction

Langston Hughes, poet, playwright, novelist, short story writer, essayist, is one of the twentieth century's most distinguished men of letters. The recurring threads that inform his art and imagination center on black people's gift of song, story, and laughter, and "their struggle to achieve full citizenship."[1] In *Not without Laughter* (1930) and *Tambourines to Glory* (1958), Hughes shows us how the discourse of black America informs our cultural history and our appreciation of aesthetic American values. Hughes captures black culture in motion through blues in *Not without Laughter* and through gospel music in *Tambourines to Glory.*

Born on February 1, 1902, in Joplin, the county seat of Jasper County, Missouri, Hughes spent most of his first thirteen years in Lawrence, Kansas, living with his maternal grandmother, Mary Sampson Patterson Leary Langston. Langston's father, James, had abandoned his wife and children in large part because of the lack of opportunity available to African Americans, moving first to Cuba and then to Mexico. Although the black population in Lawrence was not large, the young Hughes experienced some of the racism associated with the post-Reconstruction South. At the time of his childhood, all blacks in Lawrence "were barred from formerly open churches, hotels, restaurants, and other social establishments."[2] The public schools reinforced this stigmatization. Black children were routinely seated in a row behind their white classmates when integration began in the fourth grade. Hughes would later refashion some of his childhood experiences and weave them into his first novel, *Not without Laughter.*

In spite of the "all-pervading desire to inculcate disdain for everything black" by a large segment of white Anglo-Saxon Protestant America,[3] Hughes's grandmother, then in her seventies, instilled in him a sense of pride in black achievement. Arnold Rampersad, his primary biographer, reminds us that Hughes was raised with the idea that "he had a

1. Richard K. Barksdale, *Langston Hughes: The Poet and His Critics* (Chicago: American Library, 1977), x.

2. Arnold Rampersad, *The Life of Langston Hughes* (New York: Oxford University Press, 1986–1988), 1:8.

3. W. E. B. Du Bois, *The Souls of Black Folk* (1903; New York: Penguin, 1989), 10.

messianic obligation to the Afro-American people, and through them to America."[4] This obligation later informed his manifesto of the Harlem Renaissance, "The Negro Artist and the Racial Mountain" (1926). In this essay, as elsewhere, Hughes raises both aesthetic and cultural questions as he examines the issue of the representation and the subject position of African Americans.

In "The Negro-Art Hokum," which was published in the June 16, 1926, issue of the *Nation,* George S. Schuyler, a prominent black journalist and satirist, argued that the black man in the United States was "merely a lampblacked Anglo-Saxon."[5] Therefore, he should create art in keeping with the mainstream Western European culture, which had shaped his consciousness. It was in the next issue of the *Nation* that Hughes published "The Negro Artist and the Racial Mountain." In this rebuttal of Schuyler's article, Hughes celebrates the contributions of the black masses and the attendant modes of expression—folklore, spirituals, sermons, and the blues—that emerged out of the slaves' experience, allowing them to counter the degradations of slavery and segregation.

Evident in *Not without Laughter* and *Tambourines to Glory* are ways in which an overarching blues aesthetic can reflect survival and recovery. Hughes celebrated the people "way down," the folks who were, as he wrote, "workers, roustabouts, and singers, and job hunters on Lenox Avenue in New York, or Seventh Street in Washington or South State in Chicago—people up to day and down tomorrow, working this week and fired the next, beaten and baffled, but determined not to be wholly beaten, buying furniture on the installment plan, filling the house with roomers to help pay the rent, hoping to get a new suit for Easter—and pawning that suit before the Fourth of July."[6] Hughes's mission was to represent the common people, differing from them only in superior vision, conveying his themes with simple, natural language that is grounded in signs and codes of black culture.

As a novelist, Hughes wrote with a bold simplicity of language. His novels do not reflect great technical proficiency or experimentation in form, yet they reinforce the patterns, themes, and tone of his best-known work. The novels are often, indeed, extended riffs on subjects that Hughes presented to stunning effect in poetic vignettes. Although

4. Rampersad, *Life,* 1:4.

5. In *Voices from the Harlem Renaissance,* ed. Nathan Irvin Huggins (New York: Oxford University Press, 1976), 310.

6. *The Big Sea* (1940; New York: Hill and Wang, 1981), 264.

he emphasizes characters rather than plot in his novels, these characters are not developed in copious narrative detail, and there is little studied reflection on the part of his characters or even his narrator. However, the discerning observer notes Hughes's commitment to a faithful realism in his depiction of black life. In *Not without Laughter* and *Tambourines to Glory,* Hughes transforms important aspects of the mythology of African American expressive culture, with its southern roots in music and religion, into narrative.

Not without Laughter

With the accolades still ringing from the publication of his first two books of poetry, *The Weary Blues* (1926) and *Fine Clothes to the Jew* (1927), Hughes began writing his autobiographical first novel, *Not without Laughter,* during his junior year at Lincoln University in Pennsylvania. Mrs. Charlotte Osgood Mason, his patron, served as advisory editor. Seeking inspiration, he turned to his boyhood in Lawrence, Kansas, where he had spent his formative years until the age of fifteen living primarily with his grandmother.

In *Not without Laughter,* Hughes offers a polite but firm critique of and corrective to the images of black people as depicted in the most sensational novels of the age: Carl Van Vechten's *Nigger Heaven* (1926) and Claude McKay's *Home to Harlem* (1928). He depicts the lives of common, working-class people who, because of the color of their skin, have been largely excluded from full participation in the American Dream.

Like Paul Laurence Dunbar's *The Sport of the Gods* (1902), the prototypical novel of black dislocation, *Not without Laughter* reflects on the fate of the Great Black Migration to the northern cities, the focal point also of later works by Hughes such as *Shakespeare in Harlem* (1942), *Montage of a Dream Deferred* (1951), *Simple Takes a Wife* (1953), *The Sweet Flypaper of Life* (1955), and *Tambourines to Glory* (1958). Hughes shows what it means to be black in America at the turn of the twentieth century and how members of a largely invisible community respond to their marginalization.

Unevenness characterized the critical response to *Not without Laughter.* Although V. F. Calverton praised the novel for its "quick and intimate reality which is seldom seen in American fiction," he noted its defects of style and weakness of structure; nonetheless, he saw *Not without Laughter* as a significant achievement because "even where it fails, it fails beautifully." Walt Carmon praised Hughes's first novel as a breakthrough book, a "definite contribution to both Negro and proletarian literature in America"—one that breaks with the tradition of Negro burlesque and vulgarization sponsored by Van Vechten. W. E. B. Du Bois gave Hughes's work a passing word in "The Browsing Reader," noting that *Not without Laughter* "touches dirt, but it is not dirty and it ends with the upward note. It is well written." James Weldon Johnson praised Hughes for being a rebel in content and in form, noting that although his work is often of the surface, he has "adopted the philosophy of the folk bards, makers of the blues. That philosophy consists in choosing to laugh to keep from crying."[7]

In this bildungsroman, Hughes movingly tells the story of a black boy growing to manhood in Stanton, a small Kansas town. The story chronicles the protagonist's experiences with racism, family, class, school, work, sex, music, and religion. His grandmother, a humble and deeply religious woman, struggles to keep her family (living with her are two of her three daughters, one son-in-law, and her grandson) together on the meager income she earns by taking in washing. Unlike Hughes's grandmother, who was well educated and had always been free, the uneducated Hager Williams (fondly called Aunt Hager) had been a slave in the Deep South until the Civil War. Although she is well aware of racism on the part of whites in Stanton, she believes there are some good white folks in the town. Well known in the community, this pious figure is respected by blacks and whites alike.

The black Hager, named for the biblical Hagar (Genesis 16:1–16), is a metaphor for the status of black Americans. Even though they have been dispossessed and alienated in the land of their birth, women like her have pooled their meager resources to build the institutions of black America. Hager Williams is the idealized figure of the humble but heroic black woman in Hughes's "Mother to Son," a classic dramatic monologue in American letters.

Hughes takes a satiric jab at the black bourgeoisie (who figure prominently in the novels of Jesse Fauset and Nella Larsen, among the leading novelists of the Harlem Renaissance) in the figure of Hager's daughter Tempy, who rarely visits her mother, and her marriage to Arkins Siles, a

7. Calverton in *The Nation* 31 (August 6, 1930): 157–58; Carmon, "From Harlem," *New Masses* 6 (October 1930): 17–18; Du Bois, "The Browsing Reader," *The Crisis* 37.9 (September 1930): 313, 321; Johnson, *Black Manhattan* (New York: Knopf, 1930), 271–73.

mail clerk in the civil service. From their perch above the black masses, the Sileses set the cultural tone for the community. Reared in the Baptist faith, they have left it and joined the tonier Episcopal Church. These ambitious black Protestants think of themselves as Americans who are black rather than as blacks who are Americans.

Annjee (Annjelica), who works as a domestic "on the other side of town for a rich white lady," is married to Jimboy Rogers, an itinerant worker and bluesman who hails from Memphis, Tennessee, home of the "Father of the Blues," W. C. Handy. When Annjee leaves to join the wandering Jimboy in Detroit, Sandy, their only child, remains with his grandmother in Stanton. After Aunt Hager dies, Sandy moves in with Tempy until his mother sends for him to join her in Chicago, where she is living alone while Jimboy serves on the front lines in France.

In Jimboy Rogers, Hughes gives the reader a portrait of the artist as a bluesman. Through Jimboy, who never loses his capacity to dream or to transcend his pain through the making of music, Hughes demonstrates his understanding of the complexities of the experience of black Americans. To most Americans, Jimboy, a blues virtuoso, is a failure, a nonproductive member of society. Playing music, however, enables him to distill into art the pain inflicted upon him because of the color of his skin. Jimboy's guitar is emblematic of black people's ability to use the gift of music to bring joy to an otherwise drab existence. Although she disagrees with his way of life, Aunt Hager understands the bark and cry of the blues that Jimboy and Harriett sing in the evenings on the porch. Through music and song, the blues singer externalizes the community's suffering—and the worse the odds, the better the song.

Like Jimboy, Harriett, who as the novel begins is working at the Stanton Country Club, rejects the constraints of home and dead-end jobs. His experience merely confirms her belief that, as Hughes wrote in his poem "Same in Blues," "There's a certain / amount of traveling / in a dream deferred." She, too, has learned well the lesson that blacks have few options in this world. Many of the best and brightest have migrated from Stanton to larger cities such as Kansas City, St. Louis, and Chicago in search of opportunity. Harriett, a gifted singer, arrives at a fork in the road. She can follow in the footsteps of her mother and sister and be a loyal, faithful domestic. She nearly ends up a prostitute, but another route out of this circumscribed existence is to become an entertainer, a blues singer. Jimboy compliments her singing by comparing her to the foremost African American stage artist of the early twentieth century: "You got it, kid. . . . You do it like the stage women does. You'll be takin' Aida Walker's place if you keep on." Bravely Harriett takes this difficult road, to the dismay and shame of her mother, who does not live to see her achieve success.

Sandy's experiences both in and out of school impress upon him the cruelty of racial discrimination, prompting him to say, "Being colored is like being born in the basement of life, with the door to the light locked and barred—and the white folks live upstairs." The more he understands the subtleties of segregation in Stanton and the lack of jobs available to him, the more he longs to "live first!"

With Jimboy away fighting in World War I, the financially strapped Annjee sends money for Sandy to join her in Chicago, where she lives in a tenement. Anxious that Sandy begin earning money immediately, she is ready to terminate his last year of high school and sacrifice Aunt Hager's dream of Sandy being a "great man" like Frederick Douglass or Booker T. Washington. Enter Harriett, the prodigal daughter, who has established herself as a premier blues singer. Now billed as "The Princess of the Blues," Harriett is determined to honor her mother's "great ambition" that Sandy, a young man of intelligence and sensibility, earn his diploma and "help the whole race."

Harriett, the one member of the family on whom the sisters felt they could not depend, now provides the means to enable Sandy to continue his education. Rescued by Harriett, Sandy leaves the reader with a sense of hope that against all odds he will become, in the words of his grandmother, "a great man" and a credit to his race.

Tambourines to Glory

Hughes, long an admirer of the black gospel tradition, perhaps conceived of *Tambourines to Glory* in 1945–1946, when he wrote a *Chicago Defender* column about "the arrival of the highly paid gospel singer as a phenomenon in black entertainment."[8] The towering stars of black gospel then were Thomas Dorsey, whose best-known composition was "Precious Lord, Take My Hand," which he penned in response to a personal tragedy, and Mahalia Jackson, whose lyrical raptures moved many to tears. *Tambourines to Glory* is a testimonial to the diversity and inventiveness of the black gospel tradition.

Hughes wrote *Tambourines to Glory* initially as a musical play to accommodate the superb arrangements of Jobe Huntley, the musically

8. Rampersad, *Life,* 2:255.

precocious son of a Baptist minister from Monroe, North Carolina. Always hard pressed for money, Hughes wanted to capitalize on the commercial values of this music, then largely unknown to white America. Among blacks, the gospel performers drew audiences that rivaled the popular singers and big bands. Hughes began *Tambourines to Glory: A Play with Songs* in July 1956, and then between August 24 and September 12 converted his play into a novel by the same name. Hughes described his play as "an urban-folk-Harlem-*genre*-melodrama" based squarely on the black gospel tradition."[9] Eventually, he would be hailed as America's first gospel playwright.

Set in Harlem, *Tambourines to Glory* is an urban folk melodrama based on the black gospel tradition—a fusion of Christian hymns and spirituals with the blues. It is composed of thirty-six short chapters that together form a dramatically meaningful whole. With a mixture of story and song, Hughes captures the spirit of newly transplanted southern blacks who bend the alien rhythms of the city to the gospel sound. He takes the reader on a tour of Harlem that glitters in the imagination.

Hughes's use of historical figures and events of the day fuels his satire of religion. Among the people he singles out are the noted white evangelist Aimee Semple McPherson, who became his nemesis following the publication of his poem "Goodbye Christ" (in which she is mentioned), and the equally notorious black clergyman Reverend Dr. Becton, both of whom he considered charlatans. He also refers, among others, to a writer who had once been a preaching sensation in Harlem, James Baldwin; jazz pianist Teddy Wilson; evangelist Billy Graham; singer Sarah Vaughan; and Ed Sullivan, who began his career as a sportswriter and then took over Walter Winchell's gossip column before becoming a television host in 1948.

As with *Not without Laughter*, the reviews of *Tambourines to Glory* were also uneven. Hughes's second novel was generally praised for its sparkling simplicity and humor, while being taken to task for its lack of character development. Richard Gehman commented on the cleanness and simplicity of this funny book that should be read aloud, which he saw as reaffirming Hughes's talent and his "belief in the miracle of human behavior." Arna Bontemps noted that while the story is ribald and effortless and as artless as a folk ballad, it is no joke. Hughes's writings had become even more of an "affair of the heart with Harlem." Although Gilbert Millstein praises the novel "as a sort of Negro Elmer Gantry,"

9. Ibid.

he considers it minor in light of Hughes's other productions. In one of the more perceptive reviews, John W. Parker notes that the "fusion" of thirty-six segments is more meaningful than the individual parts in this urban folktale that begins in medias res.[10] Thus, Hughes was praised for his fidelity to black life with a minimum of sentimentality and pathos while taken to task for his lack of character development.

The action in *Tambourines to Glory,* which could be subtitled "Let Us Prey," turns on the sham and pretense of two Harlem tenement women who, with their names on the relief rolls and time on their hands, set about to establish an independent, unorthodox, and personally profitable church. Essie Belle Johnson and Laura Wright Reed, two migrants to Harlem now on welfare, are third-floor neighbors in a Harlem tenement. Their windows looks out on "a courtyard full of beer cans and sacks of garbage." Laura is the more physically attractive; she loves liquor and men and relishes the sensual, sexy part of life. Fat, easygoing Essie sits and dreams of being able to afford to have her sixteen-year-old daughter come to New York to live with her. Essie represents sensitive and compassionate humanity caught up in this spiritual con game. She lights up their otherwise drab existence with her powerful songs that beat back, if momentarily, the stormy weather brought on by those weary blues.

From a joking suggestion of Laura's on Palm Sunday that they save souls to improve their finances, the two women begin holding street corner revivals, then set up church in a brownstone first floor, and finally move to a deserted moviehouse that they christen Tambourine Temple. Laura, whose grandfather was "a jackleg preacher," came to Harlem as part of the Great Migration. She understands the preacher's discourse and freely practices its "whoopology" in her shameless promotion of prosperity gospel.

These gospel racketeers—with Essie as the conscience of these partners in crime—at first set up shop on the corner of 126th and Lenox Avenue. They tap into the suppressed dreams of others like themselves who are down on their luck. They work with the knowledge that whiskey, loose women, the numbers game, and the Gospel of Jesus Christ make strange but often compelling bedfellows. After Laura hits the numbers, she uses

10. Gehman, "Fee, Free, Enterprise," *Saturday Review* 41 (November 22, 1957): 19–20; Bontemps, "How the Money Rolled In," *New York Herald Tribune,* December 17, 1958, p. 4; Millstein, "Laura and Essie Belle," *New York Times Book Review,* November 23, 1958, p. 51; Parker, "Another Revealing Facet of the Harlem Scene," *Phylon* 20 (spring 1959): 100–101.

the money to make a down payment on a Bible. The Reed Sisters, as they elect to call themselves, are now on their way. As they advance from their street-corner church to a thousand-seat theater with their names on the marquee, they pay off law enforcement officers and receive help from a shady character named Marty, a white fixer who greases the palms of the political establishment.

Character does take a back seat to plot in this morality play. The Reed Sisters move from incident to incident with little studied reflection. They desire to escape poverty. With a streak of altruism, Essie wants to improve the quality of life for many in the downtrodden community, but Hughes depicts Laura, who preys on her fellow outcasts without any remorse, as selfish, vain, and greedy. Laura is a cousin of Simple's garish girlfriend Zarita in *Simply Heavenly* (1957). Both crave male companionship; however, they are unable to establish a fulfilling relationship. Always one to enjoy the sins of the flesh, Laura dresses in style for her young stud Big-Eyed Buddy Lomax, whom she describes as her "king-size Hershey bar." He boldly tells her, "This church racket beats show business, baby—the way they're turning all the old theatres in Harlem into churches." However, this opportunist/businessman/lover has eyes for other women, especially the young Marietta, who is finally able to come from the south to join her mother, Essie. The evil Buddy overreaches one time too many; good triumphs over evil; and the saints rejoice and lift their tambourines to glory in the rousing finale.

Hughes explores various topics here, including the politics of migration, the underlying cultural politics of the storefront church, black sexuality, and the racial mountain. While much of the dramatic attention is on Laura and the evil Buddy Lomax, Hughes touches on a deeper problem. The majority of the members of storefront churches were there because they did not feel welcome in the mainstream Afro-Protestant churches. In resisting the institutional policing of the mainline black churches, they also resisted the standardization of music. These new migrants to the city actively transformed the musical canon, producing a dynamic interaction between established and emergent traditions of American music. Behind the humor and the light satire of black religion, Hughes draws into sharper focus the American fixation on race. Against the backdrop of singing and shouting and worship as spectacle, he draws into sharper focus the cultural astigmatism that blinds white America to the humanity of black people.

Although published twenty-eight years apart, *Not without Laughter* and *Tambourines to Glory* share a concern for working-class people;

both blend humor and music with protest and depict the weariness and pain of an unending search for freedom. In both novels, Hughes celebrates the contribution of the black masses and the attendant modes of expression—folklore, spirituals, sermons, blues, and style of life—that emerged out of the slaves' experience. In his celebration of the people "way down," Hughes provides the reader with a sense of the texture of life that made the spirituals and blues so potent.

A Note on the Text

In this edition of Langston Hughes's two novels we have used the first printing of each novel for our text. All capitalization, punctuation, and word compounding has been retained as they originally appeared, although obvious typographical errors have been corrected.

Not without Laughter

(1930)

To J. E. and Amy Spingarn

Contents

Not without Laughter

One

Storm

Aunt Hager Williams stood in her doorway and looked out at the sun. The western sky was a sulphurous yellow and the sun a red ball dropping slowly behind the trees and house-tops. Its setting left the rest of the heavens grey with clouds.

"Huh! A storm's comin'," said Aunt Hager aloud.

A pullet ran across the back yard and into a square-cut hole in an unpainted piano-box which served as the roosting-house. An old hen clucked her brood together and, with the tiny chicks, went into a small box beside the large one. The air was very still. Not a leaf stirred on the green apple-tree. Not a single closed flower of the morning-glories trembled on the back fence. The air was very still and yellow. Something sultry and oppressive made a small boy in the doorway stand closer to his grandmother, clutching her apron with his brown hands.

"Sho is a storm comin'," said Aunt Hager.

"I hope mama gets home 'fore it rains," remarked the brown child holding to the old woman's apron. "Hope she gets home."

"I does, too," said Aunt Hager. "But I's skeared she won't."

Just then great drops of water began to fall heavily into the back yard, pounding up little clouds of dust where each drop struck the earth. For a few moments they pattered violently on the roof like a series of hammer-strokes; then suddenly they ceased.

"Come in, chile," said Aunt Hager.

She closed the door as the green apple-tree began to sway in the wind and a small hard apple fell, rolling rapidly down the top of the piano-box that sheltered the chickens. Inside the kitchen it was almost dark. While Aunt Hager lighted an oil-lamp, the child climbed to a chair and peered through the square window into the yard. The leaves and flowers of the morning-glory vines on the back fence were bending with the rising wind. And across the alley at the big house, Mrs. Kennedy's rear screen-door banged to and fro, and Sandy saw her garbage-pail suddenly tip over and roll down into the yard, scattering potato-peelings on the white steps.

"Sho gwine be a terrible storm," said Hager as she turned up the wick of the light and put the chimney on. Then, glancing through the window, she saw a black cloud twisting like a ribbon in the western sky, and the old woman screamed aloud in sudden terror: "It's a cyclone! It's gwine be a cyclone! Sandy, let's get over to Mis' Carter's quick, 'cause we ain't got no cellar here. Come on, chile, let's get! Come on, chile! . . . Come on, chile!"

Hurriedly she blew out the light, grabbed the boy's hand; and together they rushed through the little house towards the front. It was quite dark in the inner rooms, but through the parlor windows came a sort of sooty grey-green light that was rapidly turning to blackness.

"Lawd help us, Jesus!"

Aunt Hager opened the front door, but before she or the child could move, a great roaring sound suddenly shook the world, and, with a deafening division of wood from wood, they saw their front porch rise into the air and go hurtling off into space. Sailing high in the gathering darkness, the porch was soon lost to sight. And the black wind blew with terrific force, numbing the ear-drums.

For a moment the little house trembled and swayed and creaked as though it were about to fall.

"Help me to shut this do'," Aunt Hager screamed; "help me to shut it, Lawd!" as with all her might she struggled against the open door, which the wind held back, but finally it closed and the lock caught. Then she sank to the floor with her back against the wall, while her small grandson trembled like a leaf as she took him in her lap, mumbling: "What a storm! . . . O, Lawdy! . . . O, ma chile, what a storm!"

They could hear the crackling of timbers and the rolling limbs of trees that the wind swept across the roof. Her arms tightened about the boy.

"Dear Jesus!" she said. "I wonder where is yo' mama? S'pose she started out fo' home 'fore this storm come up!" Then in a scream: "Have mercy on ma Annjee! O, Lawd, have mercy on this chile's mamma! Have mercy on all ma chillens! Ma Harriett, an' ma Tempy, an' ma Annjee, what's maybe all of 'em out in de storm! O, Lawd!"

A dry crack of lightning split the darkness, and the boy began to wail. Then the rain broke. The old woman could not see the crying child she held, nor could the boy hear the broken voice of his grandmother, who had begun to pray as the rain crashed through the inky blackness. For a long while it roared on the roof of the house and pounded at the windows, until finally the two within became silent, hushing their cries. Then only the lashing noise of the water, coupled with the feeling that something terrible was happening, or had already happened, filled the evening air.

After the rain the moon rose clear and bright and the clouds disappeared from the lately troubled sky. The stars sparkled calmly above the havoc of the storm, and it was still early evening as people emerged from their houses and began to investigate the damage brought by the twisting cyclone that had come with the sunset. Through the rubbish-filled streets men drove slowly with horse and buggy or automobile. The fire-engine was out, banging away, and the soft tang-tang-tang of the motor ambulance could be heard in the distance carrying off the injured.

Black Aunt Hager and her brown grandson put their rubbers on and stood in the water-soaked front yard looking at the porchless house where they lived. Platform, steps, pillars, roof, and all had been blown away. Not a semblance of a porch was left and the front door opened bare into the yard. It was grotesque and funny. Hager laughed.

"Cyclone sho did a good job," she said. "Looks like I ain't never had no porch."

Madam de Carter, from next door, came across the grass, her large mouth full of chattering sympathy for her neighbor.

"But praise God for sparing our lives! It might've been worse, Sister Williams! It might've been much more calamitouser! As it is, I lost nothin' more'n a chimney and two wash-tubs which was settin' in the back yard. A few trees broke down don't 'mount to nothin'. We's livin', ain't we? And we's more importanter than trees is any day!" Her gold teeth sparkled in the moonlight.

" 'Deed so," agreed Hager emphatically. "Let's move on down de block, Sister, an' see what mo' de Lawd has 'stroyed or spared this evenin'. He's gin us plenty moonlight after de storm so we po' humans can see this lesson o' His'n to a sinful world."

The two elderly colored women picked their way about on the wet walk, littered with twigs and branches of broken foliage. The little brown boy followed, with his eyes wide at the sight of baby-carriages, window-sashes, shingles, and tree-limbs scattered about in the roadway. Large numbers of people were out, some standing on porches, some carrying lanterns, picking up useful articles from the streets, some wringing their hands in a daze.

Near the corner a small crowd had gathered quietly.

"Mis' Gavitt's killed," somebody said.

"Lawd help!" burst from Aunt Hager and Madam de Carter simultaneously.

"Mister and Mis' Gavitt's both dead," added a nervous young white man, bursting with the news. "We live next door to 'em, and their house turned clean over! Came near hitting us and breaking our side-wall in."

"Have mercy!" said the two women, but Sandy slipped away from his grandmother and pushed through the crowd. He ran round the corner to where he could see the overturned house of the unfortunate Gavitts.

Good white folks, the Gavitts, Aunt Hager had often said, and now their large frame dwelling lay on its side like a doll's mansion, with broken furniture strewn carelessly on the wet lawn —and they were dead. Sandy saw a piano flat on its back in the grass. Its ivory keys gleamed in the moonlight like grinning teeth, and the strange sight made his little body shiver, so he hurried back through the crowd looking for his grandmother. As he passed the corner, he heard a woman sobbing hysterically within the wide house there.

His grandmother was no longer standing where he had left her, but he found Madam de Carter and took hold of her hand. She was in the midst of a group of excited white and colored women. One frail old lady was saying in a high determined voice that she had never seen a cyclone like this in her whole life, and she had lived here in Kansas, if you please, going on seventy-three years. Madam de Carter, chattering nervously, began to tell them how she had recognized its coming and had rushed to the cellar the minute she saw the sky turn green. She had not come up until the rain stopped, so frightened had she been. She was extravagantly enjoying the telling of her fears as Sandy kept tugging at her hand.

"Where's my grandma?" he demanded. Madam de Carter, however, did not cease talking to answer his question.

"What do you want, sonny?" finally one of the white women asked, bending down when he looked as if he were about to cry. "Aunt Hager? . . . Why, she's inside helping them calm poor Mrs. Gavitt's niece. Your grandmother's good to have around when folks are sick or grieving, you know. Run and set on the steps like a nice boy and wait until she comes out." So Sandy left the women and went to sit in the dark on the steps of the big corner house where the niece of the dead Mrs. Gavitt lived. There were some people on the porch, but they soon passed through the screen-door into the house or went away down the street. The moonlight cast weird shadows across the damp steps where Sandy sat, and it was dark there under the trees in spite of the moon, for the old house was built far back from the street in a yard full of oaks and maples, and Sandy could see the light from an upstairs window reflecting on the wet leaves of their nearest boughs. He heard a girl screaming, too, up there where the light was burning, and he knew that Aunt Hager was putting cold cloths on her head, or rubbing her hands, or driving folks out of the room, and talking kind to her so that she would soon be better.

All the neighborhood, white or colored, called his grandmother when something happened. She was a good nurse, they said, and sick folks liked her around. Aunt Hager always came when they called, too, bringing maybe a little soup that she had made or a jelly. Sometimes they paid her and sometimes they didn't. But Sandy had never had to sit outdoors in the darkness waiting for her before. He leaned his small back against the top step and rested his elbows on the porch behind him. It was growing late and the people in the streets had all disappeared.

There, in the dark, the little fellow began to think about his mother, who worked on the other side of town for a rich white lady named Mrs. J. J. Rice. And suddenly frightful thoughts came into his mind. Suppose she had left for home just as the storm came up! Almost always his mother was home before dark—but she wasn't there tonight when the storm came—and she should have been home! This thought appalled him. She should have been there! But maybe she had been caught by the storm and blown away as she walked down Main Street! Maybe Annjee had been carried off by the great black wind that had overturned the Gavitts' house and taken his grandma's porch flying through the air! Maybe the cyclone had gotten his mother, Sandy thought. He wanted her! Where was she? Had something terrible happened to her? Where was she now?

The big tears began to roll down his cheeks—but the little fellow held back the sobs that wanted to come. He decided he wasn't going to cry and make a racket there by himself on the strange steps of these white folks' house. He wasn't going to cry like a big baby in the dark. So he wiped his eyes, kicked his heels against the cement walk, lay down on the top step, and, by and by, sniffled himself to sleep.

"Wake up, son!" Someone was shaking him. "You'll catch your death o' cold sleeping on the wet steps like this. We're going home now. Don't want me to have to carry a big man like you, do you, boy? . . . Wake up, Sandy!" His mother stooped to lift his long little body from the wide steps. She held him against her soft heavy breasts and let his head rest on one of her shoulders while his feet, in their muddy rubbers, hung down against her dress.

"Where you been, mama?" the boy asked drowsily, tightening his arms about her neck. "I been waiting for you."

"Oh, I been home a long time, worried to death about you and ma till I heard from Madam Carter that you-all was down here nursing the sick. I stopped at your Aunt Tempy's house when I seen the storm coming."

"I was afraid you got blowed away, mama," murmured Sandy sleepily. "Let's go home, mama. I'm glad you ain't got blowed away."

On the porch Aunt Hager was talking to a pale white man and two thin white women standing at the door of the lighted hallway. "Just let Mis' Agnes sleep," she was saying. "She'll be all right now, an' I'll come back in de mawnin' to see 'bout her. . . . Good-night, you-all."

The old colored woman joined her daughter and they started home, walking through the streets filled with debris and puddles of muddy water reflecting the moon.

"You're certainly heavy, boy," remarked Sandy's mother to the child she held, but he didn't answer.

"I'm right glad you come for me, Annjee," Hager said. "I wonder is yo' sister all right out yonder at de country club. . . . An' I was so worried 'bout you I didn't know what to do—skeared you might a got caught in this twister, 'cause it were cert'ly awful!"

"I was at Tempy's!" Annjee replied. "And I was nearly crazy, but I just left everything in the hands o' God. That's all." In silence they walked on, a piece; then hesitantly, to her mother: "There wasn't any mail for me today, was there, ma?"

"Not a speck!" the old woman replied shortly. "Mail-man passed on by."

For a few minutes there was silence again as they walked. Then, "It's goin' on three weeks he's been gone, and he ain't written a line," the younger woman complained, shifting the child to her right arm. "Seems like Jimboy would let a body know where he is, ma, wouldn't it?"

"Huh! That ain't nothin'! He's been gone before this an' he ain't wrote, ain't he? Here you is worryin' 'bout a letter from that good-for-nothing husband o' your'n an' there's ma house settin' up without a porch to its name! . . . Ain't you seed what de devil's done done on earth this evenin', chile? . . . An' yet de first thing you ask me 'bout is de mail-man! Lawd! Lawd! . . . You an' that Jimboy!"

Aunt Hager lifted her heavy body over fallen tree-trunks and across puddles, but between puffs she managed to voice her indignation, so Annjee said no more concerning letters from her husband. Instead they went back to the subject of the cyclone. "I'm just thankful, ma, it didn't blow the whole house down and you with it, that's all! I was certainly worried! . . . And then you-all was gone when I got home! Gone on out—nursing that white woman. . . . It's too bad 'bout poor Mis' Gavitt, though, and old man Gavitt, ain't it?"

"Yes, indeedy!" said Aunt Hager. "It's sho too bad. They was certainly good old white folks! An' her married niece is takin' it mighty hard, po' little soul. I was nigh two hours, her husband an' me, tryin' to bring her out o' de hysterics. Tremblin' like a lamb all over, she was." They were turning into the yard. "Be careful with that chile, Annjee, you don't trip on none o' them boards nor branches an' fall with him."

"Put me down, 'cause I'm awake," said Sandy.

The old house looked queer without a porch. In the moonlight he could see the long nails that had held the porch roof to the weather-boarding. His grandmother climbed slowly over the door-sill, and his mother lifted him to the floor level as Aunt Hager lit the large oil-lamp on the parlor table. Then they went back to the bedroom, where the youngster took off his clothes, said his prayers, and climbed into the high feather bed where he slept with Annjee. Aunt Hager went to the next room, but for a long time she talked back and forth through the doorway to her daughter about the storm.

"We was just startin' out fo' Mis' Carter's cellar, me an' Sandy," she said several times. "But de Lawd was with us! He held us back! Praise His name! We ain't harmed, none of us—'ceptin' I don't know 'bout ma Harriett at de club. But you's all right. An' you say Tempy's all right, too. An' I prays that Harriett ain't been touched out there in de country where she's workin'. Maybe de storm ain't passed that way."

Then they spoke about the white people where Annjee worked . . . and about the elder sister Tempy's prosperity. Then Sandy heard his grandmother climb into bed, and a few minutes after the springs screaked under her, she had begun to snore. Annjee closed the door between their rooms and slowly began to unlace her wet shoes.

"Sandy," she whispered, "we ain't had no word yet from your father since he left. I know he goes away and stays away like this and don't write, but I'm sure worried. Hope the cyclone ain't passed nowhere near wherever he is, and I hope ain't nothin' hurt him. . . . I'm gonna pray for him, Sandy. I'm gonna ask God right now to take care o' Jimboy. . . . The Lawd knows, I wants him to come back! . . . I loves him. . . . We both loves him, don't we child? And we want him to come on back!"

She knelt down beside the bed in her night-dress and kept her head bowed for a long time. Before she got up, Sandy had gone to sleep.

Two

Conversation

It was broad daylight in the town of Stanton and had been for a long time.

"Get out o' that bed, boy!" Aunt Hager yelled. "Here's Buster waitin' out in de yard to play with you, an' you still sleepin'!"

"Aw, tell him to cut off his curls," retorted Sandy, but his grandmother was in no mood for fooling.

"Stop talkin' 'bout that chile's haid and put yo' clothes on. Nine o'clock an' you ain't up yet! Shame on you!" She shouted from the kitchen, where Sandy could hear the fire crackling and smell coffee boiling.

He kicked the sheet off with his bare feet and rolled over and over on the soft feather tick. There was plenty of room to roll now, because his mother had long since got up and gone to Mrs. J. J. Rice's to work.

"Tell Bus I'm coming," Sandy yelled, jumping into his trousers and running with bare feet towards the door. "Is he got his marbles?"

"Come back here, sir, an' put them shoes on," cried Hager, stopping him on his way out. "Yo' feet'll get long as yard-sticks and flat as pancakes runnin' round barefooted all de time. An' wash yo' face, sir. Buster ain't got a thing to do but wait. An' eat yo' breakfast."

The air was warm with sunlight, and hundreds of purple and white morning-glories laughed on the back fence. Earth and sky were fresh and clean after the heavy night-rain, and the young corn-shoots stood straight in the garden, and green pea-vines wound themselves around their crooked sticks. There was the mingled scent of wet soil and golden pollen on the breeze that blew carelessly through the clear air.

Buster sat under the green apple-tree with a pile of black mud from the alley in front of him.

"Hey, Sandy, gonna make marbles and put 'em in the sun to dry," he said.

"All right," agreed Sandy, and they began to roll mud balls in the palms of their hands. But instead of putting them in the sun to dry they threw them against the back of the house, where they flattened and stuck beautifully. Then they began to throw them at each other.

Sandy's playmate was a small ivory-white Negro child with straight golden hair, which his mother made him wear in curls. His eyes were blue and doll-like and he in no way resembled a colored youngster; but he was colored. Sandy himself was the shade of a nicely browned piece of toast, with dark, brown-black eyes and a head of rather kinky, sandy hair that would lie smooth only after a rigorous application of vaseline and water. That was why folks called him Annjee's sandy-headed child, and then just—Sandy.

"He takes after his father," Sister Lowry said, " 'cept he's not so light. But he's gonna be a mighty good-lookin' boy when he grows up, that's sho!"

"Well, I hopes he does," Aunt Hager said. "But I'd rather he'd be ugly 'fore he turns out anything like that good-for-nothing Jimboy what comes here an' stays a month, goes away an' stays six, an' don't hit a tap o' work 'cept when he feels like it. If it wasn't for Annjee, don't know how we'd eat, 'cause Sandy's father sho don't do nothin' to support him."

All the colored people in Stanton knew that Hager bore no love for Jimboy Rogers, the tall good-looking yellow fellow whom her second daughter had married.

"First place, I don't like his name," she would say in private. "Who ever heard of a nigger named Jimboy, anyhow? Next place, I ain't never seen a yaller dude yet that meant a dark woman no good—an' Annjee is dark!" Aunt Hager had other objections, too, although she didn't like to talk evil about folks. But what she probably referred to in her mind was the question of his ancestry, for nobody knew who Jimboy's parents were.

"Sandy, look out for the house while I run down an' see how is Mis' Gavitt's niece. An' you-all play outdoors. Don't bring no chillen in, litterin' up de place." About eleven o'clock Aunt Hager pulled a dust-cap over her head and put on a clean white apron. "Here, tie it for me, chile," she said, turning her broad back. "An' mind you don't hurt yo'self on no rusty nails and rotten boards left from de storm. I'll be back atter while." And she disappeared around the house, walking proudly, her black face shining in the sunlight.

Presently the two boys under the apple-tree were joined by a coal-colored little girl who lived next door, one Willie-Mae Johnson, and the mud balls under her hands became mud pies carefully rounded and patted and placed in the sun on the small box where the little chickens lived. Willie-Mae was the mama, Sandy the papa, and Buster the baby as the old game of "playing house" began anew.

By and by the mail-man's whistle blew and the three children scampered towards the sidewalk to meet him. The carrier handed Sandy a letter. "Take it in the house," he said. But instead the youngsters sat on the front-door-sill, their feet dangling where the porch had been, and began to examine the envelope.

"I bet that's Lincoln's picture," said Buster.

"No, 'taint," declared Willie-Mae. "It's Rossiefelt!"

"Aw, it's Washington," said Sandy. "And don't you-all touch my mama's letter with your hands all muddy. It might be from my papa, you can't tell, and she wants it kept clean."

" 'Tis from Jimboy," Aunt Hager declared when she returned, accompanied by her old friend, Sister Whiteside, who peddled on foot fresh garden-truck she raised herself. Aunt Hager had met her at the corner.

"I knows his writin'," went on Hager. "An' it's got a postmark, K-A-N-, Kansas City! That's what 'tis! Niggers sho do love Kansas City! . . . Huh! . . . So that's where he's at. Well, yo' mama'll be glad to get it. If she knowed it was here, she'd quit work an' come home now. . . . Sit down, Whiteside. We gwine eat in a few minutes. You better have a bite with us an' stay an' rest yo'self awhile, 'cause I knows you been walkin' this mawnin'!"

" 'Deed I is," the old sister declared, dropping her basket of lettuce and peas on the floor and taking a chair next to the table in the kitchen. "An' I ain't sold much neither. Seems like folks ain't got no buyin' appetite after all that storm an' wind last night—but de Lawd will provide! I ain't worried."

"That's right," agreed Hager. "Might o' been me blowed away maself, 'stead o' just ma porch, if Jesus hadn't been with us. . . . You Sandy! Make haste and wash yo' hands, sir. Rest o' you chillens go on home, 'cause I know yo' ma's lookin' for you. . . . Huh! This wood fire's mighty low!"

Hager uncovered a pot that had been simmering on the stove all morning and dished up a great bowlful of black-eyed peas and salt pork. There was biscuit bread left from breakfast. A plate of young onions and a pitcher of lemonade stood on the white oilcloth-covered table. Heads were automatically bowed.

"Lawd, make us thankful for this food. For Christ's sake, amen," said Hager; then the two old women and the child began to eat.

"That's Elvira's boy, ain't it—that yaller-headed young-one was here playin' with Sandy?" Sister Whiteside had her mouth full of onions and beans as she asked the question.

"Shsss! . . . That's her child!" said Hager. "But it ain't Eddie's!" She gave her guest a meaning glance across the table, then lowered her voice, pretending all the while that Sandy's ears were too young to hear. "They say she had that chile 'fore she married Eddie. An' black as Eddie is, you knows an' I knows ain't due to be no golden hair in de family!"

"I knowed there must be something funny," whispered the old sister, screwing up her face. "That's some white man's chile!"

"Sho it is!" agreed Hager. . . . "I knowed it all de time. . . . Have some mo' meat, Whiteside. Help yo'self! We ain't got much, but such as 'tis, you're welcome. . . . Yes, sir, Buster's some white man's chile. . . . Stop reachin' cross de table for bread, Sandy. Where's yo' manners, sir? I declare, chillens do try you sometimes. . . . Pass me de onions."

"Truth, they tries you, yit I gits right lonesome since all ma young-ones is gone." Sister Whiteside worked her few good teeth vigorously, took a long swallow of lemonade, and smacked her lips. "Chillen an' grandchillen all in Chicago an' St. Louis an' Wichita, an' nary chick nor child left with me in de house. . . . Pass me de bread, thank yuh. . . . I feels kinder sad an' sorry at times, po' widder-woman that I is. I has ma garden an' ma hens, but all ma chillens done grown and married. . . . Where's yo' daughter Harriett at now, Hager? Is she married, too? I ain't seen her lately."

Hager pulled a meat skin through her teeth; then she answered: "No, chile, she too young to marry yet! Ain't but sixteen, but she's been workin' out this summer, waitin' table at de Stanton County Country Club. Been in de country three weeks now, since school closed, but she comes in town on Thursdays, though. It's nigh six miles from here, so de women-help sleeps there at night. I's glad she's out there, Sister. Course Harriett's a good girl, but she likes to be frisky—wants to run de streets 'tendin' parties an' dances, an' I can't do much with her no mo', though I hates to say it."

"But she's a songster, Hager! An' I hears she's sho one smart chile, besides. They say she's up with them white folks when it comes to books. An' de high school where she's goin' ain't easy. . . . All ma young ones quit 'fore they got through with it—wouldn't go—ruther have a good time runnin' to Kansas City an' galavantin' round."

"De Lawd knows it's a hard job, keepin' colored chillens in school, Sister Whiteside, a mighty hard job. De niggers don't help 'em, an' de white folks don't care if they stay or not. An' when they gets along sixteen an' seventeen, they wants this, an' they wants that, an' t'other—an' when you ain't got it to give to 'em, they quits school an' goes to work. . . . Harriett say she ain't goin' back next fall. I feels right hurt over it, but she 'clares she ain't goin' back to school. Says there ain't no use in learnin' books fo' nothin' but to work in white folks' kitchens when she's graduated."

"Do she, Hager? I's sho sorry! I's gwine to talk to that gal. Get Reverend Berry to talk to her, too. . . . You's struggled to bring up yo' chillens, an' all we Christians in de church ought to help you! I gwine see Reverend Berry, see can't he 'suade her to stay in school." The old woman reached for the onions. "But you ain't never raised no boys, though, has you, Hager?"

"No. I ain't. My two boy-chillens both died 'fore they was ten. Just these three girls—Tempy, an' Annjee, an' Harriett—that's all I got. An' this here grandchile, Sandy. . . . Take yo' hands off that meat, sir! You had 'nough!"

"Lawd, you's been lucky! I done raised seven grandchillen 'sides eight o' ma own. An' they don't thank me. No, sir! Go off and kick up they heels an' git married an' don't thank me a bit! Don't even write, some of 'em. . . . Waitin' fo' me to die, I reckon, so's they can squabble over de little house I owns an' ma garden." The old visitor pushed back her chair. "Huh! Yo' dinner was sho good! . . . Waitin' fo' me to die."

"Unhuh! . . . That's de way with 'em, Sister Whiteside. Chillens don't care—but I reckon we old ones can't kick much. They's got to get off fo' themselves. It's natural, that's what 'tis. Now, my Tempy, she's married and doin' well. Got a fine house, an' her husband's a mail-clerk in de civil service makin' good money. They don't 'sociate no mo' with none but de high-toned colored folks, like Dr. Mitchell, an' Mis' Ada Walls, an' Madam C. Frances Smith. Course Tempy don't come to see me much 'cause I still earns ma livin' with ma arms in de tub. But Annjee run in their house out o' the storm last night an' she say Tempy's just bought a new pianer, an' de house looks fine. . . . I's glad fo' de chile."

"Sho, sho you is, Sister Williams, you's a good mother an' I knows you's glad. But I hears from Reverend Berry that Tempy's done withdrawed from our church an' joined de Episcopals!"

"That's right! She is. Last time I seed Tempy, she told me she couldn't stand de Baptist no mo'—too many low niggers belonging, she say, so she's gonna join Father Hill's church, where de best people go. . . . I told her I didn't think much o' joinin' a church, so far away from God that they didn't want nothin' but yaller niggers for members, an' so full o' forms an' fashions that a good Christian couldn't shout—but she went on an' joined. It's de stylish temple, that's why, so I ain't said no mo'. Tempy's goin' on thirty-five now, she's ma oldest chile, an' I reckon she knows how she wants to act."

"Yes, I reckon she do. . . . But there ain't no church like de Baptist, praise God! Is there, Sister? If you ain't been dipped in that water an' half drowned, you ain't saved. Tempy don't know like we do. No, sir, she don't know!"

There was no fruit or dessert, and the soiled plates were not removed from the table for a long time, for the two old women, talking about their children, had forgotten the dishes. Young flies crawled over the biscuit bread and hummed above the bowl of peas, while the wood fire died in the stove, and Sandy went out into the sunshine to play.

"Now, ma girl, Maggie," said Sister Whiteside; "de man she married done got to be a big lawyer in St. Louis. He's in de politics there, an' Maggie's got a fine job herself—social servin', they calls it. But I don't hear from her once a year. An' she don't send me a dime. Ma boys looks out for me, though, sometimes, round Christmas. There's Lucius, what runs on de railroad, an' then Andrew, what rides de horses, an' John, in Omaha, sends me a little change now an' then—all but Charlie, an' he never was thoughtful 'bout his mother. He ain't never sent me nothin'."

"Well, you sho is lucky," said Hager; " 'cause they ain't no money comes in this house, Christmas nor no other time, less'n me an' Annjee brings it here. Jimboy ain't no good, an' what Harriett makes goes for clothes and parties an' powderin'-rags. Course, I takes some from her every week, but I gives it right back for her school things. An' I ain't taken nothin' from her these three weeks she's been workin' at de club. She say she's savin' her money herself. She's past sixteen now, so I lets her have it. . . . Po' little thing! . . . She does need to look purty." Hager's voice softened and her dark old face was half abashed, kind and smiling. "You know, last month I bought her a gold watch—surprise fo' her birthday, de kind you hangs on a little pin on yo' waist. Lawd knows, I couldn't 'ford it—took all de money from three week's o' washin', but I knowed she'd been wantin' a watch. An' this front room—I moved ma bed out last year an' bought that new rug at de second-hand store an' them lace curtains so's she could have a nice place to entertain her comp'ny. . . . But de chile goes with such a kinder wild crowd o' young folks, Sister Whiteside! It worries me! The boys, they cusses, an' the girls, they paints, an' some of 'em live in de Bottoms. I been tried to get her out of it right along, but seems like I can't. That's why I's glad she's in de country fo' de summer an' comes in but only once a week, an' then she's home with me. It's too far to come in town at night, she say, so she gets her rest now, goin' to bed early an' all, with de country air round her. I hopes she calms down from runnin' round when she comes back here to stay in de fall. . . . She's a good chile. She don't lie to me 'bout where she goes, nor nothin' like that, but she's just wild, that's all, just wild."

"Is she a Christian, Sister Williams?"

"No, she ain't. I's sorry to say it of a chile o' mine, but she ain't. She's been on de moaner's bench time after time, Sunday mawnin's an' prayer-meetin' evenin's, but she never would rise. I prays for her."

"Well, when she takes Jesus, she'll see de light! That's what de matter with her, Sister Williams, she ain't felt Him yit. Make her go to church when she comes back here. . . . I reckon you heard 'bout when de big revival's due to come off this year, ain't you?"

"No, I ain't, not yet."

"Great colored tent-meetin' with de Battle-Ax of de Lawd, Reverend Braswell preachin'! Yes, Sir! Gwine start August eighteenth in de Hickory Woods yonder by de edge o' town."

"Good news," cried Hager. "Mo' sinners than enough's in need o' savin'. I's gwine to take Sandy an' get him started right with de Lawd. An' if that onery Jimboy's back here, I gwine make him go, too, an' look Jesus in de face. Annjee an' me's saved, chile! . . . You Sandy, bring us some drinkin'-water from de pump." Aunt Hager rapped on the window with her knuckles to the boy playing outside! "An' stop wrastlin' with that gal."

Sandy rose triumphant from the prone body of black little Willie-Mae, lying squalling on the cinder-path near the back gate. "She started it," he yelled, running towards the pump. The girl began a reply, but at that moment a rickety wagon drawn by a white mule and driven by a grey-haired, leather-colored old man came rattling down the alley.

"Hy, there, Hager!" called the old Negro, tightening his reins on the mule, which immediately began to eat corn-tops over the back fence. "How you been treatin' yo'self?"

"Right tolable," cried Hager, for she and Sister Whiteside had both emerged from the kitchen and were approaching the driver. "How you doin', Brother Logan?"

"Why, if here ain't Sis' Whiteside, too!" said the old beau, sitting up straight on his wagon-seat and showing a row of ivory teeth in a wide grin. "I's doin' purty well for a po' widower what ain't got nobody to bake his bread. Doin' purty well. Hee! Hee! None o' you all ain't sorry for me, is you? How de storm treat you, Hager? . . . Says it carried off yo' porch? . . . That's certainly too bad! Well, it did some o' these white folks worse'n that. I got 'nough work to do to last me de next fo' weeks, cleanin' up yards an' haulin' off trash, me an' dis mule here. . . . How's yo' chillen, Sis' Williams?"

"Oh, they all right, thank yuh. Annjee's still at Mis' Rice's, an' Harriet's in de country at de club."

"Is she?" said Brother Logan. "I seed her in town night 'fore last down on Pearl Street 'bout ten o'clock."

"You ain't seed Harriett no night 'fore last," disputed Hager vigorously. "She don't come in town 'ceptin' Thursday afternoons, an' that's tomorrow."

"Sister, I ain't blind," said the old man, hurt that his truth should be doubted. "I—seen—Harriett Williams on Pearl Street . . . with Maudel Smothers an' two boys 'bout ten o'clock day before yestidy night! An' they was gwine to de Waiters' Ball, 'cause I asked Maudel where they was gwine, an' she say so. Then I says to Harriett: 'Does yo' mammy know you's out this late?' an' she laughed an' say: 'Oh, that's all right!' . . . Don't tell me I ain't seen Harriett, Hager."

"Well, Lawd help!" Aunt Hager cried, her mouth open. "You done seed my chile in town an' she ain't come anear home! Stayed all night at Maudel's, I reckon. . . . I tells her 'bout runnin' with that gal from de Bottoms. That's what makes her lie to me—tellin' me she don't come in town o' nights. Maudel's folks don't keep no kind o' house, and mens goes there, an' they sells licker, an' they gambles an' fights. . . . Is you sho that's right, Brother Logan, ma chile done been in town an' ain't come home?"

"It ain't wrong!" said old man Logan, cracking his long whip on the white mule's haunches. "Gitti-yap! You ole jinny!" and he drove off.

"Um-uh!" said Sister Whiteside to Hager as the two toil-worn old women walked toward the house. "That's de way they does you!" The peddler gathered up her things. "I better be movin', 'cause I got these greens to sell yit, an' it's gittin' 'long towards evenin'. . . . That's de way chillens does you, Sister Williams! I knows! That's de way they does!"

Three

Jimboy's Letter

Kansas City, Mo.
13 June 1912

Dear Annjelica,

I been laying off to written you ever since I left home but you know how it is. Work has not been so good here. Am with a section gang of coloreds and greeks and somehow strained my back on the Union Pacific laying ties so I will be home on Saturday. Will do my best to try and finish out weak here. Love my darling wife also kiss my son Sandy for me. Am dying to see you,

affectionately as ever and allways
till the judgment day,
Jimboy Rogers

"Strained his back, has he? Unhuh! An' then comes writin' 'bout till de judgment day!" Hager muttered when she heard it. "Always something wrong with that nigger! He'll be back here now, layin' 'round, doin' nothin' fo' de rest o' de summer, turnin' ma house into a theatre with him an' Harriett singin' their rag-time, an' that guitar o' his'n wangin' ever' evenin'! 'Tween him an' Harriett both it's a wonder I ain't plumb crazy. But Harriett do work fo' her livin'. She ain't no loafer. . . . Huh! . . . Annjee, you was sho a fool when you married that boy, an' you still is! . . . I's gwine next do' to Sister Johnson's!" Aunt Hager went out the back and across the yard, where, next door, Tom and Sarah Johnson, Willie-Mae's grandparents, sat on a bench against the side-wall of an unpainted shanty. They were both quietly smoking their corn-cob pipes in the evening dusk.

Sandy, looking at the back of the letter that his mother held, stood at the kitchen-table rapidly devouring a large piece of fresh lemon pie, which she had brought from Mrs. J. J. Rice's. Annjee had said to save the two cold fried lamb chops until tomorrow, or Sandy would have eaten those, too.

"Wish you'd brought home some more pie," the boy declared, his lips white with meringue, but Annjee, who had just got in from work, paid no attention to her son's appreciative remarks on her cookery.

Instead she said: "Ma certainly ain't got no time for Jimboy, has she?"

and then sat down with the open letter still in her hand—a single sheet of white paper pencilled in large awkward letters. She put it on the table, rested her dark face in her hands, and began to read it again. . . . She knew how it was, of course, that her husband hadn't written before. That was all right now. Working all day in the hot sun with a gang of Greeks, a man was tired at night, besides living in a box-car, where there was no place to write a letter anyway. He was a great big kid, that's what Jimboy was, cut out for playing. But when he did work, he tried to outdo everybody else. Annjee could see him in her mind, tall and well-built, his legs apart, muscles bulging as he swung the big hammer above his head, driving steel. No wonder he hurt his back, trying to lay more ties a day than anybody else on the railroad. That was just like Jimboy. But she was kind of pleased he had hurt it, since it would bring him home.

"Ain't you glad he's comin', Sandy?"

"Sure," answered the child, swallowing his last mouthful of pie. "I hope he brings me that gun he promised to buy last Easter." The boy wiped his sticky hands on the dish-cloth and ran out into the back yard, calling: "Willie-Mae! Willie-Mae!"

"Stay right over yonder!" answered his grandmother through the dusk. "Willie-Mae's in de bed, sir, an' we old folks settin' out here tryin' to have a little peace." From the tone of Hager's voice he knew he wasn't wanted in the Johnsons' yard, so he went back into the house, looked at his mother reading her letter again, and then lay down on the kitchen-floor.

"Affectionately as ever and allways till the judgment day," she read, "Jimboy Rogers."

He loved her, Annjee was sure of that, and it wasn't another woman that made him go away so often. Eight years they'd been married. No, nine—because Sandy was nine, and he was ready to be born when they had had the wedding. And Jimboy left the week after they were married, to go to Omaha, where he worked all winter. When he came back, Sandy was in the world, sitting up sucking meat skins. It was springtime and they bought a piano for the house—but later the instalment man came and took it back to the store. All that summer her husband stayed home and worked a little, but mostly he fished, played pool, taught Harriett to buck-dance, and quarrelled with Aunt Hager. Then in the winter he went to Jefferson City and got a job at the Capitol.

Jimboy was always going, but Aunt Hager was wrong about his never working. It was just that he couldn't stay in one place all the time. He'd been born running, he said, and had run ever since. Besides, what was there in Stanton anyhow for a young colored fellow to do except dig sewer ditches for a few cents an hour or maybe porter around a store for seven dollars a week. Colored men couldn't get many jobs in Stanton, and foreigners were coming in, taking away what little work they did have. No wonder he didn't stay home. Hadn't Annjee's father been in Stanton forty years and hadn't he died with Aunt Hager still taking in washings to help keep up the house?

There was no well-paid work for Negro men, so Annjee didn't blame Jimboy for going away looking for something better. She'd go with him if it wasn't for her mother. If she went, though, Aunt Hager wouldn't have anybody for company but Harriett, and Harriett was the youngest and wildest of the three children. With Pa Williams dead going on ten years, Hager washing every day, Tempy married, and Annjee herself out working, there had been nobody to take much care of the little sister as she grew up. Harriett had had no raising, even though she was smart and in high school. A female child needed care. But she could sing! Lawdy! And dance, too! That was another reason why Aunt Hager didn't like Jimboy. The devil's musicianer, she called him, straight from hell, teaching Harriett buck-and-winging! But when he took his soft-playing guitar and picked out spirituals and old-time Christian hymns on its sweet strings, Hager forgot she was his enemy, and sang and rocked with the rest of them. When Jimboy was home, you couldn't get lonesome or blue.

"Gee, I'll be glad when he comes!" Annjee said to herself. "But if he goes off again, I'll feel like dying in this dead old town. I ain't never been away from here nohow." She spoke aloud to the dim oil-lamp smoking on the table and the sleeping boy on the floor. "I believe I'll go with him next time. I declare I do!" And then, realizing that Jimboy had never once told her when he was leaving or for what destination, she amended her utterance. "I'll follow him, though, as soon as he writes." Because, almost always after he had been away two or three weeks, he would write. "I'll follow him, sure, if he goes off again. I'll leave Sandy here and send money back to mama. Then Harriett could settle down and take care of ma and stop runnin' the streets so much. . . . Yes, that's what I'll do next time!"

This going away was a new thought, and the dark, strong-bodied young woman at the table suddenly began to dream of the cities she had never seen to which Jimboy would lead her. Why, he had been as far north as Canada and as far south as New Orleans, and it wasn't anything for him to go to Chicago or Denver any time! He was a travelling man—and she, Annjee, was too meek and quiet, that's what she was—too stay-athomish. Never going nowhere, never saying nothing back to those who scolded her or talked about her, not even sassing white folks when they got beside themselves. And every colored girl in town said that Mrs. J. J. Rice was no easy white woman to work for, yet she had been there now five years, accepting everything without a murmur! Most young folks, girls and boys, left Stanton as soon as they could for the outside world, but here she was, Annjelica Williams, going on twenty-eight, and had never been as far as Kansas City!

"I want to travel," she said to herself. "I want to go places, too."

But that was why Jimboy married her, because she wasn't a runabout. He'd had enough of those kind of women before he struck Stanton, he said. St. Louis was full of them, and Chicago running over. She was the first nice girl he'd ever met who lived at home, so he took her. . . . There were mighty few dark women had a light, strong, good-looking young husband, really a married husband, like Jimboy, and a little brown kid like Sandy.

"I'm mighty lucky," Annjee thought, "even if he ain't here." And two tears of foolish pride fell from the bright eyes in her round black face. They trickled down on the letter, with its blue lines and pencil-scrawled message, and some of the words on the paper began to blur into purple blots because the pencil had [not] been an indelible one. Quickly she fumbled for a handkerchief to wipe the tears away, when a voice made her start.

"You Annjee!" cried Aunt Hager in the open door. "Go to bed, chile! Go on! Settin' up here this late, burnin' de light an' lurin' all sorts o' night-bugs an' creepers into de house!" The old woman came in out of the dark. "Lawd! I might anigh stumbled over this boy in de middle o' de flo'! An' you ain't even took off yo' hat since you got home from work! Is you crazy? Settin' up here at night with yo' hat on, an' lettin' this chile catch his death o' cold sleepin' down on de flo' long after his bedtime!"

Sheepishly Annjee folded her letter and got up. It was true that she still had on her hat and the sweater she had worn to Mrs. Rice's. True, too, the whole room was alive with soft-winged moths fluttering against the hot glass of the light—and on the kitchen floor a small, brown-skin, infinitely lovable edition of Jimboy lay sprawled contentedly in his grandmother's path, asleep!

"He's my baby!" Annjee said gently, stooping to pick him up. "He's my baby—me and Jimboy's baby!"

Four

Thursday Afternoon

Hager had risen at sunrise. On Thursdays she did the Reinharts' washing, on Fridays she ironed it, and on Saturdays she sent it home, clean and beautifully white, and received as pay the sum of seventy-five cents. During the winter Hager usually did half a dozen washings a week, but during the hot season her customers had gone away, and only the Reinharts, on account of an invalid grandmother with whom they could not travel, remained in Stanton.

Wednesday afternoon Sandy, with a boy named Jimmy Lane, called at the back door for their soiled clothes. Each child took a handle and between them carried the large wicker basket seven blocks to Aunt Hager's kitchen. For this service Jimmy Lane received five cents a trip, although Sister Lane had repeatedly said to Hager that he needn't be given anything. She wanted him to learn his Christian duties by being useful to old folks. But Jimmy was not inclined to be Christian. On the contrary, he was a very bad little boy of thirteen, who often led Sandy astray. Sometimes they would run with the basket for no reason at all, then stumble and spill the clothes out on the sidewalk—Mrs. Reinhart's summer dresses, and drawers, and Mr. Reinhart's extra-large B.V.D.'s lying generously exposed to the public. Sometimes, if occasion offered, the youngsters would stop to exchange uncouth epithets with strange little white boys who called them "niggers." Or, again, they might neglect their job for a game of marbles, or a quarter-hour of scrub baseball on a vacant lot; or to tease any little colored girl who might tip timidly by with her hair in tight, well-oiled braids—while the basket of garments would be left forlornly in the street without guardian. But when the clothes were safe in Aunt Hager's kitchen, Jimmy would usually buy candy with his nickel and share it with Sandy before he went home.

After soaking all night, the garments were rubbed through the suds in the morning; and in the afternoon the colored articles were on the line while the white pieces were boiling seriously in a large tin boiler on the kitchen-stove.

"They sho had plenty this week," Hager said to her grandson, who sat on the stoop eating a slice of bread and apple butter. "I's mighty late gettin' 'em hung out to dry, too. Had no business stoppin' this mawnin' to go see sick folks, and me here got all I can do maself! Looks like this warm weather old Mis' Reinhart must change ever' piece from her dress to her shimmy three times a day—sendin' me a washin' like this here!" They heard the screen-door at the front of the house open and slam. "It's a good thing they got me to do it fo' 'em! . . . Sandy, see who's that at de do'."

It was Harriett, home from the country club for the afternoon, cool and slender and pretty in her black uniform with its white collar, her smooth black face and neck powdered pearly, and her crinkly hair shining with pomade. She smelled nice and perfumy as Sandy jumped on her like a dog greeting a favorite friend. Harriett kissed him and let him hang to her arm as they went through the bedroom to the kitchen. She carried a brown cardboard suit-case and a wide straw hat in one hand.

"Hello, mama," she said.

Hager poked the boiling clothes with a vigorous splash of her round stick. The steam rose in clouds of soapy vapor.

"I been waitin' for you, madam!" her mother replied in tones that were not calculated to welcome pleasantly an erring daughter. "I wants to know de truth—was you in town last Monday night or not?"

Harriett dropped her suit-case against the wall. "You seem to have the truth," she said carelessly. "How'd you get it? . . . Here, Sandy, take this out in the yard and eat it, seed and all." She gave her nephew a plum she had brought in her pocket. "I *was* in town, but I didn't have time to come home. I had to go to Maudel's because she's making me a dress."

"To Maudel's! . . . Unhuh! An' to de Waiters' Ball, besides galavantin' up an' down Pearl Street after ten o'clock! I wouldn't cared so much if you'd told me beforehand, but you said you didn't come in town 'ceptin' Thursday afternoon, an' here I was believing yo' lies."

"It's no lies! I haven't been in town before."

"Who brung you here at night anyhow—an' there ain't no trains runnin'?"

"O, I came in with the cook and some of the boys, mama, that's who! They hired an auto for the dance. What would be the use coming home, when you and Annjee go to bed before dark like chickens?"

"That's all right, madam! Annjee's got sense—savin' her health an' strength!"

Harriett was not impressed. "For what? To spend her life in Mrs. Rice's kitchen?" She shrugged her shoulders.

"What you bring yo' suit-case home fo'?"

"I'm quitting the job Saturday," she said. "I've told them already."

"Quitting!" her mother exclaimed. "What fo'? Lawd, if it ain't one thing, it's another!"

"What for?" Harriett retorted angrily. "There's plenty what for! All that work for five dollars a week with what little tips those pikers give you. And white men insulting you besides, asking you to sleep with 'em. Look at my finger-nails, all broke from scrubbing that dining-room floor." She thrust out her dark slim hands. "Waiting table and cleaning silver, washing and ironing table-linen, and then scrubbing the floor besides—that's too much of a good thing! And only three waitresses on the job. That old steward out there's a regular white folks' nigger. He don't care how hard he works us girls. Well, I'm through with the swell new Stanton County Country Club this coming Saturday—I'm telling everybody!" She shrugged her shoulders again.

"What you gonna do then?"

"Maudel says I can get a job with her."

"Maudel? . . . Where?" The old woman had begun to wring the clothes dry and pile them in a large dish-pan.

"At the Banks Hotel, chambermaid, for pretty good pay."

Hager stopped again and turned decisively towards her daughter. "You ain't gonna work in no hotel. You hear me! They's dives o' sin, that's what they is, an' a child o' mine ain't goin' in one. If you was a boy, I wouldn't let you go, much less a girl! They ain't nothin' but strumpets works in hotels."

"Maudel's no strumpet." Harriett's eyes narrowed.

"I don't know if she is or ain't, but I knows I wants you to stop runnin' with her—I done tole you befo'. . . . Her mammy ain't none too straight neither, raisin' them chillen in sin. Look at Sammy in de reform school 'fore he were fifteen for gamblin'. An' de oldest chile, Essie, done gone to Kansas City with that yaller devil she ain't married. An' Maudel runnin' de streets night an' day, with you tryin' to keep up with her! . . . Lawd a mercy! . . . Here, hang up these clothes!"

Her mother pointed to the tin pan on the table filled with damp, twisted, white underwear. Harriett took the pan in both hands. It was heavy and she trembled with anger as she lifted it to her shoulders.

"You can bark at me if you want to, mama, but don't talk about my friends. I don't care what they are! Maudel'd do anything for me. And her brother's a good kid, whether he's been in reform school or not. They oughtn't to put him there just for shooting dice. What's that? I like him, and I like Mrs. Smothers, too. She's not always scolding people for wanting a good time and for being lively and trying to be happy."

Hot tears raced down each cheek, leaving moist lines in the pink powder. Sandy, playing marbles with Buster under the apple-tree, heard her sniffling as she shook out the clothes and hung them on the line in the yard.

"You Sandy," Aunt Hager called loudly from the kitchen-door. "Come in here an' get me some water an' cut mo' firewood." Her black face was wet with perspiration and drawn from fatigue and worry. "I got to get the rest o' these clothes out yet this evenin'. . . . That chile Harriett's aggravatin' me to death! Help me, Sandy, honey."

They ate supper in silence, for Hager's attempts at conversation with her young daughter were futile. Once the old woman said: "That onery Jimboy's comin' home Saturday," and Harriett's face brightened a moment.

"Gee, I'm glad," she replied, and then her mouth went sullen again. Sandy began uncomfortably to kick the table-leg.

"For Christ's sake!" the girl frowned, and the child stopped, hurt that his favorite aunt should yell at him peevishly for so slight an offense.

"Lawd knows, I wish you'd try an' be mo' like yo' sisters, Annjee an' Tempy," Hager began as she washed the dishes, while Harriett stood near the stove, cloth in hand, waiting to dry them. "Here I is, an old woman, an' you tries ma soul! After all I did to raise you, you don't even hear me when I speak." It was the old theme again, without variation. "Now, there's Annjee, ain't a better chile livin'—if she warn't crazy 'bout Jimboy. An' Tempy married an' doin' well, an' respected ever'where. . . . An' you runnin' wild!"

"Tempy?" Harriett sneered suddenly, pricked by this comparison. "So respectable you can't touch her with a ten-foot pole, that's Tempy! . . . Annjee's all right, working herself to death at Mrs. Rice's, but don't tell me about Tempy. Just because she's married a mail-clerk with a little property, she won't even see her own family any more. When niggers get up in the world, they act just like white folks—don't pay you no mind. And Tempy's that kind of a nigger—she's up in the world now!"

"Close yo' mouth, talking that way 'bout yo' own sister! I ain't asked her to be always comin' home, is I, if she's satisfied in her own house?"

"No, you aren't asking her, mama, but you're always talking about her being so respectable. . . . Well, I don't want to be respectable if I have to be stuck up and dicty like Tempy is. . . . She's colored and I'm colored and I haven't seen her since before Easter. . . . It's not being black that matters with her, though, it's being poor, and that's what we are, you and me and Annjee, working for white folks and washing clothes and going in back doors, and taking tips and insults. I'm tired of it, mama! I want to have a good time once in a while."

"That's 'bout all you does have is a good time," Hager said. "An' it ain't right, an' it ain't Christian, that's what it ain't! An' de Lawd is takin' notes on you!" The old woman picked up the heavy iron skillet and began to wash it inside and out.

"Aw, the church has made a lot of you old Negroes act like Salvation Army people," the girl returned, throwing the dried knives and forks on the table. "Afraid to even laugh on Sundays, afraid for a girl and boy to look at one another, or for people to go to dances. Your old Jesus is white, I guess, that's why! He's white and stiff and don't like niggers!"

Hager gasped while Harriett went on excitedly, disregarding her mother's pain: "Look at Tempy, the highest-class Christian in the family—Episcopal, and so holy she can't even visit her own mother. Seems like all the good-time people are bad, and all the old Uncle Toms and mean, dried-up, long-faced niggers fill the churches. I don't never intend to join a church if I can help it."

"Have mercy on this chile! Help her an' save her from hell-fire! Change her heart, Jesus!" the old woman begged, standing in the middle of the kitchen with uplifted arms. "God have mercy on ma daughter."

Harriett, her brow wrinkled in a steady frown, put the dishes away, wiped the table, and emptied the water with a splash through the kitchen-door. Then she went into the bedroom that she shared with her mother, and began to undress. Sandy saw, beneath her thin white underclothes, the soft black skin of her shapely young body.

"Where you goin'?" Hager asked sharply.

"Out," said the girl.

"Out where?"

"O, to a barbecue at Willow Grove, mama! The boys are coming by in an auto at seven o'clock."

"What boys?"

"Maudel's brother and some fellows."

"You ain't goin' a step!"

A pair of curling-irons swung in the chimney of the lighted lamp on the dresser. Harriett continued to get ready. She was making bangs over her forehead, and the scent of scorching hair-oil drifted by Sandy's nose.

"Up half de night in town Monday, an' de Lawd knows how late ever' night in de country, an' then you comes home to run out agin! . . . You ain't goin'!" continued her mother.

Harriett was pulling on a pair of red silk stockings, bright and shimmering to her hips.

"You quit singin' in de church choir. You say you ain't goin' back to school. You won't keep no job! Now what *is* you gonna do? Yo' pappy said years ago, 'fore he died, you was too purty to 'mount to anything, but I ain't believed him. His last dyin' words was: 'Look out fo' ma baby Harriett.' You was his favourite chile. . . . Now look at you! Runnin' de streets an' wearin' red silk stockings!" Hager trembled. " 'Spose yo' pappy was to come back an' see you?"

Harriett powdered her face and neck, pink on ebony, dashed white talcum at each arm-pit, and rubbed her ears with perfume from a thin bottle. Then she slid a light blue dress of many ruffles over her head. The skirt ended midway between the ankle and the knee, and she looked very cute, delicate, and straight, like a black porcelain doll in a Vienna toy shop.

"Some o' Maudel's makin's, that dress—anybody can tell," her mother went on quarrelling. "Short an' shameless as it can be! Regular bad gal's dress, that's what 'tis. . . . What you puttin' it on fo' anyhow, an' I done told you you ain't goin' out? You must think I don't mean ma words. Ain't more'n sixteen last April an' runnin' to barbecues at Willer Grove! De idee! When I was yo' age, wasn't up after eight o'clock, 'ceptin' Sundays in de church house, that's all. . . . Lawd knows where you young ones is headin'. An' me prayin' an' washin' ma fingers to de bone to keep a roof over yo' head."

The sharp honk of an automobile horn sounded from the street. A big red car, full of laughing brown girls gaily dressed, and coatless, slick-headed black boys in green and yellow silk shirts, drew up at the curb. Somebody squeezed the bulb of the horn a second time and another loud and saucy honk! struck the ears.

"You Sandy," Hager commanded. "Run out there an' tell them niggers to leave here, 'cause Harriett ain't goin' no place."

But Sandy did not move, because his young and slender aunt had gripped him firmly by the collar while she searched feverishly in the dresser-drawer for a scarf. She pulled it out, long and flame-colored, with fiery, silky fringe, before she released the little boy.

"You ain't gwine a step this evenin'!" Hager shouted. "Don't you hear me?"

"O, no?" said Harriett coolly in a tone that cut like knives. "You're the one that says I'm not going—*but I am!*"

Then suddenly something happened in the room—the anger fell like a veil from Hager's face, disclosing aged, helpless eyes full of fear and pain.

"Harriett, honey, I wants you to be good," the old woman stammered. The words came pitiful and low—not a command any longer—as she faced her terribly alive young daughter in the ruffled blue dress and the red silk stockings. "I just wants you to grow up decent, chile. I don't want you runnin' to Willer Grove with them boys. It ain't no place fo' you in the night-time —an' you knows it. You's mammy's baby girl. She wants you to be good, honey, and follow Jesus, that's all."

The baritone giggling of the boys in the auto came across the yard as Hager started to put a timid, restraining hand on her daughter's shoulder—but Harriett backed away.

"You old fool!" she cried. "Lemme go! You old Christian fool!"

She ran through the door and across the sidewalk to the waiting car, where the arms of the young men welcomed her eagerly. The big machine sped swiftly down the street and the rapid sput! sput! sput! of its engine grew fainter and fainter. Finally, the auto was only a red tail-light in the summer dusk. Sandy, standing beside his grandmother in the doorway, watched it until it disappeared.

Five

Guitar

Throw yo' arms around me, baby,
Like de circle round de sun!
Baby, throw yo' arms around me
Like de circle round de sun,
An' tell yo' pretty papa
How you want yo' lovin' done!

Jimboy was home. All the neighborhood could hear his rich low baritone voice giving birth to the blues. On Saturday night he and Annjee went to bed early. On Sunday night Aunt Hager said: "Put that guitar right up, less'n it's hymns you plans on playin'. An' I don't want too much o' them, 'larmin' de white neighbors."

But this was Monday, and the sun had scarcely fallen below the horizon before the music had begun to float down the alley, over back fences and into kitchen-windows where nice white ladies sedately washed their supper dishes.

Did you ever see peaches
Growin' on a watermelon vine?
Says did you ever see peaches
On a watermelon vine?
Did you ever see a woman
That I couldn't get for mine?

Long, lazy length resting on the kitchen-door-sill, back against the jamb, feet in the yard, fingers picking his sweet guitar, left hand holding against its finger-board the back of an old pocket-knife, sliding the knife upward, downward, getting thus weird croons and sighs from the vibrating strings:

O, I left ma mother
An' I cert'ly can leave you.
Indeed I left ma mother
An' I cert'ly can leave you,
For I'd leave any woman
That mistreats me like you do.

Jimboy, remembering brown-skin mamas in Natchez, Shreveport, Dallas; remembering Creole women in Baton Rouge, Louisiana:

O, yo' windin' an' yo' grindin'
Don't have no effect on me,
Babe, yo' windin' an' yo' grindin'
Don't have no 'fect on me,
'Cause I can wind an' grind
Like a monkey round a coconut-tree!

Then Harriett, standing under the ripening apple-tree, in the back yard, chiming in:

Now I see that you don't want me,
So it's fare thee, fare thee well!
Lawd, I see that you don't want me,
So it's fare—thee—well!
I can still get plenty lovin',
An' you can go to—Kansas City!

"O, play it, sweet daddy Jimboy!" She began to dance.

Then Hager, from her seat on the edge of the platform covering the well, broke out: "Here, madam! Stop that prancin'! Bad enough to have all this singin' without turnin' de yard into a show-house." But Harriett kept on, her hands picking imaginary cherries out of the stars, her hips speaking an earthly language quite their own.

"You got it, kid," said Jimboy, stopping suddenly, then fingering his instrument for another tune. "You do it like the stage women does. You'll be takin' Aida Walker's place if you keep on."

"Wha! Wha! . . . You chillen sho can sing!" Tom Johnson shouted his compliments from across the yard. And Sarah, beside him on the bench behind their shack, added: "Minds me o' de ole plantation times, honey! It sho do!"

"Unhuh! Bound straight fo' de devil, that's what they is," Hager returned calmly from her place beside the pump. "You an' Harriett both—singin' an' dancin' this stuff befo' these chillens here." She pointed to Sandy and Willie-Mae, who sat on the ground with their backs against the chicken-box. "It's a shame!"

"I likes it," said Willie-Mae.

"Me too," the little boy agreed.

"Naturally you would—none o' you-all's converted yet," countered the old woman to the children as she settled back against the pump to listen to some more.

The music rose hoarse and wild:

> I wonder where ma easy rider's gone?
> He done left me, put ma new gold watch in pawn.

It was Harriett's voice in plaintive moan to the night sky. Jimboy had taught her that song, but a slight, clay-colored brown boy who had hopped bells at the Clinton Hotel for a couple of months, on his way from Houston to Omaha, discovered its meaning to her. Puppy-love, maybe, but it had hurt when he went away, saying nothing. And the guitar in Jimboy's hands echoed that old pain with an even greater throb than the original ache itself possessed.

Approaching footsteps came from the front yard.

"Lord, I can hear you-all two blocks away!" said Annjee, coming around the house, home from work, with a bundle of food under her left arm. "Hello! How are you, daddy? Hello, ma! Gimme a kiss Sandy. . . . Lord, I'm hot and tired and most played out. This late just getting from work! . . . Here, Jimboy, come on in and eat some of these nice things the white folks had for supper." She stepped across her husband's outstretched legs into the kitchen. "I brought a mighty good piece of cold ham for you, hon', from Mis' Rice's."

"All right, sure, I'll be there in a minute," the man said, but he went on playing *Easy Rider,* and Harriett went on singing, while the food was forgotten on the table until long after Annjee had come outdoors again and sat down in the cool, tired of waiting for Jimboy to come in to her.

Off and on for nine years, ever since he had married Annjee, Jimboy and Harriett had been singing together in the evenings. When they started, Harriett was a little girl with braided hair, and each time that her roving brother-in-law stopped in Stanton, he would amuse himself by teaching her the old Southern songs, the popular rag-time ditties, and the hundreds of varying verses of the blues that he would pick up in the big dirty cities of the South. The child, with her strong sweet voice (colored folks called it alto) and her racial sense of rhythm, soon learned to sing the songs as well as Jimboy. He taught her the *parse me la,* too, and a few other movements peculiar to Southern Negro dancing, and sometimes together they went through the buck and wing and a few taps. It was all great fun, and innocent fun except when one stopped to think, as white folks did, that some of the blues lines had, not only double, but triple meanings, and some of the dance steps required very definite movements of the hips. But neither Harriett nor Jimboy soiled their minds by thinking. It was music, good exercise—and they loved it.

"Do you know this one, Annjee?" asked Jimboy, calling his wife's name out of sudden politeness because he had forgotten to eat her food, had hardly looked at her, in fact, since she came home. Now he glanced towards her in the darkness where she sat plump on a kitchen-chair in the yard, apart from the others, with her back to the growing corn in the garden. Softly he ran his fingers, light as a breeze, over his guitar strings, imitating the wind rustling through the long leaves of the corn. A rectangle of light from the kitchen-door fell into the yard striking sidewise across the healthy orange-yellow of his skin above the unbuttoned neck of his blue laborer's shirt.

"Come on, sing it with us, Annjee," he said.

"I don't know it," Annjee replied, with a lump in her throat, and her eyes on the silhouette of his long, muscular, animal-hard body. She loved Jimboy too much, that's what was the matter with her! She knew there was nothing between him and her young sister except the love of music, yet he might have dropped the guitar and left Harriett in the yard for a little while to come eat the nice cold slice of ham she had brought him. She hadn't seen him all day long. When she went to work this morning, he was still in bed—and now the blues claimed him.

In the starry blackness the singing notes of the guitar became a plaintive hum, like a breeze in a grove of palmettos; became a low moan, like the wind in a forest of live-oaks strung with long strands of hanging moss. The voice of Annjee's golden, handsome husband on the door-step rang high and far away, lonely-like, crying with only the guitar, not his wife, to understand; crying grotesquely, crying absurdly in the summer night:

> I got a mule to ride.
> I got a mule to ride.
> Down in the South somewhere
> I got a mule to ride.

Then asking the question as an anxious, left-lonesome girl-sweetheart would ask it:

You say you goin' North.
You say you goin' North.
How 'bout yo' . . . lovin' gal?
You say you goin' North.

Then sighing in rhythmical despair:

O, don't you leave me here.
Babe, don't you leave me here.
Dog-gone yo' comin' back!
Said don't you leave me here.

On and on the song complained, man-verses and woman-verses, to the evening air in stanzas that Jimboy had heard in the pine-woods of Arkansas from the lumber-camp workers; in other stanzas that were desperate and dirty like the weary roads where they were sung; and in still others that the singer created spontaneously in his own mouth then and there:

O, I done made ma bed,
Says I done made ma bed.
Down in some lonesome grave
I done made ma bed.

It closed with a sad eerie twang.

"That's right decent," said Hager. "Now I wish you-all'd play some o' ma pieces like *When de Saints Come Marchin' In* or *This World Is Not Ma Home*—something Christian from de church."

"Aw, mama, it's not Sunday yet," said Harriett.

"Sing *Casey Jones*," called old man Tom Johnson. "That's ma song."

So the ballad of the immortal engineer with another mama in the Promised Land rang out promptly in the starry darkness, while everybody joined in the choruses.

"Aw, pick it, boy," yelled the old man. "Can't nobody play like you."

And Jimboy remembered when he was a lad in Memphis that W. C. Handy had said: "You ought to make your living out of that, son." But he hadn't followed it up—too many things to see, too many places to go, too many other jobs.

"What song do you like, Annjee?" he asked, remembering her presence again.

"O, I don't care. Any ones you like. All of 'em are pretty." She was pleased and petulant and a little startled that he had asked her.

"All right, then," he said. "Listen to me:"

Here I is in de mean ole jail.
Ain't got nobody to go ma bail.
Lonesome an' sad an' chain gang bound—
Ever' friend I had's done turned me down.

"That's sho it!" shouted Tom Johnson in great sympathy. "Now, when I was in de Turner County Jail . . ."

"Shut up yo' mouth!" squelched Sarah, jabbing her husband in the ribs.

The songs went on, blues, shouts, jingles, old hits: *Bon Bon Buddy, the Chocolate Drop; Wrap Me in Your Big Red Shawl; Under the Old Apple Tree; Turkey in the Straw*—Jimboy and Harriett breaking the silence of the small-town summer night until Aunt Hager interrupted:

"You-all better wind up, chillens, 'cause I wants to go to bed. I ain't used to stayin' 'wake so late, nohow. Play something kinder decent there, son, fo' you stops."

Jimboy, to tease the old woman, began to rock and moan like an elder in the Sanctified Church, patting both feet at the same time as he played a hymn-like, lugubrious tune with a dancing overtone:

Tell me, sister,
Tell me, brother,
Have you heard de latest news?

Then seriously as if he were about to announce the coming of the Judgment:

A woman down in Georgia
Got her two sweet-men confused.

How terrible! How sad! moaned the guitar.

One knocked on de front do',
One knocked on de back—

Sad, sad . . . sad, sad! said the music.

Now that woman down in Georgia's
Door-knob is hung with black.

O, play that funeral march, boy! while the guitar laughed a dirge.

An' de hearse is comin' easy
With two rubber-tired hacks!

Followed by a long-drawn-out, churchlike:

Amen . . . !

Then with rapid glides, groans, and shouts the instrument screamed of a sudden in profane frenzy, and Harriett began to ball-the-jack, her arms flopping like the wings of a headless pigeon, the guitar strings whining in ecstasy, the player rocking gaily to the urgent music, his happy mouth crying: "Tack 'em on down, gal! Tack 'em on down, Harrie!"

But Annjee had risen.

"I wish you'd come in and eat the ham I brought you," she said as she picked up her chair and started towards the house. "And you, Sandy! Get up from under that tree and go to bed." She spoke roughly to the little fellow, whom the songs had set a-dreaming. Then to her husband: "Jimboy, I wish you'd come in."

The man stopped playing, with a deep vibration of the strings that seemed to echo through the whole world. Then he leaned his guitar against the side of the house and lifted straight up in his hairy arms Annjee's plump, brown-black little body while he kissed her as she wriggled like a stubborn child, her soft breasts rubbing his hard body through the coarse blue shirt.

"You don't like my old songs, do you, baby? You don't want to hear me sing 'em," he said, laughing. "Well, that's all right. I like you, anyhow, and I like your ham, and I like your kisses, and I like everything you bring me. Let's go in and chow down." And he carried her into the kitchen, where he sat with her on his knees as he ate the food she so faithfully had brought him from Mrs. J. J. Rice's dinner-table.

Outside, Willie-Mae went running home through the dark. And Harriett pumped a cool drink of water for her mother, then helped her to rise from her low seat, Sandy aiding from behind, with both hands pushing firmly in Aunt Hager's fleshy back. Then the three of them came into the house and glanced, as they passed through the kitchen, at Annjee sitting on Jimboy's lap with both dark arms tight around his neck.

"Looks like you're clinging to the Rock of Ages," said Harriett to her sister. "Be sure you don't slip, old evil gal!"

But at midnight, when the owl that nested in a tree near the corner began to hoot, they were all asleep—Annjee and Jimboy in one room, Harriett and Hager in another, with Sandy on the floor at the foot of his grandmother's bed. Far away on the railroad line a whistle blew, lonesome and long.

Six

Work

The sunflowers in Willie-Mae's back yard were taller than Tom Johnson's head, and the holly-hocks in the fence corners were almost as high. The nasturtiums, blood-orange and gold, tumbled over themselves all around Madam de Carter's house. Aunt Hager's sweet-william, her pinks, and her tiger-lilies were abloom and the apples on her single tree would soon be ripe. The adjoining yards of the three neighbors were gay with flowers. "Watch out for them dogs!" his grandmother told Sandy hourly, for the days had come when the bright heat made gentle animals go mad. Bees were heavy with honey, great green flies hummed through the air, yellow-black butterflies suckled at the rambling roses . . . and watermelons were on the market.

The Royal African Knights and Ladies of King Solomon's Scepter were preparing a drill for the September Emancipation celebration, a "Drill of All Nations," in which Annjee was to represent Sweden. It was not to be given for a month or more, but the first rehearsal would take place tonight.

"Sandy," his mother said, shaking him early in the morning as he lay on his pallet at the foot of Aunt Hager's bed, "listen here! I want you to come out to Mis' Rice's this evening and help me get through the dishes so's I can start home early, in time to wash and dress myself to go to the lodge hall. You hears me?"

"Yes'm," said Sandy, keeping his eyes closed to the bright stream of morning sunlight entering the window. But half an hour later, when Jimboy kicked him and said: "Hey, bo! You wanta go fishin'?" he got up at once, slid into his pants; and together they went out in the garden to dig worms. It was seldom that his father took him anywhere, and, of course, he wanted to go. Sandy adored Jimboy, but Jimboy, amiable and indulgent though he was, did not often care to be bothered with his ten-year-old son on his fishing expeditions.

Harriett had gone to her job, and Hager had long been at the tubs under the apple-tree when the two males emerged from the kitchen-door. "Huh! You ain't workin' this mawnin', is you?" the old woman grunted, bending steadily down, then up, over the wash-board.

"Nope," her tall son-in-law answered. "Donahoe laid me off yesterday on account o' the white bricklayers said they couldn't lay bricks with a nigger."

"Always something to keep you from workin'," panted Hager.

"Sure is," agreed Jimboy pleasantly. "But don't worry, me and Sandy's gonna catch you a mess o' fish for supper today. How's that, ma?"

"Don't need no fish," the old woman answered. "An' don't come ma-in' me! Layin' round here fishin' when you ought to be out makin' money to take care o' this house an' that chile o' your'n." The suds rose foamy white about her black arms as the clothes plushed up and down on the zinc wash-board. "Lawd deliver me from a lazy darky!"

But Jimboy and Sandy were already behind the tall corn, digging for bait near the back fence.

"Don't never let no one woman worry you," said the boy's father softly, picking the moist wriggling worms from the upturned loam. "Treat 'em like chickens, son. Throw 'em a little corn and they'll run after you, but don't give 'em too much. If you do, they'll stop layin' and expect you to wait on 'em."

"Will they?" asked Sandy.

The warm afternoon sun made the river a languid sheet of muddy gold, glittering away towards the bridge and the flour-mills a mile and a half off. Here in the quiet, on the end of a rotting jetty among the reeds, Jimboy and his son sat silently. A long string of small silver fish hung down into the water, keeping fresh, and the fishing-lines were flung far out in the stream, waiting for more bites. Not a breeze on the flat brown-gold river, not a ripple, not a sound. But once the train came by behind them, pouring out a great cloud of smoke and cinders and shaking the jetty.

"That's Number Five," said Jimboy. "Sure is flyin'," as the train disappeared between rows of empty box-cars far down the track, sending back a hollow clatter as it shot past the flour-mills, whose stacks could be dimly seen through the heat haze. Once the engine's whistle moaned shrilly.

"She's gone now," said Jimboy as the last click of the wheels died away. And, except for the drone of a green fly about the can of bait, there was again no sound to disturb the two fishermen.

Jimboy gazed at his lines. Across the river Sandy could make out, in the brilliant sunlight, the gold of wheat-fields and the green of trees on the hills. He wondered if it would be nice to live over there in the country.

"Man alive!" his father cried suddenly, hauling vigorously at one of the lines. "Sure got a real bite now. . . . Look at this catfish." From the water he pulled a large flopping lead-colored creature, with a fierce white mouth bleeding and gaping over the hook.

"He's on my line!" yelled Sandy. "I caught him!"

"Pshaw!" laughed Jimboy. "You was setting there dreaming."

"No, I wasn't!"

But just then, at the mills, the five-o'clock whistles blew. "Oh, gee, dad!" cried the boy, frightened. "I was s'posed to go to Mis' Rice's to help mama, and I come near forgetting it. She wants to get through early this evenin' to go to lodge meeting. I gotta hurry and go help her."

"Well, you better beat it then, and I'll look out for your line like I been doing and bring the fishes home."

So the little fellow balanced himself across the jetty, scrambled up the bank, and ran down the railroad track towards town. He was quite out of breath when he reached the foot of Penrose Street, with Mrs. Rice's house still ten blocks away, so he walked awhile, then ran again, down the long residential street, with its large houses sitting in green shady lawns far back from the sidewalk. Sometimes a sprinkler attached to a long rubber hose sprayed fountain-like jets of cold water on the thirsty grass. In one yard three golden-haired little girls were playing under an elm-tree, and in another a man and some children were having a leisurely game of croquet.

Finally Sandy turned into a big yard. The delicious scent of frying beefsteak greeted the sweating youngster as he reached the screen of the white lady's kitchen-door. Inside, Annjee was standing over the hot stove seasoning something in a saucepan, beads of perspiration on her dark face, and large damp spots under the arms of her dress.

"You better get here!" she said. "And me waiting for you for the last hour. Here, take this pick and break some ice for the tea." Sandy climbed up on a stool and raised the ice-box lid while his mother opened the oven and pulled out a pan of golden-brown biscuits. "Made these for your father," she remarked. "The white folks ain't asked for 'em, but they like 'em, too, so they can serve for both. . . . Jimboy's crazy about biscuits. . . . Did he work today?"

"No'm," said Sandy, jabbing at the ice. "We went fishing."

At that moment Mrs. Rice came into the kitchen, tall and blond, in a thin flowered gown. She was a middle-aged white woman with a sharp nasal voice.

"Annjee, I'd like the potatoes served just as they are in the casserole. And make several slices of very thin toast for my father. Now, be sure they *are* thin!"

"Yes, m'am," said Annjee stirring a spoonful of flour into the frying-pan, making a thick brown gravy.

"Old thin toast," muttered Annjee when Mrs. Rice had gone back to the front. "Always bothering round the kitchen! Here 'tis lodge-meeting night—dinner late anyhow—and she coming telling me to stop and make toast for the old man! He ain't too indigestible to eat biscuits like the rest of 'em. . . . White folks sure is a case!" She laid three slices of bread on top of the stove. "So spoiled with colored folks waiting on 'em all their days! Don't know what they'll do in heaven, 'cause I'm gonna sit down up there myself."

Annjee took the biscuits, light and brown, and placed some on a pink plate she had warmed. She carried them, with the butter and jelly, into the dining-room. Then she took the steak from the warmer, dished up the vegetables into gold-rimmed serving-dishes, and poured the gravy, which smelled deliciously onion-flavored.

"Gee, I'm hungry," said the child, with his eyes on the big steak ready to go in to the white people.

"Well, just wait," replied his mother. "You come to work, not to eat. . . . Whee! but it's hot today!" She wiped her wet face and put on a large white bungalow apron that had been hanging behind the door. Then she went with the iced tea and a pitcher of water into the dining-room, struck a Chinese gong, and came back to the kitchen to get the dishes of steaming food, which she carried in to the table.

It was some time before she returned from waiting on the table; so Sandy, to help her, began to scrape out the empty pans and put them to soak in the sink. He ate the stewed corn that had stuck in the bottom of one, and rubbed a piece of bread in the frying-pan where the gravy had been. His mother came out with the water-pitcher, broke some ice for it, and returned to the dining-room where Sandy could hear laughter, and the clinking of spoons in tea-glasses, and women talking. When Annjee came back into the kitchen, she took four custards from the ice-box and placed them on gold-rimmed plates.

"They're about through," she said to her son. "Sit down and I'll fix you up."

Sandy was very hungry and he hoped Mrs. Rice's family hadn't eaten all the steak, which had looked so good with its brown gravy and onions.

Shortly, his mother returned carrying the dishes that had been filled with hot food. She placed them on the kitchen-table in front of Sandy, but they were no longer full and no longer hot. The corn had thickened to a paste, and the potatoes were about gone; but there was still a ragged piece of steak left on the platter.

"Don't eat it all," said Annjee warningly. "I want to take some home to your father."

The bell rang in the dining-room. Annjee went through the swinging door and returned bearing a custard that had been but little touched.

"Here, sonny—the old man says it's too sweet for his stomach, so you can have this." She set the yellow cornstarch before Sandy. "He's seen these ripe peaches out here today and he wants some, that's all. More trouble than he's worth, po' old soul, and me in a hurry!" She began to peel the fruit. "Just like a chile, 'deed he is!" she added, carrying the sliced peaches into the dining-room and leaving Sandy with a plate of food before him, eating slowly. "When you rushing to get out, seems like white folks tries theirselves."

In a moment she returned, ill-tempered, and began to scold Sandy for taking so long with his meal.

"I asked you to help me so's I can get to the lodge on time, and you just set and chew and eat! . . . Here, wipe these dishes, boy!" Annjee began hurriedly to lay plates in a steaming row on the shelf of the sink; so Sandy got up and, between mouthfuls of pudding, wiped them with a large dish-towel.

Soon Mrs. Rice came into the kitchen again, briskly, through the swinging door and glanced about her. Sandy felt ashamed for the white woman to see him eating a left-over pudding from her table, so he put the spoon down.

"Annjee," the mistress said sharply. "I wish you wouldn't put quite so much onion in your sauce for the steak. I've mentioned it to you several times before, and you know very well we don't like it."

"Yes, m'am," said Annjee.

"And do *please* be careful that our drinking water is cold before meals are served. . . . You were certainly careless tonight. You must think more about what you are doing, Annjee."

Mrs. Rice went out again through the swinging door, but Sandy stood near the sink with a burning face and eyes that had suddenly filled with angry tears. He couldn't help it—hearing his sweating mother reprimanded by this tall white woman in the flowered dress. Black, hard-working Annjee answered: "Yes, m'am," and that was all—but Sandy cried.

"Dry up," his mother said crossly when she saw him, thinking he was crying because she had asked him to work. "What's come over you, anyway?—can't even wipe a few plates for me and act nice about it!"

He didn't answer. When the dining-room had been cleared and the kitchen put in order, Annjee told him to empty the garbage while she wrapped in newspapers several little bundles of food to carry to Jimboy. Then they went out the back door, around the big house to the street, and trudged the fourteen blocks to Aunt Hager's, taking short cuts through alleys, passing under arc-lights that sputtered whitely in the deepening twilight, and greeting with an occasional "Howdy" other poor colored folks also coming home from work.

"How are you, Sister Jones?"

"Right smart, I thank yuh!" as they passed.

Once Annjee spoke to her son. "Evening's the only time we niggers have to ourselves!" she said. "Thank God for night . . .'cause all day you gives to white folks."

Seven

White Folks

When they got home, Aunt Hager was sitting in the cool of the evening on her new porch, which had been rebuilt for thirty-five dollars added to the mortgage. The old woman was in her rocking-chair, with Jimboy, one foot on the ground and his back against a pillar, lounging at her feet. The two were quarrelling amicably over nothing as Annjee and Sandy approached.

"Good-evenin', you-all," said Annjee. "I brought you a nice piece o' steak, Jimboy-sugar, and some biscuits to go with it. Come on in and eat while I get dressed to go to the drill practice. I got to hurry."

'We don't want no steak now," Jimboy answered without moving. "Aunt Hager and me had fresh fish for supper and egg-corn-bread and we're full. We don't need nothin' more."

"Oh! . . ." said Annjee disappointedly. "Well, come on in anyhow, honey, and talk while I get dressed." So he rose lazily and followed his wife into the house.

Shortly, Sister Johnson, pursued by the ever-present Willie-Mae, came through the blue-grey darkness from next door. "Good-evenin', Sister Williams; how you been today?"

"Tolable," answered Hager, " 'ceptin' I's tired out from washin' an' rinsin'. Have a seat. . . . You Sandy, go in de house an' get Sister Johnson a settin' chair. . . . Where's Tom?"

"Lawd, chile, he done gone to bed long ago. That there sewer-diggin' job ain't so good fer a man old as Tom. He 'bout played out. . . . I done washed fer Mis' Cohn maself today. . . . Umh! dis cheer feels good! . . . Looked like to me she had near 'bout fifty babies' diddies in de wash. You know she done got twins, 'sides dat young-'un born last year."

The conversation of the two old women rambled on as their grandchildren ran across the front yard laughing, shrieking, wrestling; catching fire-flies and watching them glow in closed fists, then releasing them to twinkle in the sultry night-air.

Harriett came singing out of the house and sat down on the edge of the porch. "Lord, it's hot! . . . How are you, Mis' Johnson? I didn't see you in the dark."

"Jest tolable, chile," said the old woman, "but I can't kick. Honey, when you gits old as I is, you'll be doin' well if you's livin' a-tall, de way you chillens runs round now 'days! How come you ain't out to some party dis evenin'?"

"O, there's no party tonight," said Harriett laughing. "Besides, this new job of mine's a heart-breaker, Mis' Johnson. I got to stay home and rest now. I'm kitchen-girl at that New Albert Restaurant, and time you get through wrestling with pots and arguing with white waitresses and colored cooks, you don't feel much like running out at night. But the shifts aren't bad, though, food's good, and—well, you can't expect everything." She shrugged her shoulders against the two-by-four pillar on which her back rested.

"'Long's it keeps you off de streets, I's glad," said Hager, rocking contentedly. "Maybe I can git you goin' to church agin now."

"Aw, I don't like church," the girl replied.

"An', chile, I can't blame you much," said Sister Johnson, fumbling in the pocket of her apron. "De way dese churches done got now'days. . . . Sandy, run in de house an' ask yo' pappy fo' a match to light ma pipe. . . . It ain't 'Come to Jesus' no mo' a-tall. Ministers dese days an' times don't care nothin' 'bout po' Jesus. 'Stead o' dat it's rally dis an' collection dat, an' de aisle wants a new carpet, an' de pastor needs a 'lectric fan fer his red-hot self." The old sister spat into the yard. "Money! That's all 'tis! An' white folkses' religion—Lawd help! 'Taint no use in mentionin' them."

"True," agreed Hager.

"'Cause if de gates o' heaven shuts in white folkses' faces like de do's o' dey church in us niggers' faces, it'll be too bad! Yes, sir! One thing sho, de Lawd ain't prejudiced!"

"No," said Hager; "but He don't love ugly, neither in niggers nor in white folks."

"Now, talking about white folks' religion," said Annjee, emerging from the house with a fresh white dress on, "why, Mis' Rice where I work don't think no more about playing bridge on Sunday than she does about praying—and I ain't never seen her pray yet."

"You're nuts," said Jimboy behind her. "People's due to have a little fun on Sundays. That's what's the matter with colored folks now—work all week and then set up in church all day Sunday, and don't even know what's goin' on in the rest of the world."

"Huh!" grunted Hager.

"Well, we won't argue, daddy," Annjee smiled. "Come on and walk a piece with me, sweetness. Here 'tis nearly nine and I should a been at the hall at eight, but colored folks are always behind the clock. Come on, Jimboy."

"Good-bye, mama," yelled Sandy from the lawn as his parents strolled up the street together.

"Jimboy's right," said Harriett. "Darkies do like the church too much, but white folks don't care nothing about it at all. They're too busy getting theirs out of this world, not from God. And I don't blame 'em, except that they're so mean to niggers. They're right, though, looking out for themselves . . . and yet I hate 'em for it. They don't have to mistreat us besides, do they?"

"Honey, don't talk that way," broke in Hager. "It ain't Christian, chile. If you don't like 'em, pray for 'em, but don't feel evil against 'em. I was in slavery, Harrie, an' I been knowin' white folks all ma life, an' they's good as far as they can see—but when it comes to po' niggers, they just can't see far, that's all."

Harriett opened her mouth to reply, but Jimboy, who left Annjee at the corner and had returned to the porch, beat her to it. "We too dark for 'em, ma," he laughed. "How they gonna see in the dark? You colored folks oughta get lighter, that's what!"

"Shut up yo' mouth, you yaller rooster!" said Sister Johnson. "White folks is white folks, an' dey's mean! I can't help what Hager say," the old woman disagreed emphatically with her crony. "Ain't I been knowin' crackers sixty-five years, an' ain't dey de cause o' me bein' here in Stanton 'stead o' in ma home right today? De dirty buzzards! Ain't I nussed t'ree of 'em up from babies like ma own chillens, and ain't dem same t'ree boys done turned round an' helped run me an' Tom out o' town?"

The old sister took a long draw on her corn-cob pipe, and a fiery red spot glowed in its bowl, while Willie-Mae and Sandy stopped playing and sat down on the porch as she began a tale they had all heard at least a dozen times.

"I's tole you 'bout it befo', ain't I?" asked Sister Johnson.

"Not me," lied Jimboy, who was anxious to keep her going.

"No, you haven't," Harriett assured her.

"Well, it were like dis," and the story unwound itself, the preliminary details telling how, as a young freed-girl after the Civil War, Sister Johnson had gone into service for a white planter's family in a Mississippi town near Vicksburg. While attached to this family, she married Tom Johnson, then a field-hand, and raised five children of her own during the years that followed, besides caring for three boys belonging to her white mistress, nursing them at her black breasts and sometimes leaving her own young ones in the cabin to come and stay with her white charges when they were ill. These called her mammy, too, and when they were men and married, she still went to see them and occasionally worked for their families.

"Now, we niggers all lived at de edge o' town in what de whites called Crowville, an' most of us owned little houses an' farms, an' we did right well raisin' cotton an' sweet 'taters an' all. Now, dat's where de trouble started! We was doin' too well, an' de white folks said so! But we ain't paid 'em no 'tention, jest thought dey was talkin' fer de pastime of it. . . . Well, we all started fixin' up our houses an' paintin' our fences, an' Crowville looked kinder decent-like when de white folks 'gin to 'mark, so's we servants could hear 'em, 'bout niggers livin' in painted houses an' dressin' fine like we was somebody! . . . Well, dat went on fer some time wid de whites talkin' an' de coloreds doin' better'n better year by year, sellin' mo' cotton ever' day an' gittin' nice furniture an' buyin' pianers, till by an' by a prosp'rous nigger named John Lowdins up an' bought one o' dese here new autimobiles—an' dat settled it! . . . A white man in town one Sat'day night tole John to git out o' dat damn car 'cause a nigger ain't got no business wid a autimobile nohow! An' John say: 'I ain't gonna git out!' Den de white man, what's been drinkin', jump up on de runnin'-bo'ad an' bust John in de mouth fer talkin' back to him—he a white man, an' Lowdins nothin' but a nigger. 'De very idee!' he say, and hit John in de face six or seven times. Den John drawed his gun! One! two! t'ree! he fiah, hit dis old red-neck cracker in de shoulder, but he ain't dead! Ain't nothin' meant to kill a cracker what's drunk. But John think he done kilt this white man, an' so he left him kickin' in de street while he runs that car o' his'n lickety-split out o' town, goes to Vicksburg, an' catches de river boat. . . . Well, sir! Dat night Crowville's plumb full o' white folks wid dogs an' guns an' lanterns, shoutin' an' yellin' an' scarin' de wits out o' us coloreds an' wakin' us up way late in de night-time lookin' fer John, an' dey don't find him. . . . Den dey say dey gwine teach dem Crowville niggers a lesson, all of 'em, paintin' dey houses an' buyin' cars an' livin' like white folks, so dey comes to our do's an' tells us to leave our houses—git de hell out in de fields, 'cause dey don't want to kill nobody there dis evenin'! . . . Well, sir! Niggers in night-gowns an' underwear an' shimmies, half-naked an' barefooted, was runnin' ever' which way in de dark, scratchin' up dey legs in de briah patches, fallin' on dey faces, scared to death! Po' ole Pheeny, what ain't moved from her bed wid de paralytics fo' six years, dey made her daughters carry her out, screamin' an' wall-eyed, an' set her in de middle o' de cotton-patch. An'

Brian, what was sleepin' naked, jumps up an' grabs his wife's apron and runs like a rabbit with not another blessed thing on! Chillens squallin' ever'where, an' mens a-pleadin' an' a-cussin', an' womens cryin' 'Lawd 'a' Mercy' wid de whites of dey eyes showin'! . . . Den looked like to me 'bout five hundred white mens took torches an' started burnin' wid fiah ever' last house, an' hen-house, an' shack, an' barn, an' privy, an' shed, an' cow-slant in de place! An' all de niggers, when de fiah blaze up, was moanin' in de fields, callin' on de Lawd fer help! An' de fiah light up de whole country clean back to de woods! You could smell fiah, an' you could see it red, an' taste de smoke, an' feel it stingin' yo' eyes. An' you could hear de bo'ads a-fallin' an' de glass a-poppin', an' po' animals roastin' an' fryin' an' a-tearin' at dey halters. An' one cow run out, fiah all ovah, wid her milk streamin' down. An' de smoke roll up, de cotton-fields were red . . . an' dey ain't been no mo' Crowville after dat night. No, sir! De white folks ain't left nothin' fer de niggers, not nary bo'ad standin' one 'bove another, not even a dog-house. . . . When it were done—nothin' but ashes! . . . De white mens was ever'where wid guns, scarin' de po' blacks an' keepin' 'em off, an' one of 'em say: 'I got good mind to try yo'-all's hide, see is it bullet proof—gittin' so prosp'rous, paintin' yo' houses an' runnin ovah white folks wid yo' damn gasoline buggies! Well, after dis you'll damn sight have to bend yo' backs an' work a little!' . . . Dat's what de white man say. . . . But we didn't—not yit! 'Cause ever' last nigger moved from there dat Sunday mawnin'. It were right funny to see ole folks what ain't never been out o' de backwoods pickin' up dey feet an' goin'. Ma Bailey say: 'De Lawd done let me live eighty years in one place, but ma next eighty'll be spent in St. Louis.' An' she started out walkin' wid neither bag nor baggage. . . . An' me an' Tom took Willie-Mae an' went to Cairo, an' Tom started railroad-workin' wid a gang; then we come on up here, been five summers ago dis August. We ain't had not even a rag o' clothes when we left Crowville—so don't tell me 'bout white folks bein' good, Hager, 'cause I knows 'em. . . . Yes, indeedy, I really knows 'em. . . . Dey done made us leave our home."

The old woman knocked her pipe against the edge of the porch, emptying its dead ashes into the yard, and for a moment no one spoke. Sandy, trembling, watched a falling star drop behind the trees. Then Jimboy's deep voice, like a bitter rumble in the dark, broke the silence.

"I know white folks, too," he said. "I lived in the South."

"And I ain't never been South," added Harriett hoarsely, "but I know 'em right here . . . and I hate 'em!"

"De Lawd hears you," said Hager.

"I don't care if He does hear me, mama! You and Annjee are too easy. You just take whatever white folks give you—*coon* to your face, and *nigger* behind your backs—and don't say nothing. You run to some white person's back door for every job you get, and then they pay you one dollar for five dollars' worth of work, and fire you whenever they get ready."

"They do that all right," said Jimboy. "They don't mind firin' you. Wasn't I layin' brick on the *Daily Leader* building and the white union men started sayin' they couldn't work with me because I wasn't in the union? So the boss come up and paid me off. 'Good man, too,' he says to me, 'but I can't buck the union.' So I said I'd join, but I knew they wouldn't let me before I went to the office. Anyhow, I tried. I told the guys there I was a bricklayer and asked 'em how I was gonna work if I couldn't be in the union. And the fellow who had the cards, secretary I guess he was, says kinder sharp, like he didn't want to be bothered: 'That's your look-out, big boy, not mine.' So you see how much the union cares if a black man works or not."

"Ain't Tom had de same trouble?" affirmed Sister Johnson. "Got put off de job mo'n once on 'count o' de white unions."

"O, they've got us cornered, all right," said Jimboy. "The white folks are like farmers that own all the cows and let the niggers take care of 'em. Then they make you pay a sweet price for skimmed milk and keep the cream for themselves—but I reckon cream's too rich for rusty-kneed niggers anyhow!"

They laughed.

"That's a good one!" said Harriett. "You know old man Wright, what owns the flour-mill and the new hotel—how he made his start off colored women working in his canning factory? Well, when he built that orphan home for colored and gave it to the city last year, he had the whole place made just about the size of the dining-room at his own house. They got the little niggers in that asylum cooped up like chickens. And the reason he built it was to get the colored babies out of the city home, with its nice playgrounds, because he thinks the two races oughtn't to mix! But he don't care how hard he works his colored help in that canning factory of his, does he? Wasn't I there thirteen hours a day in tomato season? Nine cents an hour and five cents overtime after ten hours—and you better work overtime if you want to keep the job! . . . As for the races mixing—ask some of those high yellow women who work there. They know a mighty lot about the races mixing!"

"Most of 'em lives in de Bottoms, where de sportin' houses are," said Hager. "It's a shame de way de white mens keeps them sinful places goin'."

"It ain't Christian, is it?" mocked Harriett. . . . "White folks!" . . . And she shrugged her shoulders scornfully. Many disagreeable things had happened to her through white folks. Her first surprising and unpleasantly lasting impression of the pale world had come when, at the age of five, she had gone alone one day to play in a friendly white family's yard. Some mischievous small boys there, for the fun of it, had taken hold of her short kinky braids and pulled them, dancing round and round her and yelling: "Blackie! Blackie! Blackie!" while she screamed and tried to run away. But they held her and pulled her hair terribly, and her friends laughed because she *was* black and she *did* look funny. So from that time on, Harriett had been uncomfortable in the presence of whiteness, and that early hurt had grown with each new incident into a rancor that she could not hide and a dislike that had become pain.

Now, because she could sing and dance and was always amusing, many of the white girls in high school were her friends. But when the three-thirty bell rang and it was time to go home, Harriett knew their polite "Good-bye" was really a kind way of saying: "We can't be seen on the streets with a colored girl." To loiter with these same young ladies had been all right during their grade-school years, when they were all younger, but now they had begun to feel the eyes of young white boys staring from the windows of pool halls, or from the tennis-courts near the park—so it was not proper to be seen with Harriett.

But a very unexpected stab at the girl's pride had come only a few weeks ago when she had gone with her class-mates, on tickets issued by the school, to see an educational film of the under-sea world at the Palace Theatre, on Main Street. It was a special performance given for the students, and each class had had seats allotted to them beforehand; so Harriett sat with her class and had begun to enjoy immensely the strange wonders of the ocean depths when an usher touched her on the shoulder.

"The last three rows on the left are for colored," the girl in the uniform said.

"I—But—But I'm with my class," Harriett stammered. "We're all supposed to sit here."

"I can't help it," insisted the usher, pointing towards the rear of the theatre, while her voice carried everywhere. "Them's the house rules. No argument now—you'll have to move."

So Harriett rose and stumbled up the dark aisle and out into the sunlight, her slender body hot with embarrassment and rage. The teacher saw her leave the theatre without a word of protest, and none of her white classmates defended her for being black. They didn't care.

"All white people are alike, in school and out," Harriett concluded bitterly, as she told of her experiences to the folks sitting with her on the porch in the dark.

Once, when she had worked for a Mrs. Leonard Baker on Martin Avenue, she accidentally broke a precious cut-glass pitcher used to serve some out-of-town guests. And when she tried to apologize for the accident, Mrs. Baker screamed in a rage: "Shut up, you impudent little black wench! Talking back to me after breaking up my dishes. All you darkies are alike—careless sluts—and I wouldn't have a one of you in my house if I could get anybody else to work for me without paying a fortune. You're all impossible."

"So that's the way white people feel," Harriett said to Aunt Hager and Sister Johnson and Jimboy, while the two children listened. "They wouldn't have a single one of us around if they could help it. It don't matter to them if we're shut out of a job. It don't matter to them if niggers have only the back row at the movies. It don't matter to them when they hurt our feelings without caring and treat us like slaves down South and like beggars up North. No, it don't matter to them. . . . White folks run the world, and the only thing colored folks are expected to do is work and grin and take off their hats as though it don't matter. . . . O, I hate 'em!" Harriett cried, so fiercely that Sandy was afraid. "I hate white folks!" she said to everybody on the porch in the darkness. "You can pray for 'em if you want to, mama, but I hate 'em! . . . I hate white folks! . . . I hate 'em all!"

Eight

Dance

Mrs. J. J. Rice and family usually spent ten days during the August heat at Lake Dale, and thither they had gone now, giving Annjee a forced vacation with no pay. Jimboy was not working, and so his wife found ten days of rest without income not especially agreeable. Nevertheless, she decided that she might as well enjoy the time; so she and Jimboy went to the country for a week with Cousin Jessie, who had married one of the colored farmers of the district. Besides, Annjee thought that Jimboy might help on the farm and so make a little money. Anyway, they would get plenty to eat, because Jessie kept a good table. And since Jessie had eight children of her own, they did not take Sandy with them—eight were enough for a woman to be worried with at one time!

Aunt Hager had been ironing all day on the Reinharts' clothes—it was Friday. At seven o'clock Harriet came home, but she had already eaten her supper at the restaurant where she worked.

"Hello, mama! Hy, Sandy!" she said, but that was all, because she and her mother were not on the best of terms. Aunt Hager was attempting to punish her youngest daughter by not allowing her to leave the house after dark, since Harriett, on Tuesday night, had been out until one o'clock in the morning with no better excuse than a party at Maudel's. Aunt Hager had threatened to whip her then and there that night.

"You ain't had a switch on yo' hide fo' three years, but don't think you's gettin' too big fo' me not to fan yo' behind, madam. 'Spare de rod an' spoil de chile,' that's what de Bible say, an' Lawd knows you sho is spoiled! De idee of a young gal yo' age stayin' out till one o'clock in de mawnin', an' me not knowed where you's at. . . . Don't you talk back to me! . . . You rests in this house ever' night this week an' don't put yo' foot out o' this yard after you comes from work, that's what you do. Lawd knows I don't know what I's gonna do with you. I works fo' you an' I prays fo' you, an' if you don't mind, I's sho gonna whip you, even if you is goin' on seventeen years old!"

Tonight as soon as she came from work Harriett went into her mother's room and lay across the bed. It was very warm in the little four-room house, and all the windows and doors were open.

"We's got some watermelon here, daughter," Hager called from the kitchen. "Don't you want a nice cool slice?"

"No," the girl replied. She was fanning herself with a palm-leaf fan, her legs in their cheap silk stockings hanging over the side of the bed, and her heels kicking the floor. Benbow's Band played tonight for the dance at Chaver's Hall, and everybody was going—but her. Gee, it was hard to have a Christian mother! Harriett kicked her slippers off with a bang and rolled over on her stomach, burying her powdery face in the pillows. . . . Somebody knocked at the back door.

A boy's voice was speaking excitedly to Hager: "Hemorrhages . . . and papa can't stop 'em . . . she's coughin' something terrible . . . says can't you please come over and help him"— frightened and out of breath.

"Do, Jesus!" cried Hager. "I'll be with you right away, chile. Don't worry." She rushed into the bedroom to change her apron. "You Harriett, listen; Sister Lane's taken awful sick an' Jimmy says she's bleedin' from de mouth. If I ain't back by nine o'clock, see that that chile Sandy's in de bed. An' you know you ain't to leave this yard under no circumstances. . . . Po' Mis' Lane! She sho do have it hard." In a whisper: "I 'spects she's got de T. B., that what I 'spects!" And the old woman hustled out to join the waiting youngster. Jimmy was leaning against the door, looking at Sandy, and neither of the boys knew what to say. Jimmy Lane wore his mother's cast-off shoes to school, and Sandy used to tease him, but tonight he didn't tease his friend about his shoes.

"You go to bed 'fore it gets late," said his grandmother, starting down the alley with Jimmy.

"Yes'm," Sandy called after her. "So long, Jim!" He stood under the apple-tree and watched them disappear.

Aunt Hager had scarcely gotten out of sight when there was a loud knock at the front door, and Sandy ran around the house to see Harriett's boy friend, Mingo, standing in the dusk outside the screen-door, waiting to be let in.

Mingo was a patent-leather black boy with wide, alive nostrils and a mouth that split into a lighthouse smile on the least provocation. His body was heavy and muscular, resting on bowed legs that curved backward as though the better to brace his chunky torso; and his hands were hard from mixing concrete and digging ditches for the city's new water-mains.

"I know it's tonight, but I can't go," Sandy heard his aunt say at the door. They were speaking of Benbow's dance. "And his band don't come here often, neither. I'm heart-sick having to stay home, dog-gone it all, especially this evening!"

"Aw, come on and go anyway," pleaded Mingo. "After I been savin' up my dough for two weeks to take you, and got my suit cleaned and pressed and all. Heck! If you couldn't go and knew it yesterday, why didn't you tell me? That's a swell way to treat a fellow!"

"Because I wanted to go," said Harriett; "and still want to go. . . . Don't make so much difference about mama, because she's mad anyhow . . . but what could we do with this kid? We can't leave him by himself." She looked at Sandy, who was standing behind Mingo listening to everything.

"You can take me," the child offered anxiously, his eyes dancing at the delightful prospect. "I'll behave, Harrie, if you take me, and I won't tell on you either. . . . Please lemme go, Mingo. I ain't never seen a big dance in my life. I wanta go."

"Should we?" asked Harriett doubtfully, looking at her boy friend standing firmly on his curved legs.

"Sure, if we got to have him . . . damn 'im!" Mingo replied. "Better the kid than no dance. Go git dressed." So Harriett made a dash for the clothes-closet, while Sandy ran to get a clean waist from one of his mother's dresser-drawers, and Mingo helped him put it on, cussing softly to himself all the while. "But it ain't your fault, pal, is it?" he said to the little boy.

"Sure not," Sandy replied. "I didn't tell Aunt Hager to make Harrie stay home. I tried to 'suade grandma to let her go," the child lied, because he liked Mingo. "I guess she won't care about her goin' to just one dance." He wanted to make everything all right so the young man wouldn't be worried. Besides, Sandy very much wanted to go himself.

"Let's beat it," Harriett shrilled excitedly before her dress was fastened, anxious to be gone lest her mother come home. She was powdering her face and neck in the next room, nervous, happy, and afraid all at once. The perfume, the voice, and the pat, pat, pat of the powder-puff came out to the waiting gentleman.

"Yo' car's here, madam," mocked Mingo. "Step right this way and let's be going!"

> Wonder where ma easy rider's gone—
> He done left me, put ma new gold watch in pawn!

Like a blare from hell the second encore of *Easy Rider* filled every cubic inch of the little hall with hip-rocking notes. Benbow himself was leading and the crowd moved like jelly-fish dancing on individual sea-shells, with Mingo and Harriett somewhere among the shakers. But they were not of them, since each couple shook in a world of its own, as, with a weary wail, the music abruptly ceased.

Then, after scarcely a breath of intermission, the band struck up again with a lazy one-step. A tall brown boy in a light tan suit walked his partner straight down the whole length of the floor and, when he reached the corner, turned leisurely in one spot, body riding his hips, eyes on the ceiling, and his girl shaking her full breasts against his pink silk shirt. Then they recrossed the width of the room, turned slowly, repeating themselves, and began again to walk rhythmically down the hall, while the music was like a lazy river flowing between mountains, carving a canyon coolly, calmly, and without insistence. The *Lazy River One-Step* they might have called what the band was playing as the large crowd moved with the greatest ease about the hall. To drum-beats barely audible, the tall boy in the tan suit walked his partner round and round time after time, revolving at each corner with eyes uplifted, while the piano was the water flowing, and the high, thin chords of the banjo were the mountains floating in the clouds. But in sultry tones, alone and always, the brass cornet spoke harshly about the earth.

Sandy sat against the wall in a hard wooden folding chair. There were other children scattered lonesomely about on chairs, too, watching the dancers, but he didn't seem to know any of them. When the music stopped, all the chairs quickly filled with loud-talking women and girls in brightly colored dresses who fanned themselves with handkerchiefs and wiped their sweating brows. Sandy thought maybe he should give his seat to one of the women when he saw Maudel approaching.

"Here, honey," she said. "Take this dime and buy yourself a bottle of something cold to drink. I know Harriett ain't got you on her mind out there dancin'. This music is certainly righteous, chile!" She laughed as she handed Sandy a coin and closed her pocket-book. He liked Maudel, although he knew his grandmother didn't. She was a large good-natured brown-skinned girl who walked hippishly and used too much rouge on her lips. But she always gave Sandy a dime, and she was always laughing.

He went through the crowd towards the soft-drink stand at the end of the hall. "Gimme a bottle o' cream soda," he said to the fat orange-colored man there, who had his sleeves rolled up and a white butcher's-apron covering his barrel-like belly. The man put his hairy arms down into a zinc tub full of ice and water and began pulling out bottles, looking at their caps, and then dropping them back into the cold liquid.

"Don't seem like we got no cream, sonny. How'd a lemon do you?" he asked above the bedlam of talking voices.

"Naw," said Sandy. "It's too sour."

On the improvised counter of boards the wares displayed consisted of cracker-jacks, salted peanuts, a box of gum, and Sen Sens, while behind the counter was a lighted oil-stove holding a tin pan full of spare-ribs, sausage, and fish; and near it an ice-cream freezer covered with a brown sack. Some cases of soda were on the floor beside the zinc tub filled with bottles, in which the man was still searching.

"Nope, no cream," said the fat man.

"Well, gimme a fish sandwich then," Sandy replied, feeling very proud because some kids were standing near, looking at him as he made his purchase like a grown man.

"Buy me one, too," suggested a biscuit-colored little girl in a frilly dirty-white dress.

"I only got a dime," Sandy said. "But you can have half of mine." And he gallantly broke in two parts the double square of thick bread, with its hunk of greasy fish between, and gravely handed a portion to the grinning little girl.

"Thanks," she said, running away with the bread and fish in her hands.

"Shame on you!" teased a small boy, rubbing his forefingers at Sandy. "You got a girl! You got a girl!"

"Go chase yourself!" Sandy replied casually, as he picked out the bones and smacked his lips on the sweet fried fish. The orchestra was playing another one-step, with the dancers going like shuttles across the floor. Sandy saw his Aunt Harriett and a slender yellow boy named Billy Sanderlee doing a series of lazy, intricate steps as they wound through the crowd from one end of the hall to the other. Certain less accomplished couples were watching them with admiration.

Sandy, when he had finished eating, decided to look for the wash-room, where he could rinse his hands, because they were greasy and smelled fishy. It was at the far corner of the hall. As he pushed open the door marked GENTS, a thick grey cloud of cigarette-smoke drifted out. The stench of urine and gin and a crowd of men talking, swearing, and drinking licker surrounded the little boy as he elbowed his way towards the wash-bowls. All the fellows were shouting loudly to one another and making fleshy remarks about the women they had danced with.

"Boy, you ought to try Velma," a mahogany-brown boy yelled. "She sure can go."

"Hell," answered a whisky voice somewhere in the smoke. "That nappy-headed black woman? Gimme a high yaller for mine all de time. I can't use no coal!"

"Well, de blacker de berry, de sweeter de juice," protested a slick-haired ebony youth in the center of the place. . . . "Ain't that right, sport?" he demanded of Sandy, grabbing him jokingly by the neck and picking him up.

"I guess it is," said the child, scared, and the men laughed.

"Here, kid, buy yourself a drink," the slick-headed boy said, slipping Sandy a nickel as he set him down gently at the door. "And be sure it's pop not gin."

Outside, the youngster dried his wet hands on a handkerchief, blinked his smoky eyes, and immediately bought the soda, a red strawberry liquid in a long, thick bottle.

Suddenly and without warning the cornet blared at the other end of the hall in an ear-splitting wail: "Whaw! . . . Whaw! . . . Whaw! . . . Whaw!" and the snare-drum rolled in answer. A pause . . . then the loud brassy notes were repeated and the banjo came in, "Plinka, plink, plink," like timid drops of rain after a terrific crash of thunder. Then quite casually, as though nothing had happened, the piano lazied into a slow drag, with all the other instruments following. And with the utmost nonchalance the drummer struck into time.

"Ever'body shake!" cried Benbow, as a ribbon of laughter swirled round the hall.

Couples began to sway languidly, melting together like candy in the sun as hips rotated effortlessly to the music. Girls snuggled pomaded heads on men's chests, or rested powdered chins on men's shoulders, while wild young boys put both arms tightly around their partners' waists and let their hands hang down carelessly over female haunches. Bodies moved ever so easily together—ever so easily, as Benbow turned towards his musicians and cried through cupped hands: "Aw, screech it, boys!"

A long, tall, gangling gal stepped back from her partner, adjusted her hips, and did a few easy, gliding steps all her own before her man grabbed her again.

"Eu-o-oo-ooo-oooo!" moaned the cornet titillating with pain, as the banjo cried in stop-time, and the piano sobbed aloud with a rhythmical, secret passion. But the drums kept up their hard steady laughter—like somebody who don't care.

"I see you plowin', Uncle Walt," called a little autumn-leaf brown with switching skirts to a dark-purple man grinding down the center of the floor with a yellow woman. Two short prancing blacks stopped in their tracks to quiver violently. A bushy-headed girl threw out her arms, snapped her fingers, and began to holler: "Hey! . . . Hey!" while her perspiring partner held doggedly to each hip in an effort to keep up with her. All over the hall, people danced their own individual movements to the scream and moan of the music.

"Get low . . . low down . . . down!" cried the drummer, bouncing like a rubber ball in his chair. The banjo scolded in diabolic glee, and the cornet panted as though it were out of breath, and Benbow himself left the band and came out on the floor to dance slowly and ecstatically with a large Indian-brown woman covered with diamonds.

"Aw, do it, Mister Benbow!" one of his admirers shouted frenziedly as the ball itself seemed to tremble.

"High yallers, draw nigh! Brown-skins, come near!" somebody squalled. "But black gals, stay where you are!"

"Whaw! Whaw! Whaw!" mocked the cornet—but the steady tomtom of the drums was no longer laughter now, no longer even pleasant: the drum-beats had become sharp with surly sound, like heavy waves that beat angrily on a granite rock. And under the dissolute spell of its own rhythm the music had got quite beyond itself. The four black men in Benbow's wandering band were exploring depths to which mere sound had no business to go. Cruel, desolate, unadorned was their music now, like the body of a ravished woman on the sun-baked earth; violent and hard, like a giant standing over his bleeding mate in the blazing sun. The odors of bodies, the stings of flesh, and the utter emptiness of soul when all is done—these things the piano and the drums, the cornet and the twanging banjo insisted on hoarsely to a beat that made the dancers move, in that little hall, like pawns on a frenetic checker-board.

"Aw, play it, Mister Benbow!" somebody cried.

The earth rolls relentlessly, and the sun blazes for ever on the earth, breeding, breeding. But why do you insist like the earth, music? Rolling and breeding, earth and sun for ever relentlessly. But why do you insist like the sun? Like the lips of women? Like the bodies of men, relentlessly?

"Aw, play it, Mister Benbow!"

But why do you insist, music?

Who understands the earth? Do you, Mingo? Who understands the sun? Do you, Harriett? Does anybody know—among you high yallers, you jelly-beans, you pinks and pretty daddies, among you sealskin browns, smooth blacks, and chocolates-to-the-bone—does anybody know the answer?

"Aw, play it, Benbow!"

"It's midnight. De clock is strikin' twelve, an . . ."

"Aw, play it, Mister Benbow!"

During intermission, when the members of the band stopped making music to drink gin and talk to women, Harriett and Mingo bought Sandy a box of cracker-jacks and another bottle of soda and left him standing in the middle of the floor holding both. His young aunt had forgotten time, so Sandy decided to go upstairs to the narrow unused balcony that ran the length of one side of the place. It was dusty up there, but a few broken chairs stood near the railing and he sat on one of them. He leaned his arms on the banister, rested his chin in his hands, and when the music started, he looked down on the mass of moving couples crowding the floor. He had a clear view of the energetic little black drummer eagle-rocking with staccato regularity in his chair as his long, thin sticks descended upon the tightly drawn skin of his small drum, while his foot patted the pedal of his big bass-drum, on which was painted in large red letters: "BENBOW'S FAMOUS KANSAS CITY BAND."

As the slow shuffle gained in intensity (and his cracker-jacks gave out), Sandy looked down drowsily on the men and women, the boys and girls, circling and turning beneath him. Dresses and suits of all shades and colors, and a vast confusion of bushy heads on swaying bodies. Faces gleaming like circus balloons—lemon-yellow, coal-black, powder-grey, ebony-black, blue-black faces; chocolate, brown, orange, tan, creamy-gold faces—the room full of floating balloon faces—Sandy's eyes were beginning to blur with sleep—colored balloons with strings, and the music pulling the strings. No! Girls pulling the strings—each boy a balloon by a string. Each face a balloon.

Sandy put his head down on the dusty railing of the gallery. An odor of hair-oil and fish, of women and sweat came up to him as he sat there alone, tired and a little sick. It was very warm and close, and the room was full of chatter during the intervals. Sandy struggled against sleep, but his eyes were just about to close when, with a burst of hopeless sadness, the *St. Louis Blues* spread itself like a bitter syrup over the hall. For a moment the boy opened his eyes to the drowsy flow of sound, long enough to pull two chairs together; then he lay down on them and closed his eyes again. Somebody was singing:

St Louis woman with her diamond rings . . .

as the band said very weary things in a loud and brassy manner and the dancers moved in a dream that seemed to have forgotten itself:

Got ma man tied to her apron-strings . . .

Wah! Wah! Wah! . . . The cornet laughed with terrible rudeness. Then the drums began to giggle and the banjo whined an insulting leer. The piano said, over and over again: "St. Louis! That big old dirty town where the Mississippi's deep and wide, deep and wide . . ." and the hips of the dancers rolled.

Man's got a heart like a rock cast in de sea . . .

while the cynical banjo covered unplumbable depths with a plinking surface of staccato gaiety, like the sparkling bubbles that rise on deep water over a man who has just drowned himself:

Or else he never would a gone so far from me . . .

then the band stopped with a long-drawn-out wail from the cornet and a flippant little laugh from the drums.

A great burst of applause swept over the room, and the musicians immediately began to play again. This time just blues, not the *St. Louis,* nor the *Memphis,* nor the *Yellow Dog*—but just the plain old familiar blues, heart-breaking and extravagant, ma-baby's-gone-from-me blues.

Nobody thought about anyone else then. Bodies sweatily close, arms locked, cheek to cheek, breast to breast, couples rocked to the pulse-like beat of the rhythm, yet quite oblivious each person of the other. It was true that men and women were dancing together, but their feet had gone down through the floor into the earth, each dancer's alone—down into the center of things—and their minds had gone off to the heart of loneliness, where they didn't even hear the words, the sometimes lying, sometimes laughing words that Benbow, leaning on the piano, was singing against this background of utterly despondent music:

When de blues is got you,
Ain't no use to run away.
When de blue-blues got you,

Ain't no use to run away,
'Cause de blues is like a woman
That can turn yo' good hair grey.

Umn-ump! . . . Umn! . . . Umn-ump!

Well, I tole ma baby,
Says baby, baby, babe, be mine,
But ma baby was deceitful.
She must a thought that I was blind.

De-da! De-da! . . . De da! De da! Dee!

O, Lawdy, Lawdy, Lawdy,
Lawdy, Lawdy, Lawd . . . Lawd . . . Lawd!
She quit me fo' a Texas gambler,
So I had to git another broad.

Whaw-whaw! . . . Whaw-whaw-whaw! As though the laughter of a cornet could reach the heart of loneliness.

These mean old weary blues coming from a little orchestra of four men who needed no written music because they couldn't have read it. Four men and a leader—Rattle Benbow from Galveston; Benbow's buddy, the drummer, from Houston; his banjoist from Birmingham; his cornetist from Atlanta; and the pianist, long-fingered, sissyfied, a coal-black lad from New Orleans who had brought with him an exaggerated rag-time which he called jazz.

"I'm jazzin' it, creepers!" he sometimes yelled as he rolled his eyes towards the dancers and let his fingers beat the keys to a frenzy. . . . But now the piano was cryin' the blues!

Four homeless, plug-ugly niggers, that's all they were, playing mean old loveless blues in a hot, crowded little dance-hall in a Kansas town on Friday night. Playing the heart out of loneliness with a wide-mouthed leader, who sang everybody's troubles until they became his own. The improvising piano, the whanging banjo, the throbbing bass-drum, the hard-hearted little snare-drum, the brassy cornet that laughed, "Whaw-whaw-whaw. . . . Whaw!" were the waves in this lonesome sea of harmony from which Benbow's melancholy voice rose:

You gonna wake up some mawnin'
An' turn yo' smilin' face.

Wake up some early mawnin',
Says turn yo' smilin' face,
Look at yo' sweetie's pillow—
An' find an' empty place!

Then the music whipped itself into a slow fury, an awkward, elemental, foot-stamping fury, with the banjo running terrifiedly away in a windy moan and then coming back again, with the cornet wailing like a woman who don't know what it's all about:

Then you gonna call yo' baby,
Call yo' lovin' baby dear—
But you can keep on callin',
'Cause I won't be here!

And for a moment nothing was heard save the shuf-shuf-shuffle of feet and the immense booming of the bass-drum like a living vein pulsing at the heart of loneliness.

"Sandy! . . . Sandy! . . . My stars! Where is that child? . . . Has anybody seen my little nephew?" All over the hall. . . . "Sandy! . . . Oh-o-o, Lord!" Finally, with a sigh of relief: "You little brat, darn you, hiding up here in the balcony where nobody could find you! . . . Sandy, wake up! It's past four o'clock and I'll get killed."

Harriett vigorously shook the sleeping child, who lay stretched on the dusty chairs; then she began to drag him down the narrow steps before he was scarcely awake. The hall was almost empty and the chubby little black drummer was waddling across the floor carrying his drums in canvas cases. Someone was switching off the lights one by one. A mustard-colored man stood near the door quarrelling with a black woman. She began to cry and he slapped her full in the mouth, then turned his back and left with another girl of maple-sugar brown. Harriett jerked Sandy past this linked couple and pulled the boy down the long flight of stairs into the street, where Mingo stood waiting, with a lighted cigarette making a white line against his black skin.

"You better git a move on," he said. "Daylight ain't holdin' itself back for you!" And he told the truth, for the night had already begun to pale.

Sandy felt sick at the stomach. To be awakened precipitately made him cross and ill-humored, but the fresh, cool air soon caused him to feel less sleepy and not quite so ill. He took a deep breath as he trotted rapidly along on the sidewalk beside his striding aunt and her boy friend. He watched the blue-grey dawn blot out the night in the sky; and then pearl-grey blot out the blue, while the stars faded to points of dying fire. And he listened to the birds chirping and trilling in the trees as though they were calling the sun. Then, as he became fully awake, the child began to feel very proud of himself, for this was the first time he had ever been away from home all night.

Harriett was fussing with Mingo. "You shouldn't've kept me out like that," she said. "Why didn't you tell me what time it was? . . . I didn't know."

And Mingo came back: "Hey, didn't I try to drag you away at midnight and you wouldn't come? And ain't I called you at one o'clock and you said: 'Wait a minute'—dancin' with some yaller P. I. from St. Joe, with your arms round his neck like a life-preserver? . . . Don't tell me I didn't want to leave, and me got to go to work at eight o'clock this mornin' with a pick and shovel when the whistle blows! What de hell?"

But Harriett did not care to quarrel now when there would be no time to finish it properly. She was out of breath from hurrying and almost in tears. She was afraid to go home.

"Mingo, I'm scared."

"Well, you know what you can do if your ma puts you out," her escort said quickly, forgetting his anger. "I can take care of you. We could get married."

"Could we, Mingo?"

"Sure!"

She slipped her hand in his. "Aw, daddy!" and the pace became much less hurried.

When they reached the corner near which Harriett lived, she lifted her dark little purple-powdered face for a not very lingering kiss and sent Mingo on his way. Then she frowned anxiously and ran on. The sky was a pale pearly color, waiting for the warm gold of the rising sun.

"I'm scared to death!" said Harriett. "Lord, Sandy, I hope ma ain't up! I hope she didn't come home last night from Mis' Lane's. We shouldn't 've gone, Sandy . . . I guess we shouldn't 've gone." She was breathing hard and Sandy had to run fast to keep up with her. "Gee, I'm scared!"

The grass was diamond-like with dew, and the red bricks of the sidewalk were damp, as the small boy and his young aunt hurried under the leafy elms along the walk. They passed Madam de Carter's house and cut through the wet grass into their own yard as the first rays of the morning sun sifted through the trees. Quietly they tiptoed towards the porch; quickly and quietly they crossed it; and softly, ever so softly, they opened the parlor door.

In the early dusk the oil-lamp still burned on the front-room table, and in an old arm-chair, with the open Bible on her lap, sat Aunt Hager Williams, a bundle of switches on the floor at her feet.

Nine

Carnival

Between the tent of Christ and the tents of sin there stretched scarcely a half-mile. Rivalry reigned: the revival and the carnival held sway in Stanton at the same time. Both were at the south edge of town, and both were loud and musical in their activities. In a dirty white tent in the Hickory Woods the Reverend Duke Braswell conducted the services of the Lord for the annual summer tent-meeting of the First Ethiopian Baptist Church. And in Jed Galoway's meadow lots Swank's Combined Shows, the World's Greatest Midway Carnival, had spread canvas for seven days of bunko games and cheap attractions. The old Negroes went to the revival, and the young Negroes went to the carnival, and after sundown these August evenings the mourning songs of the Christians could be heard rising from the Hickory Woods while the profound syncopation of the minstrel band blared from Galoway's Lots, strangely intermingling their notes of praise and joy.

Aunt Hager with Annjee and Sandy went to the revival every night (Sandy unwillingly), while Jimboy, Harriett, and Maudel went to the carnival. Aunt Hager prayed for her youngest daughter at the meetings, but Harriett had not spoken to her mother, if she could avoid it, since the morning after the dance, when she had been whipped. Since their return from the country Annjee and Jimboy were not so loving towards each other, either, as they had been before. Jimboy tired of Jessie's farm, so he came back to town three days before his wife returned. And now the revival and the carnival widened the breach between the Christians and the sinners in Aunt Hager's little household. And Sandy would rather have been with the sinners—Jimboy and Harriett—but he wasn't old enough; so he had to go to meetings until, on Thursday morning, when he and Buster were climbing over the coal-shed in the back yard, Sandy accidentally jumped down on a rusty nail, which penetrated the heel of his bare foot. He set up a wail, cried until noon over the pain, and refused to eat any dinner; so finally Jimboy said that if he would only hush hollering he'd take him to the carnival that evening.

"Yes, take de rascal," said Aunt Hager. "He ain't doin' no good at de services, wiggling and squirming so's we can't hardly hear de sermon. He ain't got religion in his heart, that chile!"

"I hope he ain't," said his father, yawning.

"All you wants him to be is a good-fo'-nothin' rounder like you is," retorted Hager. And she and Jimboy began their daily quarrel, which lasted for hours, each of them enjoying it immensely. But Sandy kept pulling at his father and saying: "Hurry up and let's go," although he knew well that nothing really started at the carnival until sundown. Nevertheless, about four o'clock, Jimboy said: "All right, come on," and they started out in the hot sun towards Galoway's Lots, the man walking tall and easy while the boy hobbled along on his sore foot, a rag tied about his heel.

At the old cross-bar gate on the edge of town, through which Jed Galoway drove his cows to pasture, there had been erected a portable arch strung with electric lights spelling out "SWANK'S SHOWS" in red and yellow letters, but it was not very impressive in the day-time, with the sun blazing on it, and no people about. And from this gate, extending the whole length of the meadow on either side, like a roadway, were the tents and booths of the carnival: the Galatea illusion, the seal and sea-lion circus, the Broadway musical-comedy show, the freaks, the games of chance, the pop-corn- and lemonade-stands, the colored minstrels, the merry-go-round, the fun house, the hoochie-coochie, the Ferris wheel, and, at the far end, a canvas tank under a tiny platform high in the air from which the World's Most Dangerous and Spectacular High Dive took place nightly at ten-thirty.

"We gonna stay to see that, ain't we, papa?" Sandy asked.

"Sure," said Jimboy. "But didn't I tell you there wouldn't be nothin' runnin' this early in the afternoon? See! Not even the band playin', and ain't a thing open but the freak-show and I'll bet all the freaks asleep." But he bought Sandy a bag of peanuts and planked down twenty cents for two tickets into the sultry tent where a perspiring fat woman and a tame-looking wild-man were the only attractions to be found on the platforms. The sword-swallower was not yet at work, nor the electric marvel, nor the human glass-eater. The terrific sun beat fiercely through the canvas on this exhibit of two lone human abnormalities, and the few spectators in the tent kept wiping their faces with their handkerchiefs.

Jimboy struck up a conversation with the Fat Woman, a pink and white creature who said she lived in Columbus, Ohio; and when Jimboy said he'd been there, she was interested. She said she had always lived right next door to colored people at home, and she gave Sandy a postcard picture of herself for nothing, although it had "10¢" marked on the back. She kept saying she didn't see how anybody could stay in Kansas and it a dry state where a soul couldn't even get beer except from a bootlegger.

When Sandy and his father came out, they left the row of tents and went across the meadow to a clump of big shade-trees beneath which several colored men who worked with the show were sitting. A blanket had been spread on the grass, and a crap game was going on to the accompaniment of much arguing and good-natured cussing. But most of the men were just sitting around not playing, and one or two were stretched flat on their faces, asleep. Jimboy seemed to know several of the fellows, so he joined in their talk while Sandy watched the dice roll for a while, but since the boy didn't understand the game, he decided to go back to the tents.

"All right, go ahead," said his father. "I'll pick you up later when the lights are lit and things get started; then we can go in the shows."

Sandy limped off, walking on the toe of his injured foot. In front of the sea-lion circus he found Earl James, a little white boy in his grade at school; the two of them went around together for a while, looking at the large painted canvas pictures in front of the shows or else lying on their stomachs on the ground to peep under the tents. When they reached the minstrel-show tent near the end of the midway, they heard a piano tinkling within and the sound of hands clapping as though someone was dancing.

"Jeezus! Let's see this," Earl cried, so the two boys got down on their bellies, wriggled under the flap of the tent on one side, and looked in.

A battered upright piano stood on the ground in front of the stage, and a fat, bald-headed Negro was beating out a rag. A big white man in a checkered vest was leaning against the piano, derby on head, and a long cigar stuck in his mouth. He was watching a slim black girl, with skirts held high and head thrown back, prancing in a mad circle of crazy steps. Two big colored boys in red uniforms were patting time, while another girl sat on a box, her back towards the peeping youngsters staring up from under the edge of the tent. As the girl who was dancing whirled about, Sandy saw that it was Harriett.

"Pretty good, ain't she, boss?" yelled the wrinkle-necked Negro at the piano as he pounded away.

The white man nodded and kept his eyes on Harriett's legs. The two black boys patting time were grinning from ear to ear.

"Do it, Miss Mama!" one of them shouted as Harriett began to sashay gracefully.

Finally she stopped, panting and perspiring, with her lips smiling and her eyes sparkling gaily. Then she went with the white man and the colored piano-player behind the canvas curtains to the stage. One of the show-boys put his arms around the girl sitting on the box and began tentatively to feel her breasts.

"Don't be so fresh, hot papa," she said. And Sandy recognized Maudel's voice, and saw her brown face as she leaned back to look at the showman. The boy in the red suit bent over and kissed her several times, while the other fellow kept imitating the steps he had just seen Harriett performing.

"Let's go," Earl said to Sandy, rolling over on the ground. The two small boys went on to the next tent, where one of the carnival men caught them, kicked their behinds soundly, and sent them away.

The sun was setting in a pink haze, and the show-grounds began to take on an air of activity. The steam calliope gave a few trial hoots, and the merry-go-round circled slowly without passengers, the paddle-wheels and the get-'em-hot men, the lemonade-sellers and the souvenir-venders were opening their booths to the evening trade. A barker began to ballyhoo in front of the freak-show. By and by there would be a crowd. The lights came on along the Midway, the Ferris wheel swept languidly up into the air, and when Sandy found his father, the colored band had begun to play in front of the minstrel show.

"I want to ride on the merry-go-round," Sandy insisted. "And go in the Crazy House." So they did both; then they bought hamburger sandwiches with thick slices of white onion and drank strawberry soda and ate pop-corn with butter on it. They went to the sea-lion circus, tried to win a Kewpie doll at the paddle-wheel booth, and watched men losing money on the hidden pea, then trying to win it back at four-card monte behind the Galatea attraction. And all the while Sandy said nothing to his father about having seen Harriett dancing in the minstrel tent that afternoon.

Sandy had lived too long with three women not to have learned to hold his tongue about the private doings of each of them. When Annjee paid two dollars a week on a blue silk shirt for his father at Cohn's cut-rate credit store, and Sandy saw her make the payments, he knew without being told that the matter was never to be mentioned to Aunt Hager. And if his grandmother sometimes threw Harriett's rouge out in the alley, Sandy saw it with his eyes, but not with his mouth. Because he loved all three of them—Harriett and Annjee and Hager—he didn't carry tales on any one of them to the others. Nobody would know he had watched his Aunt Harrie dancing on the carnival lot today in front of a big fat white man in a checkered vest while a Negro in a red suit played the piano.

"We got a half-dollar left for the minstrel show," said Jimboy. "Come on, let's go." And he pulled his son through the crowd that jammed the long Midway between the booths.

All the bright lights of the carnival were on now, and everything was running full blast. The merry-go-round whirled to the ear-splitting hoots of the calliope; bands blared; the canvas paintings of snakes and dancing-girls, human skeletons, fire-eaters, billowed in the evening breeze; pennants flapped, barkers shouted, acrobats twirled in front of a tent; a huge paddle-wheel clicked out numbers. Folks pushed and shoved and women called to their children not to get lost. In the air one smelled the scent of trampled grass, peanuts, and hot dogs, animals and human bodies.

The large white man in the checkered vest was making the ballyhoo in front of the minstrel show, his expansive belly turned towards the crowd that had been attracted by the band. One hand pointed towards a tawdry group of hard-looking Negro performers standing on the platform.

"Here we have, ladies and gents, Madam Caledonia Watson, the Dixie song-bird; Dancing Jenkins, the dark strutter from Jacksonville; little Lizzie Roach, champeen coon-shouter of Georgia; and last, but not least, Sambo and Rastus, the world's funniest comedians. Last performance this evening! . . . Strike her up, perfesser! . . . Come along, now, folks!"

The band burst into sound, Madam Watson and Lizzie Roach opened their brass-lined throats, the men dropped into a momentary clog-dance, and then the whole crowd of performers disappeared into the tent. The ticket-purchasing townspeople followed through the public opening beneath a gaudily painted sign picturing a Mississippi steamboat in the moonlight, and two black bucks shooting gigantic dice on a street-corner.

Jimboy and Sandy followed the band inside and took seats, and soon the frayed curtain rose, showing a plantation scene in the South, where three men, blackened up, and two women in bandannas sang longingly about Dixie. Then Sambo and Rastus came out with long wooden razors and began to argue and shoot dice, but presently the lights went out and a ghost appeared and frightened the two men away, causing them to leave all the money on the stage. (The audience thought it screamingly funny—and just like niggers.) After that one of the women sang a rag-time song and did the eagle-rock. Then a man with a banjo in his hands began to play, but until then the show had been lifeless.

"Listen to him," Jimboy said, punching Sandy. "He's good!"

The piece he was picking was full of intricate runs and trills long drawn out, then suddenly slipping into tantalizing rhythms. It ended with a vibrant whang!—and the audience yelled for more. As an encore he played a blues and sang innumerable verses, always ending:

> An' Ah can't be satisfied,
> 'Cause all Ah love has
> Done laid down an' died.

And to Sandy it seemed like the saddest music in the world—but the white people around him laughed.

Then the stage lights went on, the band blared, and all the black actors came trooping back, clapping their hands before the cotton-field curtain as each one in turn danced like fury, vigorously distorting agile limbs into the most amazing positions, while the scene ended with the fattest mammy and the oldest uncle shaking jazzily together.

The booths were all putting out their lights as the people poured through the gate towards town. Sandy hobbled down the road beside his father, his sore heel, which had been forgotten all evening, paining him terribly until Jimboy picked him up and carried him on his shoulder. Automobiles and buggies whirled past them in clouds of gritty dust, and young boys calling vulgar words hurried after tittering girls. When Sandy and his father reached home, Aunt Hager and Annjee had not yet returned from the revival. Jimboy said he thought maybe they had stopped at Mrs. Lane's to sit up all night with the sick woman, so Sandy spread his pallet on the floor at the foot of his grandmother's bed and went to sleep. He did not hear his Aunt Harriett when she came home, but late in the night he woke up with his heel throbbing painfully, his throat dry, and his skin burning, and when he tried to bend his leg, it hurt him so that he began to cry.

Harriett, awakened by his moans, called drowsily: "What's the matter, honey?"

"My foot," said Sandy tearfully.

So his young aunt got out of bed, lit the lamp, and helped him to the kitchen, where she heated a kettle of water, bathed his heel, and covered the nail-wound with vaseline. Then she bound it with a fresh white rag.

"Now that ought to feel better," she said as she led him back to his pallet, and soon they were both asleep again.

The next morning when Hager came from the sick-bed of her friend, she sent to the butcher-shop for a bacon rind, cut from it a piece of fat meat, and bound it to Sandy's heel as a cure.

"Don't want you havin' de blood-pisen here," she said. "An' don't you run round an' play on that heel. Set out on de porch an' study yo' reader, 'cause school'll be startin' next month." Then she began Mrs. Reinhart's ironing.

The next day, Saturday, the last day of the carnival, Jimboy carried the Reinharts' clothes home for Hager, since Sandy was crippled and Jimmy Lane's mother was down in bed. But after delivering the clothes Jimboy did not come home for supper. When Annjee and Hager wanted to leave for the revival in the early evening, they asked Harriett if she would stay home with the little boy, for Sandy's heel had swollen purple where the rusty nail had penetrated and he could hardly walk at all.

"You been gone ever' night this week," Hager said to the girl. "An' you ain't been anear de holy tents where de Lawd's word is preached; so you ought to be willin' to stay home one night with a po' little sick boy."

"Yes'm," Harriett muttered in a noncommittal tone. But shortly after her mother and Annjee had gone, she said to her nephew: "You aren't afraid to stay home by yourself, are you?"

And Sandy answered: "Course not, Aunt Harrie."

She gave him a hot bath and put a new piece of fat meat on his festering heel. Then she told him to climb into Annjee's bed and go to sleep, but instead he lay for a long time looking out the window that was beside the bed. He thought about the carnival—the Ferris wheel sweeping up into the air, and the minstrel show. Then he remembered Benbow's dance a few weeks ago and how his Aunt Harriett had stood sullenly the next morning while Hager whipped her—and hadn't cried at all, until the welts came under her silk stockings. . . . Then he wondered what Jimmy Lane would do if his sick mother died from the T. B. and he were left with nobody to take care of him, because Jimmy's step-father was no good. . . . Eu-uuu! His heel hurt! . . . When school began again, he would be in the fifth grade, but he wished he'd hurry up and get to high school, like Harriett was. . . . When he got to be a man, he was going to be a railroad engineer. . . . Gee, he wasn't sleepy—and his heel throbbed painfully.

In the next room Harriett had lighted the oil-lamp and was moving swiftly about taking clothes from the dresser-drawers and spreading them on the bed. She thought Sandy was asleep, he knew—but he couldn't go to sleep the way his foot hurt him. He could see her through the doorway folding her dresses in little piles and he wondered why she was doing that. Then she took an old suit-case from the closet and began to pack it, and when it was full, she pulled a new bag from under the bed, and into it she dumped her toilet-articles, powder, vaseline, nail-polish, straightening comb, and several pairs of old stockings rolled in balls. Then she sat down on the bed between the two closed suit-cases for a long time with her hands in her lap and her eyes staring ahead of her.

Finally she rose and closed the bureau-drawers, tidied up the confusion she had created, and gathered together the discarded things she had thrown on the floor. Then Sandy heard her go out into the back yard towards the trash-pile. When she returned, she put on a tight little hat and went into the kitchen to wash her hands, throwing the water through the back door. Then she tip-toed into the room where Sandy was lying and kissed him gently on the head. Sandy knew that she thought he was asleep, but in spite of himself he suddenly threw his arms tightly around her neck. He couldn't help it.

"Where you going, Aunt Harriett?" he said, sitting up in bed, clutching the girl.

"Honey, you won't tell on me, will you?" Harriett asked.

"No," he answered, and she knew he wouldn't. "But where are you going, Aunt Harrie?"

"You won't be afraid to stay here until grandma comes?"

"No," burying his face on her breast. "I won't be afraid."

"And you won't forget Aunt Harrie?"

"Course not."

"I'm leaving with the carnival," she told him.

For a moment they sat close together on the bed. Then she kissed him, went into the other room and picked up her suit-cases—and the door closed.

Ten

Punishment

Old white Dr. McDillors, beloved of all the Negroes in Stanton, came on Sunday morning, swabbed Sandy's festering foot with iodine, bound it up, and gave him a bottle of green medicine to take, and by the middle of the week the boy was able to hobble about again without pain; but Hager continued to apply fat meat instead of following the doctor's directions.

When Harriett didn't come back, Sandy no longer slept on a pallet on the floor. He slept in the big bed with his grandma Hager, and the evenings that followed weren't so jolly, with his young aunt off with the carnival, and Jimboy spending most of his time at the pool hall or else loafing on the station platform watching the trains come through—and nobody playing music in the back yard.

They went to bed early these days, and after that eventful week of carnival and revival, a sore heel, and a missing Aunt Harriett, the muscles of Sandy's little body often twitched and jerked in his sleep and he would awaken suddenly from dreaming that he heard sad raggy music playing while a woman shouted for Jesus in the Gospel tent, and a girl in red silk stockings cried because the switches were cutting her legs. Sometimes he would lie staring into the darkness a long time, while Aunt Hager lay snoring at his side. And sometimes in the next room, where Annjee and Jimboy were, he could hear the slow rhythmical creaking of the bedsprings and the low moans of his mother, which he already knew accompanied the grown-up embraces of bodily love. And sometimes through the window he could see the moonlight glinting on the tall, tassel-crowned stalks of corn in the garden. Perhaps he would toss and turn until he had awakened Aunt Hager and she would say drowsily: "What's de matter with you, chile? I'll put you back on de flo' if you can't be still!" Then he would go to sleep again, and before he knew it, the sun would be flooding the room with warm light, and the coffee would be boiling on the stove in the kitchen, and Annjee would have gone to work.

Summer days were long and drowsy for grown-ups, but for Sandy they were full of interest. In the mornings he helped Aunt Hager by feeding the chickens, bringing in the water for her wash-tubs and filling the buckets from which they drank. He chopped wood, too, and piled it behind the kitchen-stove; then he would take the broom and sweep dust-clean the space around the pump and under the apple-tree where he played. Perhaps by that time Willie-Mae would come over or Buster would be there to shoot marbles. Or maybe his grandmother would send him to the store to get a pound of sugar or ten cents' worth of meal for dinner, and on the way there was certain to be an adventure. Yesterday he had seen two bad little boys from the Bottoms, collecting scrap-iron and junk in the alleys, get angry at each other and pretend to start a fight.

The big one said to the smaller one: "I'm a fast-black and you know I sho won't run! Jest you pick up that piece o' iron that belongs to me. Go ahead, jest you try!"

And the short boy replied: "I'm your match, long skinny! Strike me an' see if you don't get burnt up!" And then they started to play the dozens, and Sandy, standing by, learned several new and very vulgar words to use when talking about other peoples' mothers.

The tall kid said finally: "Aw, go on, you little clay-colored nigger, you looks too much like mustard to me anyhow!" Picking up the disputed piece of scrap-iron, he proceeded on his quest for junk, looking into all the trash-piles and garbage-cans along the alley, but the smaller of the two boys took his gunny-sack and went in the opposite direction alone.

"Be careful, sissy, and don't break your dishes," his late companion called after his retreating buddy, and Sandy carefully memorized the expression to try on Jimmy Lane some time—that is, if Jimmy's mother got well, for Mrs. Lane now was in the last stages of consumption. But if she got better, Sandy was going to tell her son to be careful and not break his dishes—always wearing his mother's shoes, like a girl.

By that time he had forgotten what Hager sent him to the store to buy, and instead of getting meal he bought washing-powder. When he came home, after nearly an hour's absence, his grandmother threatened to cut an elm switch, but she satisfied herself instead by scolding him for staying so long, and then sending him back to exchange the washing-powder for meal—and she waiting all that time to make corn dumplings to put in the greens!

In the afternoon Sandy played in his back yard or next door at the Johnsons', but Hager never allowed him outside their block. The white children across the street were frequently inclined to say "Nigger," so he was forbidden to play there. Usually Buster, who looked like a white kid, and Willie-Mae, who couldn't have been blacker, were his companions.

The three children would run at hide-and-seek, in the tall corn; or they would tag one another in the big yard, or play house under the apple-tree.

Once when they were rummaging in the trash-pile to see what they could find, Sandy came across a pawn ticket which he took into the kitchen to Hager. It was for a watch his Aunt Harriett had pawned the Saturday she ran away.

Sometimes in the late afternoon the children would go next door to Madam de Carter's and she would give them ginger cookies and read to them from the *Bible Story Reader.* Madam de Carter looked very pompous and important in her silk waist as she would put on her *pince-nez* and say: "Now, children, seat yourselves and preserve silence while I read you-all this moralizing history of Samson's treacherous hair. Now, Buster, who were Samson? Willie-Mae, has you ever heard of Delilah?"

Sometimes, if Jimboy was home, he would take down his old guitar and start the children to dancing in the sunlight—but then Hager would always call Sandy to pump water or go to the store as soon as she heard the music.

"Out there dancin' like you ain't got no raisin'!" she would say. "I tells Jimboy 'bout playin' that ole rag-time here! That's what ruint Harriett!"

And on Sundays Sandy went to Sabbath school at the Shiloh Baptist Church, where he was given a colored picture card with a printed text on it. The long, dull lessons were taught by Sister Flora Garden, who had been to Wilberforce College, in Ohio. There were ten little boys in Sandy's class, ranging from nine to fourteen, and they behaved very badly, for Miss Flora Garden, who wore thick-lensed glasses on her roach-colored face, didn't understand little boys.

"Where was Moses when the lights went out?" Gritty Smith asked her every Sunday, and she didn't even know the answer.

Sandy didn't think much of Sunday-school, and frequently instead of putting his nickel in the collection basket he spent it for candy, which he divided with Buster—until one very hot Sunday Hager found it out. He had put a piece of the sticky candy in his shirt-pocket and it melted, stuck, and stained the whole front of his clean clothes. When he came home, with Buster behind him, the first thing Hager said was: "What's all this here stuck up in yo' pocket?" and Buster commenced to giggle and said Sandy had bought candy.

"Where'd you get the money, sir?" demanded Aunt Hager searchingly of her grandson.

"I—we—er—Madam Carter gimme a nickel," Sandy replied haltingly, choosing the first name he could think of, which would have been all right had not Madam de Carter herself stopped by the house, almost immediately afterwards, on her way home from church.

"Is you give Sandy a nickel to buy candy this mawnin'?" Hager asked her as soon as she entered the parlor.

"Why, no, Sister Williams, I isn't. I had no coins about me a-tall at services this morning."

"Umn-huh! I thought so!" said Hager. "You Sandy!"

The little boy, guilt written all over his face, came in from the front porch, where he had been sitting with his father after Buster went home.

"Where'd you tell me you got that nickel this mawnin'?" And before he could answer, she spat out: "I'm gonna whip you!"

"Jehovah help us! Children sure is bad these days," said Madam de Carter, shaking her head as she left to go next door to her own house. "They sure *are* bad," she added, self-consciously correcting her English.

"I'm gonna whip you," Hager continued, sitting down amazed in her plush chair. "De idee o' withholdin' yo' Sunday-school money from de Lawd an' buyin' candy."

"I only spent a penny," Sandy lied, wriggling.

"How you gwine get so much candy fo' a penny that you has some left to gum up in yo' pocket? Tell me that, how you gonna do it?"

Sandy, at a loss for an answer, was standing with lowered eyelids, when the screen door opened and Jimboy came in. Sandy looked up at him for aid, but his father's usually amiable face was stern this time.

"Come here!" he said. The man towered very tall above the little fellow who looked up at him helplessly.

"I's gwine whip him!" interposed Hager.

"Is that right, you spent your Sunday-school nickel for candy?" Jimboy demanded gravely.

Sandy nodded his head. He couldn't lie to his father, and had he spoken now, the sobs would have come.

"Then you told a lie to your grandma—and I'm ashamed of you," his father said.

Sandy wanted to turn his head away and escape the slow gaze of Jimboy's eyes, but he couldn't. If Aunt Hager would only whip him, it would be better; then maybe his father wouldn't say any more. But it was awful to stand still and listen to Jimboy talk to him this way—yet there he stood, stiffly holding back the sobs.

"To take money and use it for what it ain't s'posed to be used is the same as stealing," Jimboy went on gravely to his son. "That's what you done today, and then come home and lie about it. Nobody's ugly as a liar, you know that! . . . I'm not much, maybe. Don't mean to say I am. I won't work a lot, but what I do I do honest. White folks gets rich lyin' and stealin'—and some niggers gets rich that way, too—but I don't need money if I got to get it dishonest, with a lot o' lies trailing behind me, and can't look folks in the face. It makes you feel dirty! It's no good! . . . Don't I give you nickels for candy whenever you want 'em?"

The boy nodded silently, with the tears trickling down his chin.

"And don't I go with you to the store and buy you ice-cream and soda-pop any time you ask me?"

The child nodded again.

"And then you go and take the Sunday-school nickel that your grandma's worked hard for all the week, spend it on candy, and come back home and lie about it. So that's what you do! And then lie!"

Jimboy turned his back and went out on the porch, slamming the screen door behind him. Aunt Hager did not whip her grandson, but returned to the kitchen and left him standing disgraced in the parlor. Then Sandy began to cry, with one hand in his mouth so no one could hear him, and when Annjee came home from work in the late afternoon, she found him lying across her bed, head under the pillows, still sobbing because Jimboy had called him a liar.

Eleven

School

Some weeks later the neighbors were treated to an early morning concert:

> I got a high yaller
> An' a little short black,
> But a brown-skin gal
> Can bring me right on back!
> I'm singin' brown-skin!
> Lawdy! . . . Lawd!
> Brown-skin! . . . O, ma Lawd!

"It must be Jimboy," said Hager from the kitchen. "A lazy coon, settin' out there in the cool singin', an' me in here sweatin' and washin' maself to dust!"

> Kansas City Southern!
> I mean de W. & A.!
> I'm gonna ride de first train
> I catch goin' out ma way.
> I'm got de railroad blues—

"I wish to God you'd go on, then!" mumbled Hager over the wash-boilers.

> But I ain't got no railroad fare!
> I'm gwine to pack ma grip an'
> Beat ma way away from here!

"Learn me how to pick a cord, papa," Sandy begged as he sat beside his father under the apple-tree, loaded with ripe fruit.

"All right, look a-here! . . . You put your thumb like this. . . ." Jimboy began to explain. "But, dog-gone, your fingers ain't long enough yet!"

Still they managed to spend a half-day twanging at the old instrument, with Sandy trying to learn a simple tune.

The sunny August mornings had become September mornings, and most of Aunt Hager's "white folks" had returned from their vacations;

her kitchen was once more a daily laundry. Great boilers of clothes steamed on the stove and, beside the clothes, pans of apple juice boiled to jelly, and the peelings of peaches simmered to jam.

There was no news from the runaway Harriett. . . . Mrs. Lane died one sultry night, with Hager at the bedside, and was buried by the lodge with three hacks and a fifty-dollar coffin. . . . The following week the Drill of All Nations, after much practising by the women, was given with great success and Annjee, dressed in white and wrapped in a Scandinavian flag, marched proudly as Sweden. . . . Madam de Carter's house was now locked and barred, as she had departed for Oklahoma to organize branches of the lodge there. . . . Tempy had stopped to see Hager one afternoon, but she didn't stay long. She told her mother she was out collecting rents and that she and her husband were buying another house. . . . Willie-Mae had a new calico dress. . . . Buster had learned to swear better than Sandy. . . . And next Monday was to be the opening of the new school term.

Sandy hated even to think about going back to school. He was having much fun playing, and Jimboy had been teaching him to box. Then the time to go to classes came.

"Wash yo' face good, sir, put on yo' clean waist, an' polish yo' shoes," Aunt Hager said bright and early, " 'cause I don't want none o' them white teachers sayin' I sends you to school dirty as a 'cuse to put you back in de fourth grade. You hear me, sir!"

"Yes'm," Sandy replied.

This morning he was to enter the "white" fifth grade, having passed last June from the "colored" fourth, for in Stanton the Negro children were kept in separate rooms under colored teachers until they had passed the fourth grade. Then, from the fifth grade on, they went with the other children, and the teachers were white.

When Sandy arrived on the school grounds with his face shining, he found the yard already full of shouting kids. On the girls' side he saw Willie-Mae jumping rope. Sandy found Earl and Buster and some boys whom he knew playing mumble-peg on the boys' side, and he joined them. When the bell rang, they all crowded into the building, as the marching-lines had not yet been formed. Miss Abigail Minter, the principal, stood at the entrance, and there were big signs on all the room doors marking the classes. Sandy found the fifth-grade room upstairs and went in shyly. It was full of whispering youngsters huddled in little groups. He saw two colored children among them, both girls whom he didn't know, but there were no colored boys. Soon the teacher rapped briskly on her desk, and silence ensued.

"Take seats, all of you, please," she rasped out. "Anywhere now until we get order." She rapped again impatiently with the ruler. "Take seats at once." So the children each selected a desk and sat down, most of the girls at the front of the room and most of the boys together at the back, where they could play and look out the windows.

Then the teacher, middle-aged and wearing glasses, passed out tiny slips of paper to each child in the front row, with the command that they be handed backwards, so that every student received one slip.

"Now, write your names on the paper, turning it longways," she said. "Nothing but your names, that's all I want today. You will receive forms to fill out later, but I want to get your seats assigned this morning, however."

Amid much confusion and borrowing of pencils, the slips were finally signed in big awkward letters, and collected by the teacher, who passed up and down the aisles. Then she went to her desk, and there was a delightful period of whispering and wriggling as she sorted the slips and placed them in alphabetical order. Finally she finished.

"Now," she said, "each child rise as I call out your names, so I can see who you are."

The teacher stood up with the papers in her hand.

"Mary Atkins . . . Carl Dietrich . . . Josephine Evans," she called slowly glancing up after each name. "Franklin Rhodes . . . James Rogers." Sandy stood up quickly. "Ethel Shortlidge . . . Roland Thomas." The roll-call continued, each child standing until he had been identified, then sitting down again.

"Now," the teacher said, "everybody rise and make a line around the walls. Quietly! No talking! As I call your names this time, take seats in order, starting with number one in the first row near the window. . . . Mary Atkins . . . Carl Dietrich. . . ." The roll was repeated, each child taking a seat as she had commanded. When all but four of the children were seated, the two colored girls and Sandy still were standing.

"Albert Zwick," she said, and the last white child sat down in his place. "Now," said the teacher, "you three colored children take the seats behind Albert. You girls take the first two, and you," pointing to Sandy, "take the last one. . . . Now I'm going to put on the board the list of books to buy and I want all of you to copy them correctly." And she went on with her details of schoolroom routine.

One of the colored girls turned round to Sandy and whispered: "She just put us in the back cause we're niggers." And Sandy nodded gravely. "My name's Sadie Butler and she's put me behind the Z cause I'm a nigger."

"An old heifer!" said the first little colored girl, whispering loudly. "I'm gonna tell my mama." But Sandy felt like crying. And he was beginning to be ashamed of crying because he was no longer a small boy. But the teacher's putting the colored children in the back of the room made him feel like crying.

At lunch-time he came home with his list of books, and Aunt Hager pulled her wet arms out of the tub, wiped her hands, and held them up in horror.

"Lawdy! Just look! Something else to spend money for. Ever' year more an' more books, an' chillens learn less an' less! Used to didn't have nothin' but a blue-backed speller, and now look ahere—a list as long as ma arm! Go out there in de yard an' see is yo' pappy got any money to give you for 'em, 'cause I ain't."

Sandy found Jimboy sitting dejectedly on the well-stoop in the sunshine, with his head in his hands. "You got any money, papa?" he asked.

Jimboy looked at the list of books written in Sandy's childish scrawl and slowly handed him a dollar and a half.

"You see what I got left, don't you?" said his father as he turned his pants-pockets inside out, showing the little boy a jack-knife, a half-empty sack of Bull Durham, a key, and a dime. But he smiled, and took Sandy awkwardly in his arms and kissed him. "It's all right, kid."

That afternoon at school they had a long drill on the multiplication table, and then they had a spelling-match, because the teacher said that would be a good way to find out what the children knew. For the spelling-bee they were divided into two sides—the boys and the girls, each side lining up against an opposite wall. Then the teacher gave out words that they should have learned in the lower grades. On the boys' side everyone was spelled down except Sandy, but on the girls' side there were three proud little white girls left standing and Sandy came near spelling them down, too, until he put the *e* before *i* in "chief," and the girls' side won, to the disgust of the boys, and the two colored girls, who wanted Sandy to win.

After school Sandy went uptown with Buster to buy books, but there was so large a crowd of children in the bookstore that it was five o'clock before he was waited on and his list filled. When he reached home, Aunt Hager was at the kitchen-stove frying an egg-plant for supper.

"You stayin' out mighty long," she said without taking her attention from the stove.

"Where's papa?" Sandy asked eagerly. He wanted to show Jimboy his new books—a big geography, with pictures of animals in it, and a *Nature Story Reader* that he knew his father would like to see.

"Look in yonder," said Hager, pointing towards Annjee's bedroom.

Sandy rushed in, then stopped, because there was no one there. Suddenly a queer feeling came over him and he put his books down on the bed. Jimboy's clothes were no longer hanging against the wall where his working-shirts and overalls were kept. Then Sandy looked under the bed. His father's old suit-case was not there either, nor his work-shoes, nor his Sunday patent-leathers. And the guitar was missing.

"Where's papa?" he asked again, running back to the kitchen.

"Can't you see he ain't here?" replied his grandmother, busily turning slices of egg-plant with great care in the skillet. "Gone—that's where he is—a lazy nigger. Told me to tell Annjee he say goodbye, 'cause his travellin' blues done come on . . . ! Huh! Jimboy's yo' pappy, chile, but he sho ain't worth his salt! . . . an' I's right glad he's took his clothes an' left here, maself."

Twelve

Hard Winter

September passed and the corn-stalks in the garden were cut. There were no more apples left on the trees, and chilly rains came to beat down the falling leaves from the maples and the elms. Cold and drearily wet October passed, too, with no hint of Indian summer or golden forests. And as yet there was no word from the departed Jimboy. Annjee worried herself sick as usual, hoping every day that a letter would come from this wandering husband whom she loved. And each night she hurried home from Mrs. Rice's, looked on the parlor table for the mail, and found none. Harriett had not written, either, since she went away with the carnival, and Hager never mentioned her youngest daughter's name. Nor did Hager mention Jimboy except when Annjee asked her, after she could hold it no longer: "Are you sure the mail-man ain't left me a letter today?" And then Aunt Hager would reply impatiently: "You think I'd a et it if he did? You know that good-for-nothin', upsettin' scoundrel ain't wrote!"

But in spite of daily disappointments from the postal service Annjee continued to rush from Mrs. Rice's hot kitchen as soon after dinner as she could and to trudge through the chill October rains, anxious to feel in the mail-box outside her door, then hope against hope for a letter inside on the little front-room table—which would always be empty. She caught a terrible cold tramping through the damp streets, forgetting to button her cloak, then sitting down with her wet shoes on when she got home, a look of dumb disappointment in her eyes, too tired and unhappy to remove her clothes.

"You's a fool," said her mother, whose tongue was often much sharper than the meaning behind it. "Mooning after a worthless nigger like Jimboy. I tole you years ago he were no good, when he first come, lookin' like he ought to be wearin' short pants, an' out here courtin' you. Ain't none o' them bell-hoppin', racehoss-followin' kind o' darkies worth havin', an' that's all Jimboy was when you married him an' he ain't much mo'n that now. An' you older'n he is, too!"

"But you know why I married, don't you?"

"You Sandy, go outdoors an' get me some wood fo' this stove. . . . Yes, I knows why, because he were de father o' that chile you was 'bout to bring here, but I don't see why it couldn't just well been some o' these steady, hard-workin' Stanton young men's what was courtin' you at de same time. . . . But, chile or no chile, I couldn't hear nothin' but Jimboy, Jimboy, Jimboy! I told you you better stay in de high school an' get your edication, but no, you had to marry this Jimboy. Now you see what you got, don't you?"

"Well, he ain't been so bad, ma! And I don't care, I love him!"

"Umn-huh! Try an' live on love, daughter! Just try an' live on love. . . . You's made a mistake, that's all, honey. . . . But I guess there ain't no use talkin' 'bout it now. Take off yo' wet shoes 'fore you catch yo' death o' cold!"

On Thanksgiving at Mrs. Rice's, so Annjee reported, they had turkey with chestnut dressing; but at Aunt Hager's she and Sandy had a nice juicy possum, a present from old man Logan, parboiled and baked sweet and brown with yams in the pan. Aunt Hager opened a jar of peach preserves. And she told Sandy to ask Jimmy Lane in to dinner because, since his mother died, he wasn't faring so well and the people he was staying with didn't care much about him. But since Jimmy had quit school, Sandy didn't see him often; and the day before Thanksgiving he couldn't find him at all, so they had no company to help them eat the possum.

The week after Thanksgiving Annjee fell ill and had to go to bed. She had the grippe, Aunt Hager said, and she began to dose her with quinine and to put hot mustard-plasters on her back and gave her onion syrup to drink, but it didn't seem to do much good, and finally she had to send Sandy for Dr. McDillors.

"System's all run down," said the doctor. "Heavy cold on the chest—better be careful. And stay in the bed!" But the warning was unnecessary. Annjee felt too tired and weak ever to rise, and only the mail-man's whistle blowing at somebody else's house would cause her to try to lift her head. Then she would demand weakly: "Did he stop here?"

Hager's home now was like a steam laundry. The kitchen was always hung with lines of clothes to dry, and in the late afternoon and evenings the ironing-board was spread from the table to a chair-back in the middle of the floor. All of the old customers were sending their clothes to Hager again during the winter. And since Annjee was sick, bringing no money into the house on Saturdays, the old woman had even taken an extra washing to do. Being the only wage-earner, Hager kept the suds flying—but with the wet weather she had to dry the clothes in the kitchen most of the time, and when Sandy came home from school for lunch, he would eat under dripping lines of white folks' garments while he listened to his mother coughing in the next room.

In the other rooms of the house there were no stoves, so the doors were kept open in order that the heat might pass through from the kitchen. They couldn't afford to keep more than one fire going; therefore the kitchen was living-room, dining-room, and work-room combined. In the mornings Sandy would jump out of bed and run with his clothes in his hands to the kitchen-stove, where his grandmother would have the fire blazing, the coffee-pot on, and a great tub of water heating for the washings. And in the evenings after supper he would open his geography and read about the strange countries far away, the book spread out on the oilcloth-covered kitchen-table. And Aunt Hager, if her ironing was done, would sit beside the stove and doze, while Annjee tossed and groaned in her chilly bedroom. Only in the kitchen was it really bright and warm.

In the afternoons when Sandy came home from school he would usually find Sister Johnson helping Hager with her ironing, and keeping up a steady conversation.

"Dis gonna be a hard winter. De papers say folks is out o' work ever' where, an', wid all dis sleet an' rain, it's a terror fo' de po' peoples, I tells you! Now, ma Tom, he got a good job tendin' de furnace at de Fair Buildin', so I ain't doin' much washin' long as he's workin'—but so many colored men's out o' work here, wid Christmas comin', it sho is too bad! An' you, Sis Williams, wid yo' daughter sick in bed! Any time yo' clothes git kinder heavy fo' you, I ain't mind helpin' you out. Jest send dis chile atter me or holler 'cross de yard if you kin make me hear! . . . How you press dis dress, wid de collar turn up or down? Which way do Mis' Dunset like it?"

"I always presses it down," returned Hager, who was ironing handkerchiefs and towels on the table. "Better let me iron that, an' you take these here towels."

"All right," agreed Sister Johnson, " 'cause you knows how yo' white folks likes dey things, an' I don't. Folks have so many different ways!"

"Sho do," said Hager. "I washed for a woman once what even had her sheets starched."

"But you's sure got a fine repertation as a washer, Sis Williams. One o' de white ladies what I washes fo' say you washes beautiful."

"I reckon white folks does think right smart of me," said Hager proudly. "They always likes you when you tries to do right."

"When you tries to do yo' work right, you means. Dey ain't carin' nothin' 'bout you 'yond workin' fo' 'em. Ain't dey got all de little niggers settin' off in one row at dat school whar Sandy an' Willie-Mae go at? I's like Harriett—ain't got no time fo' white folks maself, 'ceptin' what little money dey pays me. You ain't been run out o' yo' home like I is, Hager. . . . Sandy, make haste go fetch my pipe from over to de house, an' don't stay all day playin' wid Willie-Mae! Tote it here quick! . . . An' you oughter hear de way white folks talks 'bout niggers. Says dey's lazy, an' says dey stinks, an' all. Huh! Dey ought to smell deyselves! You's smelled white peoples when dey gets to sweatin' ain't you? Smells jest like sour cream, only worser, kinder sickenin' like. And some o' dese foriners what's been eating garlic—phew! Lawdy!"

When Sandy returned with the pipe, the conversation had shifted to the deaths in the colored community. "Hager, folks dyin' right an' left already dis winter. We's had such a bad fall, dat's de reason why. You know dat no-'count Jack Smears passed away last Sunday. Dey had his funeral yesterday an' I went. Good thing he belonged to de lodge, too, else he'd been buried in de po'-field, 'cause he ain't left even de copper cents to put on his eyes. Lodge beared his funeral bill, but I heard more'n one member talkin' 'bout how dey was puttin' a ten-dollar nigger in a hundred-dollar coffin! . . . An' his wife were at de funeral. Yes, sir! A hussy! After she done left him last year wid de little chillens to take care of, an' she runnin' round de streets showin' off. Dere she sot, big as life, in front wid de moaners, long black veil on her face and done dyed her coat black, an' all de time Reverend Butler been preachin' 'bout how holy Jack were, she turn an' twist an' she coughed an' she whiffled an' blowed an' she wiped—tryin' her best to cry an' couldn't, deceitful as she is! Then she jest broke out to screamin', but warn't a tear in her eye; makin' folks look at her, dat's all, 'cause she ain't cared nothin' 'bout Jack. She been livin' in de Bottoms since last Feb'ary wid a young bell-hop ain't much older'n her own son, Bert!"

"Do Jesus!" said Hager. "Some womens is awful."

"Worse'n dat," said Sister Johnson. . . . "Lawdy! Listen at dat sleet beatin' on dese winders! Sho gwine be a real winter! An' how time do pass. Ain't but three mo' weeks till Christmas!"

"Truth," said Sandy's grandmother. "An' we ain't gwine have no money a-tall. Ain't no mo'n got through payin' ma taxes good, an' de interest on ma mortgage, when Annjee get sick here! Lawd, I tells you, po' colored womens have it hard!"

"Sho do!" said Sister Johnson, sucking at her pipe as she ironed. "How long you been had this house, Sis Williams?"

"Fo' nigh on forty years, even sence Cudge an' me come here from Montgomery. An' I been washin' fo' white folks ever' week de Lawd sent sence I been here, too. Bought this house washin', and made as many payments myself as Cudge come near; an' raised ma chillens washin'; an' when Cudge taken sick an' laid on his back for mo'n a year, I taken care o' him washin'; an' when he died, paid de funeral bill washin', cause he ain't belonged to no lodge. Sent Tempy through de high school and edicated Annjee till she marry that onery pup of a Jimboy, an' Harriett till she left home. Yes, sir. Washin', an' here I is with me arms still in de tub! . . . But they's one mo' got to go through school yet, an' that's ma little Sandy. If de Lawd lets me live, I's gwine make a edicated man out o' him. He's gwine be another Booker T. Washington." Hager turned a voluminous white petticoat on the ironing-board as she carefully pressed its embroidered hem. "I ain't never raised no boy o' ma own yet, so I wants this one o' Annjee's to 'mount to something. I wants him to know all they is to know, so's he can help this black race o' our'n to come up and see de light and take they places in de world. I wants him to be a Fred Douglass leadin' de people, that's what, an' not followin' in de tracks o' his good-for-nothin' pappy, worthless an' wanderin' like Jimboy is."

"O, don't say that, ma," Annjee cried weakly from her bed in the other room. "Jimboy's all right, but he's just too smart to do this heavy ditch-digging labor, and that's all white folks gives the colored a chance at here in Stanton; so he had to leave."

"There you go excitin' yo'self agin, an' you sick. I thought you was asleep. I ain't meant nothin', honey. Course he's all right," Hager said to quiet her daughter, but she couldn't resist mumbling: "But I ain't seen him doin' you no good."

"Well, he ain't beat her, has he?" asked Sister Johnson, who, for the sake of conversation, often took a contrary view-point. "I's knowed many a man to beat his wife. Tom used to tap me a few times 'fo' I found out a way to stop him, but dat ain't nedder here nor dere!" She folded a towel decisively and gave it a vigorous rub with the hot iron. "Did I ever tell you 'bout de man lived next do' to us in Cairo what cut his wife in de stomach wid a razor an' den stood ovah her when de doctor was sewin' her up moanin': 'I don't see why I cut her in de stomach! O, Lawd! She always told me she ain't want to be cut in de stomach!' . . . An' it warn't two months atter dat dat he done sliced her in de stomach agin when she was tryin' to git away from him! He were a mean nigger, that man were!"

"Annjee, is you taken yo' medicine yet? It's past fo' o'clock," Hager called. "Sandy, here, take this fifteen cents, chile, and run to de store an' get me a soup bone. I gwine try an' make a little broth for yo' mother. An' don't be gone all day neither, 'cause I got to send these clothes back to Mis' Dunset." Hager was pressing out the stockings as she turned her attention to the conversation again. "They tells me, Sister Johnson, that Seth Jones done beat up his wife something terrible."

"He did, an' he oughter! She was always stayin' way from home an' settin' up in de church, not even cookin' his meals, an' de chillens runnin' ragged in de street."

"She's a religious frantic, ain't she?" asked Hager. . . . "You Sandy, hurry up, sir! an' go get that soup bone!"

"No, chile, 'tain't that," said Sister Johnson. "She ain't carin' so much 'bout religion. It's Reverend Butler she's runnin' atter. Ever' time de church do' opens, there she sets in de preacher's mouth, tryin' to 'tract de shepherd from his sheep. She de one what taken her husband's money an' bought Reverend Butler dat gold-headed walkin'-cane he's got. I ain't blame Seth fer hittin' her bap on de head, an' she takin' his money an' buyin' canes fer ministers!"

"Sadie Butler's in my school," said Sandy, putting on his stocking cap. "Reverend Butler's her step-father."

"Shut up! You hears too much," said Hager. "Ain't I told you to go on an' get that soup bone?"

"Yes'm. I'm going."

"An' I reckon I'll be movin' too," said Sister Johnson, placing the iron on the stove. "It's near 'bout time to be startin' Tom's supper. I done told Willie-Mae to peel de taters 'fo' I come ovah here, but I spects she ain't done it. Dat's de worse black gal to get to work! Soon as she eat, she run outdo's to de privy to keep from washin' de dishes!"

Sandy started to the store, and Sister Johnson, with an old coat over her head, scooted across the back yard to her door. It was a chill December afternoon and the steady sleet stung Sandy in the face as he ran along, but the air smelled good after the muggy kitchen and the stale scent of Annjee's sick-room. Near the corner Sandy met the mail-man, his face red with cold.

"Got anything for us?" asked the little boy.

"No," said the man as he went on without stopping.

Sandy wished his mother would get well soon. She looked so sad lying there in bed. And Aunt Hager was always busy washing and ironing. His grandmother didn't even have time to mend his stockings any more and there were great holes in the heels when he went to school. His shoes were worn out under the bottoms, too. Yesterday his mother had said: "Honey, you better take them high brown shoes of mine from underneath the bed and put 'em on to keep your feet dry this wet weather. I can't afford to buy you none now, and you ain't got no rubbers."

"You want me to wear old women's shoes like Jimmy Lane?" Sandy objected. "I won't catch cold with my feet wet."

But Hager from the kitchen overruled his objections. "Put on them shoes, sir, an' don't argue with yo' mother, an' she sick in de bed! Put 'em on an' hush yo' mouth, till you get something better."

So this morning at recess Sandy had to fight a boy for calling him "sissy" on account of his mother's shoes he was wearing.

But only a week and a half more and the Christmas vacation would come! Uptown the windows were already full of toys, dolls, skates, and sleds. Sandy wanted a Golden Flyer sled for Christmas. That's all he wanted—a Golden Flyer with flexible rudders, so you could guide it easy. Boy! Wouldn't he come shooting down that hill by the Hickory Woods where the fellows coasted every year! They cost only four dollars and ninety-five cents and surely his grandma could afford that for him, even if his mother was sick and she had just paid her taxes. Four ninety-five—but he wouldn't want anything else if Aunt Hager would buy that sled for Santa Claus to bring him! Every day, after school, he passed by the store, where many sleds were displayed, and stood for a long time looking at this Golden Flyer of narrow hard-wood timbers varnished a shiny yellow. It had bright red runners and a beautiful bar with which to steer.

When he told Aunt Hager about it, all she said was: "Boy, is you crazy?" But Annjee smiled from her bed and answered: "Wait and see." Maybe they would get it for him—but Santa Claus was mean to poor kids sometimes, Sandy knew, when their parents had no money.

"Fifteen cents' worth of hamburger," he said absent-mindedly to the butcher when he reached the market. . . . And when Sandy came home, his grandmother whipped him for bringing ground meat instead of the soup bone for which she had sent him.

So the cold days passed, heavy and cloudy, with Annjee still in bed, and the kitchen full of garments hanging on lines to dry because, out of doors, the frozen rain kept falling. Always in Hager's room a great pile of rough-dried clothes eternally waited to be ironed. Sandy helped his grandmother as much as he could, running errands, bringing in coal and wood, pumping water in the mornings before school, and sitting by his mother in the evenings, reading to her from his *Nature Story Reader* when it wasn't too cold in her bedroom.

Annjee was able to sit up now and she said she felt better, but she looked ashen and tired. She wanted to get back to work, so she would have a little money for Christmas and be able to help Hager with the doctor's bill, but she guessed she couldn't. And she was still worrying about Jimboy. Three months had passed since he went away—a longer time than usual that he hadn't written. Maybe something *had* happened to him. Maybe he was out of work and hungry, because this was a hard winter. *Maybe he was dead!*

"O, my God, no!" Annjee cried as the thought struck her.

But one Sunday morning, ten days before Christmas, the door-bell rang violently and a special-delivery boy stood on the front porch. Annjee's heart jumped as she sat up in bed. She had seen the youngster approaching from the window. Word from Jimboy surely—or word about him!

"Ma! Sandy! Go quick and see what it is!"

"Letter for Mrs. Annjelica Rogers," said the boy, stamping the snow from his feet. "Sign here."

While Sandy held the door open, letting the cold wind blow through the house, Hager haltingly scrawled something on the boy's pink pad. Then, with the child behind her, the old woman hurried to her daughter's bed with the white envelope.

"It's from him! " Annjee cried; "I know it's from Jimboy," as she tore open the letter with trembling fingers.

A scrap of dirty tablet-paper fell on the quilt, and Annjee quickly picked it up. It was written in pencil in a feminine hand.

> Dear Sister,
>
> I am stranded in Memphis, Tenn. and the show has gone on to New Orleans. I can't buy anything to eat because I am broke and don't know anybody in this town. Annjee, please send me my fare to come home and mail it to the Beale Street Colored Hotel. I'm sending my love to you and mama.
>
> Your baby sister,
> Harriett

Thirteen

Christmas

"Po' little thing," said Hager. "Po' little thing. An' here we ain't got no money."

The night before, on Saturday, Hager had bought a sack of flour, a chunk of salt pork, and some groceries. Old Dr. McDillors had called in the afternoon, and she had paid him, too.

"I reckon it would take mo'n thirty dollars to send fo' Harriett, an' Lawd knows we ain't got three dollars in de house."

Annjee lay limply back on her pillows staring out of the window at the falling snow. She had been crying.

"But never mind," her mother went on, "I's gwine see Mr. John Frank tomorrow an' see can't I borry a little mo' money on this mortgage we's got with him."

So on Monday morning the old lady left her washing and went uptown to the office of the money-lender, but the clerk there said Mr. Frank had gone to Chicago and would not be back for two weeks. There was nothing the clerk could do about it, since he himself could not lend money.

That afternoon Annjee sat up in bed and wrote a long letter to Harriett, telling her of their troubles, and before she sealed it, Sandy saw his mother slip into the envelope the three one-dollar bills that she had been guarding under her pillow.

"There goes your Santa Claus," she said to her son, "but maybe Harriett's hungry. And you don't want Aunt Harrie to be hungry, do you?"

"No'm," Sandy said.

The grey days passed and Annjee was able to get up and sit beside the kitchen-stove while her mother ironed. Every afternoon Sandy went downtown to look at the shop windows, gay with Christmas things. And he would stand and stare at the Golden Flyer sleds in Edmondson's hardware-shop. He could feel himself coasting down a long hill on one of those light, swift, red and yellow coasters, the envy of all the other boys, white and colored, who looked on.

When he went home, he described the sled minutely to Annjee and Aunt Hager and wondered aloud if that might be what he would get for

Christmas. But Hager would say: "Santa Claus are just like other folks. He don't work for nothin'!" And his mother would add weakly from her chair: "This is gonna be a slim Christmas, honey, but mama'll see what she can do." She knew his heart was set on a sled, and he could tell that she knew; so maybe he would get it.

One day Annjee gathered her strength together, put a woollen dress over her kimono, wrapped a heavy cloak about herself, and went out into the back yard. Sandy, from the window, watched her picking her way slowly across the frozen ground towards the outhouse. At the trash-pile near the alley fence she stopped and, stooping down, began to pull short pieces of boards and wood from the little pile of lumber that had been left there since last summer by the carpenters who had built the porch. Several times in her labor she rose and leaned weakly against the back fence for support, and once Sandy ran out to see if he could help her, but she told him irritably to get back in the house out of the weather or she would put him to bed without any supper. Then, after placing the boards that she had succeeded in unearthing in a pile by the path, she came wearily back to the kitchen, trembling with cold.

"I'm mighty weak yet," she said to Hager, "but I'm sure much better than I was. I don't want to have the grippe no more. . . . Sandy, look in the mail-box and see has the mail-man come by yet."

As the little boy returned empty-handed, he heard his mother talking about old man Logan, who used to be a carpenter.

"Maybe he can make it," she was saying, but stopped when she heard Sandy behind her. "I guess I'll lay back down now."

Aunt Hager wrung out the last piece of clothes that she had been rinsing. "Yes, chile," she said, "you go on and lay down. I's gwine make you some tea after while." And the old woman went outdoors to take from the line the frozen garments blowing in the sharp north wind.

After supper that night Aunt Hager said casually: "Well, I reckon I'll run down an' see Brother Logan a minute whilst I got nothin' else to do. Sandy, don't you let de fire go out, and take care o' yo' mama."

"Yes'm," said the little boy, drawing pictures on the oilcloth-covered table with a pin. His grandmother went out the back door and he looked through the frosty window to see which way she was going. The old woman picked up the boards that his mother had piled near the alley fence, and with them in her arms she disappeared down the alley in the dark.

After a little, Aunt Hager returned puffing and blowing.

"Can he do it?" Annjee demanded anxiously from the bedroom when she heard her mother enter.

"Yes, chile," Hager answered. "Lawd, it sho is cold out yonder! Whee! Lemme git here to this stove!"

That night it began to snow again. The great heavy flakes fell with languid gentility over the town and silently the whiteness covered everything. The next morning the snow froze to a hard sparkling crust on roofs and ground, and in the late afternoon when Sandy went to return the Reinharts' clothes, you could walk on top of the snow without sinking.

At the back door of the Reinharts' house a warm smell of plum-pudding and mince pies drifted out as he waited for the cook to bring the money. When she returned with seventy-five cents, she had a nickel for Sandy, too. As he slid along the street, he saw in many windows gay holly wreaths with red berries and big bows of ribbon tied to them. Sandy wished he could buy a holly wreath for their house. It might make his mother's room look cheerful. At home it didn't seem like Christmas with the kitchen full of drying clothes, and no Christmas-tree.

Sandy wondered if, after all, Santa Claus might, by some good fortune, bring him that Golden Flyer sled on Christmas morning. How fine this hard snow would be to coast on, down the long hill past the Hickory Woods! How light and swift he would fly with his new sled! Certainly he had been a good boy, carrying Aunt Hager's clothes for her, waiting on his mother when she was in bed, emptying the slops and cutting wood every day. And at night when he said his prayers:

> Now I lay me down to sleep.
> Pray the Lord my soul to keep.
> If I should die before I wake,
> Pray the Lord my soul to take. . . .

he had added with great earnestness: "And let Santa bring me a Golden Flyer sled, please, Lord. Amen."

But Sandy knew very well that there wasn't really any Santa Claus! He knew in his heart that Hager and his mother were Santa Claus—and that they didn't have any money. They were poor people. He was wearing his mama's shoes, as Jimmy Lane had once done. And his father and Harriett, who used to make the house gay, laughing and singing, were far away somewhere. . . . There wasn't any Santa Claus.

"I don't care," he said, tramping over the snow in the twilight on his way from the Reinharts'.

Christmas Eve. Candles and poinsettia flowers. Wreaths of evergreen. Baby trees hung with long strands of tinsel and fragile ornaments of colored glass. Sandy passed the windows of many white folks' houses where the curtains were up and warm floods of electric light made bright the cozy rooms. In Negro shacks, too, there was the dim warmth of oil-lamps and Christmas candles glowing. But at home there wasn't even a holly wreath. And the snow was whiter and harder than ever on the ground.

Tonight, though, there were no clothes drying in the kitchen when he went in. The ironing-board had been put away behind the door, and the whole place was made tidy and clean. The fire blazed and crackled in the little range; but nothing else said Christmas—no laughter, no tinsel, no tree.

Annjee had been about all day, still weak, but this afternoon she had made a trip to the store for a quarter's worth of mixed candies and nuts and a single orange, which she had hidden away until morning. Hager had baked a little cake, but there was no frosting on it such as there had been in other years, and there were no strange tissue-wrapped packages stuck away in the corners of trunks and drawers days ahead of time.

Although the little kitchen was warm enough, the two bedrooms were chilly, and the front room was freezing-cold because they kept the door there closed all the time. It was hard to afford a fire in one stove, let alone two, Aunt Hager kept saying, with nobody working but herself.

"I's thinking about Harriett," she remarked after their Christmas Eve supper as she rocked before the fire, "and how I's always tried to raise her right."

"And I'm thinking about—well, there ain't no use mentionin' him," Annjee said.

A sleigh slid by with jingling bells and shouts of laughter from the occupants, and a band of young people passed on their way to church singing carols. After a while another sleigh came along with a jolly sound.

"Santa Claus!" said Annjee, smiling at her serious little son. "You better hurry and go to bed, because he'll be coming soon. And be sure to hang up your stocking."

But Sandy was afraid that she was fooling, and, as he pulled off his clothes, he left his stockings on the floor, stuck into the women's shoes he had been wearing. Then, leaving the bedroom door half open so that the heat and a little light from the kitchen would come in, he climbed into his mother's bed. But he wasn't going to close his eyes yet. Sandy had discovered long ago that you could hear and see many things by not going to sleep when the family expected you to; therefore he remained awake tonight.

His mother was talking to Aunt Hager now: "I don't think he'll charge us anything, do you, ma?" And the old woman answered: "No, chile, Brother Logan's been tryin' to be ma beau for twenty years, an' he ain't gonna charge us nothin'."

Annjee came into the half-dark bedroom and looked at Sandy, lying still on the side of the bed towards the window. Then she took down her heavy coat from the wall and, sitting on the edge of a chair, began to pull on her rubbers. In a few moments he heard the front door close softly. His mother had gone out.

Where could she be going, he wondered, this time of night? He heard her footsteps crunching the hard snow and, rolling over close to the window, he pulled aside the shade a little and looked out. In the moonlight he saw Annjee moving slowly down the street past Sister Johnson's house, walking carefully over the snow like a very weak woman.

"Mama's still sick," the child thought, with his nose pressed against the cold window-pane. "I wish I could a bought her a present today."

Soon an occasional snore from the kitchen told Sandy that Hager dozed peacefully in her rocker beside the stove. He sat up in bed, wrapped a quilt about his shoulders, and remained looking out the window, with the shade hanging behind his back.

The white snow sparkled in the moonlight, and the trees made striking black shadows across the yard. Next door at the Johnsons' all was dark and quiet, but across the street, where white folks lived, the lights were burning brightly and a big Christmas-tree with all its candles aglow stood in the large bay window while a woman loaded it with toys. Sandy knew that four children lived there, three boys and a girl, whom he had often watched playing on the lawn. Sometimes he wished he had a brother or sister to play with him, too, because it was very quiet in a house with only grown-ups about. And right now it was dismal and lonely to be by himself looking out the window of a cold bedroom on Christmas Eve.

Then a woman's cloaked figure came slowly back past Sister Johnson's house in the moonlight, and Sandy saw that it was his mother returning, her head down and her shadow moving blackly on the snow. You could hear the dry grate of her heels on the frozen whiteness as she walked, leaning forward, dragging something heavy behind her. Sandy prepared to lie down quickly in bed again, but he kept his eyes against the window-pane to see what Annjee was pulling, and, as she came closer to the house, he could distinguish quite clearly behind her a solid, home-made sled bumping rudely over the snow.

Before Annjee's feet touched the porch, he was lying still as though he had been asleep a long time.

The morning sunlight was tumbling brightly into the windows when Sandy opened his eyes and blinked at the white world outside.

"Aren't you ever going to get up?" asked Annjee, smiling timidly above him. "It's Christmas morning, honey. Come see what Santa Claus brought you. Get up quick."

But he didn't want to get up. He knew what Santa Claus had brought him and he wanted to stay in bed with his face to the wall. It wasn't a Golden Flyer sled—and now he couldn't even hope for one any longer. He wanted to pull the covers over his head and cry, but, "Boy! You ain't up yet?" called Aunt Hager cheerily from the kitchen. "De little Lawd Jesus is in His manger fillin' all de world with light. An' old Santa done been here an' gone! Get out from there, chile, an' see!"

"I'm coming, grandma," said Sandy slowly, wiping his tear-filled eyes and rolling out of bed as he forced his mouth to smile wide and steady at the few little presents he saw on the floor—for the child knew he was expected to smile.

"O! A sled!" he cried in a voice of mock surprise that wasn't his own at all; for there it stood, heavy and awkward, against the wall and beside it on the floor lay two picture-books from the ten-cent store and a pair of white cotton gloves. Above the sled his stocking, tacked to the wall, was partly filled with candy, and the single orange peeped out from the top.

But the sled! Home-made by some rough carpenter, with strips of rusty tin nailed along the wooden runners, and a piece of clothes-line to pull it with!

"It's fine," Sandy lied, as he tried to lift it and place it on the floor as you would in coasting; but it was very heavy, and too wide for a boy to run with in his hands. You could never get a swift start. And a board was warped in the middle.

"It's a nice sled, grandma," he lied. "I like it, mama."

"Mr. Logan made it for you," his mother answered proudly, happy that he was pleased. "I knew you wanted a sled all the time."

"It's a nice sled," Sandy repeated, grinning steadily as he held the heavy object in his hands. "It's an awful nice sled."

"Well, make haste and look at de gloves, and de candy, and them pretty books, too," called Hager from the kitchen, where she was frying strips of salt pork. "My, you sho is a slow chile on Christmas mawnin'! Come 'ere and lemme kiss you." She came to the bedroom and picked him up in her arms. "Christmas gift to Hager's baby chile! Come on, Annjee, bring his clothes out here behind de stove an' bring his books, too. . . . This here's Little Red Riding Hood and the Wolf, and this here's Hansee and Gretsle on de cover—but I reckon you can read 'em better'n I can. . . . Daughter, set de table. Breakfast's 'bout ready now. Look in de oven an' see 'bout that corn-bread. . . . Lawd, this here Sandy's just like a baby lettin' ole Hager hold him and dress him. . . . Put yo' foot in that stocking, boy!" And Sandy began to feel happier, sitting on his grandmother's lap behind the stove.

Before noon Buster had come and gone, showing off his new shoes and telling his friend about the train he had gotten that ran on a real track when you wound it up. After dinner Willie-Mae appeared bringing a naked rag doll and a set of china dishes in a blue box. And Sister Johnson sent them a mince pie as a Christmas gift.

Almost all Aunt Hager's callers knocked at the back door, but in the late afternoon the front bell rang and Annjee sent Sandy through the cold parlor to answer it. There on the porch stood his Aunt Tempy, with several gaily wrapped packages in her arms. She was almost a stranger to Sandy, yet she kissed him peremptorily on the forehead as he stood in the doorway. Then she came through the house into the kitchen, with much the air of a mistress of the manor descending to the servants' quarters.

"Land sakes alive!" said Hager, rising to kiss her.

Tempy hugged Annjee, too, before she sat down, stiffly, as though the house she was in had never been her home. To little black Willie-Mae she said nothing.

"I'm sorry I couldn't invite you for Christmas dinner today, but you know how Mr. Siles is," Tempy began to explain to her mother and sister. "My husband is home so infrequently, and he doesn't like a house full of company, but of course Dr. and Mrs. Glenn Mitchell will be in later in the evening. They drop around any time. . . . But I had to run down and bring you a few presents. . . . You haven't seen my new piano yet, have you, mother? I must come and take you home with me some nice afternoon." She smiled appropriately, but her voice was hard.

"How is you an' yo' new church makin' it?" asked Hager, slightly embarrassed in the presence of her finely dressed society daughter.

"Wonderful!" Tempy replied. "Wonderful! Father Hill is so dignified, and the services are absolutely refined! There's never anything niggerish about them—so you know, mother, they suit me."

"I's glad you likes it," said Hager.

There was an awkward silence; then Tempy distributed her gifts, kissed them all as though it were her Christian duty, and went her way, saying that she had calls to make at Lawyer and Mrs. Moore's, and Professor Booth's, and Madam Temple's before she returned home. When she had gone, everybody felt relieved—as though a white person had left the house. Willie-Mae began to play again, and Hager pushed her feet out of her shoes once more, while Annjee went into the bedroom and lay down.

Sandy sat on the floor and untied his present, wrapped in several thicknesses of pink tissue paper, and found, in a bright Christmas box, a big illustrated volume of *Andersen's Fairy Tales* decorated in letters of gold. With its heavy pages and fine pictures, it made the ten-cent-store books that Hager had bought him appear cheap and thin. It made his mother's sled look cheap, too, and shamed all the other gifts the ones he loved had given him.

"I don't want it," he said suddenly, as loud as he could. "I don't want Tempy's old book!" And from where he was sitting, he threw it with all his might underneath the stove.

Hager gasped in astonishment. "Pick that up, sir," she cried amazed. "Yo' Aunt Tempy done bought you a fine purty book an' here you throwin' it un'neath de stove in de ashes! Lawd have mercy! Pick it up, I say, this minute!"

"I won't!" cried Sandy stubbornly. "I won't! I like my sled what you-all gave me, but I don't want no old book from Tempy! I won't pick it up!"

Then the astonished Hager grabbed him by the scruff of the neck and jerked him to his feet.

"Do I have to whip you yet this holy day? . . . Pick up that book, sir!"

"No!" he yelled.

She gave him a startled rap on the head with the back of her hand. "Talkin' sassy to yo' old grandma an' tellin' her no!"

"What is it?" Annjee called from the bedroom, as Sandy began to wail.

"Nothin'," Hager replied, " 'ceptin' this chile's done got beside hisself an' I has to hit him—that's all!"

But Sandy was not hurt by his grandmother's easy rap. He was used to being struck on the back of the head for misdemeanors, and this time he welcomed the blow because it gave him, at last, what he had been looking for all day—a sufficient excuse to cry. Now his pent-up tears flowed without ceasing while Willie-Mae sat in a corner clutching her rag doll to her breast, and Tempy's expensive gift lay in the ashes beneath the stove.

Fourteen

Return

After Christmas there followed a period of cold weather, made bright by the winter sun shining on the hard crusty snow, where children slid and rolled, and over which hay-wagons made into sleighs on great heavy runners drove jingling into town from the country. There was skating on the frozen river and fine sledding on the hills beyond the woods, but Sandy never went out where the crowds were with his sled, because he was ashamed of it.

After New Year's Annjee went back to work at Mrs. Rice's, still coughing a little and still weak. But with bills to pay and Sandy in need of shoes and stockings and clothes to wear to school, she couldn't remain idle any longer. Even with her mother washing and ironing every day except the Sabbath, expenses were difficult to meet, and Aunt Hager was getting pretty old to work so hard. Annjee thought that Tempy ought to help them a little, but she was too proud to ask her. Besides, Tempy had never been very affectionate towards her sisters even when they were all girls together—but she ought to help look out for their mother. Hager, however, when Annjee brought up the subject of Tempy's help, said that she was still able to wash, thank God, and wasn't depending on any of her children for anything—not so long as white folks wore clothes.

At school Sandy passed all of his mid-year tests and, along with Sadie Butler, was advanced to the fifth A, but the other colored child in the class, a little fat girl named Mary Jones, failed and had to stay behind. Mary's mother, a large sulphur-yellow woman who cooked at the Drummer's Hotel, came to the school and told the teacher, before all the children, just what she thought of her for letting Mary fail—and her thoughts were not very complimentary to the stiff, middle-aged white lady who taught the class. The question of color came up, too, during the discussion.

"Look at ma chile settin' back there behind all de white ones," screamed the sulphur-yellow woman. "An' me payin' as much taxes as anybody! You treats us colored folks like we ain't citizerzens—that's what you does!" The argument had to be settled in the principal's office, where the teacher went with the enraged mother, while the white children giggled that a fat, yellow colored lady should come to school to quarrel about her daughter's not being promoted. But the colored children in the class couldn't laugh.

St. Valentine's day came and Sadie Butler sent Sandy a big red heart. But for Annjee, "the mail-man passed and didn't leave no news," because Jimboy hadn't written yet, nor had Harriett thanked her for the three dollars she had mailed to Memphis before Christmas. There were no letters from anybody.

The work at Mrs. Rice's was very heavy, because Mrs. Rice's sister, with two children, had come from Indiana to spend the winter, and Annjee had to cook for them and clean their rooms, too. But she was managing to save a little money every week. She bought Sandy a new blue serge suit with a Norfolk coat and knickerbocker pants. And then he sat up very stiffly in Sterner's studio and had his picture taken.

The freckled-faced white boy, Paul Biggers, who sat across from Sandy in school, delivered the *Daily Leader* to several streets in Sandy's neighborhood, and Sandy sometimes went with him, helping to fold and throw the papers in the various doorways. One night it was almost seven o'clock when he got home.

"I had a great mind not to wait for you," said Aunt Hager, who had long had the table set for supper. "Wash yo' face an' hands, sir! An' brush that snow off yo' coat 'fo' you hang it up."

His grandmother took a pan of hot spoon-bread from the oven and put it on the table, where the little oil-lamp glowed warmly and the plain white dishes looked clean and inviting. On the stove there was a skillet full of fried apples and bacon, and Hager was making a pot of tea.

"Umn-nn! Smells good!" said Sandy, speaking of everything at once as he slid into his chair. "Gimme a lot o' apples, grandma."

"Is that de way you ask fo' 'em, sir? Can't you say please no mo'?"

"Please, ma'am," said the boy, grinning, for Hager's sharpness wasn't serious, and her old eyes were twinkling.

While they were eating, Annjee came in from work with a small bucket of oyster soup in her hands. They heated this and added it to their supper, and Sandy's mother sat down in front of the stove, with her feet propped up on the grate to dry quickly. It was very comfortable in the little kitchen.

"Seems like the snow's melting," said Annjee. "It's kinder sloppy and nasty underfoot. . . . Ain't been no mail today, has they?"

"No, honey," said Hager. "Leastwise, I been washin' so hard ain't had no time to look in de box. Sandy, run there to de front do' an' see. But I knows there ain't nothin', nohow."

"Might be," said Annjee as Sandy took a match and went through the dark bedroom and parlor to the front porch. There was no mail. But Sandy saw, coming across the slushy dirty-white snow towards the house, a slender figure approaching in the gloom. He waited, shivering in the doorway a moment to see who it was; then all at once he yelled at the top of his lungs: "Aunt Harrie's here!"

Pulling her by the hand, after having kissed and hugged and almost choked her, he ran back to the kitchen. "Look, here's Aunt Harrie!" he cried. "Aunt Harrie's home!" And Hager turned from the table, upsetting her tea, and opened wide her arms to take her to her bosom.

"Ma chile!" she shouted. "Done come home again! Ma baby chile come home!"

Annjee hugged and kissed Harriett, too, as her sister sat on Hager's knees—and the kitchen was filled with sound, warm and free and loving, for the prodigal returned.

"Ma chile's come back!" her mother repeated over and over. "Thank de Lawd! Ma chile's back!"

"You want some fried apples, Harrie?" asked Sandy, offering her his plate. "You want some tea?"

"No, thank you, honey," she replied when the excitement had subsided and Aunt Hager had released her, with her little black hat askew and the powder kissed off one side of her face.

She got up, shook herself, and removed her hat to brush down her hair, but she kept her faded coat on as she laid her little purse of metal mesh on the table. Then she sat down on the chair that Annjee offered her near the fire. She was thinner and her hair had been bobbed, giving her a boyish appearance, like the black pages in old Venetian paintings. But her lips were red and there were two little spots of rouge burning on each cheek, although her eyes were dark with heavy shadows as though she had been ill.

Hager was worried. "Has you been sick, chile?" she asked.

"No, mama," Harriett said. "I've been all right—just had a hard time, that's all. I got mad, and quit the show in Memphis, and they wouldn't pay me—so that was that! The minstrels left the carnival for the winter and started playing the theatres, and the new manager was a cheap skate. I couldn't get along with him."

"Did you get my letter and the money?" Annjee asked. "We didn't have no more to send you, and afterwards, when you didn't write, I didn't know if you got it."

"I got it and meant to thank you, sis, but I don't know—just didn't get round to it. But, anyway, I'm out of the South now. It's a hell—I mean it's an awful place if you don't know anybody! And more hungry niggers down there! I wonder who made up that song about *Dear Old Southland*. There's nothing dear about it that I can see. Good God! It's awful! . . . But I'm back." She smiled. "Where's Jimboy? . . . O, that's right, Annjee—you told me in the letter. But I sort-a miss him around here. Lord, I hope he didn't go to Memphis!"

"Did you find a job down there?" Annjee asked, looking at her sister's delicate hands.

"Sure, I found a *job* all right," Harriett replied in a tone that made Annjee ask no more questions. "Jobs are like hen's teeth—try and find 'em." And she shrugged her shoulders as Sandy had so often seen her do, but she no longer seemed to him like a little girl. She was grown-up and hard and strange now, but he still loved her.

"Aunt Harrie, I passed to the fifth A," he announced proudly.

"That's wonderful," she answered. "My, but you're smart! You'll be a great man some day, sure, Sandy."

"Where's yo' suit-case, honey?" Hager interrupted, too happy to touch her food on the table or to take her eyes away from the face of her returned child. "Didn't you bring it back with you? Where is it?"

"Sure, I got it. . . . But I'm gonna live at Maudel's this time, mama. . . . I left it at the station. I didn't think you-all'd want me here." She tried to make the words careless-like, but they were pitifully forced.

"Aw, honey!" Annjee cried, the tears coming.

The shadow of inner pain passed over Hager's black face, but the only reply she made was: "You's growed up now, chile. I reckon you knows what you's doin'. You's been ten thousand miles away from yo' mammy, an' I reckon you knows. . . . Come on, Sandy, let's we eat." Slowly the old woman returned to the cold food on her plate. "Won't you eat something with us, daughter?"

Harriett's eyes lowered and her shoulders drooped. "No, mama, thank you. I'm—not hungry."

Then a long, embarrassing silence followed while Hager gulped at her tea, Sandy tried to swallow a mouthful of bread that seemed to choke him, and Annjee stared stupidly at the stove.

Finally Harriett said: "I got to go now." She stood up to button her coat and put on her hat. Then she took her metal purse from the table.

"Maudel'll be waiting for me, but I'll be seeing you-all again soon, I guess. Good-bye, Sandy honey! I got to go. . . . Annjee, I got to go now. . . . Good-bye, mama!" She was trembling. As she bent down to kiss Hager, her purse slipped out of her hands and fell in a little metal heap on the floor. She stooped to pick it up.

"I got to go now."

A tiny perfume-bottle in the bag had broken from the fall, and as she went through the cold front room towards the door, the odor of cheap and poignant drugstore violets dripped across the house.

Fifteen

One by One

You could smell the spring.

" 'Tain't gwine be warm fo' weeks yet!" Hager said.

Nevertheless, you could smell the spring. Little boys were already running in the streets without their overcoats, and the ground-hog had seen its shadow. Snow remained in the fence corners, but it had melted on the roofs. The yards were wet and muddy, but no longer white.

It was a sunny afternoon in late March that a letter came. On his last delivery the mail-man stopped, dropped it in the box—and Sandy saw him. It was addressed to his mother and he knew it must be from Jimboy.

"Go on an' take it to her," his grandma said, as soon as she saw the boy coming with it in his hand. "I knows that's what you want to do. Go on an' take it." And she bent over her ironing again.

Sandy ran almost all the way to Mrs. Rice's, dropping the letter more than once on the muddy sidewalk, so excited he did not think to put it in his pocket. Into the big yard and around to the white lady's back door he sped—and it was locked! He knocked loudly for a long time, and finally an upper window opened and Annjee, a dust-rag around her head, looked down, squinting in the sunlight.

"Who's there?" she called stridently, thinking of some peddler or belated tradesman for whom she did not wish to stop her cleaning.

Sandy pantingly held up the letter and was about to say something when the window closed with a bang. He could hear his mother almost falling down the back stairs, she was coming so fast. Then the key turned swiftly in the lock, the door opened, and, without closing it, Annjee took the letter from him and tore it open where she stood.

"It's from Jimboy!"

Sandy stood on the steps looking at his mother, her bosom heaving, her sleeves rolled up, and the white cloth tied about her head, doubly white against her dark-brown face.

"He's in Detroit, it says. . . . Umn! I ain't never seen him write such a long letter. 'I had a hard time this winter till I landed here,' it says, 'but things look pretty good now, and there is lots of building going on and plenty of work opening up in the automobile plants . . . a mighty lot of colored folks here . . . hope you and Sandy been well. Sorry couldn't send you nothing Xmas, but I was in St. Paul broke. . . . Kiss my son for me. Tell ma hello even if she don't want to hear it. Your loving husband, Jimboy Rogers.' "

Annjee did her best to hold the letter with one hand and pick up Sandy with the other, but he had grown considerably during the winter and she was still a little weak from her illness; so she bent down to his level and kissed him several times before she re-read the letter.

"From your daddy!" she said. "Umn-mn. . . . Come on in here and warm yourself. Lemme see what he says again!" . . . She lighted the gas oven in the white kitchen and sat down in front of it with her letter, forgetting the clock and the approaching time for Mrs. Rice's dinner, forgetting everything. "A letter from my daddy! From my far-off sugar-daddy!"

"From *my* daddy," corrected Sandy. . . . "Say, gimme a nickel to buy some marbles, mama. I wanta go play."

Without taking her eyes from the precious note Annjee fumbled in her apron and found a coin. "Take it and go on!" she said.

It was a dime. Sandy skipped around the house and down the street in the chilly sunshine. He decided to stop at Buster's for a while before going home, since he had to pass there anyway, and he found his friend in the house trying to carve boats from clothes-pins with a rusty jack-knife.

Buster's mother was a seamstress, and, after opening the front door and greeting Sandy with a cheery "Hello," she returned to her machine and a friend who was calling on her. She was a tall young light-mulatto woman, with skin like old ivory. Maybe that was why Buster was so white. But her husband was a black man who worked on the city's garbage-trucks and was active politically when election time came, getting colored men to vote Republican. Everybody said he made lots of money, but that he wasn't really Buster's father.

The golden-haired child gave Sandy a butcher-knife and together they whacked at the clothes-pins. You could hear the two women talking plainly in the little sewing-room, where the machine ran between snatches of conversation.

"Yes," Buster's mother was saying, "I have the hardest time keeping that boy colored! He goes on just like he was white. Do you know what he did last week? Cut all the blossoms off my geranium plants here in the house, took them to school, and gave them to Dorothy Marlow, in his grade. And you know who Dorothy is, don't you? Senator Marlow's daughter! . . . I said: 'Buster, if you ever cut my flowers to carry to any little girl again, I'll punish you severely, but if you cut them to carry to little white girls, I don't know what I'll do with you. . . . Don't you know they hang colored boys for things like that?' I wanted to scare him—because you know there might be trouble even among kids in school over such things. . . . But I had to laugh."

Her friend laughed too. "He's a hot one, taking flowers to the women already, and a white girl at that! You've got a fast-working son, Elvira, I must say. . . . But, do you know, when you first moved here and I saw you and the boy going in and out, I thought sure you were both white folks. I didn't know you was colored till my husband said: 'That's Eddie's wife!' You-all sure looked white to me."

The machine started to whir, making the conversation inaudible for a few minutes, and when Sandy caught their words again, they were talking about the Elks' club-house that the colored people were planning to build.

"Can you go out?" Sandy demanded of Buster, since they were making no headway with the tough clothes-pins and dull knives.

"Maybe," said Buster. "I'll go see." And he went into the other room and asked his mother.

"Put on your overcoat," she commanded. "It's not summer yet. And be back in here before dark."

"All right, Vira," the child said.

The two children went to Mrs. Rumford's shop on the corner and bought three cents' worth of candy and seven cents' worth of peewees with which to play marbles when it got warm. Then Sandy walked back past Buster's house with him and they played for a while in the street before Sandy turned to run home.

Aunt Hager was making mush for supper. She sent him to the store for a pint bottle of milk as soon as he arrived, but he forgot to take the bottle and had to come back for it.

"You'd forget yo' head if it wasn't tied to you!" the old woman reminded him.

They were just finishing supper when Annjee got home with two chocolate éclairs in her coat-pocket, mashed together against Jimboy's letter.

"Huh! I'm crazy!" she said, running her hand down into the sticky mess. "But listen, ma! He's got a job and is doing well in Detroit, Jimboy says. . . . And I'm going to him!"

"You what?" Hager gasped, dropping her spoon in her mush-bowl. "What you sayin'?"

"I said I'm going to him, ma! I got to!" Annjee stood with her coat and hat still on, holding the sticky letter. "I'm going where my heart is, ma! . . . Oh, not today." She put her arms around her mother's neck. "I don't mean today, mama, nor next week. I got to save some money first. I only got a little now. But I mean I'm going to him soon's I can. I can't help it, ma—I love him!"

"Lawd, is you foolish?" cried Hager. "What's you gwine do with this chile, trapesin' round after Jimboy? What you gwine do if he leaves you in Detroiter or wherever he are? What you gwine do then? You loves him! Huh!"

"But he ain't gonna leave me in Detroit, 'cause I'm going with him everywhere he goes," she said, her eyes shining. "He ain't gonna leave me no more!"

"An' Sandy?"

"Couldn't he stay with you, mama? And then maybe we'd come back here and live, Jimboy and me, some time, when we get a little money ahead, and could pay off the mortgage on the house. . . . But there ain't no use arguing, mama, I got to go!"

Hager had never seen Annjee so positive before; she sat speechless, looking at the bowl of mush.

"I got to go where it ain't lonesome and where I ain't unhappy—and that's where Jimboy is! I got to go soon as I can."

Hager rose to put some water on the stove to heat for the dishes.

"One by one you leaves me—Tempy, then Harriett, then you," she said. "But Sandy's gonna stick by me, ain't you, son? He ain't gwine leave his grandma."

The youngster looked at Hager, moving slowly about the kitchen putting away the supper things.

"And I's gwine to make a fine man out o' you, Sandy. I's gwine raise one chile right yet, if de Lawd lets me live—just one chile right!" she murmured.

That night the March wind began to blow and the window-panes rattled. Sandy woke up in the dark, lying close and warm beside his mother. When he went back to sleep again, he dreamed that his Aunt Tempy's Christmas book had been turned into a chariot, and that he was riding through the sky with Tempy standing very dignifiedly beside him as he drove. And he couldn't see anybody down on earth, not even Hager.

When his mother rolled out at six o'clock to go to work, he woke up again, and while she dressed, he lay watching his breath curl mistily upwards in the cold room. Outside the window it was bleak and grey and the March wind, humming through the leafless branches of the trees, blew terrifically. He heard Aunt Hager in the kitchen poking at the stove, making up a blaze to start the coffee boiling. Then the front door closed when his mother went out and, as the door slammed, the wind howled fiercely. It was nice and warm in bed, so he lay under the heavy quilts half dreaming, half thinking, until his grandmother shook him to get up. And many were the queer, dream-drowsy thoughts that floated through his mind—not only that morning, but almost every morning while he lay beneath the warm quilts until Hager had called him three or four times to get ready for school.

He wondered sometimes whether if he washed and washed his face and hands, he would ever be white. Someone had told him once that blackness was only skin-deep. . . . And would he ever have a big house with electric lights in it, like his Aunt Tempy—but it was mostly white people who had such fine things, and they were mean to colored. . . . Some white folks were nice, though. Earl was nice at school, but not the little boys across the street, who called him "nigger" every day . . . and not Mrs. Rice, who scolded his mother. . . . Aunt Harrie didn't like any white folks at all. . . . But Jesus was white and wore a long, white robe, like a woman's, on the Sunday-school cards. . . . Once Jimmy Lane said: "God damn Jesus" when the teacher scolded him for not knowing his Bible lesson. He said it out loud in church, too, and the church didn't fall down on him, as Sandy thought it might. . . . Grandma said it was a sin to cuss and swear, but all the fellows at school swore—and Jimboy did, too. But every time Sandy said "God damn," he felt bad, because Aunt Hager said God was mighty good and it was wrong to take His name in vain. But he would like to learn to say "God damn" without feeling anything like most boys said it—just "God damn! . . . God damn! . . . God damn!" without being ashamed of himself. . . . The Lord never seemed to notice, anyhow. . . . And when he got big, he wanted to travel like Jimboy. He wanted to be a railroad engineer, but Harriett had said there weren't any colored engineers on trains. . . . What would he be, then? Maybe a doctor; but it was more fun being an engineer and travelling far away.

Sandy wished Annjee would take him with her when she went to join Jimboy—but then Aunt Hager would be all by herself, and grandma was so nice to him he would hate to leave her alone. Who would cut wood for her then? . . . But when he got big, he would go to Detroit. And maybe New York, too, where his geography said they had the tallest buildings in the world, and trains that ran under the river. . . . He wondered if there were any colored people in New York. . . . How ugly African colored folks looked in the geography—with bushy heads and wild eyes!

Aunt Hager said her mother was an African, but she wasn't ugly and wild; neither was Aunt Hager; neither was little dark Willie-Mae, and they were all black like Africans. . . . And Reverend Braswell was as black as ink, but he knew God. . . . God didn't care if people were black, did He? . . . What was God? Was He a man or a lamb or what? Buster's mother said God was a light, but Aunt Hager said He was a King and had a throne and wore a crown—she intended to sit down by His side by and by. . . . Was Buster's father white? Buster was white and colored both. But he didn't look like he was colored. What made Buster not colored? . . . And what made girls different from boys? . . . Once when they were playing house, Willie-Mae told him how girls were different from boys, but they didn't know why. Now Willie-Mae was in the seventh grade and had hard little breasts that stuck out sharp-like, and Jimmy Lane said dirty things about Willie-Mae. . . . Once he asked his mother what his navel was for and she said, "Layovers to catch meddlers." What did that mean? . . . And how come ladies got sick and stayed in bed when they had babies? Where did babies come from, anyhow? Not from storks—a fairy-story like Santa Claus. . . . Did God love people who told fairy-stories and lied to kids about storks and Santa Claus? . . . Santa Claus was no good, anyhow! God damn Santa Claus for not bringing him the sled he wanted Christmas! It was all a lie about Santa Claus!

The sound of Hager pouring coal on the fire and dragging her wash-tubs across the kitchen-floor to get ready for work broke in on Sandy's drowsy half-dreams, and as he rolled over in bed, his grandmother, hearing the springs creak, called loudly: "You Sandy! Get up from there! It's seven and past! You want to be late gettin' to yo' school?"

"Yes'm, I'm coming, grandma!" he said under the quilts. "But it's cold in here."

"You knows you don't dress in yonder! Bring them clothes on out behind this stove, sir."

"Yes'm." So with a kick of the feet his covers went flying back and Sandy ran to the warmth of the little kitchen, where he dressed, washed, and ate. Then he yelled for Willie-Mae—when he felt like it—or else went on to school without her, joining some of the boys on the way.

So spring was coming and Annjee worked diligently at Mrs. Rice's day after day. Often she did something extra for Mrs. Rice's sister and her children—pressed a shirtwaist or ironed some stockings—and so added a few quarters or maybe even a dollar to her weekly wages, all of which she saved to help carry her to Jimboy in Detroit.

For ten years she had been cooking, washing, ironing, scrubbing—and for what? For only the few weeks in a year, or a half-year, when Jimboy would come home from some strange place and take her in his strong arms and kiss her and murmur: "Annjee, baby!" That's what she had been working for—then the dreary months were as nothing, and the hard years faded away. But now he had been gone all winter, and, from his letter, he might not come back soon, because he said Detroit was a fine place for colored folks. . . . But Stanton—well, Annjee thought there must surely be better towns, where a woman wouldn't have to work so hard to live. . . .. And where Jimboy was.

So before the first buds opened on the apple-tree in the back yard, Annjee had gone to Detroit, leaving Sandy behind with his grandmother. And when the apple blossoms came in full bloom, there was no one living in the little house but a grey-headed old woman and her grandchild.

"One by one they leaves you," Hager said slowly. "One by one yo' chillen goes."

Sixteen

Nothing but Love

"A year ago tonight was de storm what blowed ma porch away! You 'members, honey? . . . Done seem like this year took more'n ma porch, too. My baby chile's left home an' gone to stay down yonder in de Bottoms with them triflin' Smothers family, where de piano's goin' night an' day. An' yo' mammy's done gone a-trapesin' after Jimboy. . . . Well, I thanks de Lawd you ain't gone too. You's mighty little an' knee-high to a duck, but you's ma stand-by. You's all I got, an' you ain't gwine leave yo' old grandma, is you?"

Hager had turned to Sandy in these lonely days for comfort and companionship. Through the long summer evenings they sat together on the front porch and she told her grandchild stories. Sometimes Sister Johnson came over and sat with them for a while smoking. Sometimes Madam de Carter, full of chatter and big words about the lodge and the race, would be there. But more often the two were alone—the black wash-woman with the grey hair and the little brown boy. Slavery-time stories, myths, folk-tales like the Rabbit and the Tar Baby; the war, Abe Lincoln, freedom; visions of the Lord; years of faith and labor, love and struggle filled Aunt Hager's talk of a summer night, while the lightning-bugs glowed and glimmered and the katydids chirruped, and the stars sparkled in the far-off heavens.

Sandy was getting to be too big a boy to sit in his grandmother's lap and be rocked to sleep as in summers gone by; now he sat on a little stool beside her, leaning his head on her legs when he was tired. Or else he lay flat on the floor of the porch listening, and looking up at the stars. Tonight Hager talked about love.

"These young ones what's comin' up now, they calls us ole fogies, an' handkerchief heads, an' white folks' niggers 'cause we don't get mad an' rar' up in arms like they does 'cause things is kinder hard, but, honey, when you gets old, you knows they ain't no sense in gettin' mad an' sourin' yo' soul with hatin' peoples. White folks is white folks, an' colored folks is colored, an' neither one of 'em is bad as t'other make out. For mighty nigh seventy years I been knowin' both of 'em, an' I ain't never had no room in ma heart to hate neither white nor colored.

When you starts hatin' people, you gets uglier than they is—an' I ain't never had no time for ugliness, 'cause that's where de devil comes in—in ugliness!

"They talks 'bout slavery time an' they makes out now like it were de most awfullest time what ever was, but don't you believe it, chile, 'cause it weren't all that bad. Some o' de white folks was just as nice to their niggers as they could be, nicer than many of 'em is now, what makes 'em work for less than they needs to eat. An' in those days they had to feed 'em. An' they ain't every white man beat his slaves neither! Course I ain't sayin' 'twas no paradise, but I ain't going to say it were no hell either. An' maybe I's kinder seein' it on de bestest side 'cause I worked in de big house an' ain't never went to de fields like most o' de niggers did. Ma mammy were de big-house cook an' I grewed up right with her in de kitchen an' played with little Miss Jeanne. An' Miss Jeanne taught me to read what little I knowed. An' when she growed up an' I growed up, she kept me with her like her friend all de time. I loved her an' she loved me. Miss Jeanne were de mistress' daughter, but warn't no difference 'tween us 'ceptin' she called me Hager an' I called her Miss Jeanne. But what difference do one word like 'Miss' make in yo' heart? None, chile, none. De words don't make no difference if de love's there.

"I disremembers what year it were de war broke out, but white folks was scared, an' niggers, too. Didn't know what might happen. An' we heard talk o' Abraham Lincoln 'way down yonder in de South. An' de ole marster, ole man Winfield, took his gun an' went to war, an' de young son, too, an' de superintender and de overseer—all of 'em gone to follow Lee. Ain't left nothin' but womens an' niggers on de plantation. De womens was a-cryin' an' de niggers was, too, 'cause they was sorry for de po' grievin' white folks.

"Is I ever told you how Miss Jeanne an' Marster Robert was married in de springtime o' de war, with de magnolias all a-bloomin' like candles for they weddin'? Is I ever told you, Sandy? . . . Well, I must some time. An' then Marster Robert had to go right off with his mens, 'cause he's a high officer in de army an' they heard Sherman were comin'. An' he left her a-standin' with her weddin'-clothes on, leanin' 'gainst a pillar o' de big white porch, with nobody but me to dry her eyes—ole Missis done dead an' de men-folks all gone to war. An' nobody in that big whole mansion but black ole deaf Aunt Granny Jones, what kept de house straight, an' me, what was stayin' with ma mistress.

"O, de white folks needed niggers then mo'n they ever did befo', an' they ain't a colored person what didn't stick by 'em when all they men-folks were gone an' de white womens was a-cryin' an' a-faintin' like they did in them days.

"But lemme tell you 'bout Miss Jeanne. She just set in her room an' cry. A-holdin' Marster Bob's pitcher, she set an' cry, an' she ain't come out o' her room to see 'bout nothin'—house, horses, cotton—nothin'. But de niggers, they ain't cheat her nor steal from her. An' come de news dat her brother done got wounded an' died in Virginia, an' her cousins got de yaller fever. Then come de news that Marster Robert, Miss Jeanne's husband, ain't no mo'! Killed in de battle! An' I thought Miss Jeanne would like to go crazy. De news say he died like a soldier, brave an' fightin'. But when she heard it, she went to de drawer an' got out her weddin'-veil an' took her flowers in her hands like she were goin' to de altar to meet de groom. Then she just sink in de flo' an' cry till I pick her up an' hold her like a chile.

"Well, de freedom come, an' all de niggers scatter like buck-shot, goin' to live in town. An' de yard niggers say I's a ole fool! I's free now—why don't I come with them? But I say no, I's gwine stay with Miss Jeanne—an' I stayed. I 'lowed ain't nary one o' them colored folks needed me like Miss Jeanne did, so I ain't went with 'em.

"An' de time pass; it pass an' it pass, an' de ole house get rusty for lack o' paint, an' de things, they 'gin to fall to pieces. An' Miss Jeanne say: 'Hager, I ain't got nobody in de world but you.' An' I say: 'Miss Jeanne, I ain't got nobody in de world but you neither.'

"And then she'd start talkin' 'bout her young husband what died so handsome an' brave, what ain't even had time that last day fo' to 'scort her to de church for de weddin', nor to hold her in his arms 'fore de orders come to leave. An' we would set on de big high ole porch, with its tall stone pillars, in de evenin's twilight till de bats start flyin' overhead an' de sunset glow done gone, she in her wide white skirts a-billowin' round her slender waist, an' me in ma apron an' cap an' this here chain she gimme you see on ma neck all de time an' what's done wore so thin.

"They was a ole stump of a blasted tree in de yard front o' de porch 'bout tall as a man, with two black pieces o' branches raised up like arms in de air. We used to set an' look at it, an' Miss Jeanne could see it from her bedroom winder upstairs, an' sometimes this stump, it look like it were movin' right up de path like a man.

"After she done gone to bed, late one springtime night when de moon were shinin', I hear Miss Jeanne a-cryin': 'He's come! . . . Hager, ma Robert's come back to me!' An' I jumped out o' ma bed in de next room where I were sleepin' an' run in to her, an' there she was in her long, white night-clothes standin' out in de moonlight on de little balcony, high up in de middle o' that big stone porch. She was lookin' down into de yard at this stump of a tree a-holdin' up its arms. An' she thinks it's Marster Robert a-callin' her. She thinks he's standin' there in his uniform, come back from de war, a-callin' her. An' she say: 'I'm comin', Bob, dear;' . . . I can hear her now. . . . She say: 'I'm comin'!' . . . An 'fore I think what she's doin', Miss Jeanne done stepped over de little rail o' de balcony like she were walkin' on moonlight. An' she say: 'I'm comin', Bob!'

"She ain't left no will, so de house an' all went to de State, an' I been left with nothin'. But I ain't care 'bout that. I followed her to de grave, an' I been with her all de time, 'cause she's ma friend. An' I were sorry for her, 'cause I knowed that love were painin' her soul, an' warn't nobody left to help her but me.

"An' since then I's met many a white lady an' many a white gentleman, an' some of 'em's been kind to me an' some of 'em ain't; some of 'em's cussed me an' wouldn't pay me fo' ma work; an' some of 'em's hurted me awful. But I's been sorry fo' white folks, fo' I knows something inside must be aggravatin' de po' souls. An' I's kept a room in ma heart fo' 'em, 'cause white folks needs us, honey, even if they don't know it. They's like spoilt chillens what's got too much o' ever'thing—an' they needs us niggers, what ain't got nothin'.

"I's been livin' a long time in yesterday, Sandy chile, an' I knows there ain't no room in de world fo' nothin' mo'n love. I knows, chile! Ever'thing there is but lovin' leaves a rust on yo' soul. An' to love sho 'nough, you got to have a spot in yo' heart fo' ever'body—great an' small, white an' black, an' them what's good an' them what's evil—'cause love ain't got no crowded-out places where de good ones stays an' de bad ones can't come in. When it gets that way, then it ain't love.

"White peoples maybe mistreats you an' hates you, but when you hates 'em back, you's de one what's hurted, 'cause hate makes yo' heart ugly—that's all it does. It closes up de sweet door to life an' makes ever'thing small an' mean an' dirty. Honey, there ain't no room in de world fo' hate, white folks hatin' niggers, an' niggers hatin' white folks. There ain't no room in this world fo' nothin' but love, Sandy chile. That's all they's room fo'— nothin' but love."

Seventeen

Barber-Shop

Mr. Logan, hearing that Aunt Hager had an empty room since all her daughters were gone, sent her one evening a new-comer in town looking for a place to stay. His name was Wim Dogberry and he was a brickmason and hod-carrier, a tall, quiet, stoop-shouldered black man, neither old nor young. He took, for two dollars and a half a week, the room that had been Annjee's, and Hager gave him a key to the front door.

Wim Dogberry was carrying hod then on a new moving-picture theatre that was being built. He rose early and came in late, face, hands, and overalls covered with mortar dust. He washed in a tin basin by the pump and went to bed, and about all he ever said to Aunt Hager and Sandy was "Good-mornin' " and "Good-evenin'," and maybe a stumbling "How is you?" But on Sunday mornings Hager usually asked him to breakfast if he got up on time—for on Saturday nights Wim drank licker and came home mumbling to himself a little later than on week-day evenings, so sometimes he would sleep until noon Sundays.

One Saturday night he wet the bed, and when Hager went to make it up on the Sabbath morning, she found a damp yellow spot in the middle. Of this act Dogberry was so ashamed that he did not even say "Good-mornin' " for several days, and if, from the corner, he saw Aunt Hager and her grandson sitting on the porch in the twilight when he came towards home, he would pass his street and walk until he thought they had gone inside to bed. But he was a quiet roomer, he didn't give anyone any trouble, and he paid regularly. And since Hager was in no position to despise two dollars and a half every week, she rather liked Dogberry.

Now Hager kept the growing Sandy close by her all the time to help her while she washed and ironed and to talk to her while she sat on the porch in the evenings. Of course, he played sometimes in his own yard whenever Willie-Mae or Buster or, on Sundays, Jimmy Lane came to the house. But Jimmy Lane was running wild since his mother died, and Hager didn't like him to visit her grandson any more. He was bad.

When Sandy wanted to go to the vacant lot to play baseball with the neighbor boys, his grandmother would usually not allow him to leave her. "Stay here, sir, with Hager. I needs you to pump ma water fo' me an' fill up these tubs," she would say. Or else she would yell: "Ain't I told you you might get hurt down there with them old rough white boys? Stay here in yo' own yard, where you can keep out o' mischief."

So he grew accustomed to remaining near his grandmother, and at night, when the other children would be playing duck-on-the-rock under the arc-light at the corner, he would be sitting on the front porch listening to Aunt Hager telling her tales of slavery and talking of her own far-off youth. When school opened in the fall, the old woman said: "I don't know what I's gwine do all day without you, Sandy. You sho been company to me, with all my own chillens gone." But Sandy was glad to get back to a roomful of boys and girls again.

One Indian-summer afternoon when Aunt Hager was hanging up clothes in the back yard while the boy held the basket of clothes-pins, old man Logan drove past on his rickety trash-wagon and bowed elaborately to Hager. She went to the back fence to joke and gossip with him as usual, while his white mule switched off persistent flies with her tail.

Before the old beau drove away, he said: "Say, Hager, does you want that there young one o' your'n to work? I knows a little job he can have if you does," pointing to Sandy.

"What'll he got to do?" demanded Hager.

"Well, Pete Scott say he need a boy down yonder at de barber-shop on Saturdays to kinder clean up where de kinks fall, an' shine shoes fo' de customers. Ain't nothin' hard 'bout it, an' I was thinkin' it would just 'bout be Sandy's size. He could make a few pennies ever' week to kinder help things 'long."

"True, he sho could," said Hager. "I'll have him go see Pete."

So Sandy went to see Mr. Peter Scott at the colored barber-shop on Pearl Street that evening and was given his first regular job. Every Saturday, which was the barber-shop's only busy day, when the working-men got paid off, Sandy went on the job at noon and worked until eight or nine in the evening. His duties were to keep the place swept clean of the hair that the three barbers sheared and to shine the shoes of any customer who might ask for a shine. Only a few customers permitted themselves that last luxury, for many of them came to the shop in their working-shoes, covered with mud or lime, and most of them shined their own boots at home on Sunday mornings before church. But occasionally Cudge Windsor, who owned a pool hall, or some of the dressed-up bootleggers, might climb on the stand and permit their shoes to be cleaned by the brown youngster, who asked shyly: "Shine, mister?"

The barber-shop was a new world to Sandy, who had lived thus far tied to Aunt Hager's apron-strings. He was a dreamy-eyed boy who had grown to his present age largely under the dominant influence of women—Annjee, Harriett, his grandmother—because Jimboy had been so seldom home. But the barber-shop then was a man's world, and, on Saturdays, while a dozen or more big laborers awaited their turns, the place was filled with loud man-talk and smoke and laughter. Baseball, Jack Johnson, race-horses, white folks, Teddy Roosevelt, local gossip, Booker Washington, women, labor prospects in Topeka, Kansas City, Omaha, religion, politics, women, God—discussions and arguments all afternoon and far up into the night, while crisp kinks rolled to the floor, cigarette and cigar-butts were thrown on the hearth of the monkey-stove, and Sandy called out: "Shine, mister?"

Sometimes the boy earned one or two dollars from shines, but on damp or snowy days he might not make anything except the fifty cents Pete Scott paid him for sweeping up. Or perhaps one of the barbers, too busy to go out for supper, would send Sandy for a sandwich and a bottle of milk, and thus he would make an extra nickel or dime.

The patrons liked him and often kidded him about his sandy hair. "Boy, you's too dark to have hair like that. Ain't nobody but white folks s'posed to have sandy-colored hair. An' your'n's nappy at that!" Then Sandy would blush with embarrassment—if the change from a dry chocolate to a damp chocolate can be called a blush, as he grew warm and perspired—because he didn't like to be kidded about his hair. And he hadn't been around uncouth fellows long enough to learn the protective art of turning back a joke. He had discovered already, though, that so-called jokes are often not really jokes at all, but rather unpleasant realities that hurt unless you can think of something equally funny and unpleasant to say in return. But the men who patronized Pete Scott's barber-shop seldom grew angry at the hard pleasantries that passed for humor, and they could play the dozens for hours without anger, unless the parties concerned became serious, when they were invited to take it on the outside. And even at that a fight was fun, too.

After a winter of Saturday nights at Pete's shop Sandy himself became pretty adept at "kidding"; but at first he was timid about it and afraid to joke with grown-up people, or to give smart answers to strangers when they teased him about his crinkly, sand-colored head. One day, however, one of the barbers gave him a tin of Madam Walker's and told him: "Lay that hair down an' stop these niggers from laughin' at you." Sandy took his advice.

Madam Walker's—a thick yellow pomade—and a good wetting with water proved most efficacious to the boy's hair, when aided with a stocking cap—the top of a woman's stocking cut off and tied in a knot at one end so as to fit tightly over one's head, pressing the hair smooth. Thereafter Sandy appeared with his hair slick and shiny. And the salve and water together made it seem a dark brown, just the color of his skin, instead of the peculiar sandy tint it possessed in its natural state. Besides he soon advanced far enough in the art of "kidding" to say: "So's your pa's," to people who informed him that his head was nappy.

During the autumn Harriett had been home once to see her mother and had said that she was working as a chambermaid with Maudel at the hotel. But in the barber-shop that winter Sandy often heard his aunt's name mentioned in less proper connections. Sometimes the boy pretended not to hear, and if Pete Scott was there, he always stopped the men from talking.

"Tired o' all this nasty talk 'bout women in ma shop," he said one Saturday night. "Some o' you men better look after your own womenfolks if you got any."

"Aw, all de womens in de world ain't worth two cents to me," said a waiter sitting in the middle chair, his face covered with lather. "I don't respect no woman but my mother."

"An' neither do I," answered Greensbury Jones. "All of em's evil, specially if they's black an' got blue gums."

"I's done told you to hush," said Pete Scott behind the first chair, where he was clipping Jap Logan's hair. "Ma wife's black herself, so don't start talkin' 'bout no blue gums! I's tired o' this here female talk anyhow. This is ma shop, an' ma razors sho can cut somethin' else 'sides hair—so now just keep on talkin' 'bout blue gums!"

"I see where Bryant's runnin' for president agin," said Greensbury Jones.

But one Saturday, while the proprietor was out to snatch a bite to eat, a discussion came up as to who was the prettiest colored girl in town. Was she yellow, high-brown, chocolate, or black? Of course, there was no agreement, but names were mentioned and qualities were described. One girl had eyes like Eve herself; another had hips like Miss Cleopatra; one smooth brown-skin had legs like—like—like—

"Aw, man! De Statue of Liberty!" somebody suggested when the name of a famous beauty failed the speaker's memory.

"But, feller, there ain't nothin' in all them rainbow shades," a young teamster argued against Uncle Dan Givens, who preferred high yellows.

"Gimme a cool black gal ever' time! They's too dark to fade—and when they are good-looking, I mean they *are* good-looking! I'm talkin' 'bout Harrietta Williams, too! That's who I mean! Now, find a better-looking gal than she is!"

"I admits Harrietta's all right," said the old man; "all right to look at but—sput-t-tsss!" He spat contemptuously at the stove.

"O, I know that!" said the teamster; "but I ain't talkin' 'bout what she is! I'm talkin' 'bout how she looks. An' a songster out o' this world don't care if she is a—!"

"S-s-s-sh! Soft-pedal it brother." One of the men nudged the speaker. "There's one o' the Williamses right here—that kid over yonder shinin' shoes's Harriett's nephew or somethin' 'nother."

"You niggers talks too free, anyhow," one of the barbers added. "Somebody gwine cut your lips off some o' these days. De idee o' ole Uncle Dan Givens' arguin' 'bout women and he done got whiskers all round his head like a wore-out cheese."

"That's all right, you young whip-snapper," squeaked Uncle Dan heatedly. "Might have whiskers round ma head, but I ain't wore out!"

Laughter and smoke filled the little shop, while the winter wind blew sleet against the big plate-glass window and whistled through the cracks in the doorway, making the gas lights flicker overhead. Sandy smacked his polishing cloth on the toes of a gleaming pair of brown button shoes belonging to a stranger in town, then looked up with a grin and said: "Yes, sir!" as the man handed him a quarter.

"Keep the change," said the new-comer grandly.

"That guy's an actor," one of the barbers said when the man went out. "He's playin' with the *Smart Set* at the Opery House tonight. I bet the top gallery'll be full o' niggers sence it's a jig show, but I ain't goin' anear there myself to be Jim-Crowed, cause I don't believe in goin' nowhere I ain't allowed to set with the rest of the folks. If I can't be the table-cloth, I won't be the dish-rag—that's my motto. And if I can't buy the seats I want at a show, I sure God can keep my change!"

"Yes, and miss all the good shows," countered a little red-eyed porter. "Just as well say if you can't eat in a restaurant where white folks eat, you ain't gonna eat."

"Anybody want a shine?" yelled Sandy above the racket. "And if you don't want a shine, stay out of my chair and do your arguing on the floor!"

A brown-skin chorus girl, on her way to the theatre, stepped into the shop and asked if she could buy a *Chicago Defender* there. The barber directed her to the colored restaurant, while all the men immediately stopped talking to stare at her until she went out.

"Whew! . . . Some legs!" the teamster cried as the door closed on a vision of silk stockings. "How'd you like to shine that long, sweet brown-skin mama's shoes, boy?"

"She wouldn't have to pay me!" said Sandy.

"Whoopee! Gallery or no gallery," shouted Jap Logan, "I'm gonna see that show! Don't care if they do Jim-Crow niggers in the white folks' Opery House!"

"Yes," muttered one of the barbers, "that's just what's the matter now—you ain't got no race-pride! You niggers ain't got no shame!"

Eighteen

Children's Day

When Easter came that spring, Sandy had saved enough money to buy himself a suit and a new cap from his earnings at the barber-shop. He was very proud of this accomplishment and so was Aunt Hager.

"You's a 'dustrious chile, sho is! Gwine make a smart man even if yo' daddy warn't nothin'. Gwine get ahead an' do good fo' yo'self an' de race, yes, sir!"

The spring came early and the clear balmy days found Hager's back yard billowing with clean white clothes on lines in the sun. Her roomer had left her when the theatre was built and had gone to work on a dam somewhere up the river, so Annjee's room was empty again. Sandy had slept with his grandmother during the cold weather, but in summer he slept on a pallet.

The boy did not miss his mother. When she had been home, Annjee had worked out all day, and she was quiet at night because she was always tired. Harriett had been the one to keep the fun and laughter going—Harriett and Jimboy, whenever he was in town. Sandy wished Harrie would live at home instead of staying at Maudel's house, but he never said anything about it to his grandmother. He went to school regularly, went to work at the barber-shop on Saturdays and to Sunday-school on Sundays, and remained with Aunt Hager the rest of his time. She was always worried if she didn't know where he was.

"Colored boys, when they gets round twelve an' thirteen, they gets so bad, Sandy," she would say. "I wants you to stay nice an' make something out o' yo'self. If Hager lives, she ain't gonna see you go down. She's gonna make a fine man out o' you fo' de glory o' God an' de black race. You gwine to 'mount to something in this world. You hear me?"

Sandy did hear her, and he knew what she meant. She meant a man like Booker T. Washington, or Frederick Douglass, or like Paul Laurence Dunbar, who did poetry-writing. Or maybe Jack Johnson. But Hager said Jack Johnson was the devil's kind of greatness, not God's.

"That's what you get from workin' round that old barber-shop where all they talks 'bout is prize-fightin' an' hossracin'. Jack Johnson done married a white woman, anyhow! What he care 'bout de race?"

The little boy wondered if Jack Johnson's kids looked like Buster. But maybe he didn't have any kids. He must ask Pete Scott about that when he went back to work on Saturday.

In the summer a new amusement park opened in Stanton, the first of its kind in the city, with a merry-go-round, a shoot-the-shoots, a Ferris wheel, a dance-hall, and a bandstand for week-end concerts. In order to help popularize the park, which was far on the north edge of town, the *Daily Leader* announced, under its auspices, what was called a Free Children's Day Party open to all the readers of that paper who clipped the coupons published in each issue. On July 26 these coupons, presented at the gate, would entitle every child in Stanton to free admittance to the park, free popcorn, free lemonade, and one ride on each of the amusement attractions—the merry-go-round, the shoot-the-shoots, and the Ferris wheel. All you had to do was to be a reader of the *Daily Leader* and present the coupons cut from that paper.

Aunt Hager and Sister Johnson both took the *Leader* regularly, as did almost everybody else in Stanton, so Sandy and Willie-Mae started to clip coupons. All the children in the neighborhood were doing the same thing. The Children's Day would be a big event for all the little people in town. None of them had ever seen a shoot-the-shoots before, a contrivance that pulled little cars full of folks high into the air and then let them come whizzing down an incline into an artificial pond, where the cars would float like boats. Sandy and Willie-Mae looked forward to thrill after thrill.

When the afternoon of the great day came at last, Willie-Mae stopped for Sandy, dressed in her whitest white dress and her new patent-leather shoes, which hurt her feet awfully. Sandy's grandmother was making him wash his ears when she came in.

"You gwine out yonder 'mongst all them white chillens, I wants you to at least look clean!" said Hager.

They started out.

"Here!" called Aunt Hager. "Ain't you gwine to take yo' coupons?" In his rush to get away, Sandy had forgotten them.

It was a long walk to the park, and Willie-Mae stopped and took off her shoes and stockings and carried them in her hands until she got near the gate; then she put them on again and limped bravely along, clutching her precious bits of newspaper. They could hear the band playing and children shouting and squealing as the cars on the shoot-the-shoots shot downward with a splash into the pond. They could see the giant Ferris wheel, larger than the one the carnival had had, circling high in the air.

"I'm gonna ride on that first," said Sandy.

There were crowds of children under the bright red and white wooden shelter at the park entrance. They were lining up at the gate—laughing, merry, clean little white children, pushing and yelling and giggling amiably. Sandy let Willie-Mae go first and he got in line behind her. The band was playing gaily inside. . . . They were almost to the entrance now . . . . There were just two boys in front of them . . . . Willie-Mae held out her black little hand clutching the coupons. They moved forward. The man looked down.

"Sorry," he said. "This party's for white kids."

Willie-Mae did not understand. She stood holding out the coupons, waiting for the tall white man to take them.

"Stand back, you two," he said, looking at Sandy as well. "I told you little darkies this wasn't your party. . . . Come on—next little girl." And the line of white children pushed past Willie-Mae and Sandy, going into the park. Stunned, the two dark ones drew aside. Then they noticed a group of a dozen or more other colored youngsters standing apart in the sun, just without the bright entrance pavilion, and among them was Sadie Butler, Sandy's class-mate. Three or four of the colored children were crying, but most of them looked sullen and angry, and some of them had turned to go home.

"My papa takes the *Leader*," Sadie Butler was saying. "And you see what it says here on the coupons, too—'Free Admittance to Every Child in Stanton.' Can't you read it, Sandy?"

"Sure, I can read it, but I guess they didn't mean colored," he answered, as the boy watched the white children going in the gate. "They wouldn't let us in."

Willie-Mae, between the painful shoes and the hurt of her disappointment, was on the verge of tears. One of the small boys in the crowd, a hard-looking little fellow from Pearl Street, was cursing childishly.

"God damn old sons of biscuit-eaters, that what they are! I wish I was a big man, dog-gone, I'd shoot 'em all, that's what I'd do!"

"I suppose they didn't mean colored kids," said Sandy again.

"Buster went in all right," said Sadie. "I seen him. But they didn't know he was colored, I guess. When I went up to the gate, the man said: 'Whoa! Where you goin'?' just like I was a horse. . . . I'm going home now and tell my papa."

She walked away, followed by five or six other little girls in their Sunday dresses. Willie-Mae was sitting on the ground taking off her shoes again, sweat and tears running down her black cheeks. Sandy saw his white schoolmate, Earl, approaching.

"What's matter, Sandy? Ain't you goin' in?" Earl demanded, looking at his friend's worried face. "Did the little girl hurt her foot?"

"No," said Sandy. "We just ain't going in. . . . Here, Earl, you can have my coupons. If you have extra ones, the papers says you get more lemonade . . . so you take 'em."

The white boy, puzzled, accepted the proffered coupons, stood dumbly for a moment wondering what to say to his brown friend, then went on into the park.

"It's yo' party, white chile!" a little tan-skin girl called after him, mimicking the way the man at the gate had talked. "Whoa! Stay out! You's a nigger!" she said to Sandy.

The other children, in spite of themselves, laughed at the accuracy of her burlesque imitation. Then, with the music of the merry-go-round from beyond the high fence and the laughter of happy children following them, the group of dark-skinned ones started down the dusty road together—and to all the colored boys and girls they met on the way they called out, "Ain't no use, jigaboos! That party's for white folks!"

When Willie-Mae and Sandy got home and told their story, Sister Johnson was angry as a wet hen.

"Crackers is devils," she cried. "I 'spected as much! Dey ain't nary hell hot 'nough to burn ole white folks, 'cause dey's devils deyselves! De dirty hounds!"

But all Hager said was: "They's po' trash owns that park what don't know no better, hurtin' chillens' feelin's, but we'll forgive 'em! Don't fret yo'self, Sister Johnson. What good can frettin' do? Come on here, let's we have a party of our own." She went out in the yard and took a watermelon from a tub of well-water where it had been cooling and cut it into four juicy slices; then they sat down on the grass at the shady side of the house and ate, trying to forget about white folks.

"Don't you mind, Willie-Mae," Hager said to the little black girl, who was still crying. "You's colored, honey, an' you's liable to have a hard time in this life—but don't cry. . . . You Sandy, run round de house an' see didn't I heard de mail-man blowin'."

"Yes'm," said Sandy when he came back. "Was the mail-man, and I got a letter from mama." The boy sat on the grass to read it, anxious to see what Annjee said. And later, when the company had gone, he read it aloud to Hager.

Dear little Son:

How have you all been? how is grandma? I get worried about you when I do not hear. You know Aunt Hager is old and can't write much so you must do it for her because she is not used to adress letters and the last one was two weeks getting here and had went all around everywhere. Your father says tell you hello. I got a job in a boarding house for old white folks what are cranky about how they beds is made. There are white and colored here in the auto business and women to. Tell Madam de Carter I will send my Lodge dues back because I do not want to be transfer as I might come home sometime. I ain't seen you all now for more'n a year. Jimboy he keeps changing jobs from one thing to another but he likes this town pretty well. You know he broke his guitar carrying it in a crowded street car. Ma says you are growing and have bought yourself a new suit last Easter. Mama certainly does right well to keep on washing and ironing at her age and worrying with you besides. Tempy ought to help ma but seem like she don't think so. Do you ever see your Aunt Harrie? I hope she is settling down in her ways. If ma wasn't all by herself maybe I could send for you to come live with us in Detroit but maybe I will be home to see you if I ever get any money ahead. Rent is so high here I never wittnessed so many folks in one house, rooming five and six together, and nobody can save a dime. Are you still working at the barber shop. I heard Sister Johnson was under the weather but I couldn't make out from ma's scribbling what was the matter with her. Did she have a physicianer? You behave yourself with Willie-Mae because you are getting to be a big boy now and she is a girl older then you are. I am going to send you some pants next time I go down town but I get off from work so late I don't have a chance to do nothing and your father eats in the restaurant count of me not home to fix for him and I don't care where you go colored folks has a hard time. I want you to mind your grandma and help her work. She is too old to be straining at the pump drawing water to wash clothes with. Now write to me. Love to you all both and seven kisses XXXXXXX right here on the paper,

Your loving mother,
Annjelica Rogers

Sandy laughed at the clumsy cross-mark kisses. He was glad to get a letter from his mother, and word in it about Jimboy. And he was sorry his father had broken his guitar. But not even watermelon and the long letter could drive away his sick feeling about the park.

"I guess Kansas is getting like the South, isn't it, ma?" Sandy said to his grandmother as they came out on the porch that evening after supper. "They don't like us here either, do they?"

But Aunt Hager gave him no answer. In silence they watched the sunset fade from the sky. Slowly the evening star grew bright, and, looking at the stars, Hager began to sing, very softly at first:

From this world o' trouble free,
Stars beyond!
Stars beyond!

And Sandy, as he stood beside his grandmother on the porch, heard a great chorus out of the black past—singing generations of toil-worn Negroes, echoing Hager's voice as it deepened and grew in volume:

There's a star fo' you an' me,
Stars beyond!

Nineteen

Ten Dollars and Costs

In the fall Sandy found a job that occupied him after school hours, as well as on Saturday and Sunday. One afternoon at the barber-shop, Charlie Nutter, a bell-hop who had come to have his hair cut, asked Sandy to step outside a minute. Once out of earshot of the barbers and loafers within, Charlie went on: "Say, kid, I got some dope to buzz to yuh 'bout a job. Joe Willis, the white guy what keeps the hotel where I work, is lookin' for a boy to kinder sweep up around the lobby every day, dust off, and sort o' help the bell-boys out sometimes. Ain't nothin' hard attached to it, and yuh can bring 'long your shine-box and rub up shoes in the lobby, too, if yuh wants to. I thought maybe yuh might like to have the job. Yuh'd make more'n yuh do here. And more'n that, too, when yuh got on to the ropes. Course yuh'd have to fix me up with a couple o' bucks o' so for gettin' yuh the job, but if yuh want it, just lemme know and I'll fix it with the boss. He tole me to start lookin' for somebody and that's what I'm doin'." Charlie Nutter went on talking, without stopping to wait for an answer. "Course a boy like you don't know nothin 'bout hotel work, but yuh ain't never too young to learn, and that's a nice easy way to start. Yuh might work up to me some time, yuh never can tell—head bell-hop! 'Cause I ain't gonna stay in this burg all my life; I figger if I can hop bells here, I can hop bells in Chicago or some place worth livin' at. But the tips ain't bad down there at the Drummer's though—lots o' sportin' women and folks like that what don't mind givin' yuh a quarter any time. . . . And yuh can get well yourself once in a while. What yuh say? Do yuh want it?"

Sandy thought quick. With Christmas not far off, his shoes about worn out, and the desire to help Aunt Hager, too—"I guess I better take it," he said. "But do I have to pay you now?"

"Hell, naw, not now! I'll keep my eye on yuh, and yuh can just slip me a little change now and then down to the hotel when you start workin'. Other boy ain't quittin' nohow till next week. S'pose yuh come round there Sunday morning and I'll kinder show yuh what to do. And don't pay no mind to Willis when he hollers at yuh. He's all right—just got a hard way about him with the help, that's all—but he ain't a bad boss. I'll see yuh, then! Drop by Sunday and lemme know for sure. So long!"

But Aunt Hager was not much pleased when Sandy came home that night and she heard the news. "I ain't never wanted none o' my chillens to work in no ole hotels," she said. "They's evil, full o' nastiness, an' you don't learn nothin' good in 'em. I don't want you to go there, chile."

"But grandma," Sandy argued, "I want to send mama a Christmas present. And just look at my shoes, all worn out! I don't make much money any more since that new colored barber-shop opened up. It's all white inside and folks don't have to wait so long 'cause there's five barbers. Jimmy Lane's got the porter's job down there . . . and I have to start working regular some time, don't I?"

"I reckons you does, but I hates to see you workin' in hotels, chile, with all them low-down Bottoms niggers, and bad womens comin' an' goin'. But I reckon you does need de job. Yo' mammy ain't sent no money here fo' de Lawd knows when, an' I ain't able to buy you nice clothes an' all like you needs to go to school in. . . . But don't forget, honey, no matter where you works—you be good an' do right. . . . I reckon you'll get along."

So Sandy found Charlie Nutter on Sunday and told him for sure he would take the job. Then he told Pete Scott he was no longer coming to work at his barber-shop, and Pete got mad and told him to go to hell, quitting when business was bad after all he had done for Sandy, besides letting him shine shoes and keep all his earnings. At other shops he couldn't have done that; besides he had intended to teach Sandy to be a barber when he got big enough.

"But go on!" said Pete Scott. "Go on! I don't need you. Plenty other boys I can find to work for me. But I bet you won't stay at that Drummer's Hotel no time, though—I can tell you that!"

The long Indian summer lingered until almost Thanksgiving, and the weather was sunny and warm. The day before Sandy went to work on his new job, he came home from school, brought in the wood for the stove, and delivered a basket of newly ironed clothes to the white folks. When he returned, he found his grandmother standing on the front porch in the sunset, reading the evening paper, which the boy had recently delivered. Sandy stopped in the twilight beside Hager, breathing in the crisp cool air and wondering what they were going to have for supper.

Suddenly his grandmother gave a deep cry and leaned heavily against the door-jamb, letting the paper fall from her hands. "O, ma Lawd!" she moaned. "O, ma Lawd!" and an expression of the uttermost pain made the old woman's eyes widen in horror. "Is I read de name right?"

Sandy, frightened, picked up the paper from the porch and found on the front page the little four-line item that his grandmother had just read:

> NEGRESSES ARRESTED
> Harrietta Williams and Maudel Smothers, two young negresses, were arrested last night on Pearl Street for street-walking. They were brought before Judge Brinton and fined ten dollars and costs.

"What does that mean, ma—street-walking?" the child asked, but his grandmother raised her apron to her eyes and stumbled into the house. Sandy stopped, perplexed at the meaning of the article, at his aunt's arrest, at his grandmother's horror. Then he followed Hager, the open newspaper still in his hands, and found her standing at the window in the kitchen, crying. Racking sobs were shaking her body and the boy, who had never seen an old person weep like that before, was terribly afraid. He didn't know that grown-up people cried, except at funerals, where it was the proper thing to do. He didn't know they ever cried alone, by themselves in their own houses.

"I'm gonna get Sister Johnson," he said, dropping the paper on the floor. "I'm gonna get Sister Johnson quick!"

"No, honey, don't get her," stammered the old woman. "She can't help us none, chile. Can't nobody help us . . . but de Lawd."

In the dusk Sandy saw that his grandmother was trying hard to make her lips speak plainly and to control her sobs.

"Let's we pray, son, fo' yo' po' lost Aunt Harriett—fo' ma own baby chile, what's done turned from de light an' is walkin' in darkness."

She dropped on her knees near the kitchen-stove with her arms on the seat of a chair and her head bowed. Sandy got on his knees, too, and while his grandmother prayed aloud for the body and soul of her daughter, the boy repeated over and over in his mind: "I wish you'd come home, Aunt Harrie. It's lonesome around here! Gee, I wish you'd come home."

Twenty

Hey, Boy!

In the lobby of the Drummer's Hotel there were six large brass spittoons—one in the center of the place, one in each corner, and one near the clerk's desk. It was Sandy's duty to clean these spittoons. Every evening that winter after school he came in the back door of the hotel, put his books in the closet where he kept his brooms and cleaning rags, swept the two short upper halls and the two flights of stairs, swept the lobby and dusted, then took the spittoons, emptied their slimy contents into the alley, rinsed them out, and polished them until they shone as brightly as if they were made of gold. Except for the stench of emptying them, Sandy rather liked this job. He always felt very proud of himself when, about six o'clock, he could look around the dingy old lobby and see the six gleaming brass bowls catching the glow of the electric lamps on their shining surfaces before they were again covered with spit. The thought that he himself had created this brightness with his own hands, aided by a can of brass-polish, never failed to make Sandy happy.

He liked to clean things, to make them beautiful, to make them shine. Aunt Hager did, too. When she wasn't washing clothes, she was always cleaning something about the house, dusting, polishing the range, or scrubbing the kitchen-floor until it was white enough to eat from. To Hager a clean thing was beautiful—also to Sandy, proud every evening of his six unblemished brass spittoons. Yet each day when he came to work, they were covered anew with tobacco juice, cigarette-butts, wads of chewing-gum, and phlegm. But to make them clean was Sandy's job—and they were beautiful when they were clean.

Charlie Nutter was right—there was nothing very hard about the work and he liked it for a while. The new kinds of life which he saw in the hotel interested and puzzled him, but, being naturally a silent child, he asked no questions, and, beyond the directions for his work, nobody told him anything. Sandy did his cleaning well and the boss had not yet had occasion to bellow at him, as he often bellowed at the two bell-boys.

The Drummer's Hotel was not a large hotel, nor a nice one. A three-story frame structure, dilapidated and run down, it had not been painted for years. In the lobby two large panes of plate glass looked on the street, and in front of these were rows of hard wooden chairs. At the rear of the lobby was the clerk's desk, a case of cigars and cigarettes, a cooler for water, and the door to the men's room. It was Sandy's duty to clean this toilet, too.

Upstairs on the second and third floors were the bedrooms. Only the poorest of travelling salesmen, transient railroad workers, occasionally a few show-people, and the ladies of the streets with their clients rented them. The night trade was always the most brisk at the Drummer's Hotel, but it was only on Saturdays that Sandy worked after six o'clock. That night he would not get home until ten or eleven, but Aunt Hager would always be waiting for him, keeping the fire warm, with the wash-tub full of water for his weekly bath.

There was no dining-room attached to the hotel, and, aside from Sandy, there were only five employees. The boss himself, Joe Willis, was usually at the desk. There were two chambermaids who worked in the mornings, an old man who did the heavy cleaning and scrubbing once or twice a week, and two bellboys—one night boy and one day boy supposedly, but both bellmen had been there so long that they arranged the hours to suit themselves. Charlie Nutter had started small, like Sandy, and had grown up there. The other bell-boy, really no boy at all, but an old man, had been in the hotel ever since it opened, and Sandy was as much afraid of him as he was of the boss.

This bellman's name was Mr. George Clark. His uniform was frayed and greasy, but he wore it with the air of a major, and he acted as though all the burdens of running the hotel were on his shoulders. He knew how everything was to be done, where everything was kept, what every old guest liked. And he could divine the tastes of each new guest before he had been there a day. Subservient and grinning to white folks, evil and tyrannical to the colored help, George was the chief authority, next to Joe Willis, in the Drummer's Hotel. He it was who found some fault with Sandy's work every day until he learned to like the child because Sandy never answered back or tried to be fly, as George said most young niggers were. After a time the old fellow seldom bothered to inspect Sandy's spittoons or to look in the corners for dust, but, nevertheless, he remained a person to be humored and obeyed if one wished to work at the Drummer's Hotel.

Besides being the boss's right-hand man, George Clark was the official bootlegger for the house, too. In fact, he kept his liquor-supply in the hotel cellar. When he was off duty, Charlie, the other bell-hop, sold it for him if there were any calls from the rooms above. They made no sales other than to guests of the house, but such sales were frequent. Some of the white women who used the rooms collected a commission from George for the sales they helped make to their men visitors.

Sandy was a long time learning the tricks of hotel work. "Yuh sure a dumb little joker," Charlie was constantly informing him. "But just stay around awhile and yuh'll get on to it."

Christmas came and Sandy sent his mother in Detroit a big box of drugstore candy. For Aunt Hager he started to buy a long pair of green ear-rings for fifty cents, but be was afraid she might not like them, so he bought her white handkerchiefs instead. And he sent a pretty card to Harriett, for one snowy December day his aunt had seen him through the windows sweeping out the lobby of the hotel and she had called him to the door to talk to her. She thrust a little piece of paper into his hand with her new address on it.

"Maudel's moved to Kansas City," she said, "so I don't live there any more. You better keep this address yourself and if mama ever needs me, you can know where I am."

Then she went on through the snow, looking very pretty in a cheap fur coat and black, high-heeled slippers, with grey silk stockings. Sandy saw her pass the hotel often with different men. Sometimes she went by with Cudge Windsor, the owner of the pool hall, or Billy Sanderlee. Almost always she was with sporty-looking fellows who wore derbies and had gold teeth. Sandy noticed that she didn't urge him to come to see her at this new house-number she had given him, so he put the paper in his pocket and went back to his sweeping, glad, anyway, to have seen his Aunt Harriett.

One Saturday afternoon several white men were sitting in the lobby smoking and reading the papers. Sandy swept around their chairs, dusted, and then took the spittoons out to clean. This work did not require his attention; while he applied the polish with a handful of soft rags, he could let his mind wander to other things. He thought about Harriett. Then he thought about school and what he would do when he was a man; about Willie-Mae, who had a job washing dinner dishes for a white family; about Jimmy Lane, who had no mama; and Sandy wondered what his own mother and father were doing in another town, and if they wanted him with them. He thought how old and tired and grey-headed Aunt Hager had become; how she puffed and blowed over the wash-tubs now, but never complained; how she waited for him on Saturday nights with the kitchen-stove blazing, so he would be warm after walking so far in the cold; and how she prayed he would be a great man some day. . . . Sitting there in the back room of the hotel, Sandy wondered how people got to be great, as, one by one, he made the spittoons bright and beautiful. He wondered how people made themselves great.

That night he would have to work late picking up papers in the lobby, running errands for the boss, and shining shoes. After he had put the spittoons around, he would go out and get a hamburger sandwich and a cup of coffee for supper; then he would come back and help Charlie if he could. . . . Charlie was a good old boy. He had taken only a dollar for getting Sandy his job and he often helped him make tips by allowing Sandy to run to the telegraph office or do some other little odd job for a guest upstairs. . . . Sure, Charlie was a nice guy.

Things were pretty busy tonight. Several men had their shoes shined as they sat tipped back in the lobby chairs while Sandy with his boot-black box let them put up a foot at a time to be polished. One tall farmer gave him a quarter tip and a pat on the head.

"Bright little feller, that," he remarked to the boss.

About ten o'clock the blond Miss Marcia McKay's bell rang, and, Charlie being engaged, Joe Willis sent Sandy up to see what she wanted. Miss McKay had just come in out of the snow a short time before with a heavy-set ugly man. Both of them were drunk. Sandy knocked timidly outside her room.

"Come in," growled the man's voice.

Sandy opened the door and saw Miss McKay standing naked in the middle of the floor combing her hair. He stopped on the threshold.

"Aw, come in," said the man. "She won't bite you! Where's that other bell-boy? We want some licker! . . . Damn it! Say, send Charlie up here! He knows what I want!"

Sandy scampered away, and when he found Charlie, he told him about Miss McKay. The child was scared because he had often heard of colored boys' being lynched for looking at white women, even with their clothes on—but the bell-boy only laughed.

"Yuh're a dumb little joker!" he said. "Just stay around here awhile and yuh'll see lots more'n that!" He winked and gave Sandy a nudge in the ribs. "Boy, I done sold ten quarts o' licker tonight," he whispered jubilantly. "And some a it was mine, too!"

Sandy went back to the lobby and the shining of shoes. A big, red-necked stranger smoking and drinking with a crowd of drummers in one corner of the room called to him "Hey, boy! Shine me up here!" So he edged into the center of the group of men with his blacking-box, got down on his knees before the big fellow, took out his cans and his cloths, and went to work.

The white men were telling dirty stories, uglier than any Sandy had heard at the colored barber-shop and not very funny— and some of them made him sick at the stomach.

The big man whose shoes he was shining said: "Now I'm gonna tell one." He talked with a Southern drawl and a soft slurring of word-endings like some old colored folks. He had been drinking, too. "This is 'bout a nigger went to see Aunt Hanner one night. . . ."

A roar of laughter greeted his first effort and he was encouraged to tell another.

"Old darky caught a gal on the levee . . ." he commenced.

Sandy finished polishing the shoes and put the cloths inside his wooden box and stood up waiting for his pay, but the speaker did not notice the colored boy until he had finished his tale and laughed heartily with the other men. Then he looked at Sandy. Suddenly he grinned.

"Say, little coon, let's see you hit a step for the boys! . . . Down where I live, folks, all our niggers can dance! . . . Come on, boy, snap it up!"

"I can't," Sandy said, frowning instead of smiling, and growing warm as he stood there in the smoky circle of grinning white men. "I don't know how to dance."

"O, you're one of them stubborn Kansas coons, heh?" said the red-necked fellow disgustedly, the thickness of whisky on his tongue. "You Northern darkies are dumb as hell, anyhow!" Then, turning to the crowd of amused lobby loungers, he announced: "Now down in Mississippi, whar I come from, if you offer a nigger a dime, he'll dance his can off . . . an' they better dance, what I mean!"

He turned to the men around him for approbation, while Sandy still waited uncomfortably to be paid for the shine. But the man kept him standing there, looking at him drunkenly, then at the amused crowd of Saturday-night loungers.

"Now, a nigger his size down South would no more think o' not dancin' if a white man asked him than he would think o' flyin'. This boy's jest tryin' to be smart, that's all. Up here you-all've got darkies spoilt, believin' they're somebody. Now, in my home we keep 'em in their places." He again turned his attention to Sandy. "Boy! I want to see you dance!" he commanded.

But Sandy picked up his blacking-box and had begun to push through the circle of chairs, not caring any longer about his pay, when the southerner rose and grabbed him roughly by the arm, exhaling alcoholic breath in the boy's face as he jokingly pulled him back.

"Com'ere, you little—" but he got no further, for Sandy, strengthened by the anger that suddenly possessed him at the touch of this white man's hand, uttered a yell that could be heard for blocks.

Everyone in the lobby turned to see what had happened, but before Joe Willis got out from behind the clerk's desk, the boy, wriggling free, had reached the street-door. There Sandy turned, raised his boot-black box furiously above his head, and flung it with all his strength at the group of laughing white men in which the drunken southerner was standing. From one end of the whizzing box a stream of polish-bottles, brushes, and cans fell clattering across the lobby while Sandy disappeared through the door, running as fast as his legs could carry him in the falling snow.

"Hey! You black bastard!" Joe Willis yelled from the hotel entrance, but his voice was blown away in the darkness. As Sandy ran, he felt the snow-flakes falling in his face.

Twenty-one

Note to Harriett

Several days later, when Sandy took out of his pocket the piece of paper that his Aunt Harriett had given him that day in front of the hotel, he noticed that the address written on it was somewhere in the Bottoms. He felt vaguely worried, so he did not show it to his grandmother, because he had often heard her say that the Bottoms was a bad place. And when he was working at the barber-shop, he had heard the men talking about what went on there—and in a sense he knew what they meant.

It was a gay place—people did what they wanted to, or what they had to do, and didn't care—for in the Bottoms folks ceased to struggle against the boundaries between good and bad, or white and black, and surrendered amiably to immorality. Beyond Pearl Street, across the tracks, people of all colors came together for the sake of joy, the curtains being drawn only between themselves and the opposite side of the railroad, where the churches were and the big white Y.M.C.A.

At night in the Bottoms victrolas moaned and banjos cried ecstatically in the darkness. Summer evenings little yellow and brown and black girls in pink or blue bungalow aprons laughed invitingly in doorways, and dice rattled with the staccato gaiety of jazz music on long tables in rear rooms. Pimps played pool; bootleggers lounged in big red cars; children ran in the streets until midnight, with no voice of parental authority forcing them to an early sleep; young blacks fought like cocks and enjoyed it; white boys walked through the streets winking at colored girls; men came in autos; old women ate pigs' feet and watermelon and drank beer; whisky flowed; gin was like water; soft indolent laughter didn't care about anything; and deep nigger-throated voices that had long ago stopped rebelling against the ways of this world rose in song.

To those who lived on the other side of the railroad and never realized the utter stupidity of the word "sin," the Bottoms was vile and wicked. But to the girls who lived there, and the boys who pimped and fought and sold licker there, "sin" was a silly word that did not enter their heads. They had never looked at life through the spectacles of the Sunday-School. The glasses good people wore wouldn't have fitted their eyes, for they hung no curtain of words between themselves and reality. To them, things were—what they were.

"Ma bed is hard, but I'm layin' in it jest de same!"

sang the raucous-throated blues-singer in her song;

"Hey! . . . Hey! Who wants to lay with me?"

It was to one of these streets in the Bottoms that Sandy came breathlessly one bright morning with a note in his hand. He knocked at the door of a big grey house.

"Is this where Harriett Williams lives?" he panted.

"You means Harrietta?" said a large, sleek yellow woman in a blue silk kimono who opened the door. "Come in, baby, and sit down. I'll see if she's up yet." Then the woman left Sandy in the parlor while she went up the stairs calling his aunt in a clear, lazy voice.

There were heavy velvet draperies at the windows and doors in this front room where Sandy sat, and a thick, well-worn rug on the floor. There was a divan, a davenport covered with pillows, a centre table, and several chairs. Through the curtains at the double door leading into the next room, Sandy saw a piano, more sofas and chairs, and a cleared oiled floor that might be used for dancing. Both rooms were in great disorder, and the air in the house smelled stale and beerish. Licker-bottles and ginger-ale bottles were underneath the center table, underneath the sofas, and on top of the piano. Ash-trays were everywhere, overflowing with cigar-butts and cigarette-ends—on the floor, under chairs, overturned among the sofa-pillows. A small brass tray under one of the sofas held a half-dozen small glasses, some of them still partly full of whisky or gin.

Sandy sat down to wait for his aunt. It was very quiet in the house, although it was almost ten o'clock. A man came down the stairs with his coat on his arm, blinking sleepily. He passed through the hall and out into the street. Bedroom-slippered feet shuffled to the head of the steps on the second floor, and the lazy woman's voice called: "She'll be down in a minute, darling. Just wait there."

Sandy waited. He heard the splash of water above and the hoarse gurgling of a bath-tub being emptied. Presently Harriett appeared in a little pink wash dress such as a child wears, the skirt striking her just above the knees. She smelled like cashmere-bouquet soap, and her face was not yet powdered, nor her hair done up, but she was smiling broadly, happy to see her nephew, as her arms went round his neck.

"My! I'm glad to see you, honey! How'd you happen to come? How'd you find me?"

"Grandma's sick," said Sandy. "She's awful sick and Aunt Tempy sent you this note."

The girl opened the letter. It read:

> Your mother is not expected to live. You better come to see her since she has asked for you. Tempy.

"O! . . . Wait a minute," said Harriett softly. "I'll hurry."

Sandy sat down again in the room full of ash-trays and licker-bottles. Many feet pattered upstairs, and, as doors opened and closed, women's voices were heard: "Can I help you, girlie? Can I lend you anything? Does you need a veil?"

When Harriett came down, she was wearing a tan coat-suit and a white turban, pulled tight on her head. Her face was powdered and her lips rouged ever so slightly. The bag she carried was beaded, blue and gold.

"Come on, Sandy," she said. "I guess I'm ready."

As they went out, they heard a man's voice in a shabby house across the street singing softly to a two-finger piano accompaniment:

> Sugar babe, I'm leavin'
> An' it won't be long. . . .

While outside, on his front door-step, two nappy-headed little yellow kids were solemnly balling-the-jack.

Two days before, Sandy had come home from school and found his grandmother lying across the bed, the full tubs still standing in the kitchen, her clothes not yet hung out to dry.

"What's the matter?" he asked.

"I's washed down, chile," said the old woman, panting. "I feels kinder tired-like, that's all."

But Sandy knew that there must be something else wrong with Aunt Hager, because he had never seen her lying on the bed in broad daylight, with her clothes still in the tubs.

"Does your back ache?" asked the child.

"I does feel a little misery," sighed Aunt Hager. "But seems to be mo' ma side an' not ma back this time. But 'tain't nothin'. I's just tired."

But Sandy was scared. "You want some soda and water, grandma?"

"No, honey." Then, in her usual tones of assumed anger: "Go on away from here an' let a body rest. Ain't I told you they ain't nothin' the matter 'ceptin' I's all washed out an' just got to lay down a minute? Go on an' fetch in yo' wood an' spin yo' top out yonder with Buster and them. Go on!"

It was nearly five o'clock when the boy came in again. Aunt Hager was sitting in the rocker near the stove then, her face drawn and ashy. She had been trying to finish her washing.

"Chile, go get Sister Johnson an' ask her if she can't wring out ma clothes fo' me—Mis' Dunset ain't sent much washin' this week, an' you can help her hang 'em up. I reckon it ain't gonna rain tonight, so's they can dry befo' mawnin'."

Sandy ran towards the door.

"Now, don't butt your brains out!" said the old lady. "Ain't no need o' runnin'."

Not only did Sister Johnson come at once and hang out the washing, but she made Hager get in bed, with a hot-water bottle on her paining side. And she gave her a big dose of peppermint and water.

"I 'spects it's from yo' stomick," she said. "I knows you et cabbage fo' dinner!"

"Maybe 'tis," said Hager.

Sister Johnson took Sandy to her house for supper that evening and he and Willie-Mae ate five sweet potatoes each.

"You-all gwine bust!" said Tom Johnson.

About nine o'clock the boy went to bed with his grandmother, and all that night Hager tossed and groaned, in spite of her efforts to lie quiet and not keep Sandy awake. In the morning she said: "Son, I reckon you better stay home from school, 'cause I's feelin' mighty po'ly. Seems like that cabbage ain't digested yet. Feels like I done et a stone. . . . Go see if you can't make de fire up an' beat me a cup o' hot water."

About eleven o'clock Madam de Carter came over. "I thought I didn't perceive you nowhere in the yard this morning and the sun 'luminating so bright and cheerful. You ain't indispensed, are you? Sandy said you was kinder ill." She chattered away. "You know it don't look natural not to see you hanging out clothes long before the noon comes."

"I ain't well a-tall this mawnin'," said Hager when she got a chance to speak. "I's feelin' right bad. I suffers with a pain in ma side; seems like it ain't gettin' no better. Sister Johnson just left here from rubbin' it, but I still suffers terrible an' can't eat nothin'. . . . You can use de phone, can't you, Sister Carter?"

"Why, yes! Yes indeedy! I oftens phones from over to Mis' Petit's. You think you needs a physicianer?"

In spite of herself a groan came from the old woman's lips as she tried to turn towards her friend. Aunt Hager, who had never moaned for lesser hurts, did not intend to complain over this one—but the pain!

"It's cuttin' me in two." She gasped. "Send fo' old Doc McDillors an' he'll come."

Madam de Carter, proud and important at the prospect of using her white neighbor's phone, rushed away.

"I didn't know you were so sick, grandma!" Sandy's eyes were wide with fright and sympathy. "I'm gonna get Mis' Johnson to come rub you again."

"O! . . . O, ma Lawd, help!" Alone for a moment with no one to hear her, she couldn't hold back the moans any longer. A cold sweat stood on her forehead.

The doctor came—the kind old white man who had known Hager for years and in whom she had faith.

"Well," he said, "It's quite a surprise to see you in bed, Aunty." Then, looking very serious and professional, he took her pulse.

"Go out and close the door," he said gently to Madam de Carter and Sister Johnson, Willie-Mae and Sandy, all of whom had gathered around the bed in the little room. "Somebody heat some water." He turned back the quilts from the woman's body and unbuttoned her gown.

Ten minutes later he said frankly, but with great kindness in his tones: "You're a sick woman, Hager, a very sick woman."

That afternoon Tempy came, like a stranger to the house, and took charge of things. Sandy felt uncomfortable and shy in her presence. This aunt of his had a hard, cold, correct way of talking that resembled Mrs. Rice's manner of speaking to his mother when Annjee used to work there. But Tempy quickly put the house in order, bathed her mother, and spread the bed with clean sheets and a white counterpane. Before evening, members of Hager's Lodge began to drop in bringing soups and custards. White people of the neighborhood stopped, too, to inquire if there was anything they could do for the old woman who had so often waited on them in their illnesses. About six o'clock old man Logan drove up the alley and tied his white mule to the back fence.

The sun was setting when Tempy called Sandy in from the back yard, where he was chopping wood for the stove. She said: "James"—how queerly his correct name struck his ears as it fell from the lips of this cold aunt!—"James, you had better send this telegram to your mother. Now, here is a dollar bill and you can bring back the change. Look on her last letter and get the correct address."

Sandy took the written sheet of paper and the money that his aunt gave him. Then he looked through the various drawers in the house for his mother's last letter. It had been nearly a month since they had heard from her, but finally the boy found the letter in the cupboard, under a jelly-glass full of small coins that his grandmother kept there. He carried the envelope with him to the telegraph office, and there he paid for a message to Annjee in Detroit:

Mother very sick, come at once. Tempy.

As the boy walked home in the gathering dusk, he felt strangely alone in the world, as though Aunt Hager had already gone away, and when he reached the house, it was full of lodge members who had come to keep watch. Tempy went home, but Sister Johnson remained in the sick-room, changing the hot-water bottles and administering, every three hours, the medicine the doctor had left.

There were so many people in the house that Sandy came out into the back yard and sat down on the edge of the well. It was cool and clear, and a slit of moon rode in a light-blue sky spangled with stars. Soon the apple-trees would bud and the grass would be growing. Sandy was a big boy. When his next birthday came, he would be fourteen, and he had begun to grow tall and heavy. Aunt Hager said she was going to buy him a pair of long pants this coming summer. And his mother would hardly know him when she saw him again, if she ever came home.

Tonight, inside, there were so many old sisters from the lodge that Sandy couldn't even talk to his grandmother while she lay in bed. They were constantly going in and out of the sick-room, drinking coffee in the kitchen, or gossiping in the parlor. He wished they would all go away. He could take care of his grandmother himself until she got well—he and Sister Johnson. They didn't even need Tempy, who, he felt, shouldn't be there, because he didn't like her.

"They callin' you inside," Willie-Mae came out to tell him as he sat by himself in the cold on the edge of the well. She was taller than Sandy now and had a regular job taking care of a white lady's baby. She no longer wore her hair in braids. She did it up, and she had a big leather pocket-book that she carried on her arm like a woman. Boys came to take her to the movies on Saturday nights. "They want you inside."

Sandy got up, his legs stiff and numb, and went into the kitchen. An elderly brown woman, dressed in black silk that swished as she moved, opened the door to Hager's bedroom and whispered to him loudly: "Be quiet, chile."

Sandy entered between a lane of old women. Hager looked up at him and smiled—so grave and solemn he appeared.

"Is they takin' care o' you?" she asked weakly. "Ain't it bedtime, honey? Is you had something to eat? Come on an' kiss yo' old grandma befo' you go to sleep. She'll be better in de mawnin'."

She couldn't seem to lift her head, so Sandy sat down on the bed and kissed her. All he said was: "I'm all right, grandma," because there were so many old women in there that he couldn't talk. Then he went out into the other room.

The air in the house was close and stuffy and the boy soon became groggy with sleep. He fell across the bed that had been Annjee's, and later Dogberry's, with all his clothes on. One of the lodge women in the room said: "You better take off yo' things, chile, an' go to sleep right." Then she said to the other sisters: "Come on in de kitchen, you-all, an' let this chile go to bed."

In the morning Tempy woke him. "Are you sure you had Annjee's address correct last night?" she demanded. "The telegraph office says she couldn't be found, so the message was not delivered. Let me see the letter."

Sandy found the letter again, and the address was verified.

"Well, that's strange," said Tempy. "I suppose, as careless and irresponsible as Jimboy is, they've got it wrong, or else moved. . . . Do you know where Harriett can be? I don't suppose you do, but mother has been calling for her all night. I suppose we'll have to try to get her, wherever she is."

"I got her address," said Sandy. "She wrote it down for me when I was working at the hotel this winter. I can find her."

"Then I'll give you a note," said Tempy. "Take it to her."

So Sandy went to the big grey house in the Bottoms that morning to deliver Tempy's message, before the girls there had risen from their beds.

Twenty-two

Beyond the Jordan

During the day the lodge members went to their work in the various kitchens and restaurants and laundries of the town. And Madam de Carter was ordered to Tulsa, Oklahoma, where a split in her organization was threatened because of the elections of the grand officers. Hager was resting easy, no pain now, but very weak.

"It's only a matter of time," said the doctor. "Give her the medicine so she won't worry, but it does no good. There's nothing we can do."

"She's going to die!" Sandy thought.

Harriett sat by the bedside holding her mother's hand as the afternoon sunlight fell on the white spread. Hager had been glad to see the girl again, and the old woman held nothing against her daughter for no longer living at home.

"Is you happy, chile?" Hager asked. "You looks so nice. Yo' clothes is right purty. I hopes you's findin' what you wants in life. You's young, honey, an' you needs to be happy. . . . Sandy!" She called so weakly that he could hardly hear her, though he was standing at the head of the bed. "Sandy, look in that drawer, chile, under ma night-gowns an' things, an' hand me that there little box you sees down in de corner."

The child found it and gave it to her, a small, white box from a cheap jeweller's. It was wrapped carefully in a soft handkerchief. The old woman took it eagerly and tried to hold it out towards her daughter. Harriett unwound the handkerchief and opened the lid of the box. Then she saw that it contained the tiny gold watch that her mother had given her on her sixteenth birthday, which she had pawned months ago in order to run away with the carnival. Quick tears came to the girl's eyes.

"I got it out o' pawn fo' you," Hager said, " 'cause I wanted you to have it fo' yo'self, chile. You know yo' mammy bought it fo' you."

It was such a little watch! Old-timy, with a breast-pin on it. Harriett quickly put her handkerchief over her wrist to hide the flashy new timepiece she was wearing on a gold bracelet.

That night Hager died. The undertakers came at dawn with their wagon and carried the body away to embalm it. Sandy stood on the front porch looking at the morning star as the clatter of the horses' hoofs echoed in the street. A sleepy young white boy was driving the undertaker's wagon, and the horse that pulled it was white.

The women who had been sitting up all night began to go home now to get their husbands' breakfasts and to prepare to go to work themselves.

"It's Wednesday," Sandy thought. "Today I'm supposed to go get Mrs. Reinhart's clothes, but grandma's dead. I guess I won't get them now. There's nobody to wash them."

Sister Johnson called him to the kitchen to drink a cup of coffee. Harriett was there weeping softly. Tempy was inside busily cleaning the room from which they had removed the body. She had opened all the windows and was airing the house.

Out in the yard a rooster flapped his wings and crowed shrilly at the rising sun. The fire crackled, and the coffee boiling sent up a fragrant aroma. Sister Johnson opened a can of condensed milk by punching it with the butcher-knife. She put some cups and saucers on the table.

"Tempy, won't you have some?"

"No, thank you, Mrs. Johnson," she called from the dead woman's bedroom.

When Aunt Hager was brought back to her house, she was in a long box covered with black plush. They placed it on a folding stand by the window in the front room. There was a crape on the door, and the shades were kept lowered, and people whispered in the house as though someone were asleep. Flowers began to be delivered by boys on bicycles, and the lodge members came to sit up again that night. The time was set for burial, and the *Daily Leader* carried this paragraph in small type on its back page:

> Hager Williams, aged colored laundress of 419 Cypress Street, passed away at her home last night. She was known and respected by many white families in the community. Three daughters and a grandson survive.

They tried again to reach Annjee in Detroit by telegram, but without success. On the afternoon of the funeral it was cold and rainy. The little Baptist Church was packed with people. The sisters of the lodge came in full regalia, with banners and insignia, and the brothers turned out with them. Hager's coffin was banked with flowers. There were many fine pieces from the families for whom she had washed and from the white neighbors she had nursed in sickness. There were offerings, too, from Tempy's high-toned friends and from Harriett's girl companions in the house in the Bottoms. Many of the bell-boys, porters, and bootleggers sent wreaths and crosses with golden letters on them: "At Rest in Jesus," "Beyond the Jordan," or simply: "Gone Home." There was a bouquet of violets from Buster's mother and a blanket of roses from Tempy herself. They were all pretty, but, to Sandy, the perfume was sickening in the close little church.

The Baptist minister preached, but Tempy had Father Hill from her church to say a few words, too. The choir sang *Shall We Meet Beyond the River?* People wept and fainted. The services seemed interminable. Then came the long drive to the cemetery in horse-drawn hacks, with a few automobiles in line behind. In at the wide gates and through a vast expanse of tombstones the procession passed, across the graveyard, towards the far, lonesome corner where most of the Negroes rested. There Sandy saw the open grave. Then he saw the casket going down . . . down . . . down, into the earth.

The boy stood quietly between his Aunt Tempy and his Aunt Harriett at the edge of the grave while Tempy stared straight ahead into the drizzling rain, and Harriett cried, streaking the powder on her cheeks.

"That's all right, mama," Harriett sobbed to the body in the long, black box. "You won't get lonesome out here. Harrie'll come back tomorrow. Harrie'll come back every day and bring you flowers. You won't get lonesome, mama."

They were throwing wet dirt on the coffin as the mourners walked away through the sticky clay towards their carriages. Some old sister at the grave began to sing:

Dark was the night,
Cold was the ground . . .

in a high weird monotone. Others took it up, and, as the mourners drove away, the air was filled with the minor wailing of the old women. Harriett was wearing Hager's gift, the little gold watch, pinned beneath her coat.

When they got back to the house where Aunt Hager had lived for so long, Sister Johnson said the mail-man had left a letter under the door that afternoon addressed to the dead woman. Harriett was about to open it when Tempy took it from her. It was from Annjee.

"Dear mama," it began.

We have moved to Toledo because Jimboy thought he would do better here and the reason I haven't written, we have been so long getting settled. I have been out of work but we both got jobs now and maybe I will be able to send you some money soon. I hope you are well, ma, and all right. Kiss Sandy for me and take care of yourself. With love and God's blessings from your daughter,

Annjee

Tempy immediately turned the letter over and wrote on the back:

We buried your mother today. I tried to reach you in Detroit, but could not get you, since you were no longer there and neglected to send us your new address. It is too bad you weren't here for the funeral. Your child is going to stay with me until I hear from you.

Tempy

Then she turned to the boy, who stood dazed beside Sister Johnson in the silent, familiar old house. "You will come home with me, James," she said. "We'll see that this place is locked first. You try all the windows and I'll fasten the doors; then we'll go out the front. . . . Mrs. Johnson, it's been good of you to help us in our troubles. Thank you."

Sister Johnson went home, leaving Harriett in the parlor. When Sandy and Tempy returned from locking the back windows and doors, they found the girl still standing there, and for a moment the two sisters looked at one another in silence. Then Tempy said coldly: "We're going."

Harriett went out alone into the drizzling rain. Tempy tried the parlor windows to be sure they were well fastened; then, stepping outside on the porch, she locked the door and put the key in her bag.

"Come on," she said.

Sandy looked up and down the street, but in the thick twilight of fog and rain Harriett had disappeared, so he followed his aunt into the waiting cab. As the hack clattered off, the boy gave an involuntary shiver.

"Do you want to hold my hand," Tempy asked, unbending a little.

"No," Sandy said. So they rode in silence.

Twenty-three

Tempy's House

"James, you must get up on time in this house. Breakfast has been ready twenty minutes. I can't come upstairs every morning to call you. You are old enough now to wake yourself and you must learn to do so—you've too far to walk to school to lie abed."

Sandy tumbled out. Tempy left the room so that he would be free to dress, and soon he came downstairs to breakfast.

He had never had a room of his own before. He had never even slept in a room alone, but here his aunt had given him a small chamber on the second floor which had a window that looked out into a tidy back yard where there was a brick walk running to the back gate. The room, which was very clean, contained only the bed, one chair, and a dresser. There was, too, a little closet in which to hang clothes, but Sandy did not have many to put in it.

The thing that impressed him most about the second floor was the bathroom. He had never lived where there was running water indoors. And in this room, too, everything was so spotlessly clean that Sandy was afraid to move lest he disturb something or splash water on the wall.

When he came downstairs for breakfast, he found the table set for two. Mr. Siles, being in the railway postal service, was out on a trip. The grapefruit was waiting as Sandy slid shyly into his place opposite the ash-brown woman who had become his guardian since his grandma's death. She bowed her bead to say a short grace; then they ate.

"Have you been accustomed to drinking milk in the mornings?" Tempy asked as they were finishing the meal. "If you have, the milkman can leave another bottle. Young people should have plenty of milk."

"Yes'm, I'd like it, but we only had coffee at home."

"You needn't say 'yes'm' in this house. We are not used to slavery talk here. If you like milk, I'll get it for you. . . . Now, how are your clothes? I see your stocking has a hole in it, and one pants-leg is hanging."

"It don't stay fastened."

"It *doesn't*, James! I'll buy you some more pants tomorrow. What else do you need?"

Sandy told her, and in a few days she took him to Wertheimer's, the city's largest store, and outfitted him completely. And, as they shopped, she informed him that she was the only colored woman in town who ran a bill there.

"I want white people to know that Negroes have a little taste; that's why I always trade at good shops. . . . And if you're going to live with me, you'll have to learn to do things right, too."

The tearful letter that came from Annjee when she heard of her mother's death said that Toledo was a very difficult place to get work in, and that she had no money to send railroad fare for Sandy, but that she would try to send for him as soon as she could. Jimboy was working on a lake steamer and was seldom home, and she couldn't have Sandy with her anyway until they got a nicer place to stay; so would Tempy please keep him a little while?

By return post Tempy replied that if Annjee had any sense, she would let Sandy remain in Stanton, where he could get a good education, and not be following after his worthless father all over the country. Mr. Siles and she had no children, and Sandy seemed like a quiet, decent child, smart in his classes. Colored people needed to encourage talent so that the white race would realize Negroes weren't all mere guitar-players and housemaids. And Sandy could be a credit if he were raised right. Of course, Tempy knew he hadn't had the correct environment to begin with—living with Jimboy and Harriett and going to a Baptist church, but undoubtedly he could be trained. He was young. "And I think it would be only fair to the boy that you let him stay with us, because, Annjee, you are certainly not the person to bring him up as he should be reared." The letter was signed: "Your sister, Tempy," and written properly with pen and ink.

So it happened that Sandy came to live with Mr. and Mrs. Arkins Siles, for that was the name by which his aunt and uncle were known in the Negro society of the town. Mr. Siles was a mail-clerk on the railroad—a position that colored people considered a high one because you were working for "Uncle Sam." He was a paste-colored man of forty-eight who had inherited three houses from his father.

Tempy, when she married, had owned houses too, one of which had been willed her by Mrs. Barr-Grant, for whom she had worked for years as personal maid. She had acquired her job while yet in high school, and Mrs. Barr-Grant, who travelled a great deal in the interest of woman suffrage and prohibition, had taken Tempy east with her. On their return to Stanton she allowed the colored maid to take charge of her home, where she also employed a cook and a parlor girl. Thus was the mistress left free to write pamphlets and prepare lectures on the various evils of the world standing in need of correction.

Tempy pleased Mrs. Barr-Grant by being prompt and exact in obeying orders and by appearing to worship her Puritan intelligence. In truth Tempy did worship her mistress, for the colored girl found that by following Mrs. Barr-Grant's early directions she had become an expert housekeeper; by imitating her manner of speech she had acquired a precise flow of language; and by reading her books she had become interested in things that most Negro girls never thought about. Several times the mistress had remarked to her maid: "You're so smart and such a good, clean, quick little worker, Tempy, that it's too bad you aren't white." And Tempy had taken this to heart, not as an insult, but as a compliment.

When the white lady died, she left one of her small houses to her maid as a token of appreciation for faithful services. By dint of saving, and of having resided with her mistress where there had been no living expenses, Tempy had managed to buy another house, too. When Mr. Siles asked her to be his wife, everybody said it was a fine match, for both owned property, both were old enough to know what they wanted, and both were eminently respectable. . . . Now they prospered together.

Tempy no longer worked out, but stayed home, keeping house, except that she went each month to collect her rents and those of her husband. She had a woman to do the laundry and help with the cleaning, but Tempy herself did the cooking, and all her meals were models of economical preparation. Just enough food was prepared each time for three people. Sandy never had a third helping of dessert in her house. No big pots of black-eyed peas and pigtails scented her front hall, either. She got her recipes from *The Ladies' Home Journal*—and she never bought a watermelon.

White people were for ever picturing colored folks with huge slices of watermelon in their hands. Well, she was one colored woman who did not like them! Her favorite fruits were tangerines and grapefruit, for Mrs. Barr-Grant had always eaten those, and Tempy had admired Mrs. Barr-Grant more than anybody else—more, of course, than she had admired Aunt Hager, who spent her days at the wash-tub, and had loved watermelon.

Colored people certainly needed to come up in the world, Tempy thought, up to the level of white people—dress like white people, talk like white people, think like white people—and then they would no longer be called "niggers."

In Tempy this feeling was an emotional reaction, born of white admiration, but in Mr. Siles, who shared his wife's views, the same attitude was born of practical thought. The whites had the money, and if Negroes wanted any, the quicker they learned to be like the whites, the better. Stop being lazy, stop singing all the time, stop attending revivals, and learn to get the dollar—because money buys everything, even the respect of white people.

Blues and spirituals Tempy and her husband hated because they were too Negro. In their house Sandy dared not sing a word of *Swing Low, Sweet Chariot,* for what had darky slave songs to do with respectable people? And rag-time belonged in the Bottoms with the sinners. (It was ironically strange that the Bottoms should be the only section of Stanton where Negroes and whites mingled freely on equal terms.) That part of town, according to Tempy, was lost to God, and the fact that she had a sister living there burned like a hidden cancer in her breast. She never mentioned Harriett to anyone.

Tempy's friends were all people of standing in the darker world—doctors, school-teachers, a dentist, a lawyer, a hairdresser. And she moved among these friends as importantly as Mrs. Barr-Grant had moved among a similar group in the white race. Many of them had had washwomen for mothers and day-laborers for fathers; but none ever spoke of that. And while Aunt Hager lived, Tempy, after getting her position with Mrs. Barr-Grant, was seldom seen with the old woman. After her marriage she was even more ashamed of her family connections—a little sister running wild, and another sister married for the sake of love—Tempy could never abide Jimboy, or understand why Annjee had taken up with a rounder from the South. One's family as a topic of conversation, however, was not popular in high circles, for too many of Stanton's dark society folks had sprung from humble family trees and low black bottoms.

"But back in Washington, where I was born," said Mrs. Doctor Mitchell once, "we really have blood! All the best people at the capital come from noted ancestry—Senator Bruce, John M. Langston, Governor Pinchback, Frederick Douglass. Why, one of our colored families on their white side can even trace its lineage back to George Washington! . . . O, yes, we have a background! But, of course, we are too refined to boast about it."

Tempy thought of her mother then and wished that black Aunt Hager had not always worn her apron in the streets, uptown and everywhere! Of course, it was clean and white and seemed to suit the old lady, but aprons weren't worn by the best people. When Tempy was in the hospital for an operation shortly after her marriage, they wouldn't let Hager enter by the front door—and Tempy never knew whether it was on account of her color or the apron! The Presbyterian Hospital was prejudiced against Negroes and didn't like them to use the elevator, but certainly her mother should not have come there in an apron!

Well, Aunt Hager had meant well, Tempy thought, even if she didn't dress right. And now this child, Sandy—James was his correct name! At that first breakfast they ate together, she asked him if he had a comb and brush of his own.

"No'm, I ain't," said Sandy.

"I haven't," she corrected him. "I certainly don't want my white neighbors to hear you saying 'ain't.' . . . You've come to live with me now and you must talk like a gentleman."

Twenty-four

A Shelf of Books

That spring, shortly after Sandy went to stay with Tempy, there was an epidemic of mumps among the schoolchildren in Stanton, and, old as he was, he was among its early victims. With jaws swollen to twice their normal size and a red sign, MUMPS, on the house, he was forced to remain at home for three weeks. It was then that the boy began to read books other than the ones be had had to study for his lessons. At Aunt Hager's house there had been no books, anyway, except the Bible and the few fairy-tales that he had been given at Christmas; but Tempy had a case full of dusty volumes that were used to give dignity to her sitting-room: a row of English classics bound in red, an *Encyclopedia of World Knowledge* in twelve volumes, a book on household medicine full of queer drawings, and some modern novels—*The Rosary, The Little Shepherd of Kingdom Come,* the newest Harold Bell Wright, and all that had ever been written by Gene Stratton Porter, Tempy's favorite author. The Negro was represented by Chesnutt's *House Behind the Cedars,* and the *Complete Poems* of Paul Laurence Dunbar, whom Tempy tolerated on account of his fame, but condemned because he had written so much in dialect and so often of the lower classes of colored people. Tempy subscribed to *Harper's Magazine,* too, because Mrs. Barr-Grant had taken it. And in her sewing-room closet there was also a pile of *The Crisis,* the thin Negro monthly that she had been taking from the beginning of its publication.

Sandy had heard of that magazine, but he had never seen a copy; so he went through them all, looking at the pictures of prominent Negroes and reading about racial activities all over the country, and about racial wrongs in the South. In every issue he found, too, stirring and beautifully written editorials about the frustrated longings of the black race, and the hidden beauties in the Negro soul. A man named Du Bois wrote them.

"Dr. William Edward Burghardt Du Bois," said Tempy, "and he is a great man."

"Great like Booker T. Washington?" asked Sandy.

"Teaching Negroes to be servants, that's all Washington did!" Tempy snorted in so acid a tone that Sandy was silent. "Du Bois wants our rights. He wants us to be real men and women. He believes in social equality. But

Washington—huh!" The fact that he had established an industrial school damned Washington in Tempy's eyes, for there were enough colored workers already. But Du Bois was a doctor of philosophy and had studied in Europe! . . . That's what Negroes needed to do, get smart, study books, go to Europe! "Don't talk to me about Washington," Tempy fumed. "Take Du Bois for your model, not some white folks' nigger."

"Well, Aunt Hager said—" then Sandy stopped. His grandmother had thought that Booker T. was the greatest of men, but maybe she had been wrong. Anyway, this Du Bois could write! Gee, it made you burn all over to read what he said about a lynching. But Sandy did not mention Booker Washington again to Tempy, although, months later, at the library he read his book called *Up from Slavery,* and he was sure that Aunt Hager hadn't been wrong. "I guess they are both great men," he thought.

Sandy's range of reading increased, too, when his aunt found a job for him that winter in Mr. Prentiss's gift-card- and printing-shop, where he kept the place clean and acted as delivery boy. This shop kept a shelf of current novels and some volumes of the new poetry—Sandburg, Lindsay, Masters—which the Young Women's Club of Stanton was then studying, to the shocked horror of the older white ladies of the town. Sandy knew of this because Mr. Prentiss's daughter, a student at Goucher College, used to keep shop and she pointed out volumes for the boy to read and told him who their authors were and what the books meant. She said that none of the colored boys they had employed before had ever been interested in reading; so she often lent him, by way of encouragement, shop-worn copies to be taken home at night and returned the next day. Thus Sandy spent much of his first year with Tempy deep in novels too mature for a fourteen-year-old boy. But Tempy was very proud of her studious young nephew. She began to decide that she had made no mistake in keeping him with her, and when he entered the high school, she bought him his first long-trouser suit as a spur towards further application.

Sandy became taller week by week, and it seemed to Tempy as if his shirt-sleeves became too short for him overnight. His voice was changing, too, and he had acquired a liking for football, but his after-school job at Prentiss's kept him from playing much. At night he read, or sometimes went to the movies with Buster—but Tempy kept him home as much as she could. Occasionally he saw Willie-Mae, who was keeping company with the second cook at Wright's Hotel. And sometimes he saw Jimmy Lane, who was a bell-hop now and hung out with a sporty crowd in the rear room of Cudge Windsor's pool hall. But whenever Sandy went into his old neighborhood, he felt sad, remembering Aunt Hager and his mother, and Jimboy, and Harriett—for his young aunt had gone away from Stanton, too, and the last he heard about her rumored that she was on the stage in Kansas City. Now the little house where Sandy had lived with his grandmother belonged to Tempy, who kept it rented to a family of strangers.

In high school Sandy was taking, at his aunt's request, the classical course, which included Latin, ancient history, and English, and which required a great deal of reading. His teacher of English was a large, masculine woman named Martha Fry, who had once been to Europe and who loved to talk about the splendors of old England and to read aloud in a deep, mannish kind of voice, dramatizing the printed words. It was from her that Sandy received an introduction to Shakespeare, for in the spring term they studied *The Merchant of Venice*. In the spring also, under Miss Fry's direction, the first-year students were required to write an essay for the freshman essay prizes of both money and medals. And in this contest Sandy won the second prize. It was the first time in the history of the school that a colored pupil had ever done anything of the sort, and Tempy was greatly elated. There was a note in the papers about it, and Sandy brought his five dollars home for his aunt to put away. But he gave his bronze medal to a girl named Pansetta Young, who was his class-mate and a new-found friend.

From the first moment in school that he saw Pansetta, he knew that he liked her, and he would sit looking at her for hours in every class that they had together—for she was a little baby-doll kind of girl, with big black eyes and a smooth pinkish-brown skin, and her hair was curly on top of her head. Her widowed mother was a cook at the Goucher College dining-hall; and she was an all-alone little girl, for Pansetta had no brothers or sisters. After Thanksgiving Sandy began to walk part of the way home with her every day. He could not accompany her all the way because he had to go to work at Mr. Prentiss's shop. But on Christmas he bought her a box of candy—and sent it to her by mail. And at Easter-time she gave him a chocolate egg.

"Unh-huh! You got a girl now, ain't you?" teased Buster one April afternoon when he caught Sandy standing in front of the high school waiting for Pansetta to come out.

"Aw, go chase yourself!" said Sandy, for Buster had a way of talking dirty about girls, and Sandy was afraid he would begin that with Pansetta; but today his friend changed the subject instead.

"Say come on round to the pool hall tonight and I'll teach you to play billiards."

"Don't think I'd better, Bus. Aunt Tempy might get sore," Sandy replied, shaking his head. "Besides, I have to study."

"Are you gonna read yourself to death?" Buster demanded indignantly. "You've got to come out some time, man! Tell her you're going to the movies and we'll go down to Cudge's instead."

Sandy thought for a moment.

"All the boys come round there at night."

"Well, I might."

"Little apron-string boy!" teased Buster.

"If I hit you a couple of times, you'll find out I'm not!" Sandy doubled up his fists in pretended anger. "I'll black your blue eyes for you!"

"Ya-a-a-a?" yelled his friend, running up the street. "See you tonight at Cudge's—apron-string boy!"

And that evening Sandy didn't finish reading, as he had planned, *Moby Dick,* which Mr. Prentiss's daughter had lent him. Instead he practised handling a cue-stick under the tutelage of Buster.

Twenty-five

Pool Hall

There were no community houses in Stanton and no recreation centres for young men except the Y.M.C.A., which was closed to you if you were not a white boy; so, for the Negro youths of the town, Cudge Windsor's pool hall was the evening meeting-place. There one could play billiards, shoot dice in a back room, or sit in summer on the two long benches outside, talking and looking at the girls as they passed. In good weather these benches were crowded all the time.

Next door to the pool hall was Cudge Windsor's lunch-room. Of course, the best colored people did not patronize Cudge's, even though his business was not in the Bottoms. It was located on Pearl Street, some three or four blocks before that thoroughfare plunged across the tracks into the low terrain of tinkling pianos and ladies who loved for cash. But since Cudge catered to what Mr. Siles called "the common element," the best people stayed away.

After months of bookishness and subjection to Tempy's prim plans for his improvement, Sandy found the pool hall an easy and amusing place in which to pass time. It was better than the movies, where people on the screen were only shadows. And it was much better than the Episcopal Church, with its stoop-shouldered rector, for here at Cudge's everybody was alive, and the girls who passed in front swinging their arms and grinning at the men were warm-bodied and gay, while the boys rolling dice in the rear room or playing pool at the tables were loud-mouthed and careless. Life sat easily on their muscular shoulders.

Adventurers and vagabonds who passed through Stanton on the main line would often drop in at Cudge's to play a game or get a bite to eat, and many times on summer nights reckless black boys, a long way from home, kept the natives entertained with tales of the road, or trips on side-door Pullmans, and of far-off cities where things were easy and women generous. They had a song that went:

> O, the gals in Texas,
> They never be's unkind.
> They feeds their men an'
> Buys 'em gin an' wine.
> But these women in Stanton,

Their hearts is hard an' cold.
When you's out of a job, they
Denies you jelly roll.

Then, often, arguments would begin—boastings, proving and fending; or telling of exploits with guns, knives, and razors, with cops and detectives, with evil women and wicked men; out-bragging and out-lying one another, all talking at once. Sometimes they would create a racket that could be heard for blocks. To the uninitiated it would seem that a fight was imminent. But underneath, all was good-natured and friendly—and through and above everything went laughter. No matter how belligerent or lewd their talk was, or how sordid the tales they told—of dangerous pleasures and strange perversities—these black men laughed. That must be the reason, thought Sandy, why poverty-stricken old Negroes like Uncle Dan Givens lived so long—because to them, no matter how hard life might be, it was not without laughter.

Uncle Dan was the world's champion liar, Cudge Windsor said, and the jolly old man's unending flow of fabulous reminiscences were entertaining enough to earn him a frequent meal in Cudge's lunch-room or a drink of licker from the patrons of the pool hall, who liked to start the old fellow talking.

One August evening when Tempy was away attending a convention of the Midwest Colored Women's Clubs, Sandy and Buster, Uncle Dan, Jimmy Lane, and Jap Logan sat until late with a big group of youngsters in front of the pool hall watching the girls go by. A particularly pretty high yellow damsel passed in a thin cool dress of flowered voile, trailing the sweetness of powder and perfume behind her.

"Dog-gone my soul!" yelled Jimmy Lane. "Just gimme a bone and lemme be your dog—I mean your salty dog!" But the girl, pretending not to hear, strolled leisurely on, followed by a train of compliments from the pool-hall benches.

"Sweet mama Venus!" cried a tall raw-bony boy, gazing after her longingly.

"If angels come like that, lemme go to heaven—and if they don't, lemme be lost to glory!" Jap exclaimed.

"Shut up, Jap! What you know 'bout women?" asked Uncle Dan, leaning forward on his cane to interrupt the comments. "Here you-all is, ain't knee-high to ducks yit, an' talkin' 'bout womens! Shut up, all o' you! Nary one o' you's past sebenteen, but when I were yo' age—Hee! Hee! You-all want to know what dey called me when I were yo' age?"

The old man warmed to his tale. "Dey called me de 'stud nigger'! Yes, dey did! On 'count o' de kind o' slavery-time work I was doin'—I were breedin' babies fo' to sell!"

"Another lie!" said Jap.

"No, 'tain't, boy! You listen here to what I's gwine tell you. I were de onliest real healthy nigger buck ma white folks had on de plantation, an' dese was ole po' white folks what can't 'ford to buy many slaves, so dey figures to raise a heap o' darky babies an' sell 'em later on—dat's why dey made me de breeder. . . . Hee! Hee! . . . An' I sho breeded a gang o' pickaninnies, too! But I were young then, jest like you-all is, an' I ain't had a pint o' sense—laying wid de womens all night, ever' night."

"Yes, we believe you," drawled Jimmy.

"An' it warn't no time befo' little yaller chillens an' black chillens an' red chillens an' all kinds o' chillens was runnin' round de yard eatin' out o' de hog-pen an' a-callin' me pappy. . . . An' here I is today gwine on ninety-three year ole an' I done outlived 'em all. Dat is, I done outlived all I ever were able to keep track on after de war, 'cause we darkies sho scattered once we was free! Yes, sah! But befo' de fightin' ended I done been pappy to forty-nine chillens—an' thirty-three of 'em were boys!"

"Aw, I know you're lying now, Uncle Dan," Jimmy laughed.

"No, I ain't, sah! . . . Hee! Hee! . . . I were a great one when I were young! Yes, sah!" The old man went on undaunted. "I went an' snuck off to a dance one night, me an' nudder boy, went 'way ovah in Macon County at ole man Laird's plantation, who been a bitter enemy to our white folks. Did I ever tell you 'bout it? We took one o' ole massa's best hosses out de barn to ride, after he done gone to his bed. . . . Well, sah! It were late when we got started, an' we rid dat hoss lickety-split uphill an' down holler, ovah de crick an' past de mill, me an' ma buddy both on his back, through de cane-brake an' up anudder hill, till he wobble an' foam at de mouth like he's 'bout to drap. When we git to de dance, long 'bout midnight, we jump off dis hoss an' ties him to a post an' goes in de cabin whar de music were—an' de function were gwine on big. Man! We grabs ourselves a gal an' dance till de moon riz, kickin' up our heels an' callin' figgers, an' jest havin' a scrumptious time. Ay, Lawd! We sho did dance! . . . Well, come 'long 'bout two o'clock in de mawnin, niggers all leavin', an' we goes out in de yard to git on dis hoss what we had left standin' at de post. . . . An' Lawd have mercy—de hoss were dead! Yes, sah! He done fell down right whar he were tied, eyeballs rolled back, mouth a-foamin', an' were stone-dead! . . . Well, we ain't knowed how we gwine git home ner what we gwine do 'bout massa's hoss—an' we was skeered, Lawdy! 'Cause we know he beat us to death if he find out we done rid his best hoss anyhow—let lone ridin' de crittur to death. . . . An' all de low-down Macon niggers what was at de party was whaw-whawin' fit to kill, laughin' cause it were so funny to see us gittin' ready to git on our hoss an' de hoss were dead! . . . Well, sah, me an' ma buddy ain't wasted no time. We took dat animule up by de hind legs an' we drug him all de way home to massa's plantation befo' day! We sho did! Uphill an' down holler, sixteen miles! Yes, sah! An' put dat damn hoss back in massa's barn like he war befo' we left. An' when de sun riz, me an' ma buddy were in de slavery quarters sleepin' sweet an' lowly-like as if we ain't been nowhar. . . . De next day old massa 'maze how dat hoss die all tied up in his stall wid his halter on! An' we niggers 'maze, too, when we heard dat massa's hoss been dead, 'cause we ain't knowed a thing 'bout it. No, sah! Ain't none o' us niggers knowed a thing! Hee! Hee! Not a thing!"

"Weren't you scared?" asked Sandy.

"Sho, we was scared," said Uncle Dan, "but we ain't act like it. Niggers was smart in them days."

"They're still smart," said Jap Logan, "if they can lie like you."

"I mean!" said Buster.

"Uncle Dan's the world's champeen liar," drawled a tall lanky boy. "Come on, let's chip in and buy him a sandwich, 'cause he's lied enough fo' one evening."

They soon crowded into the lunch-room and sat on stools at the counter ordering soda or ice-cream from the fat good-natured waitress. While they were eating, a gambler bolted in from the back room of the pool hall with a handful of coins he had just won.

"Gonna feed ma belly while I got it in ma hand," he shouted. "Can't tell when I might lose, 'cause de dice is runnin' they own way tonight. Say, Mattie," he yelled, "tell chef to gimme a beefsteak all beat up like Jim Jeffries, cup o' coffee strong as Jack Johnson, an' come flyin' like a airship so I can get back in the game. Tell that kitchen buggar sweet-papa Stingaree's out here!"

"All right, keep yo' collar on," said Mattie. "De steak's got to be cooked."

"What you want, Uncle Dan?" yelled the gambler to the old man. "While I's winnin', might as well feed you, too. Take some ham and cabbage or something. That sandwich ain't 'nough to fill you up."

Uncle Dan accepted a plate of spareribs, and Stingaree threw down a pile of nickels on the counter.

"Injuns an' buffaloes," he said loudly. "Two things de white folks done killed, so they puts 'em on de backs o' nickels. . . . Rush up that steak there, gal, I's hongry!"

Sandy finished his drink and bought a copy of the *Chicago Defender,* the World's Greatest Negro Weekly, which was sold at the counter. Across the front in big red letters there was a headline: *Negro Boy Lynched.* There was also an account of a race riot in a Northern industrial city. On the theatrical page a picture of pretty Baby Alice Whitman, the tap-dancer, attracted his attention, and he read a few of the items there concerning colored shows; but as he was about to turn the page, a little article in the bottom corner made him pause and put the paper down on the counter.

ACTRESS MAKES HIT

St. Louis, Mo., Aug. 3: Harrietta Williams, sensational young blues-singer, has been packing the Booker Washington Theatre to the doors here this week. Jones and Jones are the headliners for the all-colored vaudeville bill, but the singing of Miss Williams has been the outstanding drawing card. She is being held over for a continued engagement, with Billy Sanderlee at the piano.

"Billy Sanderlee," said Buster, who was looking over Sandy's shoulder. "That's that freckled-faced yellow guy who used to play for dances around here, isn't it? He could really beat a piano to death, all right!"

"Sure could," replied Sandy. "Gee, they must make a great team together, 'cause my Aunt Harrie can certainly sing and dance!"

"Ain't the only thing she can do!" bellowed the gambler, swallowing a huge chunk of steak. "Yo' Aunt Harrie's a whang, son!"

"Shut yo' mouth!" said Uncle Dan.

Twenty-six

The Doors of Life

During Sandy's second year at high school Tempy was busy sewing for the local Red Cross and organizing Liberty Bond clubs among the colored population of Stanton. She earnestly believed that the world would really become safe for democracy, even in America, when the war ended, and that colored folks would no longer be snubbed in private and discriminated against in public.

"Colored boys are over there fighting," she said. "Our men are buying hundreds of dollars' worth of bonds, colored women are aiding the Red Cross, our clubs are sending boxes to the camps and to the front. White folks will see that the Negro can be trusted in war as well as peace. Times will be better after this for all of us."

One day a letter came from Annjee, who had moved to Chicago. She said that Sandy's father had not long remained in camp, but had been sent to France almost immediately after he enlisted, and she didn't know what she was going to do, she was so worried and alone! There had been but one letter from Jimboy since he left. And now she needed Sandy with her, but she wasn't able to send for him yet. She said she hoped and prayed that nothing would happen to his father at the front, but every day there were colored soldiers' names on the casualty list.

"Good thing he's gone," grunted Tempy when she read the letter as they were seated at the supper-table. Then, suddenly changing the subject, she asked Sandy: "Did you see Dr. Frank Crane's beautiful article this morning?"

"No, I didn't," said the boy.

"You certainly don't read as much as you did last winter," complained his aunt. "And you're staying out entirely too late to suit me. I'm quite sure you're not at the movies all that time, either. I want these late hours stopped, young man. Every night in the week out somewhere until ten and eleven o'clock!"

"Well, boys do have to get around a little, Tempy," Mr. Siles objected. "It's not like when you and I were coming up."

"I'm raising this boy, Mr. Siles," Tempy snapped. "When do you study, James? That's what I want to know."

"When I come in," said Sandy, which was true. His light was on until after twelve almost every night. And when he did not study late, his old habit of lying awake clung to him and he could not go to sleep early.

"You think too much," Buster once said. "Stop being so smart; then you'll sleep better."

"Yep," added Jimmy Lane. "Better be healthy and dumb than smart and sick like some o' these college darkies I see with goggles on their eyes and breath smellin' bad."

"O, I'm not sick," objected Sandy, "but I just get to thinking about things at night—the war, and white folks, and God, and girls, and—O, I don't know—everything in general."

"Sure, keep on thinking," jeered Buster, "and turn right ashy after while and be all stoop-shouldered like Father Hill." (The Episcopalian rector was said to be the smartest colored man in town.) "But I'm not gonna worry about being smart myself. A few more years, boy, and I'll be in some big town passing for white, making money, and getting along swell. And I won't need to be smart, either I'll—be ofay! So if you see me some time in St. Louis or Chi with a little blond on my arm—don't recognize me, hear! I want my kids to be so yellow-headed they won't have to think about a color line."

And Sandy knew that Buster meant what he said, for his light-skinned friend was one of those people who always go directly towards the things they want, as though the road is straight before them and they can see clearly all the way. But to Sandy himself nothing ever seemed quite that clear. Why was his country going stupidly to war? . . . Why were white people and colored people so far apart? Why was it wrong to desire the bodies of women? . . . With his mind a maelstrom of thoughts as he lay in bed night after night unable to go to sleep quickly, Sandy wondered many things and asked himself many questions.

Sometimes he would think about Pansetta Young, his class-mate with the soft brown skin, and the pointed and delicate breasts of her doll-like body. He had never been alone with Pansetta, never even kissed her, yet she was "his girl" and he liked her a great deal. Maybe be loved her! . . . But what did it mean to love a girl? Were you supposed to marry her then and live with her for ever? . . . His father had married his mother—good-natured, guitar-playing Jimboy—but they weren't always together, and Sandy knew that Jimboy was enjoying the war now, just as he had always enjoyed everything else.

"Gee, he must of married early to be my father and still look so young!" he thought. "Suppose I marry Pansetta now!" But what did he really know about marriage other than the dirty fragments he had picked up from Jimmy and Buster and the fellows at the pool hall?

On his fifteenth birthday Tempy had given him a book written for young men on the subject of love and living, called *The Doors of Life,* addressed to all Christian youths in their teens—but it had been written by a white New England minister of the Presbyterian faith who stood aghast before the flesh; so its advice consisted almost entirely in how to pray in the orthodox manner, and in how *not* to love.

"Avoid evil companions lest they be your undoing (see Psalms cxix, 115–20); and beware of lewd women, for their footsteps lead down to hell (see Proverbs vii, 25–7)," said the book, and that was the extent of its instructions on sex, except that it urged everyone to marry early and settle down to a healthy, moral, Christian life. . . . But how could you marry early when you had no money and no home to which to take a wife, Sandy wondered. And who were evil companions. Neither Aunt Hager nor Annjee had ever said anything to Sandy about love in its bodily sense; Jimboy had gone away too soon to talk with him; and Tempy and her husband were too proper to discuss such subjects; so the boy's sex knowledge consisted only in the distorted ideas that youngsters whisper; the dirty stories heard in the hotel lobby where he had worked; and the fact that they sold in drugstores articles that weren't mentioned in the company of nice people.

But who were nice people anyway? Sandy hated the word "nice." His Aunt Tempy was always using it. All of her friends were nice, she said, respectable and refined. They went around with their noses in the air and they didn't speak to porters and washwomen—though they weren't nearly so much fun as the folks they tried to scorn. Sandy liked Cudge Windsor or Jap Logan better than he did Dr. Mitchell, who had been to college—and never forgotten it.

Sandy wondered if Booker T. Washington had been like Tempy's friends? Or if Dr. Du Bois was a snob just because he was a college man? He wondered if those two men had a good time being great. Booker T. was dead, but he had left a living school in the South. Maybe he could teach in the South, too, Sandy thought, if he ever learned enough. Did colored folks need to know the things he was studying in books now? Did French and Latin and Shakespeare make people wise and happy? Jap Logan never went beyond the seventh grade and he was happy. And Jimboy never attended school much either. Maybe school didn't matter. Yet to get a good job you had to be smart—and white, too. That was the trouble, you had to be white!

"But I want to learn!" thought Sandy as he lay awake in the dark after he had gone to bed at night. "I want to go to college. I want to go to Europe and study. 'Work and make ready and maybe your chance will come,' it said under the picture of Lincoln on the calendar given away by the First National Bank, where Earl, his white friend, already had a job promised him when he came out of school. . . . It was not nearly so difficult for white boys. They could work at anything—in stores, on newspapers, in offices. They could become president of the United States if they were clever enough. But a colored boy. . . . No wonder Buster was going to pass for white when he left Stanton.

"I don't blame him," thought Sandy. "Sometimes I hate white people, too, like Aunt Harrie used to say she did. Still, some of them are pretty decent—my English-teacher, and Mr. Prentiss where I work. Yet even Mr. Prentiss wouldn't give me a job clerking in his shop. All I can do there is run errands and scrub the floor when everybody else is gone. There's no advancement for colored fellows. If they start as porters, they stay porters for ever and they can't come up. Being colored is like being born in the basement of life, with the door to the light locked and barred—and the white folks live upstairs. They don't want us up there with them, even when we're respectable like Dr. Mitchell, or smart like Dr. Du Bois. . . . And guys like Jap Logan—well, Jap don't care anyway! Maybe it's best not to care, and stay poor and meek waiting for heaven like Aunt Hager did. . . . But I don't want heaven! I want to live first!" Sandy thought. "I want to live!"

He understood then why many old Negroes said: "Take all this world and give me Jesus!" It was because they couldn't get this world anyway—it belonged to the white folks. They alone had the power to give or withhold at their back doors. Always back doors—even for Tempy and Dr. Mitchell if they chose to go into Wright's Hotel or the New Albert Restaurant. And no door at all for Negroes if they wanted to attend the Rialto Theatre, or join the Stanton Y.M.C.A., or work behind the grilling at the National Bank.

The Doors of Life. . . . God damn that simple-minded book that Tempy had given him! What did an old white minister know about the doors of life for him and Pansetta and Jimmy Lane, for Willie-Mae and Buster and Jap Logan and all the black and brown and yellow youngsters standing on the threshold of the great beginning in a Western town called Stanton? What did an old white minister know about the doors of life anywhere?

And, least of all, the doors to a Negro's life? . . . Black youth. . . . Dark hands knocking, knocking! Pansetta's little brown hands knocking on the doors of life! Baby-doll hands, tiny autumn-leaf girl-hands! . . . Gee, Pansetta! The Doors of Life . . . the great big doors. . . . Sandy was asleep . . . of life.

Twenty-seven

Beware of Women

"I won't permit it," said Tempy. "I won't stand for it. You'll have to mend your ways, young man! Spending your evenings in Windsor's pool parlor and running the streets with a gang of common boys that have had no raising, that Jimmy Lane among them. I won't stand for it while you stay in my house. . . . But that's not the worst of it. Mr. Prentiss tells me you've been getting to work late after school three times this week. And what have you been doing? O, don't think I don't know! I saw you with my own eyes yesterday walking home with that girl Pansetta Young! . . . Well, I want you to understand that I won't have it!"

"I didn't walk home with her," said Sandy. "I only go part way with her every day. She's in my class in high school and we have to talk over our lessons. She's the only colored kid in my class I have to talk to."

"Lessons! Yes, I know it's lessons," said Tempy sarcastically. "If she were a girl of our own kind, it would be all right. I don't see why you don't associate more with the young people of the church. Marie Steward or Grace Mitchell are both nice girls and you don't notice them. No, you have to take up with this Pansetta, whose mother works out all day, leaving her daughter to do as she chooses. Well, she's not going to ruin you, after all I've done to try to make something out of you."

"Beware of women, son," said Mr. Siles pontifically from his deep morris-chair. It was one of his few evenings home and Tempy had asked him to talk to her nephew, who had gotten beyond her control, for Sandy no longer remained in at night even when she expressly commanded it; and he no longer attended church regularly, but slept on Sunday mornings instead. He kept up his school-work, it was true, but he seemed to have lost all interest in acquiring the respectable bearing and attitude towards life that Tempy thought he should have. She bought him fine clothes and he went about with ruffians.

"In other words, he has been acting just like a nigger, Mr. Siles!" she told her husband. "And he's taken up with a girl who's not of the best, to say the least, even if she does go to the high school. Mrs. Francis Cannon, who lives near her, tells me that this Pansetta has boys at her house all the time, and her mother is never at home until after dark. She's a cook or something somewhere. . . . A fine person for a nephew of ours to associate with, this Pansy daughter of hers!"

"Pansetta's a nice girl," said Sandy. "And she's smart in school, too. She helps me get my Latin every day, and I might fail if she didn't."

"Huh! It's little help you need with your Latin, young man! Bring it here and I'll help you. I had Latin when I was in school. And certainly you don't need to walk on the streets with her in order to study Latin, do you? First thing you know you'll be getting in trouble with her and she'll be having a baby—I see I have to be plain—and whether it's yours or not, she'll say it is. Common girls like that always want to marry a boy they think is going to amount to something—going to college and be somebody in the world. Besides, you're from the Williams family and you're good-looking! But I'm going to stop this affair right now. . . . From now on you are to leave that girl alone, do you understand me? She's dangerous!"

"Yes," grunted Mr. Siles. "She's dangerous."

Angry and confused, Sandy left the room and went upstairs to bed, but he could not sleep. What right had they to talk that way about his friends? Besides, what did they mean about her being dangerous? About his getting in trouble with her? About her wanting to marry him because her mother was a cook and he was going to college?

A white boy in Sandy's high-school class had "got in trouble" with an Italian girl and they had had to go to the juvenile court to fix it up, but it had been kept quiet. Even now Sandy couldn't quite give an exact explanation of what getting in trouble with a girl meant. Did a girl have to have a baby just because a fellow walked home with her when he didn't even go in? Pansetta had asked him into her house often, but he always had to go back uptown to work. He was due at work at four o'clock—besides he knew it wasn't quite correct to call on a young lady if her mother was not at home. But it wasn't necessarily bad, was it? And how could a girl have a baby and say it was his if it wasn't his? Why couldn't he talk to his Aunt Tempy about such things and get a clear and simple answer instead of being given an old book like *The Doors of Life* that didn't explain anything at all?

Pansetta hadn't said a word to him about babies, or anything like that, but she let him kiss her once and hold her on his lap at Sadie Butler's Christmas party. Gee, but she could kiss—and such a long time! He wouldn't care if she did make him marry her, only he wanted to travel first. If his mother would send for him now, he would like to go to

Chicago. His Aunt Tempy was too cranky, and too proper. She didn't like any of his friends, and she hated the pool hall. But where else was there for a fellow to play? Who wanted to go to those high-toned people's houses, like the Mitchells', and look bored all the time while they put Caruso's Italian records on their new victrola? Even if it was the finest victrola owned by a Negro in Stanton, as they always informed you, Sandy got tired of listening to records in a language that none of them understood.

"But this is opera!" they said. Well, maybe it was, but he thought that his father and Harriett used to sing better. And they sang nicer songs. One of them was:

> Love, O love, O careless love—
> Goes to your head like wine!

"And maybe I really am in love with Pansetta. . . . But if she thinks she can fool me into marrying her before I've travelled all around the world, like my father, she's wrong," Sandy thought. "She can't trick me, not this kid!" Then he was immediately sorry that he had allowed Tempy's insinuations to influence his thoughts.

"Pretty, baby-faced Pansetta! Why, she wouldn't try to trick anybody into anything. If she wanted me to love her, she'd let me, but she wouldn't try to trick a fellow. She wouldn't let me love her that way anyhow—like Tempy meant. Gee, that was ugly of Aunt Tempy to say that! . . . But Buster said she would. . . . Aw, he always talked that way about girls! He said no women were any good—as if he knew! And Jimmy Lane said white women were worse than colored—but all the boys who worked at hotels said that."

Let 'em talk! Sandy liked Pansetta anyhow. . . . But maybe his Aunt Tempy was right! Maybe he had better stop walking home with her. He didn't want to "get in trouble" and not be able to travel to Chicago some time, where his mother was. Maybe he could go to Chicago next summer if he began to save his money now. He wanted to see the big city, where the buildings were like towers, the trains ran overhead, and the lake was like a sea. He didn't want to "get in trouble" with Pansetta even if he did like her. Besides, he had to live with Tempy for awhile yet and he hated to be quarrelling with his aunt all the time. He'd stop going to the pool hall so much and stay home at night and study. . . . But, heck! it was too beautiful out of doors to stay in the house—especially since spring had come!

Through his open window, as he lay in bed after Tempy's tirade about the girl, he could see the stars and the tops of the budding maple-trees. A cool earth-smelling breeze lifted the white curtains, scattering the geometry papers that he had left lying on his study table. He got out of bed to pick up the papers and put them away, and stood for a moment in his pyjamas looking out of the window at the roofs of the houses and the tops of the trees under the night sky.

"I wish I had a brother," Sandy thought as he stood there. "Maybe I could talk to him about things and I wouldn't have to think so much. It's no fun being the only kid in the family, and your father never home either. . . . When I get married, I'm gonna have a lot of children; then they won't have to grow up by themselves."

The next day after school he walked nearly home with Pansetta as usual, although he was still thinking of what Tempy had said, but he hadn't decided to obey his aunt yet. At the corner of the block in which the girl lived, he gave her her books.

"I got to beat it back to the shop now. Old man Prentiss'll have a dozen deliveries waiting for me just because I'm late."

"All right," said Pansetta in her sweet little voice. "I'm sorry you can't come on down to my house awhile. Say, why don't you work at the hotel, anyway? Wouldn't you make more money there?"

"Guess I would," replied the boy. "But my aunt thinks it's better where I am."

"Oh," said Pansetta. "Well, I saw Jimmy Lane last night and he's making lots of money at the hotel. He wanted to meet me around to school this afternoon, but I told him no. I said you took me home."

"I do," said Sandy.

"Yes," laughed Pansetta; "but I didn't tell him you wouldn't ever come in."

During the sunny spring weeks that followed, Sandy did not walk home with her any more after school. Having to go to work earlier was the excuse he gave, but at first Pansetta seemed worried and puzzled. She asked him if he was mad at her, or something, but he said he wasn't. Then in a short time other boys were meeting her on the corner near the school, buying her cones when the ice-cream wagon passed and taking her home in the afternoons. To see other fellows buying her ice-cream and walking home with her made Sandy angry, but it was his own fault, he thought. And he felt lonesome having no one to walk with after classes.

Pansetta, in school, was just as pleasant as before, but in a kind of impersonal way, as though she hadn't been his girl once. And now Sandy was worried, because it had been easy to drop her, but would it be easy to get her back again if he should want her? The hotel boys had money, and once or twice he saw her talking with Jimmy Lane. Gee, but she looked pretty in her thin spring dresses and her wide straw hat.

Why had he listened to Tempy at all? She didn't know Pansetta, and just because her mother worked out in service she wanted him to snub the girl. What was that to be afraid of—her mother not being home after school? Even if Pansetta would let him go in the house with her and put his arms around her and love her, why shouldn't he? Didn't he have a right to have a girl like that, as well as the other fellows? Didn't he have a right to be free with women, too, like all the rest of the young men? . . . But Pansetta wasn't that kind of girl! . . . What made his mind run away with him? Because of what Tempy had said? . . . To hell with Tempy!

"She's just an old-fashioned darky Episcopalian, that's what Tempy is! And she wanted me to drop Pansetta because her mother doesn't belong to the Dunbar Whist Club. Gee, but I'm ashamed of myself. I'm a cad and a snob, that's all I am, and I'm going to apologize." Subconsciously he was living over a scene from an English novel he had read at the printing-shop, in which the Lord dropped the Squire's daughter for a great Lady, but later returned to his first love. Sandy retained the words "cad" and "snob" in his vocabulary, but he wasn't thinking of the novel now. He really believed, after three weeks of seeing Pansetta walking with other boys, that he had done wrong, and that Tempy was the villainess in the situation. It was worrying him a great deal; he decided to make up with Pansetta if he could.

One Friday afternoon she left school with a great armful of books. They had to write an English composition for Monday and she had taken some volumes from the school library for reference. He might have offered to carry them for her, but he hadn't. Instead he went to work—and there had been no other colored boys on the corner waiting for her as she went out. Now he could have kicked himself for his neglect, he thought, as he cleaned the rear room of Mr. Prentiss's gift-card shop. Suddenly he dropped the broom with which he was sweeping, grabbed his cap, and left the place, for the desire to make friends with Pansetta possessed him more fiercely than ever, and he no longer cared about his work.

"I'm going to see her right now," he thought, "before I go home to supper. Gee, but I'm ashamed of the way I've treated her."

On the way to Pansetta's house the lawns looked fresh and green and on some of them tulips were blooming. The late afternoon sky was aglow with sunset. Little boys were out in the streets with marbles and tops, and little girls were jumping rope on the sidewalks. Workmen were coming home, empty dinner-pails in their hands, and a band of Negro laborers passed Sandy, singing softly together.

"I must hurry," the boy thought. "It will soon be our supper-time." He ran until he was at Pansetta's house—then came the indecision: Should he go in? Or not go in? He was ashamed of his treatment of her and embarrassed. Should he go on by as if he had not meant to call? Suppose she shut the door in his face! Or, worse, suppose she asked him to stay awhile! Should he stay? What Tempy had said didn't matter any more. He wanted to be friends with Pansetta again. He wanted her to know he still liked her and wanted to walk home with her. But how could he say it? Had she seen him from the window? Maybe he could turn around and go back, and see her Monday at school.

"No! I'm not a coward," he declared. "Afraid of a girl! I'll walk right up on the front porch and knock!" But the small house looked very quiet and the lace curtains were tightly drawn together at the windows . . . . He knocked again. Maybe there was no one home. . . . Yes, he heard somebody.

Finally Pansetta peeped through the curtains of the glass in the front door. Then she opened the door and smiled surprisingly, her hair mussed and her creamy-brown skin pink from the warm blood pulsing just under the surface. Her eyes were dark and luminous, and her lips were moist and red.

"It's Sandy!" she said, turning to address someone inside the front room.

"O, come in, old man," a boy's voice called in a tone of forced welcome, and Sandy saw Jimmy Lane sitting on the couch adjusting his collar self-consciously. "How's everything, old scout?"

"All right," Sandy stammered. "Say, Pansy, I—I—Do you know — I mean, what is the subject we're supposed to write on for English Monday? I must of forgotten to take it down."

"Why, 'A Trip to Shakespeare's England.' That's easy to remember, silly. You must have been asleep. . . . Won't you sit down?"

"No, thanks, I've—I guess I got to get back to supper."

"Jesus!" cried Jimmy jumping up from the sofa. "Is it that late? I'm due on bells at six o'clock. Wait a minute, Sandy, and I'll walk up with you as far as the hotel. Boy, I'm behind time!" He picked up his coat from the floor, and Pansetta held it for him while he thrust his arms into the sleeves, glancing around meanwhile for his cap, which lay among the sofa-pillows. Then he kissed the girl carelessly on the lips as he slid one arm familiarly around her waist.

"So long, baby," he said, and the two boys went out. On the porch Jimmy lit a cigarette and passed the pack to Sandy.

Jimmy Lane looked and acted as if he were much older than his companion, but Jimmy had been out of school several years, and hopping bells taught a fellow a great deal more about life than books did—and also about women. Besides, he was supporting himself now, which gave him an air of independence that boys who still lived at home didn't have.

When they had walked about a block, the bell-boy said carelessly: "Pansetta can go! Can't she, man?"

"I don't know," said Sandy.

"Aw, boy, you're lying," Jimmy Lane returned. "Don't try to hand me that kid stuff! You had her for a year, didn't you?"

"Yes," replied Sandy slowly, "but not like you mean."

"Stop kidding," Jimmy insisted.

"No, honest, I never touched her that way," the boy said. "I never was at her house before."

Jimmy opened his mouth astonished. "What!" he exclaimed. "And her old lady out working till eight and nine every night! Say, Sandy, we're friends, but you're either just a big liar—or else a God-damn fool!" He threw his cigarette away and put both hands in his pockets. "Pansetta's easy as hell, man!"

Twenty-eight

Chicago

Chicago, Ill.
May 16, 1918

Dear Sandy:

Have just come home from work and am very tired but thought I would write you this letter right now while I had time and wasn't sleepy. You are a big boy and I think you can be of some help to me. I don't want you to stay in Stanton any longer as a burden on your Aunt Tempy. She says in her letters you have begun to stay out late nights and not pay her any mind. You ought to be with your mother now because you are all she has since I do not know what has happened to your father in France. The war is awful and so many mens are getting killed. Have not had no word from Jimboy for 7 months from Over There and am worried till I'm sick. Will try and send you how much money you need for your fare before the end of the month so when school is out in june you can come. Let me know how much you saved and I will send you the rest to come to Chicago because Mr. Harris where I stay is head elevator man at a big hotel in the Loop and he says he can put you on there in July. That will be a good job for you and maybe by saving your money you can go back to school in Sept. I will help you if I can but you will have to help me too because I have not been doing so well. Am working for a colored lady in her hair dressing parlor and am learning hairdressing myself, shampoo and straighten and give massauges on the face and all. But colored folks are hard people to work for. Madam King is from down south somewhere and these southern Negroes are not like us in their ways, but she seems to like me. Mr. Harris is from the south too in a place called Baton Rouge. They eat rice all the time. Well I must close hoping to see you soon once more because it has been five years since I have looked at my child. With love to you and Tempy, be a good boy,

Your mother,
Annjelica Rogers.

A week later another letter came to Sandy from his mother. This time it was a registered special-delivery, which said: "If you'll come right away you can get your job at once. Mr. Harris says he will have a vacancy Saturday because one of the elevator boys are quitting." And sufficient bills to cover Sandy's fare tumbled out.

With a tremendous creaking and grinding and steady clacking of wheels the long train went roaring through the night towards Chicago as Sandy, in a day coach, took from his pocket Annjee's two letters and re-read them for the tenth time since leaving Stanton. He could hardly believe himself actually at that moment on the way to Chicago!

In the stuffy coach papers littered the floor and the scent of bananas and human feet filled the car. The lights were dim and most of the passengers slumbered in the straight-backed green-plush seats, but Sandy was still awake. The thrill of his first all-night rail journey and his dream-expectations of the great city were too much to allow a sixteen-year-old boy to go calmly to sleep, although the man next to him had long been snoring.

Annjee's special-delivery letter had come that morning. Sandy had discovered it when he came home for lunch, and upon his return to the high school for the afternoon classes he went at once to the principal to inquire if he might be excused from the remaining days of the spring term.

"Let me see! Your record's pretty good, isn't it, Rogers?" said Professor Perkins looking over his glasses at the young colored fellow standing before him. "Going to Chicago, heh? Well, I guess we can let you transfer and give you full credit for this year's work without your waiting here for the examinations—there are only ten days or so of the term remaining. You are an honor student and would get through your exams all right. Now, if you'll just send us your address when you get to Chicago, we'll see that you get your report. . . . Intending to go to school there, are you? . . . That's right! I like to see your people get ahead. . . . Well, good luck to you, James." The old gentleman rose and held out his hand.

"Good old scout," thought Sandy. "Miss Fry was a good teacher, too! Some white folks *are* nice all right! Not all of them are mean. . . . Gee, old man Prentiss hated to see me quit his place. Said I was the best boy he ever had working there, even if I was late once in awhile. But I don't mind leaving Stanton. Gee, Chicago ought to be great! And I'm sure glad to get away from Tempy's house. She's too tight!"

But Tempy had not been glad to see her nephew leave. She had grown fond of the boy in spite of her almost nightly lectures to him recently on his behavior and in spite of his never having become her model youth. Not that he was bad, but he might have been so much better! She wanted to show her white neighbors a perfect colored boy—and such a boy certainly wouldn't be a user of slang, a lover of pool halls and non-Episcopalian ways. Tempy had given Sandy every opportunity to move in the best colored society and he had not taken advantage of it. Nevertheless, she cried a little as she packed a lunch for him to eat on the train. She had done all she could. He was a good-looking boy, and quite smart. Now, if he wanted to go to his mother, well—"I can only hope Chicago won't ruin you," she said. "It's a wicked city! Goodbye, James. Remember what I've tried to teach you. Stand up straight and look like you're somebody!"

Stanton, Sandy's Kansas home, was back in the darkness, and the train sped towards the great center where all the small-town boys in the whole Middle West wanted to go.

"I'm going now!" thought Sandy. "Chicago now!"

A few weeks past he had gone to see Sister Johnson, who was quite feeble with the rheumatism. As she sat in the corner of her kitchen smoking a corn-cob pipe, no longer able to wash clothes, but still able to keep up a rapid flow of conversation, she told him all the news.

"Tom, he's still at de bank keepin' de furnace goin' and sort o' handy man. . . . Willie-Mae, I 'spects you knows, is figurin' on gettin' married next month to Mose Jenkins, an' I tells her she better stay single, young as she is, but she ain't payin' me no mind. Umn-unh! Jest let her go on! . . . Did you heerd Sister Whiteside's daughter done brought her third husband home to stay wid her ma—an' five o' her first husband's chillens there too? Gals ain't got no regard for de old folks. Sister Whiteside say if she warn't a Christian in her heart she don't believe she could stand it! . . . I tells Willie-Mae she better not bring no husbands here to stay wid me—do an' I'll run him out! These mens ought be shame o' demselves comin' livin' on de womenfolks."

As the old woman talked, Sandy, thinking of his grandmother, gazed out of the window towards the house next door, where he had lived with Aunt Hager. Some small children were playing in the back yard, running and yelling. They belonged to the Southern family to whom Tempy had rented the place. . . . Madam de Carter, who still owned the second house, had been made a national grand officer in the women's division of the lodge and many of the members of the order now had on the walls of their homes a large picture of her dressed in full regalia, inscribed: "Yours in His Grace," and signed: "Madam Fannie Rosalie de Carter."

"Used to be just plain old Rose Carter befo' she got so important," said Sister Johnson, explaining her neighbor's lengthy name. "All these womens dey mammy named Jane an' Mary an' Cora, soon's dey gets a little somethin', dey changes dey names to Janette or Mariana or Corina or somethin' mo' flowery then what dey had. Willie-Mae say she gwine change her'n to Willetta-Mayola, an' I tole her if she do, I'll beat her—don't care how old she is!"

Sandy liked to listen to the rambling talk of old colored folks. "I guess there won't be many like that in Chicago," he thought, as he doubled back his long legs under the green-plush seat of the day coach. "I better try to get to sleep—there's a long ways to go until morning."

Although it was not yet June, the heat was terrific when, with the old bags that Tempy had given him, Sandy got out of the dusty train in Chicago and walked the length of the sheds into the station. He caught sight of his mother waiting in the crowd, a fatter and much older woman than he had remembered her to be; and at first she didn't know him among the stream of people coming from the train. Perhaps, unconsciously, she was looking for the little boy she left in Stanton; but Sandy was taller than Annjee now and he looked quite a young man in his blue serge suit with long trousers. His mother threw both plump arms around him and hugged and kissed him for a long time.

They went uptown in the street-cars, Annjee a trifle out of breath from helping with the bags, and both of them perspiring freely from the heat. And they were not very talkative either. A strange and unexpected silence seemed to come between them. Annjee had been away from her son for five growing years and he was no longer her baby boy, small and eager for a kiss. She could see from the little cuts on his face that he had even begun to shave on the chin. And his voice was like a man's, deep and musical as Jimboy's, but not so sure of itself.

But Sandy was not thinking of his mother as they rode uptown on the street-car. He was looking out of the windows at the blocks of dirty grey warehouses lining the streets through which they were passing. He hadn't expected the great city to be monotonous and ugly like this and he was vaguely disappointed. No towers, no dreams come true! Where were the thrilling visions of grandeur he had held? Hidden in the dusty streets? Hidden in the long, hot alleys through which he could see at a distance the tracks of the elevated trains?

"Street-cars are slower, but I ain't got used to them air lines yet," said Annjee, searching her mind for something to say. "I always think maybe them elevated cars'll fall off o' there sometimes. They go so fast!"

"I believe I'd rather ride on them, though," said Sandy, as he looked at the monotonous box-like tenements and dismal alleys on the ground level. No trees, no yards, no grass such as he had known at home, and yet, on the other hand, no bigness or beauty about the bleak warehouses and sorry shops that hugged the sidewalk. Soon, however, the street began to take on a racial aspect and to become more darkly alive. Negroes leaned from windows with heads uncombed, or sat fanning in doorways with legs apart, talking in kimonos and lounging in overalls, and more and more they became a part of the passing panorama.

"This is State Street," said Annjee. "They call it the Black Belt. We have to get off in a minute. You got your suit-case?"

She rang the bell and at Thirty-seventh Street they walked over to Wabash Avenue. The cool shade of the tiny porch that Annjee mounted was more than welcome, and as she took out her key to unlock the front door, Sandy sat on the steps and mopped his forehead with a grimy handkerchief. Inside, there was a dusky gloom in the hallway, that smelled of hair-oil and cabbage steaming.

"Guess Mis' Harris is in the kitchen," said Annjee. "Come on—we'll go upstairs and I'll show you our room. I guess we can both stay together till we can do better. You're still little enough to sleep with your mother, ain't you?"

They went down the completely dark hall on the second floor, and his mother opened a door that led into a rear room with two windows looking out into the alley, giving an extremely near view of the elevated structure on which a downtown train suddenly rushed past with an ear-splitting roar that made the entire house tremble and the window-sashes rattle. There was a wash-stand with a white bowl and pitcher in the room, Annjee's trunk, a chair, and a brass bed, covered with a fresh spread and starched pillow-covers in honor of Sandy's arrival.

"See," said Annjee. "There's room enough for us both, and we'll be saving rent. There's no closet, but we can drive a few extra nails behind the door. And with the two windows we can get plenty of air these hot nights."

"It's nice, mama," Sandy said, but he had to repeat his statement twice, because another L train thundered past so that he couldn't hear his own words as he uttered them. "It's awful nice, mama!"

He took off his coat and sat down on the trunk between the two windows. Annjee came over and kissed him, rubbing her hand across his crinkly brown hair.

"Well, you're a great big boy now. . . . Mama's baby—in long pants. And you're handsome, just like your father!" She had Jimboy's picture stuck in a corner of the wash-stand—a postcard photo in his army uniform, in which he looked very boyish and proud, sent from the training-camp before his company went to France. "But I got no time to be setting here petting you, Sandy, even if you have just come. I got to get on back to the hairdressing-parlor to make some money."

So Annjee went to work again—as she had been off only long enough to meet the train—and Sandy lay down on the bed and slept the hot afternoon away. That evening as a treat they had supper at a restaurant, where Annjee picked carefully from the cheap menu so that their bill wouldn't be high.

"But don't think this is regular. We can't afford it," she said. "I bring things home and fix them on an oil-stove in the room and spread papers on the trunk for a table. A restaurant supper's just in honor of you."

When they came back to the house that evening, Sandy was introduced to Mrs. Harris, their landlady, and to her husband, the elevator-starter, who was to give him the job at the hotel.

"That's a fine-looking boy you got there, Mis' Rogers," he said, appraising Sandy. "He'll do pretty well for one of them main lobby cars, since we don't use nothing but first-class intelligent help down where I am, like I told you. And we has only the best class o' white folks stoppin' there, too. . . . Be up at six in the mornin', buddy, and I'll take you downtown with me."

Annjee was tired, so they went upstairs to the back room and lit the gas over the bed, but the frequent roar of the L trains prevented steady conversation and made Sandy jump each time that the long chain of cars thundered by. He hadn't yet become accustomed to them, or to the vast humming of the city, which was strange to his small-town ears. And he wanted to go out and look around a bit, to walk up and down the streets at night and see what they were like.

"Well, go on if you want to," said his mother, "but don't forget this house number. I'm gonna lie down, but I guess I'll be awake when you come back. Or somebody'll be setting on the porch and the door'll be open."

At the corner Sandy stopped and looked around to be sure of his bearings when he returned. He marked in his mind the sign-board advertising CHESTERFIELDS and the frame-house with the tumble-down stairs on the outside. In the street some kids were playing hopscotch under the arc-light. Somebody stopped beside him.

"Nice evening?" said a small yellow man with a womanish kind of voice, smiling at Sandy.

"Yes," said the boy, starting across the street, but the stranger followed him, offering Pall Malls. He smelled of perfume, and his face looked as though it had been powdered with white talcum as he lit a tiny pocket-lighter.

"Stranger?" murmured the soft voice, lighting Sandy's cigarette.

"I'm from Stanton," he replied, wishing the man had not chosen to walk with him.

"Ah, Kentucky," exclaimed the perfumed fellow. "I been down there. Nice women in that town, heh?"

"But it's not Kentucky," Sandy objected. "It's Kansas."

"Oh, out west where the girls are raring to go! I know! Just like wild horses out there—so passionate, aren't they?"

"I guess so," Sandy ventured. The powdered voice was softly persistent.

"Say, kid," it whispered smoothly, touching the boy's arm, "listen, I got some swell French pictures up in my room—naked women and everything! Want to come up and see them?"

"No," said Sandy quickening his pace. "I got to go somewhere."

"But I room right around the corner," the voice insisted. "Come on by. You're a nice kid, you know it? Listen, don't walk so fast. Stop, let me talk to you."

But Sandy was beginning to understand. A warm sweat broke out on his neck and forehead. Sometimes, at the pool hall in Stanton, he had heard the men talk about queer fellows who stopped boys in the streets and tried to coax them to their rooms.

"He thinks I'm dumb," thought Sandy, "but I'm wise to him!" Yet he wondered what such men did with the boys who accompanied them. Curious, he'd like to find out—but he was afraid; so at the next corner he turned and started rapidly towards State Street, but the queer fellow kept close beside him, begging.

" . . . and we'll have a nice time. . . . I got wine in the room, if you want some, and a vic, too."

"Get away, will you!"

They had reached State Street where the lights were bright and people were passing all the time. Sandy could see the fellow's anxious face quite clearly now.

"Listen, kid . . . you . . ."

But suddenly the man was no longer beside him—for Sandy commenced to run. On the brightly lighted avenue panic seized him. He had to escape this powdered face at his shoulder. The whining voice made him sick inside—and, almost without knowing it, his legs began swerving swiftly between the crowds along the curb. When he stopped in front of the Monogram Theatre, two blocks away, he was freed of his companion.

"Gee, that's nice," panted Sandy, grinning as he stood looking at the pictures in front of the vaudeville house, while hundreds of dark people passed up and down on the sidewalk behind him. Lots of folks were going into the theatre, laughing and pushing, for one of the great blues-singing Smiths was appearing there. Sandy walked towards the ticket-booth to see what the prices were.

"Buy me a ticket, will you?" said a feminine voice beside him. This time it was a girl—a very ugly, skinny girl, whose smile revealed a row of dirty teeth.

She sidled up to the startled boy whom she had accosted and took his hand.

"I'm not going in," Sandy said shortly, as he backed away, wiping the palm of his hand on his coat-sleeve.

"All right then, stingy!" hissed the girl, flouncing her hips and digging into her own purse for the coins to buy a ticket. "I got money."

Some men standing on the edge of the sidewalk laughed as Sandy went up the street. A little black child in front of him toddled along in the crowd, seemingly by itself, licking a big chocolate ice-cream cone that dripped down the front of its dress.

So this was Chicago where the buildings were like towers and the lake was like a sea . . . State Street, the greatest Negro street in the world, where people were always happy, lights for ever bright; and where the prettiest brown-skin women on earth could be found—so the men in Stanton said.

"I guess I didn't walk the right way. But maybe tomorrow I'll see other things," Sandy thought, "the Loop and the lake and the museum and the library. Maybe they'll be better."

He turned into a side street going back towards Wabash Avenue. It was darker there, and near the alley a painted woman called him, stepping out from among the shadows.

"Say, baby, com'ere!" But the boy went on.

Crossing overhead an L train thundered by, flashing its flow of yellow light on the pavement beneath.

Sandy turned into Wabash Avenue and cut across the street. As he approached the colored Y.M.C.A., three boys came out with swimming suits on their arms, and one of them said: "Damn, but it's hot!" They went up the street laughing and talking with friendly voices, and at the corner they turned off.

"I must be nearly home," Sandy thought, as he made out a group of kids still playing under the street-light. Then he distinguished, among the other shabby buildings, the brick house where he lived. The front porch was still crowded with roomers trying to keep cool, and as the boy came up to the foot of the steps, some of the fellows seated there moved to let him pass.

"Good-evenin', Mr. Rogers," Mrs. Harris called, and as Sandy had never been called Mr. Rogers before, it made him feel very manly and a little embarrassed as he threaded his way through the group on the porch.

Upstairs he found his mother sleeping deeply on one side of the bed. He undressed, keeping on his underwear, and crawled in on the other side, but he lay awake a long while because it was suffocatingly hot, and very close in their room. The bed-bugs bit him on the legs. Every time he got half asleep, an L train roared by, shrieking outside their open windows, lighting up the room, and shaking the whole house. Each time the train came, he started and trembled as though a sudden dragon were rushing at the bed. But then, after midnight, when the elevated cars passed less frequently, and he became more used to their passing, he went to sleep.

Twenty-nine

Elevator

The following day Sandy went to work as elevator-boy at the hotel in the Loop where Mr. Harris was head bellman, and during the hot summer months that followed, his life in Chicago gradually settled into a groove of work and home—work, and home to Annjee's stuffy little room against the elevated tracks, where at night his mother read the war news and cried because there had been no letter from Jimboy. Whether Sandy's father was in Brest or Saint-Lazare with the labor battalions, or at the front, she did not know. The *Chicago Defender* said that colored troops were fighting in the Champagne sector with great distinction, but Annjee cried anew when she read that.

"No news is good news," Sandy repeated every night to comfort his mother, for he couldn't imagine Jimboy dead. "Papa's all right!" But Annjee worried and wept, half sick all the time, for ever reading the death lists fearfully for her husband's name.

That summer the heat was unbearable. Uptown in the Black Belt the air was like a steaming blanket around your head. In the Loop the sky was white-hot metal. Even on the lake front there was no relief unless you hurried into the crowded water. And there were long stretches of beach where the whites did not want Negroes to swim; so it was often dangerous to bathe if you were colored.

Sandy sweltered as he stood at the door of his box-like, mirrored car in the big hotel lobby. He wore a red uniform with brass buttons and a tight coat that had to be kept fastened no matter how warm it was. But he felt very proud of himself holding his first full-time job, helping his mother with the room rent, and trying to save a little money out of each pay in order to return to high school in the fall.

The prospects of returning to school, however, were not bright. Some weeks it was impossible for Sandy to save even a half-dollar. And Annjee said now that she believed he should stay out of school and work to take care of himself, since he was as large as a man and had more education already than she'd had at his age. Aunt Hager would not have felt that way, though, Sandy thought, remembering his grandmother's great ambition for him. But Annjee was different, less far-seeing than her mother had been, less full of hopes for her son, not ambitious about him—caring only for the war and Jimboy.

At the hotel Sandy's hours on duty were long, and his legs and back ached with weariness from standing straight in one spot all the time, opening and closing the bronze door of the elevator. He had been assigned the last car in a row of six, each manned by a colored youth standing inside his metal box in a red uniform, operating the lever that sent the car up from the basement grill to the roof-garden restaurant on the fifteenth floor and then back down again all day. Repeating up-down—up-down—up-down interminably, carrying white guests.

After two months of this there were times when Sandy felt as though he could stand it no longer. The same flow of people week after week—fashionable women, officers, business men; the fetid air of the elevator-shaft, heavy with breath and the perfume of bodies; the same doors opening at the same unchanging levels hundreds of times each innumerable, monotonous day. The L in the morning; the L again at night. The street or the porch for a few minutes of air. Then bed. And the same thing tomorrow.

"I've got to get out of this," Sandy thought. "It's an awful job." Yet some of the fellows had been there for years. Three of the elevator-men on Sandy's shift were more than forty years old—and had never gotten ahead in life. Mr. Harris had been a bell-hop since his boyhood, doing the same thing day after day—and now he was very proud of being head bell-boy in Chicago.

"I've got to get out of this," Sandy kept repeating. "Or maybe I'll get stuck here, too, like they are, and never get away. I've got to go back to school."

Yet he knew that his mother was making very little money—serving more or less as an apprentice in the hairdressing-shop, trying to learn the trade. And if he quit work, how would he live? Annjee did not favor his returning to school. And could he study if he were hungry? Could he study if he were worried about having no money? Worried about Annjee's displeasure?

"Yes! I can!" he said. "I'm going to study!" He thought about Booker Washington sleeping under the wooden pavements at Richmond—because he had had no place to stay on his way to Hampton in search of an education. He thought about Frederick Douglass—a fugitive slave, owning not even himself, and yet a student. "If they could study, I can, too! When school opens, I'm going to quit this job. Maybe I can get another one at night or in the late afternoon—but it doesn't matter—I'm going back to my classes in September. . . . I'm through with elevators."

Jimboy! Jimboy! Like Jimboy! something inside him warned, quitting work with no money, uncaring.

"Not like Jimboy," Sandy countered against himself. "Not like my father, always wanting to go somewhere. I'd get as tired of travelling all the time, as I do of running this elevator up and down day after day. . . . I'm more like Harriett—not wanting to be a servant at the mercies of white people for ever. . . . I want to do something for myself, by myself. . . . Free. . . . I want a house to live in, too, when I'm older—like Tempy's and Mr. Siles's. . . . But I wouldn't want to be like Tempy's friends—or her husband, dull and colorless, putting all his money away in a white bank, ashamed of colored people."

"A lot of minstrels—that's all niggers are!" Mr. Siles had said once. "Clowns, jazzers, just a band of dancers—that's why they never have anything. Never be anything but servants to the white people."

Clowns! Jazzers! Band of dancers! . . . Harriett! Jimboy! Aunt Hager! . . . A band of dancers! . . . Sandy remembered his grandmother whirling around in front of the altar at revival meetings in the midst of the other sisters, her face shining with light, arms outstretched as though all the cares of the world had been cast away; Harriett in the back yard under the apple-tree, eagle-rocking in the summer evenings to the tunes of the guitar; Jimboy singing. . . . But was that why Negroes were poor, because they were dancers, jazzers, clowns? . . . The other way round would be better: dancers because of their poverty; singers because they suffered; laughing all the time because they must forget. . . . It's more like that, thought Sandy.

A band of dancers. . . . Black dancers—captured in a white world. . . . Dancers of the spirit, too. Each black dreamer a captured dancer of the spirit. . . . Aunt Hager's dreams for Sandy dancing far beyond the limitations of their poverty, of their humble station in life, of their dark skins.

"I wants you to be a great man, son," she often told him, sitting on the porch in the darkness, singing, dreaming, calling up the deep past, creating dreams within the child. "I wants you to be a great man."

"And I won't disappoint you!" Sandy said that hot Chicago summer, just as though Hager were still there, planning for him. "I won't disappoint you!" he said, standing straight in his sweltering red suit in the cage of the hotel elevator. “I won’t disappoint you, Aunt Hager,” dreaming at night in the stuffy little room in the great Black Belt of Chicago. “I won’t disappoint you now,” opening his eyes at dawn when Annjee shook him to get up and go to work again.

Thirty

Princess of the Blues

One hot Monday in August Harrietta Williams, billed as "The Princess of the Blues," opened at the Monogram Theatre on State Street. The screen had carried a slide of her act the week previous, so Sandy knew she would be there, and he and his mother were waiting anxiously for her appearance. They were unable to find out before the performance where she would be living, or if she had arrived in town, but early that Monday evening Sandy hurried home from work, and he and Annjee managed to get seats in the theatre, although it was soon crowded to capacity and people stood in the aisles.

It was a typical Black Belt audience, laughing uproariously, stamping its feet to the music, kidding the actors, and joining in the performance, too. Rows of shiny black faces, gay white teeth, bobbing heads. Everybody having a grand time with the vaudeville, swift and amusing. A young tap-dancer rhymed his feet across the stage, grinning from ear to ear, stepping to the tantalizing music, ending with a series of intricate and amazing contortions that brought down the house. Then a sister act came on, with a stock of sentimental ballads offered in a wholly jazzy manner. They sang even a very melancholy mammy song with their hips moving gaily at every beat.

> O, what would I do
> Without dear you,
> Sweet mammy?

they moaned reverently, with their thighs shaking.

"Aw, step it, sweet gals!" the men and boys in the audience called approvingly. "We'll be yo' mammy and yo' pappy, too! Do it, pretty mamas!"

A pair of black-faced comedians tumbled on the stage as the girls went off, and began the usual line of old jokes and razor comedy.

"Gee, I wish Aunt Harriett's act would come on," Sandy said as he and Annjee laughed nervously at the comedians.

Finally the two blacked-up fellows broke into a song called *Walking the Dog,* flopping their long-toed shoes, twirling their middles like egg-beaters, and made their exit to a roar of laughter and applause. Then the canvas street-scene rose, disclosing a gorgeous background of blue velvet, with a piano and a floor-lamp in the centre of the stage.

"This is Harriett's part now," Sandy whispered excitedly as a tall, yellow, slick-headed young man came in and immediately began playing the piano. "And, mama, that's Billy Sanderlee!"

"Sure is!" said Annjee.

Suddenly the footlights were lowered and the spotlight flared, steadied itself at the right of the stage, and waited. Then, stepping out from among the blue curtains, Harriett entered in a dress of glowing orange, flame-like against the ebony of her skin, barbaric, yet beautiful as a jungle princess. She swayed towards the footlights, while Billy teased the keys of the piano into a hesitating delicate jazz. Then she began to croon a new song—a popular version of an old Negro melody, refashioned with words from Broadway.

"Gee, Aunt Harrie's prettier than ever!" Sandy exclaimed to his mother.

"Same old Harriett," said Annjee. "But kinder hoarse."

"Sings good, though," Sandy cried when Harriett began to snap her fingers, putting a slow, rocking pep into the chorus, rolling her bright eyes to the tune of the melody as the piano rippled and cried under Billy Sanderlee's swift fingers.

"She's the same Harrie," murmured Annjee.

When she appeared again, in an apron of blue calico, with a bandanna handkerchief knotted about her head, she walked very slowly. The man at the piano had begun to play blues—the old familiar folk-blues—and the audience settled into a receptive silence broken only by a "Lawdy! . . . Good Lawdy! Lawd!" from some southern lips at the back of the house, as Harriett sang:

> Red sun, red sun, why don't you rise today?
> Red sun, O sun! Why don't you rise today?
> Ma heart is breakin'—ma baby's gone away.

A few rows ahead of Annjee a woman cried out "True, Lawd!" and swayed her body.

> Little birds, little birds, ain't you gonna sing this morn?
> Says, little chirpin' birds, ain't you gonna sing this morn?
> I cannot sleep—ma lovin' man is gone.

"Whee-ee-e! . . . Hab mercy! . . . Moan it, gal!" exclamations and shouts broke loose in the understanding audience.

"Just like when papa used to play for her," said Sandy. But Annjee was crying, remembering Jimboy, and fumbling in her bag for a handkerchief. On the stage the singer went on—as though singing to herself—her voice sinking to a bitter moan as the listeners rocked and swayed.

> It's a mighty blue mornin' when yo' daddy leaves yo' bed.
> I says a blue, blue mornin' when yo' daddy leaves yo' bed—
> 'Cause if you lose yo' man, you'd just as well be dead!

Her final number was a dance-song which she sang in a sparkling dress of white sequins, ending the act with a mad collection of steps and a swift sudden whirl across the whole stage as the orchestra joined Billy's piano in a triumphant arch of jazz.

The audience yelled and clapped and whistled for more, stamping their feet and turning to one another with shouted comments of enjoyment.

"Gee! She's great," said Sandy. When another act finally had the stage after Harriett's encores, he was anxious to get back to the dressing-room to see her.

"Maybe they won't let us in," Annjee objected timidly.

"Let's try," Sandy insisted, pulling his mother up. "We don't want to hear this fat woman with the flag singing *Over There*. You'll start crying, anyhow. Come on, mama."

When they got backstage, they found Harriett standing in the dressing-room door laughing with one of the black-face comedians, a summer fur over her shoulders, ready for the street. Billy Sanderlee and the tap-dancing boy were drinking gin from a bottle that Billy held, and Harriett was holding her glass, when she saw Sandy coming.

Her furs slipped to the floor. "My Lord!" she cried, enveloping them in kisses. "What are you doing in Chicago, Annjee? My, I'm mighty glad to see you, Sandy! . . . I'm certainly surprised—and so happy I could cry. . . . Did you catch our act tonight? Can't Billy play the piano, though? . . . Great heavens! Sandy, you're twice as tall as me! When did you leave home? How's that long-faced sister o' mine, Tempy?"

After repeated huggings the new-comers were introduced to everybody around. Sandy noticed a certain harshness in his aunt's voice. "Smoking so much," she explained later. "Drinking, too, I guess. But a blues-singer's supposed to sing deep and hoarse, so it's all right."

Beyond the drop curtain Sandy could hear the audience laughing in the theatre, and occasionally somebody shouting at the performers.

"Come on! Let's go and get a bite to eat," Harriett suggested when they had finally calmed down enough to decide to move on. "Billy and me are always hungry. . . . Where's Jimboy, Annjee? In the war, I suppose! It'd be just like that big jigaboo to go and enlist first thing, whether he had to or not. Billy here was due to go, too, but licker kept him out. This white folk's war for democracy ain't so hot, nohow! . . . Say, how'd you like to have some chop suey instead of going to a regular restaurant?"

In a Chinese café they found a quiet booth, where the two sisters talked until past midnight—with Sandy and Billy silent for the most part. Harriett told Annjee about Aunt Hager's death and the funeral that chill rainy day, and how Tempy had behaved so coldly when it was all over.

"I left Stanton the week after," Harriett said, "and haven't been back since. Had hard times, too, but we're kinder lucky now, Billy and me—got some dates booked over the Orpheum circuit soon. Liable to get wind of us at the Palace on Broadway one o' these days. Can't tell! Things are breakin' pretty good for spade acts—since Jews are not like the rest of the white folks. They will give you a break if you've got some hot numbers to show 'em, whether you're colored or not. And Jews control the theatres."

But the conversation went back to Stanton, when Hager and Jimboy and all of them had lived together, laughing and quarrelling and playing the guitar—while the tea got cold and the chop suey hardened to a sticky mess as the sisters wept. Billy marked busily on the table-cloth meanwhile with a stubby pencil, explaining to Sandy a new and intricate system he had found for betting on the numbers.

"Harrie and me plays every day. Won a hundred forty dollars last week in Cleveland," he said.

"Gee! I ought to start playing," Sandy exclaimed. "How much do you put on each number?"

"Well, for a nickel you can win . . ."

"No, you oughtn't," checked Harriett, suddenly conscious of Billy's conversation, turning towards Sandy with a handkerchief to her eyes. "Don't you fool with those numbers, honey! . . . What are you trying to do, Billy, start the boy off on your track? . . . You've got to get your education, Sandy, and amount to something. . . . Guess you're in high school now, aren't you, kid?"

"Third year," said Sandy slowly, dreading a new argument with his mother.

"And determined to keep on going here this fall, in spite o' my telling him I don't see how," put in Annjee. "Jimboy's over yonder, Lord knows where, and I certainly can't take care of Sandy and send him to school, too. No need of my trying—since he's big enough and old enough to hold a job and make his own living. He ought to be wanting to help me, anyway. Instead of that, he's determined to go back to school."

"Make his own living!" Harriett exclaimed, looking at Annjee in astonishment. "You mean you want Sandy to stay out of school to help you? What good is his little money to you?"

"Well, he helps with the room rent," his mother said. "And gets his meals where he works. That's better'n we'd be doing with him studying and depending on me to keep things up."

"What do you mean better?" Harriett cried, glaring at her sister excitedly, forgetting they had been weeping together five minutes before. "For crying out loud—better? Why, Aunt Hager'd turn over in her grave if she heard you talking so calmly about Sandy leaving school—the way she wanted to make something out of this kid. . . . How much do you earn a week?" Harriett asked suddenly, looking at her nephew across the table.

"Fourteen dollars."

"Pshaw! Is that all? I can give you that much myself," Harriett said. "We've got straight bookings until Christmas—then cabaret work's good around here. Bill and I can always make the dough—and you go to school."

"I want to, Aunt Harrie," Sandy said, suddenly content.

"Yea, old man," put in Billy. "And I'll shoot you a little change myself—to play the numbers," he added, winking.

"Well," Annjee began, "what about. . . ."

But Harriett ignored Billy's interjection as well as her sister's open mouth. "Running an elevator for fourteen dollars a week and losing your education!" she cried. "Good Lord! Annjee, you ought to be ashamed, wanting him to keep that up. This boy's gotta get ahead—all of us niggers are too far back in this white man's country to let any brains go to waste! Don't you realize that? . . . You and me was foolish all right, breaking mama's heart, leaving school, but Sandy can't do like us. He's gotta be what his grandma Hager wanted him to be—able to help the black race, Annjee! You hear me? Help the whole race!"

"I want to," Sandy said.

"Then you'll stay in school!" Harriett affirmed, still looking at Annjee. "You surely wouldn't want him stuck in an elevator for ever—just to help you, would you, sister?"

"I reckon I wouldn't," Annjee murmured, shaking her head.

"You know damn well you wouldn't," Harriett concluded. And, before they parted, she slipped a ten-dollar bill into her nephew's hand.

"For your books," she said.

When Sandy and his mother started home, it was very late, but in a little Southern church in a side street, some old black worshippers were still holding their nightly meeting. High and fervently they were singing:

> By an' by when de mawnin' comes,
> Saints an' sinners all are gathered home. . . .

As the deep volume of sound rolled through the open door, Annjee and her son stopped to listen.

"It's like Stanton," Sandy said, "and the tent in the Hickory Woods."

"Sure is!" his mother exclaimed. "Them old folks are still singing—even in Chicago! . . . Funny how old folks like to sing that way, ain't it?"

"It's beautiful!" Sandy cried—for, vibrant and steady like a stream of living faith, their song filled the whole night:

> An' we'll understand it better by and by!

Tambourines to Glory

(1958)

To Irene

Upon this Rock I build my
Church and the gates of hell
shall not prevail against it.

St. Matthew 16:18

Contents

Tambourines to Glory

1

Palm Sunday

It was a chilly Palm Sunday and Essie Belle Johnson did not have a palm. Several of the other kitchenette dwellers in her lodgings had been to church that day and returned with leaves, sheaves and even large sprays of palm straw to stick up in their mirrors or in one corner of the frame of Mama's picture.

"I used to always go to church on Palm Sunday when I were a child," Essie said, "as well as Easter, too."

"I seldom went," said Laura, "and never regular. My mother was too beat out from Saturday night to get me up in time to go to church. My step-pa sold whiskey—you know, I growed up in bootleg days. My schooling came from bathtub likker, with some small change left over sometimes to go to movies, buy Eskimo pies."

"My mama always woke me up on the Sabbath before she went to work," mused Essie. "Her white folks only gave her one Sunday off a month. She'd give me a nickel to put in Sunday school and a dime for church, then leave something in the pot for me to eat when I got back home. In the evening, Mama would go to services by herself and turn out the light and leave me in bed until I got teen-age. Then I went to church at night, too. I loved those songs, 'Precious Lord, Take My Hand.' Oh, but that's pretty! Let's go to church Easter, Laura."

"Which one, Sanctified or Baptist?"

"Where the singing is best," said Essie.

"Sanctified," said Laura. "But you know I ain't got nothing to wear to church. On Easter Sunday I should decorate my headlights proper. Man told me last week, said, 'Woman, you got bubbies like the headlights on a Packard car sticking out like two forty-fours. Stop shooting me in the eyes that way with what you carries in front of you.' " Laura drew herself up proudly.

"An out-of-shape woman can get by with some poor rags. But you got a good figure, Laura. If you didn't put so much money into the bottle, you could get yourself some clothes."

"Girl, hush! Chilly as it is tonight, I had to get a little wine. Being Sunday, I had to pay more for it bootleg. There ought to be some heat in this old rathole."

"You could have got yourself a hat with what you paid for that wine."

"*An Easter bonnet with a blue ribbon on it,*" sang Laura. "Pshaw, child, by this time next Sunday I might have a new hat. Who knows? Maybe my new man will buy me one."

"If he does, it will be mighty near the first time. You one of these women always buying men something, instead of letting them do for you. You sure are crazy about men, Laura."

"One nice thing about being on relief is, it leaves you plenty time to be sweet to your daddy, have him something ready to eat when he comes from work, have your own head combed. I don't see much sense in a woman working, long as the Home Relief mails out checks. Of course, sometimes I has more energy being idle than I know what to do with. Essie, if I could just set on my haunches and be content like you! You don't even want a drink—just set and get fat, and you're happy."

"I ain't all that happy, Laura. I want my daughter with me. I get lonesome. If it wasn't for you dropping in all the time, I'd be more lonesome. Sure glad you're my neighbor, Laura, even if I can't keep you company with no bottle."

"A few swallows of this and you'd forget about being lonesome. You ought to learn to drink a little, Essie."

" 'I hate that old raw wine, Laura. It makes me sick at the stomach."

"Your life is empty and your belly, too. You ought to do something. At least, get yourself a man, girl, somebody, anybody."

"A man?" cried Essie. "No! Not to beat me all over the head. I'm cranky. I'm getting set in my ways. And I been long disgusted with men, low-down, no-good as they are."

"Well, smoke a reefer then. Try a little goopher dust. Dope, nope? Live out your life, instead of just setting here gathering pounds. Excite yourself, get high and fly."

"Somehow I kinder like to keep my head clear. Even if I am beat, I like to know it."

"Woman, you sound right simple," declared Laura.

"Anyhow, where would I get the money for them bad habits you're talking about, even if I wanted them?"

"The Lord helps them that helps themselves," declared Laura, shaking the last drop of sherry out of her pint bottle and laying it flat on the porcelain table. "Essie, don't you want no kind of pleasure out of living? You ain't that old. You still got breasts, legs, and what God give you. No fun, you might as well die."

"Sometimes I think so, rooming all by myself like this and living off the Welfare. About all I can do nowadays is ask the Lord to take my hand."

"Well, why don't you do that then? Get holy, sanctify yourself. The Lord is no respecter of persons if He takes a pimp's hand and makes a bishop out of him, like he did with Bishop Longjohn over there on Lenox Avenue. That saint had three whores on the block ten years ago. He's got a better racket now, the Gospel! And a rock and roll band out of this world in front of the pulpit with a piano player that beats Teddy Wilson. That bishop's found himself a great shill."

"Shill?"

"Racket, girl, racket."

"Religion don't just have to be a racket, Laura, do it? Maybe he's converted."

"Converted about as much as an atom bomb is converted to peace."

"Longjohn might be converted, Laura."

"All the money he takes in every Sunday would convert me," declared Laura. "Money! I sure wish I had some. Say, Essie, why don't you and me start a church like Mother Bradley's? We ain't doing nothing else useful, and it would beat Home Relief. You sing good. I'll preach. We'll both take up collection and split it."

"What denomination we gonna be?" asked Essie, amused at the idea.

"Start our own denomination, then we won't be beholding to nobody else," said Laura.

"Where we gonna start it?" asked Essie.

"Summer's coming, ain't it? We'll start it on the street where the bishop started his, right outdoors this summer, rent free, on the corner."

Essie grinned. "You mean, in the gutter where we are."

"On the curb above the gutter, girl. We'll save them lower down than us."

"Now, who could they be?"

"The ones who can do what you can't do, drink without getting sick, stay high on Sneaky Pete wine. Gamble away their rent. Play up their relief check on the numbers. Lay with each other without getting disgusted, no matter how many unwanted kids they produce. Use the needle, support the dope trade. Them's the ones we'll set out to convert."

"With what?"

"With Jesus. He comes free," cried Laura. "Girl, you know I think I hit upon an idea. Just ask Jesus to take your hand, in public, Essie. Then, next thing you know, somebody will think He's got your hand, and will put some cash in *yours* to see if they can make the same contact. Folks is simple. Money they're going to throw away anyhow, so they might as well throw some our way. Just walk with God, and tell the rest of them to follow you, *and pay as they go.* Dig?"

Taking it like an impossible game, Essie murmured, "Um-hum!" But Laura already saw herself as a lady preacher. Besides, the wine was gone. In her new role, she felt like singing, and she did.

"Precious Lord, take my hand,
Lead me on, let me stand.
I am weak, I am tired, I am worn."

She had a strange voice, deep, strong, wine-rusty, and wild.

"Through the storms of the night
Lead me on to the light.
Take my hand, precious Lord, lead me on."

Essie was moved. "I knowed you could sing blues, Laura, but I never knowed you knew them kind of songs before."

"Pick it up with me," said Laura. "Pick it up, girl."

Cooler, higher and sweeter than Laura's, Essie's voice picked up the song, and the drab cold kitchenette room filled with melody was no longer cold, no longer drab. Even the light seemed brighter.

"When my way grows drear,
Precious Lord, linger near.
When the day is almost gone,
Hear my cry, hear my call,
Guide my feet lest I fall.
Take my hand, precious Lord, lead me on."

"Essie, if I could sing like you, I'd be Mahalia Jackson," cried Laura. "You're a songster!"

"Mahalia is a good woman. I ain't," said Essie.

"To make her money, records and all, I'd be willing to be good myself," said Laura.

"It ain't easy to get hold of money. I've tried, Lord knows I've tried to get ahead. Ever since I come up North I been scuffling to get enough money to send for my daughter and get a little two-, three-room apartment for her and me to stay in."

"Pshaw! For love nor money can't nobody get no apartment in Harlem, unless you got enough money to pay under the table."

"Marietta's sixteen and ain't been with me, her mama, not two years hand-running since she were born. I always wanted that child with me. Never had her. Laura, I was borned to bad luck."

"Essie, it's because you don't use your talents, that's why," said Laura, looking at her portly friend with a critical eye. "All you use, like most women, is the what-you-may-call-it that you sets on, your assets instead of your head. Now, me, I got a brain, but I pay it no mind. I hope you will, though, and listen to my advice. Girl, with your voice, raise your fat disgusted self up out of that relief chair and let's we go make our fortune saving souls.

"Remember Elder Becton? Remember that white woman back in depression days, Aimee Semple McPherson, what put herself on some wings and opened up a temple and made a million dollars? Girl, we'll call ourselves sisters, use my name, the Reed Sisters. Even if we ain't no relation, we're sisters in God. You sing, I'll preach. We'll stand on the curb and let the sinners in the gutter come to us. You know, my grandpa down in North Carolina was a jackleg preacher. And when I get full of wine, I can whoop and holler real good. Listen to this spiel."

Laura jumped up from her chair with gestures. "I'll tell them Lenox Avenue sinners," she said, "You-all better come to Jesus! Yes, sinning like hell every night, you better, because the atom bomb's about to destroy this world, and you ain't ready! Get ready! Get ready! I say, aw, let Him take your hand. Yes, sisters, brothers, He's got mine! Let Him take yours and walk with Him. Now, sing with me:

"When the darkness appears,
Precious Lord, linger near.
When my life is almost gone,
At the river I stand,
Guide my feet, hold my hand.
Take my hand, precious Lord, lead me on.

"Grab the chorus, Essie. Sing it, girl, sing!"

Essie's voice rose full and persuasive, so persuasive, in fact, that melodically she persuaded herself and Laura, too, that they ought to go out into the streets and move multitudes.

"I sure wish I had me some more wine," sighed Laura when they had finished singing.

"The Wine of God is all we need," Essie said. "Laura, I'm gonna pray." She knelt down with her arms on the chair where she had been sitting. "Lord, I wish you would take my hand. Lead me on, show me the way, help me to be good. Help Sister Laura, too. And help us both to help others to be good. That I wish in my heart, Lord, I do."

"Amen!" cried Laura with her hand on her empty glass.

" 'Surely goodness and mercy shall follow me all the days of my life,' " murmured Essie.

"And never catch up with you unless you get up and do something yourself," said Laura.

2

Blue Monday

The next morning, which was a blue Monday, when Laura could hardly scrape together enough change to combinate a number and put a dime on the lead, Essie said as she washed the percolator top, "I prayed again this morning for what we was talking about last night."

Laura, who had left her bed unmade down the hall in Number 7 to tap on Essie's door in the hope of a hot cup of coffee, looked puzzled. "What?"

"That church we gonna start," said Essie. "I believe God answers prayer. In fact, that church is started."

"Started? Where?"

"Right here in this room with you and me."

"Then lemme pass the collection plate," said Laura, "because I dreamed about fish last night—782—and that is a good number to play. Here, put some change in this saucer, and I'll put the number in for you, too."

"I said I was *praying*, Laura, not playing. If we're gonna save souls, have I got to save you from sin first?"

"Oh, you talking about starting a church?" said Laura, her mind clearing of sleep a little. "Well, as soon as the weather warms up a bit, we'll buy a Bible and a tambourine and plant our feet on the rock of 126th and Lenox and start. But right now, I want me at least forty-five cents to work on these numbers. Suppose *fish* jumps out today? If it did, and I didn't catch it, I sure would be mad. Girl, pour me one little drop more of that coffee. If I could just find that old Negro who's liking me so much, so he says, I might could maybe get a dollar or two. But he never does come by here on Monday."

"Laura, you oughtn't to be encouraging that married man to be laying up with you."

"He encourages his self," yawned Laura. "Can I help it if I appeal to him whenever he can get out of his wife's sight? The Lord give me my smooth brown body, girl, and I ain't one to let it go to waste. Excuse me, I'm gonna comb my hair and go downstairs and put these numbers in. A small hit's better than none. But I sure hate to be so poor! Maybe that Chinese that winked at me from behind the lunch counter will feel in a lending mood this morning."

"A Christian woman taking up with a heathen," said Essie.

"On a blue Monday morning I would take up with a dog," said Laura, "if the dog said, 'Baby, how about a drink?' Soon as this coffee dies down, I'm gonna need something a little stronger."

Laura's carpet slippers heel-flapped their way down the hall. All the nearby kitchenettes were quiet. Everybody on that floor except these two women had gone to work. Essie sat down to think, and sat a long while, which was what she liked to do—just sit. Ten o'clock, eleven o'clock, noon. But today, she kept seeing in her mind's eye herself singing to more and more people on a corner, then in a gospel tent, then in a church, and people weeping and shouting and fainting and coming to Jesus because of her songs, and a railroad ticket, yellow and very long, that she was folding and putting into a letter and sending to her daughter in Richmond writing, "Honey, baby, daughter, child, come to your mother," and she was signing the letter with her own name, *Essie*. And suddenly she was shouting all alone by herself, "Thank you, God! Thank God! Thank God!"

Then she got up and started sweeping the floor, and imagined it was the living room of a nice apartment, and she was getting ready for Marietta to arrive. She looked out her rear window three stories down into a courtyard full of beer cans and sacks of garbage and saw, instead, a pretty view of a park—because where she lived now with her daughter was way up on the hill and there were trees outside the apartment windows. "It's all because of You, Lord," she said, "and because I am walking with God. Yes!" And she began to sing:

"Just a closer walk with Thee,
Grant it, Jesus, if you please.
Daily walking close to Thee—
Let it be! Let it be! Let it be!"

Broom in hand, she stopped. "I wonder if that winehead of a Laura has sure enough converted me? Thank God, I see some kind of light right now!

"I am weak, but Thou art strong.
Jesus, keep me from all wrong!
I'll be satisfied as long
As I walk close to Thee!"

"Sing it, girl," cried Laura, breezing past in the hall to find the Chinese counterman in the Japanese restaurant, her numbers writer, and somebody on the corner to buy her a bottle of wine.

Essie sat down again in her chair, filling it amply, and again her mind was sort of empty as it usually was. But the sun came in bright at the window, brighter than the sun had been for many months. It was spring. Vaguely Essie thought, I'll raise the window in a minute. But she sat a long, long time before she did raise the window. Essie's life had been full of long, long, very long pauses.

3

Visions of a Rock

"Well, it did not hit," said Laura, "no parts of it. The number was 413—so I did not catch the lead, I did not catch the second, and I had no change to put on the third. That Chinese man did not feel so well today. What did you do all afternoon?"

Essie had a report to make. "I priced a Bible."

"Have I done dreamed up something that you are really taking serious," said Laura, "about this church?"

"Been passing the store for months and just never noticed," said Essie, "that stuck back up there in the window of that furniture household shop, midst stoves, hassocks, floor lamps, and overstuffed chairs, is a great big Bible leaning up against a sign that says: GOLD-EDGED BIBLE ON INSTALMENT PLAN—*Two Dollars Down, Two Dollars a Month.* That Bible costs eighteen-fifty."

"Where's it at?" asked Laura.

"Bernstein's," said Essie. "Big beautiful gold-lettered Bible. We might as well buy a big Bible."

"I agree," said Laura. "If I hit tomorrow, I'll put down the first payment."

"No," said Essie. "Let's start this thing right. When my Welfare check comes, I'll put down a payment. But let's not use no numbers money to found our church."

"You are getting holier-than-thou already," said Laura. "Girl, I believe I'll go take a little nap before nightfall. Old daddy-boy-baby might come by to keep me awake after dark. Dig you remotely, doll. So long!"

Concerning Laura, "She's got a fine brown frame," observed the men in the block. "A hefty hussy," said the women, "more well-built than plump, but there's enough of her." From behind, young boys might whistle, "Whee-ooo-oo-o!" But if Laura turned around they saw she could be their mother, but a good-looking mother for true. When Laura got dressed up, her exterior decorations hung well. Sometimes emerging from the Rabbit Warren with her finery on, Laura looked good. Well ahead of her came her breasts, natural—like singers' voices in the pre-microphone days, projecting without artificial aid—colloquially termed by the local Lotharios *headlights, forty-fours, easy riders, daily doubles,*

Maes, meaning West. Concerning her legs, climbing stairs had kept them sturdy, dancing kept them graceful, pride kept them in runless stockings chosen to match her cocoa skin. Laura would buy stockings when she couldn't pay her rent. If a man said something nice about her legs on the subway, she would pull her dress down. Otherwise when seated she was careless. Guile, not modesty, generally prevailed.

Concerning the ancient building where Laura and Essie lived, well, if you didn't see all those names under the different bells, you wouldn't believe so many people lived there: B. Jenkins, Sarah Butler, J. T. K. Washington, Ben Wade, Mrs. E. B. Johnson (which was Essie), Katie Huff, Jefferson Lord, Jr., Mr. and Mrs. Titter, Sisseretta Smith, Ed Givens, Laura Wright Reed (which was Laura), and so on and on into the dozens and dozens, sometimes three or four people listed in the same room. It was an old apartment house in which a door opening onto the central hall had been cut directly into every room, and inner communicating doors sealed. Then each room no matter how small had been made into a kitchenette with a gas burner (fire laws notwithstanding) plus a sink installed in a corner for washing both face and feet, pots and privates, clothes, cutlery, dogs and dishes. The building had a name, the Marquette, but the neighborhood called it the *Rabbit Warren,* for short just the *Rabbit.*

Late that afternoon in the Rabbit, through the still-open window facing the areaway, Essie could hear kids coming home from school, romping and playing on other floors in rooms where parents had not yet come home from work. Alone, youngsters could make as much noise as they wished. Sometimes they made plenty. Essie did not mind. She kept thinking of her own child as still a little playful girl—only her daughter *couldn't* be like that any more. Marietta was sixteen. Essie had not seen her for four years, but Grandma had sent her a picture when the girl came out of junior high school, a golden-faced kid, all in white looking mighty pretty. Grandma kept that child looking washed and clean all the time.

She must be a church girl, thought Essie, because them people are religious down South. Well, when Marietta gets here, she will find me religious, too. Never was much of a sinner, nohow. I can't go for sin like Laura. Fast life tires me out.

Essie got up to pull down the window, since the sunset was chilly. She put on her coat, a shapeless, heavy old black coat, and sat down again. From the pocket of her coat she took a long pearl-handled knife, pressed a little button in its side and a thin sharp blade shot out. With the blade she began to clean her fingernails—which was about the only use she had ever had for that knife, although Essie carried it in her pocket when she went out, for protection, she said, against robberies and rapes and suchlike calamities. But nobody had ever even tried to snatch Essie's pocketbook, let alone otherwise accost her rather corpulent person.

Once in a while a man leaning on a stoop might say, "Big mama, you look good to me." But none had as yet tried to drag her into a hallway to rob her of her virtue, or pull her down a janitor's steps into a furnace room—where she had heard tell many a good woman had surrendered to males unknown. Had any man laid hands on her, "I have my knife," said Essie, as she used it to clean her fingernails.

When Essie had finished, she clicked the blade back in place, put her protector in her coat pocket, and sat for a long spell in the gathering dusk before she got up to turn on the light, wash the rice, and start to cook herself some supper. Might be maybe Laura would add something to the pot, and they would eat together. It was rather early in the week for Laura's Old Man to be coming by.

I need some rock on which to stand, suddenly thought Essie leaning over the stove. That Laura's got several rocks of an earthly nature on which she leans, men, numbers, likker, even if they do slip out from under her sometimes. While me, I just set, and set, and set. "But now I see me a rock, and that rock is Jesus!" cried Essie aloud.

Suddenly she was startled that her thoughts had become words rocking about the room, words spoken so strongly and with so much conviction that she almost dropped the spoon with which she stirred the rice.

Then much more quietly and quite aware of the fact that she was *talking,* not merely thinking, "A Rock," she cried, "I visions me a Rock."

4

Naturally Weak

"Old raccoon, you," cried Laura, "if you can't bring me nothing, then don't come by here." Essie heard her friend's voice all the way up the hall. "Just stay home, Negro!"

"So you want me to stay home, huh?" growled the man.

His walking papers, Essie thought. But they don't have to let the world know every time they fall out. Some people are too broadcast.

"I can't come handing you out money every time I look in your face," barked the old raccoon.

"I know somebody who can," cried Laura. "And he's a young man, too."

Laura's lying, thought Essie. Laura gives that young man money herself every time her Welfare check comes. Uly do not give her a thing but a hard row to go. Laura is just trying to collect from that old man to *keep* that young man on her string. That Laura, mused Essie as she cut a great big piece of Cushman's cake to go with her third cup of tea. Laura's hungry, that I know, and since that old man did not bring no change with him, this being Monday, I know she just wants to get rid of him quick so she can come on in here and eat. Payday, he'll be welcome back.

I need some rock on which to stand,
Some ground that is not shifting sand . . .

Somehow the song kept running through her mind that she had heard so often on a gospel program over the radio from Jersey City. Everywhere, Jersey City, Richmond, New York, everywhere she had ever been, everybody needed some rock on which to stand. Essie found herself eating and singing. The song was beautiful and cool in the room when Laura tapped lightly and tripped on in. Laura said, "Well, all right, now!" and joined in the song until her food got warmed up. Meanwhile some of the other tenement dwellers opened up their doors to listen since it sounded as if there might be a small revival meeting going on in the room, and Essie heard somebody say, "That singing sure sounds good!"

Laura said, "You see, girl, I'm telling you, this religious jive is something we can collect on. Look here, ain't you got no meat or nothing to go with this rice jive here? I been wrastling with that old raccoon for the last two hours, I'm hungry. Maybe Uly will be by about ten or eleven o'clock—my heart, my lover-man for true! Ain't we got a ham hock left from Sunday I can put on my plate?"

"Your memory is short," said Essie. "You know we cleaned up that ham hock and greens yesterday. Saturday, Sunday—how long you expect one pot of victuals to last?"

"The relief investigator thinks one pot ought to last a week. I sure will be glad when we ain't no longer beholding to them people. My investigator is colored, too—talking about she don't see why I can't get along on the money I draw. Also, as healthy-looking as I am, why can't I keep a job? And me, I done stooped myself over, uncombed my hair, tottered, and tried to look as sick and consumptive as I could for her benefit. We're both of the *same* race, she and me. Why does she begrudge me them white folks' money? Essie, you could at least have made some gravy for this rice. Even if I am from Carolina where it grows, I like a meat-flavor with rice, girl. I like meat! If 782 had just come out, we could have had pork chops tonight. Oh, well, tomorrow is another day. I'm sure gonna send Ulysses Walker for some wine when he gets here. Lend me a half, please."

"*Precious Lord, take my hand . . .* " Essie began to hum.

"Um-hum!" agreed Laura, "help Sister Essie, Lord, do—so she can help me—because, I swear, for some things I am weak—men, wine, and something fine—just naturally weak."

5

When Sap Rises

"When the sap rises in the trees, it's spring," said Laura. "Babes and boys start holding conferences in which actions speak louder than words. Aw, do it to me, lover!"

"I wish you would not talk that way, Laura, and you supposed to be preparing yourself for the ministry."

"I'm a she-male minister," said Laura, "and there ain't nothing in the Bible says male nor female shall not make love. Fact is, Essie, the very first book is just full of begats, which runs from Genesis through to Tabulations."

"Revelations," said Essie. "I read the Bible when I were a child."

"Which were a long time ago," murmured Laura.

"Just because I'm a few years older than you," said Essie, "you don't need to reflect on it. But if we're gonna start them meetings we been talking about, you ought to start reading up in the Bible."

"Big as that book is, don't nobody know all of what's in it," said Laura. "But I'll take up reading when the time comes. All I need is one text to start me out. And I know one, *Jesus wept.* Also I know another thing He did do. He turned the water into wine—and ever since then somebody's been drunk. Thank God, I seldom go too far."

"Sometimes you guzzle a little too much."

"A little too much is just enough for me—a pint, then I always need just *one* drink more. But what can I do on relief? Not being a street-walker, next best thing to do is be a street-stander—which we gonna be soon as it gets warm enough to stand still long enough in one place to pray."

"Your faith should keep you warm," said Essie.

"My faith and my wine together."

"Laura," cried Essie, "you ain't gonna drink no wine and be standing up preaching God's word beside me, no sir!"

"Are you telling me already what I am and ain't gonna do, Essie, and we ain't even formed our sisterhood yet? You're no relation to me, you know. If we gonna fall out before we start the Lord's work, I'm gonna go right straight and get my two dollars back I put down at Bernstein's on that Bible."

"You done made a payment on the Bible?"

"I did, went right straight and put every penny on it that I won when I caught that first digit the other day—the 4."

"Laura! No you didn't! I don't want to start nothing religious on the wages of sin."

"Wages, hell! I ain't worked a lick since Lincoln's birthday. That money come from luck. Facts are, it were manna from heaven. I had begun to believe I could not hit a number no more, never in life. Now my faith is restored. Out of gratitude, I paid that two bucks down on a Bible."

"Do, Jesus!" said Essie.

"I could have bought a whole half gallon of wine."

"I know," sighed Essie. Then she went into one of her silent pauses and did not say hardly another word to Laura the rest of the evening. So, when Laura got through looking at Essie's comic books, she went on down the hall to her room and turned the radio on to the all-night record man. Essie just sat and looked at the wall until she got ready to go to bed.

It was warm enough to leave the window open tonight for air. But it was well past the middle of June before the two women thought it warm enough to go seek a corner on which to lift their voices in song and see if anybody stopped to listen. They found at the Good Will Store a tambourine and a folding camp stool, 35¢ for the latter, and a half dollar for the tambourine.

"Including the Bible, we have invested $2.85 in this holy deal," said Laura.

"What we take up tomorrow night, if we does take up anything, goes on the Bible," said Essie.

"Beyond that, we will split it two ways," declared Laura. "A two-dollar payment to Bernstein's ought to leave a little change for the Lord's servants. We have our earthly needs."

"*All* we take up at our first meeting is going on the Bible," said Essie. "Period!"

Never having seen Essie that firm about anything before, Laura opened her mouth to speak, then closed it in surprise, opened it again, and very slowly let it close.

"Tomorrow night at seven at 126th and Lenox," continued Essie. "Leastwise, that's what you said, we raise our hymns. I think I'll wear my coat in case it's chilly."

"Yeah," said Laura, "and we might need that switchblade you keep in your coat pocket to protect our collection on the way back up these dark steps. You never can tell what folks will do when they see we got money."

"Laura, can you play a tambourine?"

"I can play it and *pass it* both," said Laura. "We gonna take up some money."

6

The Call

"It were Palm Sunday when I got the call," preached Laura. "I were setting in my room with Sister Essie here, and I heard a voice just as loud saying, 'Take up the Cross and follow Me, go out unto the highways and byways and save souls, go to the curbstones and gutters and rescue the lost, approach the river of sin and pull out the drowning.' Oh, I were drowning once, friends, but now I'm saved. I were down there in sin's gutter lower than a snake's belly—now look at me! Look at me up here on the curbstone of life reaching out with my voice to you to come and be saved, too. The Reed Sisters, folks, that's who we are, lifting our voices for God's sake. Our church is this corner, our roof is God's sky, and there's no doors, no place in our church that is not open to you because there is no doors. So come in and be one with us, one with God, and be saved. See how things will change for you—from worst to bad to better to best. Babes and boys, come in! Draw nigh! Men and women, come in! Approach! Children, stand near! Young and old, everybody, drop a nickel, dime, quarter in this tambourine as we sing:

> *"What He's done for me!*
> *What He's done for me!*
> *I never shall forget*
> *What He's done for me!*

"Sing it, Sister Essie, while I shake and pass this tambourine."

Essie's voice rose in happy song while Laura's tambourine trembled and shook in rhythm, and the words and the music spread to the crowd. The fifteen or twenty persons on the corner sang, too. Their singing made others stop to look, stop to sing, and as they sang Laura stopped shaking her music-maker to move among them, the tambourine held like a plate, and the very first nickels, dimes, and quarters bounced into it. Soon the bottom of the instrument was covered, then they didn't bounce any more, they clinked. They clinked into a rising mound which grew heavier and heavier before Laura returned to the camp stool where her tote bag was into which she poured the money.

"I never shall forget
What He's done for me!"

Laura lifted her empty tambourine in an ecstatic shimmer to the power of a song, brought it down trilling and spangling, struck it repeatedly in a drumlike rhythm against her elbow, then shouted "Amen!" Both women led the song to a joyous close, and Laura hissed to Essie, "I think it's time to stop this meeting, girl."

Their first meeting had not begun at seven o'clock as planned. In her room Essie was dressed, ready and waiting, with her old black coat hanging over a chair—but no Laura. Uly *would* come by that afternoon to fool away Laura's time. Laura's room door was locked, and when Essie went down the hall and knocked after the clock hand had passed seven-fifteen, all she got was a "I hear you, Essie! Just wait. I'll be along in due time."

It was after eight when Laura came bouncing up the hall, powdered and grinning, and Essie heard Uly's footsteps going down the stairs. By that time Essie had gone into one of her pauses, just sitting, so was not very communicative as Laura borrowed a slice of cheese from her icebox and chattered as she ate.

"Come on, let's go! Tonight's the night. You have the tambourine and the camp stool? Even if we ain't got a Bible, I got a text, 'Take up your cross and follow Me.' Come on."

"Laura, you're a cross yourself," said Essie.

"Then we'll put up with each other's crosses," laughed Laura. "Get up off your fat bohunkus and let's go see what's cooking with the public. Energize yourself, Essie! You been setting looking at these four walls for the last five or six years. Get up and give out—and see what we get back. Cast your singing bread upon the muddy waters of Harlem this evening, while I pass this tambourine amongst the sinners."

Laura grabbed the secondhand tambourine from the table and started shaking it: *Ching-a-ching! A ching-ching! Ching-ching-ching!*

"I got that old-time religion!
Got that old-time religion!
That old-time religion—
And it's good enough for me!"

Ching-ching! A ching-ching! Ching-ching! The way she shook it, it sounded good. The music pulled Essie out of her trance. She picked up the folding stool, threw her coat over her arm, fumbled for her key in her purse, turned out the light, and locked the door. Down the stairs and out into the June night went she and Laura headed for Lenox Avenue and a new life.

Auto horns were honking, taxis flying by, arc lights blinking, people passing up and down the street, restaurants and bars full, wine-o's sitting on a box just around the corner from the grocery store drinking from a common bottle, and nobody stopping for anything when Essie and Laura stopped on the corner they had chosen the day before. There Essie put down her camp stool and laid her coat on it. Laura lifted up her tambourine and shook it. Just the shaking of her tambourine was enough to make a teen-age boy stop, also a middle-aged couple, plus two children who ran past, then ran back and stood watching. Two human pebbles in the Harlem brook had begun to change the course of its water.

For a few seconds Laura shook her tambourine, then she began to sing:

> *"I got that old-time religion . . ."*

As Essie joined in, Laura hit her elbow with the tambourine—one-two! Three-four! in perfect rhythm to the song. Then one of the wine-o's yelled, "Aw, play it, sister!" as he rose unsteadily to participate. And it wasn't a minute before a dozen folks had gathered there on the corner, the two running kids were dancing to Essie and Laura's song, and an elderly woman had three times shouted "Amen!"

"Precious Lord, Take My Hand" followed. Essie prayed. Then Laura announced that it was Palm Sunday when she got the call. And that's the way they started saving souls in Harlem.

7

Bible and Bonus

"This is $11.93 more than we had this afternoon," said Laura when they got home. "Now, I wonder who in hell put them pennies in that tambourine?"

"Blessed is he that giveth, and blessed is he that receiveth," said Essie, "and pennies count, too. Maybe the poor soul did not have any more."

"Yes, but how are we gonna divide up three pennies equal?"

"Divide up?" said Essie. "This is the Lord's money, and we gonna put it all on the Bible—which means we can get the Bible out. We'll only owe five or six more dollars to have it paid for in full."

"I'll be damned," said Laura. "I will put $2 on the Bible—but the rest I need. Here, you take half—six, plus two for the Bible—which leave me $3.93 for my earthly needs. I'm going downstairs right now with mine before the likker store closes and make an investment—minus what I'm gonna save to play 319 in the morning."

"Laura!"

But Laura had gone on, out the door. Her feet were taking her down the stairs as fast as a child's. Essie sat down on a kitchen chair and went into a pause. In her mind's eye she saw the people stopping on that Lenox Avenue corner to listen to her and Laura sing. Out of their pockets had come this money on the table, and somehow Essie did not think it belonged to her. Essie thought it ought to go in some way to the works of God. So she gathered it up and put it into a spice jar marked CLOVES, on the shelf. The next morning she took it to Bernstein's and turned it in on the Bible, a heavy and beautiful book which she brought home since it was now two-thirds paid for and the store had made its profit. As a bonus, the surprised clerk gave her a little framed motto which said, GOD BLESS THIS HOME. Essie hung it on the wall beside the window.

She sat down and stared at GOD BLESS THIS HOME and whispered, "Send me my daughter home. I know You will. But I got to have a nice place for Marietta to come to first. Lord, I know You will give me that, too." And a still small voice said, "But you've got to get up off this chair and get your feet on the Rock." In her mind's eye the Rock was 126th and Lenox.

And Laura was there, too—Laura, who had managed to pull Essie out of her lifelong trance. Wine-loving, man-loving Laura. "I got to give Laura credit, Lord, for connecting me to You. Not that You wasn't in my mind, Lord, and in my soul—but I hadn't had no direct connections with You since my girlhood. Laura reached out and called Your name, and a prayer come into my mouth then and there. It has stayed murmuring in my heart since Palm Sunday. That Laura lets her prayers float away like soap bubbles and bust. But my prayers stick here, Lord. Here, Lord, here!"

Essie beat a hand against her breast, and thought about Laura right then, no doubt joking with the likker store clerk as she bought a bottle of the cheapest wine—which she would share with whomever she met in the block. Laura would share whatever anybody owned, including herself, Laura, or herself, Essie. Except over men, Laura was not selfish. But a man, if she liked him, she wanted that man for herself alone.

Neighbors for five years. When you're neighbors with people on the same floor in the same kitchenette roominghouse, you learn about them, just being neighbors. Only once in their seven years of friendship had Laura spent the night with Essie. That was the evening when a man who claimed he was real deep in love with Laura and had given her a dress, threatened to whale the living daylights out of her because she did not physically return his love. In fact, right on the public streets the man did bruise her a couple of times by planting his foot twice on the cheeks of Laura's thighs as she switched scornfully away from him in the dress he had bought and paid for. If Laura had not screamed so loudly on the corner, he might have inflicted even more solid punishment on her in places where the bruises would show. At any rate, a passing taxi which drove off with Laura slamming the door saved her before the man could grab the handle. But that night Laura was afraid to go home down the hall to her own room, so she slept with Essie.

For about a year after that a nice young man lived with Laura and was her protector, during which time older Negroes were scarce at Laura's end of the hall. But young men won't do right. They see a young girl and their heads get turned, no matter how nice an older woman is to them. No matter if she does give, rather than take.

When no man was around, Laura seldom liked to cook. Instead, she would put some change in with Essie's change and together they would stew up a pot and both would eat—which was one reason she was in and out of Essie's room so much. That was also why Essie's garbage pail had a wine bottle or two in it almost every day, although Essie herself did not drink. Essie's only bad habit was sitting. Just sitting.

"Girl, a pulpit chair is the very thing for you," said Laura. "You can set whilst I preaches, and you don't even need to get up to sing less'n you want to. When we get our own church, we gonna do just like we want to do."

"Like God wants, you mean," said Essie.

"With His guidance, and *my* mind," said Laura, "and you setting there looking all calm and sweet with not a cloud on your landscape. Essie, you can just set and look more unworried than anybody I ever seen. Me, I need to be doing something—good, bad, or indifferent—but something. No wonder you never has no misfortunes. You just sets."

"I'm setting and thinking on God these days," said Essie. "You better be thinking on Him too, Laura. Take our Bible in your room and read it tonight."

"Can't I read it here?"

"If you want to."

"Where is that part about *begat*?" asked Laura.

8

Pointed Questions

"Who will come and walk with Him, talk with Him, sing with Him?" Laura cried as old folks, young folks, boys and girls passed up and down the lighted street. But enough paused, lingered, and stood for her and Essie to maintain a crowd. With their backs to the taxis and the passing cars, in the balmy summer air they had conducted a very happy meeting that evening and many voices had joined in their songs—a little unusual for street meetings, where people stopped to *listen* to singing but seldom joined in. Essie and Laura had a way of pulling voices right out of people's throats and getting them to blend with their own in the old songs of the church that everybody knew, or in the more recent gospel songs folks heard on their radios or records. Now, with practice, Laura was beginning to beat a tambourine with rhythms like Cozy Cole's drums.

Playing and singing and talking were the only things about their corner that interested Laura, but these were the least that interested Essie. Sitting on her camp stool while Laura held forth, you'd think Essie had gone into a pause, but this was not true. Her eyes, that seemed to move so slowly, were studying faces, looking into other eyes, wondering what troubled this woman, what worried that man, what had hurt that young boy's soul, or made so bitter that girl's face. Essie, when the meetings were over, would linger and talk to folks until Laura would almost have to drag her away.

"Girl, you don't have to stand on the curb talking to these people all night. Collection is took. Come on! I'm thirsty myself." Laura would start off down the street, walking fast.

Behind her, Essie explaining, "Laura, seems like them folks think I can help them."

"You've done helped yourself. You might *can* help them," says Laura, "but why bother?"

Curving the corner of 125th and Lenox, Essie replies, "Because I think maybe that is the way to help ourselves—by helping others."

"You better help *yourself* first," passing the Lido Bar where the music's coming out. Says Laura, "Smell that fried chicken in there? If this bar wasn't so near our meeting corner, I'd stop and have me a wing and a Bud. That would help me."

"There's nothing wrong with helping somebody else besides ourselves, is there?" persists Essie. "You helped me to pull out. Now look at us, we ain't hardly started in His work, yet already we're prospering in the Lord. This month we don't have to worry."

"Then why worry?" asks Laura. "Don't worry about them folks on that corner after you get their donations. We're straight tonight. Buy yourself some barbecue to take home. I'm gonna get me a quart of the very best sherry wine and get good and high so I can sleep it off. I'm also gonna buy Uly a red sport shirt in the morning, which kind I heard him say he wanted. I like that big old no-good stud myself, I swear I do. If the Lord just takes care of me, I'll take care of my man. Aw, don't look so shocked, Essie! You're out here hustling just like me—in God's name."

"Laura," Essie asks as they cross Fifth Avenue to reach the liquor store on the other side before midnight, "is we doing right?"

"Soon as we're starting to get so we don't have to worry about being wrong, *you* start worrying about being right. Girl, good night! Go on home. I'm gonna stop by Big John's with my bottle and see is Uly playing cards up there. Are we straight on the dough?"

"I don't know," said Essie. "Keep what's in your bag."

"Then don't blame me if I got a dime more than you. And don't let nobody rob you on the way home."

"I got the same knife I been had for twenty years."

"I know it's sharp, so you're all right."

"But I'm worried about what we're doing, Laura. I'm going home and pray."

Laura stopped in her tracks. "Essie, is your wig gone?"

9

Enter Birdie Lee

"All you loose-limbed sons and daughters of Satan, jumping-jacks of sin, throwing your legs every-which-a-way, dancing, letting your feet lead you every-which-a-where, sinning, playing cards by day and fornicating by night, turn! I say turn! Turn your steps toward God this evening, join up with us, and stand up for Jesus on this corner," Laura commanded. "Talk, speak, shout, declare your determination. Who will stand up and testify for Him? If nobody else will, I will—me, Laura Wright Reed. Yes! Yes! I will! Folks, since God took my hand, I have not wanted for nothing. Rent paid, pots full, clothes on my back. Satisfied, praise God! Ain't that right, Sister Essie?"

Essie from her camp stool affirmed, "True, true! Yes, bless God, true!"

Laura continued, "It's God's doings, so I ask you all to help me stay in His footsteps. Help me to stay on the right road, people. Help me, all you-all, until you find the road yourself. Put a nickel, dime, quarter, dollar in this tambourine. Put it here and help in the Lord's work."

"I has done put a quarter in there once," said a little old lady in the crowd, "now I wants to testify."

"Speak, sister, speak," cried Essie.

She came forward, and the little old lady talked so long and so loud that she held up Laura's collection.

"My name is Birdie Lee," she said. "Once I were a child of God, but I backslid, backslid, backslid. Tonight I'm coming home. This evening I makes my determination to stay on His side from here on in—and I mean *into* the Kingdom. Sister Laura, gimme that tambourine and lemme shake it a mite to his glory." Whereupon that little old lady began a song and shook the tambourine—shook it so well that the whole corner started to rock and sway, feet to patting, hands to clapping, and Essie to shouting. So much rhythm swept up and down the street that some of the passing cars slowed to see what was happening—and it made Laura mad. But she did not show it. She sang and clapped her hands, too. But in her soul of souls Laura did not want any other woman on that corner attracting all that attention.

Who in the hell is this Birdie Lee? thought Laura without opening her mouth.

"I'm a sinner determined to be a saint," said Birdie Lee, as if she read Laura's mind. "I'm gonna join up with this band and sing and shout out here on God's street this whole blessed summer long, and nobody's gonna stop me, because—

"I want to be in that number
When the saints go marching in! . . ."

Sister Birdie Lee shook Laura's tambourine and sang the song until all of Lenox Avenue seemed like a street of gold leading right up to God's throne. When she had finished her song and Laura snatched the tambourine out of her hand and started to take up collection, money showered into the instrument. Birdie Lee went and stood beside Essie on the curb and became a part of their church. Because Birdie Lee seemed like a good investment, commercially speaking, Laura did not object.

10

The Fix

"Some of you-all are going to throw your money away anyhow, so throw some of it here," was the way Laura opened her collection speech one Friday evening. This brought a laugh and filled the tambourine with bills from the sporting element.

"How you can keep your mind on money so much, and on God at all, is more than I can fathom," said Essie gazing at Laura when they got home that night.

"God helps them that helps themselves," said Laura. "I can't help Him if I don't get mine. Them pimps and gamblers and whores on that corner was all headed for the nearest bar or cabaret, anyhow, like I would be if I was them, so why shouldn't I get mine before it goes to the paddys that owns these Harlem guzzle joints? After all, Lenox Avenue is *my* people. Let 'em drop me a little of that money on the way to the bar, instead of it all going right to the white man. Money is color-blind—but you almost have to reach over the color line to get it. Only with the Lord's help did we get what we got here tonight. And you, Essie Belle Johnson, you ain't made so much money before in one day since you been black. Have you?"

"No."

"And whose hand reached out to get it for you?"

"The Lord's."

"And *mine,*" said Laura. "These gospel songs is about the only thing the white folks ain't latched onto yet. But they will, soon as they find out there's some dough in 'em. They'll be up here in Harlem running revival meetings on our corner, I expect, in due time. Billy Graham will have a gospel chorus and Mahalia Jackson a white manager. Just you mark my words."

"Can't nobody manage God," said Essie.

"White folks've got the nerve to try," said Laura. "And I don't see nowhere in the Bible where God tells me not to pass my tambourine."

"He driv the money-changers out of the temple," said Essie.

"Money-*changers,*" said Laura. "Us is different. We are money-getters."

"I visions trouble," said Essie, and she went into a pause. Sure enough, in the midst of their singing that night a cop walked up and asked Laura if they had a license to be out there on that corner.

Laura said, "This is my license." She reached down in her tote bag and pulled out a greenback which happened to be a ten, and put it in the cop's hand—and that was that. Essie did not miss a note, nor Birdie Lee a handclap, and Laura's tambourine shook louder than ever as the policeman walked away. The next time, a few nights later, he came back with a pal in an ordinary suit, a plainclothes man of the type anybody can spot. At his appearance all the Negroes in the crowd sang louder than ever. The plainclothes man had the feeling that he might have a singing riot on his hands if he went too far, so he accepted a ten, too. But Laura and her tote bag moved off a half block from the meeting for this negotiation, out of the public eye. Meanwhile, Essie clapped the rhythm of a song while the corner continued to jump. The fix was on. For the rest of the summer whenever the Law came by for its cut, Laura would walk a few paces down the block, hand over a bill, and calmly return to her soul-saving.

By the time the summer hurricanes and the late August rains swept the trash from the gutters and the people from the sidewalks, the weather made it unfeasible to meet outdoors some nights. That did not worry Laura. When they did hold a meeting, they took up enough change to last a while.

Essie said, "Laura, what we gonna do when the cold weather comes?"

Laura said, "We'll just find ourselves an inside meeting place. For a couple of hundred dollars under the table, we'll rent some old apartment, buy some secondhand undertaker chairs, and raise a prayer."

"We need a rostrum to put the Bible on, too," said Essie. "I wonder how much does a rostrum cost. In what kind of store do you buy a rostrum?"

11

Ethiopian Eden

Shortly after the first nip of frost bit the autumn air, Essie Belle Johnson, Laura Reed, and Miss Birdie Lee descended on an old first-floor apartment between Lenox and Seventh in the West 130's with brooms, mops, and pails and proceeded to create that which is next to godliness, cleanliness, in rooms which badly needed cleaning. Three rooms, a bath, and kitchen. A front parlor and a back parlor, with big sliding double doors between, that nobody had used for parlors for years. An old brownstone converted into apartments, the parlors had become bedrooms, until the landlord put a family from Georgia out in response to Laura's under-the-table payment and three months' rent in advance.

When Essie pushed back the tall double doors and made the two big rooms one, she said, "Praise God, this is our church!" She stood like a large angel with her arms stretched out between the double doors and shouted. Whereupon Birdie Lee got to leaping and jumping and shouting, too. But Laura just stood and looked at them. Finally she said, "Saints, we better get to mopping." The next day Laura commissioned a young artist and gave him her instructions.

"I don't care what scenes from the Bible you paint on these windows," said Laura to the artist with the paint cans, "just so you make them colored. I want every last angel you paint to be brownskin. If you put the Devil in, make him white."

"I thought I would put Christ feeding His sheep on one window," said the young artist, "and the woman at the well on the other."

"God made us in His own image," said Laura, "so God must be black, or at least dark brown. As to the lambs, you know what color my Lenox Avenue lambs are."

"Yes'm," said the young man.

"So I look like a ma'am to you?" said Laura.

"No, ma'am, but—"

"I ain't all that age-able," said Laura, who had eyes for that artist. But the painter did not seem interested in anything but his work, and be made two such pretty pictures on the front windows that Laura said, "I think you had better paint me a Garden of Eden on the wall of that back parlor behind where the rostrum is gonna stand. Make me an Eve about the color of Sarah Vaughan. Put a diamond in that serpent's head, and let that apple be a Baldwin. I want Adam to look just like Joe Louis. Champeen! I love that man!" declared Laura. "And let the grass be green, green, green, all around the floor level."

"Yes, ma'am," said the young artist. "I will paint you the prettiest Garden of Eden you ever saw." Which he did.

He also painted the rostrum gold. And he found two big red chairs at the Good Will Store for the Reed Sisters to sit in. He also suggested adding ribbons to their tambourines.

"I love that artist," Laura confided to Essie. "He's got ideas. That young boy could really be my man."

"That boy ain't nothing but a baby," said Essie.

"A sugar baby to me," said Laura.

"There will be no assignations in this church," said Essie flatly. "That back bedroom behind Eden we are going to use as a powder room for the womens, and also as a place to revive them that passes out from shouting. The kitchen we will use for making coffee, tea, cocoa for our church socials. But there will be no beds nowhere."

"I was thinking of moving one in myself," said Laura, "and saving rent by using that bedroom. There's got to be some kind of caretaker here."

"The Lord is the caretaker of this church," said Essie. "Besides, there's a janitor lives downstairs. No need of you living in here all by yourself."

"Just an idea," said Laura. "But where we living now is not fit for servants of the Lord. We've both got to move. Since we got our church—which you just *had* to have first—to find a nice apartment for ourselves is the next step."

"If we prosper here," said Essie, "which I know we will."

"And I do not want no private house," said Laura. "I want a place with an elevator, janitor service, plenty of light, maybe even a doorman like they have on Riverside, everything for comfort."

"You expects to live high on the hog," said Essie.

"We both have chose the higher things of life now," said Laura, "and it's about time. You ain't no spring chicken, you know."

"Don't but a midget span separate you from me, Laura. You just happen to be well preserved, that's all."

"In wine, too," said Laura. "But you know, Essie, I'm developing a taste for Scotch."

"Wine is a mocker and strong drink is a tempter," said Essie.

"Even hard cider's got a kick to it," declared Laura. "When that serpent handed Eve that apple, he probably knew Eve could make hard cider out of it. Aw, look at that beautiful apple that artist-boy's painted for our altar! Pretty enough to eat!"

"Eve do look a lot like Sarah Vaughan," said Essie.

"Ethiopia's Garden of Eden," said Laura. "Listen, I got an idea. For our Sunday school, we gonna have some pretty brownskin cards printed too—Adam, Eve, the Lord God Jesus, Mary and Mary Magdalene all colored, black, brown, sepia, and meriney—with brownskin cherubs that our children can say, 'That's me!' This is gonna be a race church."

"We're colored ourselves," said Essie.

"When we add a man minister to our staff, he's gonna be the biggest blackest coloredest minister I can find," said Laura. "Black to the glory of God, amen!"

"I do not vision no man minister soon," said Essie.

"Then God will have to lift the veil from your eyes," stated Laura, "because male and female created He them—including ministers. So it would do no harm to have a man around now that we got our church."

"Thank God it ain't no little old store-front church neither," said Essie.

"We're eight steps up from the street," said Laura.

"We's rising," said Essie.

Laura sat down in her big red chair at the right of the rostrum in front of the Garden of Eden. She threw one shapely leg over the chair arm and turned to stare up at the bright new picture of the Garden on the wall behind her.

"Aw, just look at Joe Louis—Adam—naked as a kangaroo behind that bush—and he's peering out at Eve! Look at Joe!"

"Adam: *man*—that's what Adam means," said Essie, "*man*."

"Joe sure God is a man!" said Laura.

12

Dyed-in-the-Wool

The first convert in the new church was a man, a *real sinner,* too, not just a backslider returning to the fold. He was an old sinner who had been sinning for a long, long time. His name was Crow-For-Day—Chicken Crow-For-Day. He stood against the Garden of Eden and declared his determination.

It was a warm October evening and the front windows with the dusky lambs painted on them were open, so people in the street could hear him as he cried his new-found strength; and voices even outside the windows said "Amen!"

It was their first Sunday night in the new church. Laura was proud, Essie was happy, and their joy and happiness radiated to all the people. It was the first service they had ever held with a piano, too, and the young man who played had a rhythm and a roll that sent waves of jubilant sound rippling up and down the aisles between the folding chairs and bouncing off the walls and ceiling. Somebody said that Eve in the picture, at a certain point, even started to open her mouth and sing, and the snake gave a couple of wiggles. And at one place in the Sunday services, maybe because she was thinking about her daughter in the South, Essie was moved to stand and sing all alone "Sometimes I Feel Like a Motherless Child" and people started to cry, and Chicken Crow-For-Day jumped up and said, "I'm motherless and fatherless, too, but right now this minute I know I have found Jesus."

He shouted until Essie finished singing, then the old man took the rostrum and began to testify.

"Right now this minute I have come to God!" He was six feet tall, acknowledged sixty years old, thin as a shadow, and he said, "Right now I have found God! After all my years of sin, tonight the light!"

So many people in the church shouted simultaneously that you could hardly hear Crow-For-Day. But he went on, "Dyed-in-the-wool, dyed-in-the-wool, a dyed-in-the-wool sinner, dyed-in-the-wool with a dye so deep and a stain so dark that only the lamb of God could wash me clean. I seen these lambs in these windows and I said I'm going in. And I come—and look at me now, white, whiter than snow, washed white!" And nobody laughed that he was not white at all, because everybody was listening beyond his words and looking through him to the hope that they, too, might find some sort of joy akin to his, some kind of sin cleanser, though it be but for a moment, like this ancient reprobate had found—for you could look into his face and tell he had been until this moment a hound.

"Sniffing after women, tailing after sin, gambling on green tables, Saratoga, Trenton, High Point, North Carolina, let 'em roll! Santa Anita, Hialeah, Belmont, Miami, never read nothing but the racing forms. Harlem, nothing but the numbers columns in the *Daily News*. And for relaxations, crime in the comic books. Oh, but tonight Sister Essie has done snatched me off the ship of iniquity on which I rid down the river of sin through the most awfullest of storms, through gales of evil and hurricanes of passions, purple as devil's ink, green as gall. Yes, I tell you I shot dices. Now I've stopped. I lived off of women. Uh-uh! No more! I'll make my own living now. I carried a pistol, called it Dog—because when it shot, it barked just like a dog. I won't carry no pistol no more. Looky here! Everybody, looky here!"

Four women fainted and twenty screamed as Crow-For-Day pulled a pistol from his pocket, walked down the aisle with it above his head, and threw it out the open window into the street. Pistol out the window, gone.

"I carried a knife. Knives got me in trouble. Here goes old knife, too." And out the window went the knife, gone. As heavy as Essie was, she leaped into the air three times on the rostrum and said, "Thank God!"

"I hope, Essie, you'll throw your old switchblade away, too," said Laura on the platform but Essie did not hear her at all, or if she heard, she did not reply.

By then Crow-For-Day had come back up the aisle to the front of the church and turned to reveal still more of his sinful past to the congregation. "I drank likker," he shouted.

"Me, too," said Sister Birdie Lee.

"It made me fool-headed," cried Crow-For-Day. "Thank God I stopped last year so I don't have to stop drinking now."

"We stopped, stopped, stopped," said Birdie Lee.

"Let the man talk, Birdie," said Laura. "Let the new soul talk."

"I witnessed the chain gang," cried Chicken, "the jail, the bread line, the charity house—but look at me tonight. Look at me now!"

"Look, look, look," cried Birdie Lee.

"Bless God, I've lived to see the rooster crow for day, the sun of grace to rise, the rivers of life to flow—and I have found my determination. Help me! Help me! Brothers and sisters, help me."

Whereupon, Laura came forward with a singing cry, took the convert's hand, and appealed to the congregation on Crow-For-Day's behalf:

"When you see some sinner
Leave iniquity's dark den
And turn his feet toward Canaan,
Friends, help him to begin.
Christians, take his hand,
Show him God's his friend,
Just lead him on
And say Amen!"

The building began to rock to the song. Shaking hands and dancing feet laced the rhythm into a net of ecstasy while the piano bassed its chords of confirmation.

"Let the church say Amen!
Let the church say Amen!
When a sinner comes to Jesus
Let the church say Amen!"

13

Likker and Loot

"I got two thousand dollars in that spice jar in the cupboard," said Essie, "so I think we better take it to the bank."

"I think so, too," said Laura, "to the colored bank."

"To the Carver," said Essie.

"Yes, because that's too much loot to keep in the house any more. Who'd've ever thought this time last year, you and me would be banking money?"

"You have shook your tambourine to blessings," said Essie.

"I'm gonna shake it to a mink coat by Christmas," declared Laura, inspecting an unopened bottle of Scotch.

"I'm gonna shake mine to glory," said Essie.

"You are doing right well shaking since you bought your own self a tambourine, too. But I'm still the champion shaker—and collection taker."

"You do all right, Laura, and you deserves to buy a nice Christmas present for yourself. I wonder will I have my daughter with me by then?"

"You said you wanted to wait till we got an apartment, didn't you? A nice place to bring her to, not this old run-down joint. Essie, suppose we take this two thousand dollars and move, instead of putting it in the bank?"

"No, Laura. The church needs a nest egg. This is it. We put this away. Then maybe we start doing a little something for ourselves."

"O.K., as you say. I'm happy—I got my man to keep me warm."

"Looks like you could choose a new man out of the church."

"This one is just temporary, honey."

"Must be, 'cause I ain't even met him."

"He comes in early and goes out late," said Laura. "Lemme get on down the hall and see is he there yet."

"You gave him a key?"

"Sure—which is why I told you to keep our money in *your* room. You know I'm generous with my keys. Why, that key-man around the corner has made me so many keys to my door he must know its shape by heart."

"Ain't you scared someone of them mens will open your door some night and catch you with somebody else?"

"Don't worry, Essie, I got a night latch inside, also a bolt. Besides, when I put a man down, they usually don't fool around no more, key or no key, especially now—since they think I can put the curse of God on their sinful souls, me being a lady minister. Negroes don't play around with the church much. They take it serious."

"I wish you'd take it serious yourself," said Essie.

"As if I don't," exclaimed Laura. "But you won't catch me lending no money to nobody in the church, like you did Sister Birdie Lee last week. Facts is, I don't think you ought to start it."

"Birdie Lee paid me back."

"You're lucky. I expect she borrowed it to buy herself a tambourine."

"No, she didn't. She borrowed it to get a tooth pulled."

"Birdie's trying to tambourine herself up on the rostrum with us," said Laura, "setting in the front row playing like mad."

"She sure can shake it," confirmed Essie. "She tells me she can play drums, too. When we get our orchestra we planning, let's give her a chance."

"Essie, do you want to help every stray we pick up—and put them in the forefront, too? Let Birdie Lee set down there in the congregation where she belongs. Dried up and ugly as Birdie is, nobody wants to look at her."

"No, but her music's a different thing. Nobody wants to look at me neither, much, fat as I am, but they like to hear me sing. You are the rose of this church."

"Thank God for making me a high-breasted woman," said Laura. "But what you're probably thinking, though, is—I can tell by looking at you—that *you* are the saint and I am the devil. Well, fool, go ahead on and work and pray and worry yourself down with their problems if you want to. Lend out your money. Kill yourself over that church. Not me."

"Laura, the needs is so big up here in Harlem, and the ways of helping so little, I figure we have to work hard," said Essie.

"How come, after all these years I've knowed you, just *this* year you find so much energy all of a sudden?"

"From God," said Essie.

"With *me* propelling," said Laura.

"You God's handmaiden—even if you do not always act like a holy maiden do."

"How does a holy maiden act?" asked Laura.

"They be's not bold with their sinning," said Essie.

"It's easier for me to be a saint than to be a hypocrite. And neither my light nor my headlights will I hide under a bushel. The Lord gimme these breasts and if they look like headlights on a Packard car, it is not my fault. 'Let your light so shine,' is my belief."

"You would have led that little young artist-boy what painted our church windows to sin if you could."

"I don't believe that boy was leadable, Essie. He were of the type you call 'refined.' But he sure painted a *de*-lightful Garden of Eden. Even that serpent looks like he can be persuaded! Oh, well, lemme see if this English White Horse tastes as good as that Johnny Walker I had last night. I'm trying all the different brands of Scotch to see which one I'm gonna settle on for life. I can see my picture in a magazine now—when I get to be as famous at soul-saving as was Aimee Semple McPherson—*Sister Laura Reed endorses Vat 69 as ideal for colds and fevers, nothing else.* I will get five thousand dollars for that endorsement."

"Your mind sure runs to likker and to loot," said Essie. "But one of these days the Spirit is going to strike you dry, strike greed from your heart, lust from your body, and—"

"Make me as stupid as you are," Laura cut her off, "without a idea in your head until I put this one there—that's brought us a good living. Now you want to cramp my style."

Essie could tell Laura was angry. Suddenly the tone of voice hurt, her eyes cut, and Essie suffered. She sat down in her chair and said no more. When Laura left with her Scotch, Essie went into a pause.

14

Enter Buddy

He just walked down the aisle out of nowhere, confronted Laura, and spoke. "I saw you on the curb before you moved off the street into this church, and you certainly looked good to me."

"I did not observe you in the services tonight, did I?" asked Laura. She went toward the switch to turn out the altar lights.

"No, I just wandered in after things was over. I saw the people going out. I wondered where you had disappeared to off of Lenox Avenue. Cold weather, naturally you had to go somewhere. I traced you here."

"The Reed Sisters is flattered."

"No *sisters* to it. It's you I'm talking to. Maybe I could ride you somewhere, now that your night's work is done."

"You got a car?"

"I can call a taxi."

"I usually go for a little drink after services," smiled Laura.

"You're a woman after my own heart," grinned the young man. "I'm Buddy—Big-Eyed Buddy."

"And I'm Miss Laura Reed."

"I know. How about your partner who's shaking hands at the door? Does she drink?"

"No, she goes home like she ought to. Essie's the serious type."

"Essie looks it," said Buddy.

Valance lights out over Eden, cluster lights out on the walls, all lights out except at the door.

"Essie, you take the bag. I'm going riding with this young man for an hour. Mrs. Johnson, meet Mr. Buddy—"

"Lomax," said Buddy taking Essie's hand which had—for him—no grip.

"Hey! Taxi!"

The cab stopped and they rode down to the Roma Gardens. Buddy went to the Men's Room and when he came back, seated in her tiny booth Laura looked up, and there at the edge of the table stood a six-foot, a tower-tall, a brownskin, a large-featured, a big-handed, handsome lighthouse-grinning chocolate boy of a man.

"How old are you?" zoomed around the table. However, neither asked the question. But that is what Laura was asking in her mind of him, Buddy in his mind of her. In her mind Laura lied, "Thirty-two." Of him in her mind Laura guessed, "Twenty-four."

In his mind Buddy thought, "Forty—but *forty,*" which, accented, meant O.K.

"You're forty with me," he said aloud.

"Forty with me, too, baby," said Laura. "Set down."

Nice lights in the Roma Gardens. Cozy in the Roma Gardens. Out of the way, the Roma Gardens. Whee-ooo-oo-o! How many times in the Roma Gardens! Just as if it never happened to her anywhere before the Roma Gardens. Just as it had happened from there to the Shalimar to Eddie's to the Champagne Bar on the Hill for Buddy.

"I got news for you, I'm married," lied Buddy.

"Which makes me no difference," said Laura.

But Buddy knew it did—older women liked younger men better if they were married—spice to make the pot more tasty, age to make cheese more binding, phosphorus the light more blinding—mellow.

No, not that rat trap where I live, thought Laura. It's got to be some place fine, like the Theresa. Besides, Uly might be—

"What you drinking?"

"White Horse 69," said Laura.

"You kinder mixed up there, aren't you, kid?" Buddy grinned.

"Any kind of good Scotch," Laura laughed.

"House of Lords," the waiter smiled. "Chasers?"

"Ginger ale," Laura said.

"Give her water," Buddy laughed. "She don't know."

Laura didn't laugh. She wanted to know. "Just straight might be safer," she sighed.

"I always play it straight," vowed Buddy.

Juke box not too loud. Bar not too full, no crowd, just right to be not lonesome-looking. Knees not too close, just possible to touch. Table not too wide for a whisper to drift across. If a woman were to whisper, it could drift across. Lights not too bright, yet not too dim to see her eyes, his eyes. And table not too wide for what *what* to drift across?

The *what* that sparks the diamond in the serpent's head?

That painter-boy, remembered Laura. Thank God, Buddy is not *refined!*

Bang-bang-bang across the table the *what* that lights the diamond in the serpent's head.

15

Enter Marty

"You could sell Holy Water from the Jordan on Sundays and get a Cadillac," said Buddy. "Let's phone down for breakfast."

Below on Seventh Avenue the uptown traffic hummed through the morning sunlight.

"Bishop Lawson's sure got a great big church," said Laura looking out the double windows before coming back to bed. "How much does Holy Water cost?"

"Just turn the tap," said Buddy, "that's all. And I can get you a hundred gross of empty bottles for a little or nothing, with labels: HOLY WATER—a green river and some palms, you know—about the size of dime store Listerines."

"But you mean the water ain't really holy?"

"It's holy if you bless it," said Buddy. "You can rename the Hudson yourself."

"Essie would have a conniption fit," cried Laura. "Hey, chocolate boy with the coconut eyes, what do you want for breakfast?"

"A little Scotch, a stack of wheats, and a little more loving from you," purred Buddy.

Elevators going up and down. Voices in the hall.

"They got a radio station in this hotel," said Laura.

"WLIB," said Buddy. "Ever been interviewed on it?"

"Never."

"Want to be?"

"What should I say?"

"Pray one of your pretty prayers," said Buddy, "like you used to do on the corner. Sing one of your pretty songs. You might get a week at the Apollo on the Gospel Caravan."

"Essie would drop dead," said Laura.

"Rape Essie!" said Buddy.

Grinding of brakes in the street below as a too-fast car comes to a sudden stop.

"How much should we sell it for?" asked Laura.

"What?" said Buddy.

"The Holy Water," Laura pursued.

"A dollar a bottle." Thus the price was set. "A bottle and a label will cost you about two cents. See the profit? See the Caddy by Christmas? Hum-mm-m! Baby, you're built—no false brassieres!"

"Naturally not. Ouch! Buddy, what I want is an apartment."

"I'll call up Marty."

"Who's Marty?"

"The fixer, the man behind the men *behind* the men. Get you anything."

"Colored?"

"You know he *can't* be colored," said Buddy.

"I hear there're six hundred applications for those twenty apartments in that new building on the Hill."

"Marty'll get your application on the very top."

"I never did put in no application."

"Then he'll just get you the apartment," said Buddy.

"Money under the table?"

"Marty don't need money." White sheet, raw chocolate-brown, that Buddy without pajamas.

I got to get me some nice silk nightgowns, thought Laura, at least to put on to take off.

"Marty knows about your church," said Buddy. "You might never see Marty, but he knows about you."

"Just *who* is Marty?"

"The man."

"What man?"

"Behind the throne of Harlem," said Buddy. "And sitting in your bathroom, too."

"What?"

"All over your bathroom," said Buddy.

16

The Devil's Ham

The winter prospered them. Their two-parlor church grew until so many people wanted to attend that it could no longer hold them all and when the new young leaves were coming out in the spring, Essie found herself standing at a window high up on the ninth floor of a brand-new apartment house looking out over the prettiest edge of Harlem.

"The park! And the river down there!" said Essie. "Laura, how in God's name did you ever get this apartment for us?"

"Buddy—through Marty," said Laura. "Don't frown up—because otherwise we never would have had it. Now you can send for your daughter."

"Thank God for this ham, even if the Devil did bring it!" Essie joked—an old slavery-time joke, it was about a black mother who taught her son that it was a sin to steal; if you did steal the devil was in you. But they were both hungry and the master's smokehouse was full of hams. So one night the son took a ham from the white man's smokehouse, ran back past their cabin, and threw the ham in the window. The black mother cried, "Thank God for this ham—even if the Devil brung it!" And they ate the ham.

Essie loved the apartment. All she moved out of her old place was her motto: GOD BLESS THIS HOME. It didn't go very well with the modernistic couches and things Laura put in the parlor, but Essie hung it firmly on the wall, nevertheless, and there it stayed.

It was a big apartment. Essie had a bedroom and Laura had a bedroom. There was a dining room, an alcove room, a pantry and a kitchen. The alcove could be a bedroom, too. They paid cash for the furniture, all the fine new furniture, and it only took two weeks' collections at church. They had six girls now passing tambourines, besides the marching-up collection at the end.

"The Lord has blessed us indeed," said Essie. But the holy services were not unalloyed. For some reason, Birdie Lee was a nightly thorn in Laura's side—and Buddy was a thorn in Essie's. Birdie Lee could sing too loud to be a little woman, and the way she played the drums—they had a small combo in the church now—excited the worshipers to a frenzy and took the spotlight—had there been a spotlight—off of Laura. Without a personal spotlight, Laura was lost, whereas Essie's sweet placidity continued to glow, even as attention shifted. She just sat like a rock to which the bird of public affection continually returned. That downtown columnist who had come to Harlem to hear their singing had mentioned Essie and Birdie Lee in the paper, and wrote not a word about Laura. Marty had sent the man up there to do a funny piece about the Holy Water from Manhattan's Jordan.

That was the rub with Essie—Buddy's ideas came from the Devil. And Buddy was the Devil's shadow—Marty's Harlem handyman. Marty nobody had ever seen. That Holy Water had caused Essie to go into a series of pauses that lasted for days. It had happened long before they moved to the new apartment. When Buddy brought a dozen cases of empty little bottles with colorful stickers on them to their third-floor tenement, for some reason, maybe because Essie's room was nearest the steps, Laura wanted to pile the cases in her room and fill the bottles from *her* sink. But, in Laura's own words, "Essie pitched a bitch."

"After you left, Buddy," Laura related, "she pitched a bitch. 'Take them lying vessels out of here,' she hollered. And Essie would not let me run a drop of water from her sink. Essie said she wouldn't have no parts of this Holy Water jive—when she knew it didn't come from the Jordan, but right out of a New York tap. As for blessing it, Essie said she hoped the Lord would strike me dead if I blessed such low deceit. Oh, well, Essie's getting old. So I got all them bottles corked up in my room, ready for you to take over to the church, case by case, as we need them. Essie says she won't even set on the rostrum while I sell them, so I told her to go mediate in the backroom then while the selling ceremony is going on—it being *my* rostrum as well as hers. She allows as how she will not only mediate, but pray for my soul."

"That Essie's too holy for her own good," said Buddy.

But that is exactly what happened—on the nights when Laura sold Holy Water for a dollar a bottle, Essie withdrew to the bedroom behind the Garden of Eden and got down on her knees and prayed for the serpent to drop its apple of greed. In her mind Buddy was the serpent.

"How simple can people get," scorned Buddy, "buying Holy Water from the Jordan at a buck a bottle! Ha-ha! Always looking for some kind of lucky stuff here in Harlem. I depend on *myself,* myself."

"Me, too," said Laura. "But Essie depends on God—and *me*. Without me and my ideas where would she have been? Still on relief!"

Yet Essie would touch none of the money from the sale of Holy Water. So Laura told her, "All right, then, I'll put it on a Cadillac car." And she did. She bought a car.

17

Lights Out

Smoldering coals plus quick young sparks produce murky fires beneath the grills of love. Laura had purchased her new nightgowns. But even in her cold old room before they moved, Buddy did not wear pajamas, never. "I sleep too restless," he said. Meanwhile Laura had changed the lock on her kitchenette door before she moved, and she had stopped giving out keys. Only one to Buddy, and a key to the Cadillac for him when the car was delivered. After all, Buddy had gotten her—and Essie—the apartment to move into as soon as the building would be completed. Oh, happy moving day!

"I'm your stick man," said Buddy, brown head on white pillow with a white cigarette between his chocolate lips. "I've got your extra dice up my sleeve. The Reed Sisters, ha! Some nerve! The greatest gospel team in the business. Got to give it to you-all! And you're the slick one—I admire you, kid. But any angles you women don't know, or can't work, Laura, leave to Papa Buddy."

"Chocolate boy with the coconut eyes," cooed Laura, "kiss me."

"I just got through kissing you," said Buddy. "Listen, Marty give me a new idea for you-all the other day."

"You told me about us maybe doing TV programs with the chorus, and getting our gospel quartet on the air, building them up for a night club act after we get our bigger church."

"Naw, not that," said Buddy, offering Laura a puff from his Camel. "Something easier."

"What?"

"Numbers."

"What do you mean, numbers?" cried Laura. "We can't write no numbers in the church."

"Not write 'em, baby, just pronounce 'em," drawled Buddy.

"Pronounce them?"

"Give numbers out in services. You know, you-all got a mighty big following here in Harlem, and when you move to that old theatre you'll have a bigger—"

"Do you think we're really gonna get that empty old theatre? I hear it's condemned."

"Leave it to Marty. With a white man to front for you, baby, you can get anything. Leave it to me and Marty. Marty can get your records played on the air. Marty can get you a lot of recording dates, and he knows a juke box combine. You'll be interviewed on Doc Wheeler's Gospel Show, aw, baby you'll go places. Now, if you'd just eliminate Essie."

"Buddy, we—"

"O.K., skip it. But I'm going to start working on this record deal soon. The Ward Sisters have sold a million copies of their records. So did Mahalia. With a thousand-seat theatre to fill—"

"Church," corrected Laura.

"Church to fill—you gonna need a bigger draw than just singing and praying. Let the word get around that you give out lucky digits every Sunday—and it will be full."

"Buddy, Essie wouldn't even let me mention numbers in our pulpit."

"You won't need to mention numbers. But, anyhow, we gonna have to get rid of Essie—in due time. She's too straight. In fact, she's so straight, she's square. But right now, that's neither here nor there. You won't have to mention numbers, not in the gambling sense. You just give out some holy hymns from the pulpit, or Bible texts with three numbers, that's all, and let the folks write the numbers down. What happens after that is not your business, nor Essie's. If they play 'em, then they play 'em. See, I'll get the bartenders and the poolhall boys to spread the word around that one of your figures hit for big money the very next week, whether it did or not. From then on, your church will be packed, believe me, baby."

"Big-Eyed Buddy, boy, you got an idea," said Laura kissing him square on the lips as his cigarette in his enormous hand hung over the side of the bed.

"Marty's idea," said Buddy. "Him and his syndicate back the biggest numbers bank in Manhattan. But lately business has been slow, particularly in Harlem. High prices and everything, folks are not playing as much as they used to. It needs a shot in the arm—like Marty's uncle says that minister back in the twenties, who used to give out lucky numbers in his pulpit, gave the whole setup. Hundreds of Harlem saints took down the numbers of his hymns—Lucky Hymns—every Sunday and played them all week long. Get the point?"

"Um-hum," hummed Laura. "If that minister had lucky hymns, I could have texts—Lucky Texts."

"Laura Reed's Lucky Texts," mused Buddy. "And each time you give out a text, pass the tambourine for a quarter, else the players won't be lucky the next day."

"And I wouldn't get mine either," said Laura, "without the tambourines."

"Baby, that'll add a few more hundreds regular to the bank account every week—and the government can't tax no church income."

"Amen!" said Laura.

"Amen's right, baby," purred Buddy, putting an electric arm around her neck and drawing her close. "I want you to get me a red Caddy, sports model, convertible."

"Ain't one Cadillac in the family enough, sugar?"

"I never did like dark-colored cars like yours," he murmured, rolling over. "How about it, baby? You know damn well I got a birthday next month."

"Well, maybe . . ."

Without moving his lips from hers, Buddy reached up to turn out the light at the head of the bed, so Laura did not finish her sentence.

18

Stray Cats, Stray Dogs

"Into my church, yes. Into my home, maybe. But into my bed, no!" said Essie squatting on a kitchen chair in their new apartment. "I takes no stray cats."

"If you're gonna throw a hint, throw it clean," said Laura. "I know you're talking about Buddy."

"He's too good-looking to be any good, anyhow," said Essie. "That boy was cut out for a pimp."

"He's got higher ideas," said Laura. "In fact, he's got more than ideas. He's got get-up-and-go, do something about things—which is more than some people I know ever had. Besides, Buddy's no stray cat. He's young, he's healthy, he's smart, he's clean."

"But he ain't no saint. If he's so interested in our church, why don't he get religion?"

"Converted? Buddy?" Laura started to laugh. Then she said, thoughtfully, "He would if I told him to."

"You're not the one to do the telling," said Essie. "That's the spark that comes from God."

"Through me and you in our temple," said Laura, "I believe I'll spark up a few sparks and see what I can do with Buddy."

"You know," mused Essie, "I took in a stray dog once, so frisky and friendly in the street, and clean-looking. After I had him two or three days around home—this were down in Richmond—I found out that that dog had everything a hound could have. He was so frisky and leaped and jumped so much because he had worms. He scooted and slid across the floor so funny because he had the itching piles. He sneezed so cute because he had distemper. Also he had fleas. Besides, when I took that dog to the vet's and paid out my good ten dollars, the man said he had a patch of ringworm behind his ear, which is catching to children and humans. I had to get rid of that dog I had taken into my home. Another time I took a kitten borned of an alley cat, but cute. That kitten grew up to claw one of my neighbor's children in the face, bit me, and had a temper like a tiger. Stray cats, stray dogs, stray people, you can never tell about 'em," said Essie. "You can never tell."

"We got a church full of 'em," said Laura, "and ain't but one turned out bad—that boy that used to come damn near every night to sing and pray, then would go off down the street and light a fire in somebody's house and try to burn them up. Thank God, he never lit no fire in our church before they caught him. I would hate to see my Garden of Eden burnt up."

"When peoples is under the spell of Christ, they most in generally behaves themselves," stated Essie. "But even religion do not touch every heart in time to save it from a life of hellishness and hell. Look how long it took Crow-For-Day to get converted and do right—in his sixty-fifth year before he found salvation—because he told me himself he lied when he said he was only sixty on the night of his conversion."

"Crow's a right good old deacon, even if he did start out his first testimony with a lie. But what's a year more or less? If I told my right age, some folks would be startled."

"Big-Eyed Buddy, for instance," said Essie.

"Lay off of my king-size Hershey bar," said Laura. "Buddy's gonna be my business manager."

"You can have him," said Essie.

"My idea man! That boy's got ways of making loot I ain't never knew existed—also of making love. And if I have my way I'm gonna wrap him up in money like a Hershey bar is wrapped in tin foil."

"Loot, loot, and likker, his speed!"

"Unholy trinity," said Laura. "I think I ought to bring that man to the fold. Imagine what a shouting there would be if Buddy got converted some Sunday!"

"What about Monday?"

"Meaning by that?"

"You should be as good on Monday as you are on Sunday."

"Buddy *is* sort of untamable like, ain't he?"

"Stray cats, stray dogs, stray people!" said Essie.

"But are you forgetting what we said in the beginning, Sister Saintly—that our aim was to save them *lower* down than us?" asked Laura. "You done got on a mighty high horse of late, Miss Essie. I hope you don't be riding for a fall."

Having the last word and already at the door, Laura withdrew, breasts higher than ever, head higher still.

19

God's Marquee

"Not quite a year," said Laura, dusting off the Bible preparatory to evening services, "and already we got a little church and a big apartment. Soon we gonna have a big church. Essie, I signed the lease on that old showhouse today."

"It look mighty rundown to me."

"They gonna paint it up, turn the stage into a rostrum, and put our names in big lights outside where it used to say JOAN CRAWFORD IN THE LOVES OF PASSION, or some such jive. We're gonna fix up that big room down under the stage for the robing room. And you and me'll have dressing rooms down there, too, when they get 'em built. But I guess I can robe with the choir at first—except we ain't gonna call it a choir no more after we move. We gonna call it the Tambourine Chorus, and our church the Tambourine Temple."

"Which was whose idea?" asked Essie.

"Buddy's," said Laura. "He's an idea man! We're gonna get two pianos, one on either side of the stage—rostrum—and everybody in the chorus will have a tambourine."

"I bet Birdie'll buy herself a new set of drums."

"She'll pay for 'em herself, too," said Laura, "much as she has to run to the toilet during services. That woman must have had a busted bladder once."

"Birdie Lee had a hard life before she come back to Jesus," said Essie.

"She's one of your stray cats for true," said Laura.

" 'Our church has no doors,' you stated yourself out there on that corner, Laura."

"There comes that little old varmint of a Birdie Lee now," said Laura. "Look, she's heading straight up the side aisle, I'll bet toward the bathroom."

"Birdie's always ahead of time for services. Good evening, Sister Lee."

"Good evening, all. I'll see you in a minute. When you got to go, you got to go!" Birdie disappeared behind the Garden of Eden and down the back hall.

"Birdie's being cute," said Laura. "And she never did buy one of my bottles of Holy Water yet."

"Birdie ain't so simple," said Essie. "She knows the score."

"Look, people coming already. Why don't you raise a hymn, Essie, while I go back and make myself a pot of coffee. I neglected to eat my supper tonight."

"Out riding?"

"Yes, out riding—in my Cadillac."

Laura disappeared as Sister Essie went down on the floor level to shake hands with the folks who were coming in. "Sister Jenkins, howdy! . . . Mrs. Longshaw, how you been? . . . Brother Bullworth, good evening to you! . . . Deacon Crow-For-Day, come in! . . . God bless you, Sister Jones."

"Blessed assurance, Jesus is mine!
Oh, what a fortress of glory divine! . . ."

On the day when they moved their church into the renovated theatre, as soon as their numerous members got off from work almost everybody turned out to help, and Deacon Crow-For-Day carried the Bible. Laura carred the rostrum in her big new Cadillac with Buddy driving. Essie took the bus up to the old reconverted theatre which, sure enough, had their names up in great big lights: THE REED SISTER'S TAMBOURINE TEMPLE with the possessive in the wrong place. Nobody noticed that. Besides it was day-dusk so the lights were not yet on.

"God's marquee," said Buddy, "with your name on it—Reed. You're a businesswoman, kid, runner-up to Rose Meta—without having to bother with heads."

"I once thought of going into the beauty business," said Laura. "Never could get the capital. I'm glad I didn't now."

"You'd of been a beauty," complimented Buddy.

"Sweet daddy, I'd kiss you if we wasn't in front of the church."

One thousand seats, and each seat bottom folded back. A balcony that used to be for smoking, but no more. "I wonder if we'll fill the upstairs?" asked Laura.

"Try them Lucky Texts," Buddy advised.

"I'll have to spring that deal on Essie by surprise," said Laura. "I better not do it the first Sunday night. I want a little peace for the dedication."

"You got enough on your program for the opener. Save the Bible luckies for next week," Bud counseled. "Start your shot in the arm on another go-round. Get up there on the rostrum now and lemme see how you look."

Laura mounted the stage. They had rented an enormous golden curtain as a background for the chorus.

"I'm gonna get me a red robe to wear up here," said Laura, "and a purple one to change off. Essie's so big, let her wear black for sin, or white for goodness."

"Baby, you would look gorgeous with nothing on," cried Buddy from the back of the auditorium. "And when that spotlight strikes you . . ."

Essie came panting in and looked around the vast playhouse. "They did clean it up right nice for us, didn't they? And the rostrum looks wonderful with that gold velvet drape. But I miss our Garden of Eden."

"Adam's here," said Buddy, pointing a thumb at himself, "and yonder's Eve."

Laura laughed, but Essie wilted silently into a folding seat at the back and went into a pause, a heaviness in her heart. The other saints were bustling around inspecting the place, and Deacon Crow-For-Day proudly placed the Bible on the rostrum which Buddy eventually brought down to the stage. Birdie Lee emerged from the bathroom and set up her drums, took out her sticks, and rolled a jolly gospel roll. Whereupon, in the darkened auditorium, Essie came to life and cried, "Amen!"

20

Strong Branch

Now in their new apartment, they each had big, beautiful bedrooms. Essie slept alone. Laura—well, there were men's coats hanging in Laura's closet, and male pajamas in her laundry—not for sleeping—pajamas with a red B embroidered in silk on the jacket pocket. Naturally they belonged to that big *black* Negro (which is what Laura called him when she got mad—otherwise he was *dark brownskin*) by name of Buddy. Buddy said he liked the shower with the glass doors in the bathroom, which is why he often slept at their place, just so he could get up in the morning and take a shower.

Essie said "Huh!" at that one.

Water! Wonderful water, cleanliness next to godliness! Buddy was clean, teeth shining, nails polished, Sugar Ray's Barber Shop giving his hair a gleam. Sharp-moving like a boxer, like a beast. Tiger of a boy! Coconut eyes, hair which crackled sometimes when Laura ran a comb through it. For Laura, who had never touched the Holy Grail, Buddy was the nearest thing to such a vessel.

"I thrills when I touches the Bible," said Essie.

"I thrill when I touch that man," grinned Laura.

But it was in their new apartment in the late watch of evening that an unsmiling Laura often poured too many drinks. And it was in the late watch of evening that she occasionally talked too much—or rather too freely, for she always talked. But especially on nights when Buddy was not there, she would go to the case in the pantry and pull out another bottle if the built-in cabinet in the living room was dry. In the day, before services, Laura seldom, if ever, drank. But nighttime, with Buddy off somewhere, the hours were so long!

Essie, being a sleepyhead, seldom kept her company. Essie's new Beautyrest mattress in the big cool bedroom in the new apartment was too comfortable! Besides, she had her books to read, slowly going through the whole Bible, plus Howard Thurman with his rolling sentences concerning Jehovah God, and Norman Vincent Peale telling people how to behave themselves easily. But sometimes Laura would start one of her glass-in-hand talking jags early, before Essie turned in, and it was hard for Essie to be so impolite as to go to bed in the middle of an exposition.

When Laura was even just a little drunk, her conversations had a way of weaving continuous links that had no end—for in truth, the end was not yet. Tonight Laura was talking about her mother. It had begun with the lighted cross in the living-room panel which Laura said the writer from *Ebony* that afternoon had called a *symbol.* "And I thought a *cymbal* was something on a drum," said Laura.

"Crosses and nothing else holy don't mean a thing if you don't live right," said Essie, "whatever you may call 'em. And you, Laura, singing and preaching and praying in church half the night and drinking at home the rest, you are burning your candle at both ends."

"My mama burned hers at both ends, also in the middle too," said Laura. "Did I ever tell you really about my mama? Hell-raisingest woman in Charlotte society! North Carolina ain't forgot Mama yet. My mother was from a good family, but the family claimed she did their name no good. They put her out when I was born—I'm illegitimate, you know. The principal of the school was my father—married and a father twice before he fathered me. He never would graduate my mama from that school after she became pregnant, which he did not consider respectable for a student to do. I was born in Raleigh after all of Charlotte knew I was coming—too late for Grandpa, who was a mail carrier and a preacher, to send Mama away before the news leaked out—which is why she was always in disgrace at home. Do you think Mama cared? Never cared! She went on back to Charlotte from Raleigh and stayed right there until the day she died having her thirteenth baby at the age of forty-four. Mama should have knowed better, but she kept on producing black, yellow, and brownskin children for thirty years. Had so many marriage licenses around the house, one overlapped the other. Every time Mama got drunk, she wanted to go get married. Me, being the first one, was the only child not blessed by some kind of wedlock—Catholic, Protestant, or Justice of the Peace. I told that reporter from *Ebony* today, don't go digging too far back into my past—write about the *now,* not the *then.*"

"How come they want to write about you in the magazine?"

"Because he says you and me've got the biggest independent church in Harlem—not belonging to no denomination but our own. He asked me in what did I believe. I said, 'In myself.' Of course, I added, 'For publication, you better fix that statement up a little. Shall I grease your palm? Or do they pay you well on your magazine?' He said, 'We don't accept money from others.' So all I said was, 'Do Jesus! Have a drink.' We got on fine. Sorry you was taking your nap, Essie, when he was here interviewing. You're always resting somewhere, so you miss a lot of what's happening. But Mr. Morrison's coming back with a photographer. They gonna take pictures of our lighted cross and me in my mink coat, me in my car, me singing in the pulpit with a tambourine. Girl, our church is getting famous! Had my mama lived to see me now, she'd of forgot I was a bastard."

"Laura!"

"Well, I was—which is maybe why I'm what that *Ebony* man calls a personality—you know, like Eartha Kitt—with that little something extra on the ball. Essie, I got it from my mama. My mother could jive a man back, make him run and butt his head against the wall, lay down his month's salary at her feet, then beg her for a nickel."

"You just the other way around," yawned Essie, growing sleepy, "giving away money."

"I know. I took after my mother in reverse. Skip it! Tell a story! Mama could make a bar full of people laugh or cry, whichever way her tale went, or if it was about ghosts, scare the hell out of 'em. Mama never saw a ghost in her life, no more than I ever saw Jesus, but she could make up ghost stories to raise the hair on your head. That's where I get my gift of making up visions. I can tell 'em in church so well that even *you* believe me, Essie, and get to shouting up there in the pulpit. Sometimes, sister, I think you're real square."

"Laura, sometimes I do think you are telling the truth in the pulpit, but you just don't believe it yourself. Your experiences is stronger than your faith."

"I been through a plenty, girl, but never seen no visions. What I been through is *real*—robbed, raped, knocked down, plus being kicked on both haunches by that old Negro that bought me that new dress that time I run to you to hide. I have had experiences, Essie, not visions. High on hard likker when I was ten, converted Baptist and half drowned at baptism when I was twelve, married when I was sixteen, divorced when I was twenty, then married again by twenty-one to a simple old Negro who wanted to take care of me.

"I said, 'Baby, I can take care of myself. Don't I look like it?'

"He said, 'You're a fine figure of a woman, Laura—which is why I am willing to buy you new dishes every day just to throw at my head.' I had a temper at that time—broke two chicken platters and a gravy bowl on his bald spot. Sometimes, all of a sudden, Essie, I would coo at him real sweet—and be reaching at the same time for something to bust that man's brains out. But I hate to be kicked in the street where the lampposts is all cemented down. Otherwise, I would have picked one of them posts up and brained that joker that night I run to you. Sometimes my meanness comes out, Laura—which, I guess, is from my mother, too. My mama took a red-hot poker in Winston-Salem one night and stuck it square up a Negro's middle hole whilst he slept."

"Fatheration!" said Essie, trying to keep her eyes open.

"I admired my mother," affirmed Laura. "Sometimes I wish I had her gumption. Ball all night, play all day, drink a bootlegger dry, and still looked like a chippie when she died! Mama protected herself from all evil and got her share of life. This Haig and Haig I'm downing would be a soft drink to my mama. And that Negro Buddy—that I'm so weak about that I'm worried as to where he's at right now—to her would be nothing but a play-toy. Take Buddy serious? Not Mama! She'd bust his conk wide open. They made women in them days—and I take somewhat after her myself. But the rest of Mama's children turned out to be nothing—all fell by the wayside—except me, Sister Laura Reed. I'm a strong branch of a bitch myself."

Essie was snoring politely in a gray silk chair from Sloane's, so she made no comment. Laura poured another drink, lifted her glass, and made a toast to herself in the mirror.

"To Miss Bitch!" she said.

21

Enter Marietta

When June came all over the U.S.A. and Marietta's school was out down South, it came about that at last she was coming to live in Harlem with her mother. Essie had sent her the money for two new dresses and a magic ticket North on the bus. In New York, Essie went down to the Greyhound Terminal to meet her.

Wonderland of the North—where white folks and colored folks all sit anywhere on a bus. The North where you can be colored but still get a Coca-Cola in any drugstore without having to carry it outside to drink it. The North—where young folks all go to school together. The North where New York is, Chicago, Detroit—and Harlem.

They all had come originally from the South—Essie, Laura, Buddy, plus just about everybody else in their church, too. Mighty magnet of the colored race—the North! Roll bus! Roll across that Jim Crow River called the Potomac! Roll past the white dome of the Capitol! Roll down the New Jersey Turnpike, through the Holland Tunnel and up and out from under the river into the North! New York! Roll into the magic streets of Manhattan! Harlem, a chocolate ice cream cone in New York's white napkin.

"Chocolate candy of a boy! Buddy, baby, daddy, do you want another little nip of Scotch now before Essie gets back here tonight with her daughter? We'd better put these drinking things away before that teenager arrives."

"I expect that kid's smelled likker before," growled Buddy.

"But I'm gonna be her 'Aunt Laura,' so no bad examples the first day."

"What are you looking at *me* for?" asked Buddy. "Do I look like a bad example?"

"Doll-baby boy," purred Laura behind the silky couch on which Buddy lounged, "lean back your head and let me kiss your sugar lips." Cool records on the victrola, rippling vibes, somebody like Milt Jackson playing "Willow, Weep For Me," cool, cool, cool, coo-ooo-oo-ol, "Baby-doll!"

"Don't call me such cute names—I'm not a poodle," growled Buddy.

Laura clawed him gently on the shoulder. "Tomcat then! Billy goat! Big black bar-stud! Mama's beautiful bastard!"

"Don't get me roused up *again* this early in the evening. Unhand me, woman!"

"You sweet old honeycomb of a joker! Tonight's Saturday—no services for me. But I'm going to bed early so's to be fresh for church tomorrow—I love that big funny old theatre we moved into!"

"You look sharp upon that stage, too, sugar—just like a grand piano, as I told you before—full front, streamlined rear."

"Soon as the backstage painting's done, I'm gonna take that big dressing room downstairs with the star on it for my robing room. Before it turned to movies, they tell me that house used to be an old vaudeville theatre. Seems like I can still smell make-up. I always did want to be in show business and have myself a dressing room."

"This church racket beats show business, baby—the way they're turning all the old theatres in Harlem into churches."

"You know what Mahalia Jackson says: 'The church will be here when the night clubs are gone.' The church is the rock. I reckon me and Essie picked a good rock on which to stand."

"That Essie's a little *too* holy and sanctified," growled Buddy. "Telling me I ought to change my ways! Kid, I've been a hustler too long now to be anything else *but.* And if it hadn't been for me, Laura, you-all Reed Sisters never would have got that old firetrap of a theatre cleared by the inspector."

The Scotch stood on the coffee table before them and now Laura was on the silky couch with Buddy.

"I'm glad you know the right people," she cooed, "in with the politicianers."

"Connections, sugar, connections! Marty can fix anything. Even in the rackets, a Negro's got to have a white man to front for him."

Laura rubbed her thumb and forefinger together indicating money. "I must say, the do-re-mi helped a little too, didn't it?"

"Greasing palms always helps, kiddo! I could do with a little change myself tonight—a few Abe Lincolns and some tens. Since you say you're going to bed early, I might take a hand of poker up at Shoofly's. How about table stakes?"

"Table stakes?"

"Say, fifty simoleons."

"Aw, honey, that's a lot of money to gamble away."

Buddy shrugged. "I can't sleep here tonight, so Essie informs me. With that young girl coming, I got to blasé my time away somewhere. Something tells me that kid's going to be in our way around here, Laura."

"Essie's daughter is no kid, Buddy. She's sixteen."

Buddy grinned. "Sweet sixteen—but I bet she's been kissed."

"Maybe not. Marietta was raised by her grandmother," said Laura, "and down South they generally raise kids right—not running wild like they do up here in Harlem. God's been good to Essie, and at last she'll have her daughter with her. I wonder if that child'll get off the bus hungry."

"I don't know about that child, but me, I could give a steak hell right now—rare, with the blood oozing out."

"They'll be here soon, then me and Essie'll fix dinner. I told her to bring in some groceries. Meanwhile I better get decent and put on a dress, heh? Also let's put this likker away *right now,* and rinse out the glasses. You do it, Daddy, while I get pretty. Be sweet."

"O.K.," said Buddy, "go ahead and make like Lena Horne."

Laura went down the hall to her room and Buddy took a couple straight before he put the House of Lords away in a built-in cabinet in the wall opposite the lighted panel of a cross. When all the other lights were out in the living room, the cross glowed softly. Above it was Essie's motto: God Bless This Home.

That must be her now putting a key in the lock. It was. And behind Essie, came Marietta. When Buddy looked up, in the door there stood a tiny, a well-formed, a golden-skinned, a delicate-featured, a doll-handed, a pretty-as-a-picture, a blossoming peaches-and-cream of a girl.

"Why, good evening! I didn't know you'd still be here, Buddy," Essie said. "Marietta, meet Mr. Lomax. Mr. Lomax, my daughter."

Buddy stood up. Slowly his lighthouse smile spread. Then softly he took the young girl's hand. "Pleased to know you, Marietta. Essie, you got a bee-ooo-tiful daughter!"

Marietta's eyes were big as saucers, almost as big as Buddy's. When he finally dropped her hand, she cried, "Mama, it's so pretty in here! Oh, Mama, what a nice place you've got—so modernistic! And a lighted cross in the wall!"

"We're blessed, honey! But just wait until you see our new church tomorrow. All of this is the Lord's own miracle, Marietta. But where is Laura?" Essie called, "Laura, Laura!"

"I'm coming, coming," strong voice from down the hall. Then cool in her summer frock, Laura came, arms out to Marietta. "Child, I'm your Aunt Laura."

"This is my old friend who's stuck by me through thick and thin," said Essie. "This is Laura."

"I'm glad you're here, Marietta! This is your house." Laura took her in her arms.

"I wish *I* was related, too," grinned Buddy. But Essie didn't hear him.

"Thank God! I just thank God for all," Essie said glowing.

"God—and your tambourines," laughed Buddy. "Marietta, can you play a tambourine?"

Shyly, "I used to try sometimes in church down home."

"Then you'll fit," said Buddy.

"Are you part of the choir at the church?" asked Marietta.

"No, baby," he said, "I'm just a backstage man."

"Buddy," Laura's tone was sharp, "her name's Marietta, not *baby*."

"She's a baby to me," said Buddy. "And I'm sure glad you got here, little old gal, so we can have dinner."

"Oh, my goodness!" Essie exclaimed. "Meeting Marietta, I was so excited I clean forgot to bring the chops. Ain't that awful!"

"No," said Buddy, "not so bad—because my mouth's set on steaks anyhow, so I'll go get 'em. Umm-m—with the blood oozing out! Come on, Marietta, lemme show you where the stores are in this neighborhood, since you'll be living here. We'll get some sirloins, ice cream, and beer. What else do you need, Laura?"

"Potatoes," said Laura drily, as her eyes narrowed.

"Marietta, ain't you kinder tired?" asked Essie.

"Not really, Mama."

"Oh, let the girl see what our block looks like—take a little squint at Harlem," said Buddy. "Come on, kid." Marietta looked at Essie eagerly. "All right, Mama?"

"You-all come directly back then," said Essie weakly, "and while you're gone we'll set the table."

Had Laura said anything at all then, she would have screamed. As soon as the door closed, she went to the cabinet and got a drink. "I'll steal one while your child's out," she said, "so she won't think right off the bat that I'm a likker-head." Then she turned and smiled at Essie. "She's a mighty pretty girl, Essie—I'm afraid too pretty for this city of sin. Don't you think maybe Marietta should just stay here for a *little* visit, then go on back to her grandma down in the simple old South?"

"After all these years," said Essie, "I want to keep my child with me."

"She's at the age, you know—" warned Laura.

"Well, there's some mighty nice young mens in Harlem—in our church," Essie said. "I already told young C.J. my daughter was coming, and to drop around tonight."

"Oh, God, I hope C.J. don't bring that guitar of his! The last thing I want to hear is gospel music on my night off. I be's good all the week in front of the public, *plus on Sunday.* But on Saturday night I feel like letting my hair down."

"I hope you won't drink so much, now that Marietta is here."

"I'll do my damndest to respect your child, Essie, I swear I will. But you know I ain't no saint. You've just naturally got goodness in you. Long as I've known you, you never was inclined to do nothing much—but set on your big fat behind and let the city pay your rent. Me, I'm active. But you, you just take whatever comes. Thank God, for all our sakes, it's money coming these days."

"I wrestles with temptation, too, Laura, in my heart. But somehow or another, I always did want to *try* to be good. Once I thought—just like you said about me—being good was doing nothing, I guess, so I done nothing for half my life. Now, I'm trying to do *something*—and be good, too. That's harder. It's easy to preach holy, but hard to live holy."

"You're reading a mighty lot lately"—Laura pointed to the pile of books on the table—"which is strangely for you, who never even read the Bible till we started this church. Now you're *buying* books."

"Just Thurman, and Reverend Robinson and Norman Vincent Peale. I want to see what them men say about being good."

"I don't trust nothing white folks write, especially about being good, the way they behave down South."

"Howard Thurman ain't white. He's a colored preacher. So's Reverend Robinson. As for that Mr. Peale, I'm no respecter of race, Laura. Some white folks is good, some bad, just like the rest of us. What I'm trying to do, now that I've got the time—"

"And money," interrupted Laura.

"And money to set down and meditate, is to try to unscramble the good from the bad—in myself and others. If I can just separate the good in this world, the wheat from the tares, maybe I can hold onto it. I found a verse in the Bible I been studying over and over, says, 'Canst thou by searching find out God?' "

"What verse is that?" asked Laura sitting up straight. "Where is it?"

"Job 11–7."

"What a number!" cried Laura. "11–7, wow! 7–11."

"Laura, you thinking about the numbers, and I'm thinking about finding God—finding out what *is* God in terms of what we is—us, you and me—on this earth. Reverend Thurman says—"

"Reverend Thurman don't know no more than you do about God. He ain't nothing but a man, and we're all made in God's image, both men and women. I'm gonna try to stay as good-looking as I can myself. It takes money to go to Rose Meta's—which is one more *fine* beauty shop—but I intend to go every week."

"It takes money to run a good church, too. And now that we got a big place, Laura, I wants me a day nursery in the basement of our church where mothers what goes to work can leave their children and—oh, sister, there's so many ways to do good and *be* good that we ain't found yet."

"Listen, Essie, *how* good do you want to be—so good you ain't got a dime? I'm trying to figure out how we can make *plenty* of money. My mink coat's costing me Three Thousand Dollars! And now you got a daughter here in New York to educate. Takes money to put a young girl through school right."

"I wants other people's daughters to get through school too. There ain't no being good and keeping goodness to yourself. Is there, Laura?"

"It's good to me when it's just *all* mine, Essie. It's like love—like Buddy. I don't want to share Buddy with nobody."

"You talking about flesh-kind of love, not spirit."

"The spirit works in mysterious ways. When I open my mouth to sing, it feels just like when I open it for a kiss—*so good*, like being in bed with Buddy."

"Laura!"

"Well it does—same kind of thrill—especially when I hit them high notes in swing time. Ow! But by the way, I wonder where is Buddy?"

22

Steak for Dinner

The bell rang, but it was C.J. at the door, and he *did* have his guitar. Essie made him welcome, for C.J. was one of the nice young men in their gospel choir, or rather in the singing band at one side of the rostrum that accompanied the choir. There Birdie Lee had set up her drums along with the guitar, trumpet, and an old man who blowed on a flute, while the two pianos at either side of the stage sometimes drowned them all out, except the drums. Nobody could top Birdie Lee when her sticks really got going.

C.J. played a nice gospel guitar. "And I'm working on some brand-new spiritual riffs out of this world, Sister Essie, for that new song the Tambourine Chorus is trying out tomorrow night."

"Some saints can overdo, C.J.," said Laura, leaving for the kitchen to start the coffee boiling. "You just set down and rest yourself. Put your gitfiddle in the corner. You can serenade the young lady when she comes."

"Bless God, son, you do play pretty!"

"Does your daughter sing?" C.J. asked Essie.

"To tell the truth, I don't know, C.J., but I hope she do. You ask her."

"I will," said C.J. "Where's she at?"

"She'll be here directly."

Sure enough, directly Marietta and Buddy arrived loaded down with things to eat and drink, including Buddy's carrying a dozen cans of beer, three of which he promptly opened, handing one to C.J. and offering another to Marietta. But she declined. C.J. demurred, saying he did not drink beer. But Buddy made him feel like less than a man if he couldn't drink that weak stuff. No kid likes to be made out a sissy in front of a pretty girl, even if he is a junior saint, so C.J. drank the beer, and shortly felt it. Meanwhile, in spite of Buddy, he got acquainted with Marietta.

"That's a pretty name."

"And yours," asked Marietta, "what really is your first name?"

"My first name's just C.J."

"What does C.J. stand for?"

"C.J., that's all," said the young man. "I only got initials for a first name."

But Buddy cut in, "Christ Jesus, baby, Christ Jesus, that's what it stands for."

"Mr. Lomax is just kidding, Marietta," said C.J.

"C.J. is one of them holy and sanctified boys," said Buddy.

"I was raised up in a gospel church, but—"

"Probably won't even take a chick to the movies."

"Sure I will," bristled C.J.

"Never see you around the pool halls," insisted Buddy.

"Well, with school work and all—"

"Where do you go to school, C.J.?" asked Marietta.

"First year college at City," said C.J.

"Can I look at your guitar, kid?" asked Buddy. "I used to beat out a mean blues before I left Savannah."

"A blues? Sure, if the Sisters don't mind."

"A little blues won't hurt the Sisters. Hum-mm! You got a nice box here."

"I play in the college orchestra sometimes."

"You're lucky to be in college," said Marietta.

"My Korean GI money," said C.J.

"What are you taking up?"

"Chemistry. I can analyze that Holy Water Sister Laura dispenses in church. I wish she'd let me test a bottle while I'm here tonight, so I can tell what makes Jordan Water different from that we have in New York City."

"That Jordan Water costs a dollar a bottle, boy," drawled Buddy, "so nobody's giving none away."

"Well, maybe I'll buy a bottle at church tomorrow."

"I would advise you to leave that water alone," said Buddy.

"Why?" asked C.J., puzzled.

"Just advice, that's all," said Buddy as the first eight bars of a down-home stomp rolled off the guitar strings. "How do you like my blues, boy?"

"Right nice, Mr. Lomax. Marietta, whereabouts are you in school—high, or what?"

"Second year high school. But you know the schools down South aren't very good, especially for colored, and—" She was speaking louder and louder as Buddy's blues mounted, too. "Well, I'm afraid I won't match the girls up North here."

"You look real smart to me, Marietta. Besides, you're so pretty you scare me." But the boy had to shout his last few words. Buddy was drowning them out with the blues, sniffing at the same time at the scent of food from the back of the house.

Apron on from the kitchen, Essie put a stop to it. "I knowed that couldn't be C.J. playing that loud. Buddy, the neighbors! They'll hear all them blues coming out of our apartment and think we've forgot the gospel."

With a belly chord, Buddy tossed the guitar to C.J. "Here, kid, you can play the kind of stuff the Sisters like. But them gospel songs sound just like blues to me."

"Buddy! At least our words is different. But we don't need no music now, boys, nohow. We're about to put the steaks on the fire. Anybody want to wash up for dinner?"

"I'm a clean boy myself, thanks," said Buddy.

But C.J. spoke up. "I do, Sister Essie."

"I'll show you the place," said Essie, "and when you've washed your hands, son, come on out in the kitchen and cut the watermelon. Dinner'll soon be ready." C.J. followed Essie down the hall.

"He's country," said Buddy, with a head-down smile. He was looking at Marietta. "Baby, I'd like to show you something."

"On the guitar?" asked Marietta.

"No, not on the guitar."

"What?" He was very near her now.

"You've only met two men in New York so far."

"Why, I've only been here an—"

"I know. You met *me* first," said Buddy. "It's up to me to school you."

"School me?"

"That's right. That gospel boy of a C.J. ain't dry behind the ears yet. Men don't start asking a sharp little chick like you what school you're in."

"Sharp?"

"Stacked, solid, neat-all-reet, copasetic, baby!"

"Thank you, Mr. Buddy."

"Don't *Mister* Buddy me. Just call me Buddy, that's all—Big-Eyed Buddy—with eyes for you."

"Mama told me you're Miss Laura's friend."

"Marietta, Laura is as old as your mama—and I'm mighty near as young as you."

"Still and yet, you're her friend, aren't you?"

"I'm her friend. But, Marietta, I'm gonna show you something. I'm gonna show you how fast a real Harlem stud moves in."

"Moves in?"

"On a chick." Before she could pass, Buddy's arm swept her to him. His body was warm. The old symbol of the earth suddenly sounded as if beaten by the sun in the first Garden. "We start like this," he breathed. Buddy kissed her.

"You told me you liked your steaks rare—with the blood oozing out," said Laura very quietly from the doorway. She had come to call them to dinner.

Before Marietta could struggle free, he dropped his arms. "I do," Buddy said.

"And your women tender?"

"Could be," said Buddy.

"You, Miss Marietta, I guess you're not as innocent as you look."

"I tried to get past, Aunt Laura, but—"

"Then get past, honey, *get past quick!* As for you, Buddy-boy—"

"Aw, come, old chick, don't get blood in your eyes."

"Nor on my hands?" asked Laura. "I never knowed a Negro yet that didn't bleed—if cut."

Essie's voice rang out in the hall. "Let's go, everybody, dinner!"

"Come on, Buddy, get your steak," said Laura.

23

Lucky Texts

After Marietta came, Laura didn't bring Buddy home so often. After services they went elsewhere in Laura's car. The big new apartment was quiet, and Essie had a chance to get acquainted with her daughter. Only C.J. was there sometimes, properly courting the kid. Essie liked C.J. for he was a clean, quiet gospel boy, bright and not bad-looking. Marietta liked him, too. But even when he held her tightly in his arms on the silky couch, nothing electric happened as had happened that one and only time when Buddy moved in behind the magnet of his chocolate shadow. About that, no one said a thing to Essie—not Laura, Buddy, or Marietta. Now Marietta avoided Buddy.

The Tambourine Choir filled the new church with music, and Marietta became a part of the singing. When her mother introduced her to the congregation she had, all alone, begun a chorus of "Rise and Shine and Give God the Glory." All the instruments and voices had supported her and the whole church sang too, along with the singing in Essie's heart that her daughter had come to her at last. That night, taking advantage of the wave of wonder in the church, Laura chose to introduce the Lucky Texts of which Essie had no inkling. As Marietta took her seat in the banked choir loft and the singing died down and Essie sat fanning in her big red chair, Laura stepped forward and thanked God for Essie, Marietta, and the Tambourine Chorus.

"And now," she said, "I've got something new for you, church. After this fine chorus that you are going to hear on the air waves of the nation soon, and before I introduce our up-and-coming TV quartet, the Gloriettas, I got a surprise for everybody, right out of the Book—the Bible. And not one, but four surprises. I am going to give you four texts for the week—Lucky Texts, picked out with prayer and meditation on my part from the Holy Book. For each Lucky Text, members and friends, I want you to drop a quarter—or a dollar for all four—in the tambourines as they pass. Girls of the Offeratory, circulate amongst the congregation for their free-will gifts."

Essie leaned forward. "Laura, you gonna stop the services to take up a collection now?"

"I am," whispered Laura. "This is a special collection, so just hold your horses, Essie."

She turned again to the people, opened the big Bible on the rostrum and fingered its gilt-edged pages.

"Friends, I want you-all to write down the numbers of these Lucky Texts, and study these texts all during the week—until I give out some more next Sunday. Get your quarters ready, your dollar bills, and your pencils. Now write."

Laura pretended to look at the Bible, wetting her thumb to turn its pages, but what she really looked at was a slip of paper she had lying on the rostrum.

"Psalms 9 and 20," she said. "Got that? 9 and 20. Now drop a quarter in the tambourines. For each text a quarter. Give God His, folks, and you'll get yours! . . . Next text: Leviticus 2–16, Chapter 2, verse 16. Take down all three numbers: 2-1-6. Twenty-five cents. You'll have no luck if you don't give God His'n. 2–16, yes! Aw, let 'em clink! Let the holy coins clink! . . . Now, again, ready? Revelations 12–3. Got it? 12–3. Let me read that text to you. Listen: And there appeared another wonder in heaven; and behold a great red dragon, having seven heads and ten horns, and seven crowns upon his heads.' What a text! What a mighty text! Revelations 12–3! Yes, one-two-three! And in the text itself, *seven* heads and *ten* horns—the number *seven* and the number *ten*. Look up this text yourself—Revelations 12–3. . . . And now the last one. Oh, what a great text, too—Sister Essie's favorite! But I ain't gonna tell you what this one is. Just write the number on your pads, then look it up yourself. Read it and see for yourself. So take the numbers down—Job 11–7. Carefully, now! Write it right—Job 11–7. I said 7, 7–11, or 11–7 either way. Yes, bless God, children! 11–7, that's right. Job 11–7."

The rhythm of Laura's phrases and the magic of the numbers, the 3, the 11, and the 7 to top them all, caused many among the crowd to cry aloud "Thank you, Sister Laura! Thank you! Thanks, thanks! Thank you!" The tambourines were filled with money when the ushers returned to the rostrum. Laura estimated two, maybe three hundred dollars.

"There'll be some numbers played tomorrow," Buddy could not resist crying from his third-row seat.

Essie said, "Just listen at that Buddy taking everything wrong."

Laura said, "Amen!" as if she had not heard. "Now a little holy music. Let me introduce to you for another happy time our singing pride, our Temple's fine young women, the Four Gloriettas."

The two gleaming grand pianos trilled, C.J.'s guitar joined the pianos, Birdie's drums rolled, the trumpet played a golden note, and four buxom girls came forward shod in golden slippers and mauve robes to sing a song about the glory of touching God's garment that ended:

> *"There will be a shower of stars!*
> *There will be a blaze of light!*
> *All around my Saviour's head*
> *A diadem so bright!*
> *You will see it from afar*
> *As you stand beside His throne.*
> *Oh, when you touch His garment*
> *He will claim you for His own!"*

For many there living in the tenements of Harlem, to believe in such wonder was worth every penny the tambourines collected.

24

Set to Ascend

"Seventeen converts last night, including the man with one eye and one arm. This church is growing, Essie. But big as it is, it's already busting at the seams."

In the big room under the stage of Tambourine Temple as the mid-week preliminary song service drew toward its close, with the choir singing upstairs, Laura and Essie were robing to make their entrance. As usual Laura was talking.

"Since I gave Buddy that red car for his birthday, Essie, I've been having to drive myself—or else get a chauffeur. So what do you think? I'm gonna *get* a chauffeur."

"Ostentation is a sin, Laura."

"So's having too much money, according to you. But there's nothing I love as much as *too* much money. And the way it's pouring in every night upstairs, I'm gonna stack up loot on the living room table next year and stare at it."

"Laura!"

"You can buy anything with money, honey, which is why I love it."

"Sister, darling, I hope you won't mind what I say—but don't you think maybe money can do harm sometimes? I hope you ain't spoiling yourself—and Buddy."

"Do I mingle and meddle in your affairs, Essie?"

"I wouldn't say nothing if you wasn't my friend."

"Sometimes friendship can rile even a friend, Sister. Just look out for yourself and your little girl, and I'll look out for me, see! And whilst I'm on the subject of Marietta, maybe you ought to send her back down South—or else move to the suburbs, one."

"Thanks for the hint, Laura. I reckon you feel crowded, now that Marietta's come. I didn't want to leave you—unless you told me to."

"Girl, you ain't Ruth, and I ain't Naomi. And you got your daughter's morals to protect. They call this thing a tiara," murmured Laura, putting on her head a gold band with a cross in front. "Goes nice with this robe, don't it, Essie?"

"Um-humm!" said Essie. "But I wonder what is Marietta and C.J.

doing outside in the door so long. Why don't them kids come on in here?"

"Necking," said Laura. "I hope you don't think C.J. really is named after Christ, do you?"

"Aw, now, Laura, them children—"

"Children, my eye!"

"I got shoes, you got shoes
All of God's chillun got shoes!
When I get to heaven
Gonna put on my shoes!
Gonna walk all over God's heaven . . . "

Laura took a few syncopated steps to the music rollicking down from above.

"Heaven! Heaven!
Everybody talks about
Heaven ain't going there . . ."

"Just listen at that fine singing upstairs, girl!" Laura cried. "We got some good gospel musicianers, I mean!"

"You really organized a fine band, Laura. You're the backbone of it all."

"Entertain people at Tambourine Temple, that's what I say. You sing and pray, Sister, and I will arrange the show."

"It's more than a show, Laura. You've done better than you know—God is in this church."

"I still got feet of clay, Essie. You're the soul. But please powder your face a little before you go upstairs. That spotlight on the rostrum shows up your liver spots."

Laura handed Essie her compact. While she stood in front of the mirror, Marietta and C.J. came running in.

"Mama," panted Marietta, "C.J. wants to know can he take me out for a hamburger tonight after services?"

"I'll bring her right home," swore C.J.

"Not to your home—*ours,* I hope," said Laura.

"Yes'm, Sister Laura."

"I guess it's all right, son, if she wants to go," said Essie. "But behave your-all's selves."

"That's settled," said Laura, "so get on up with the band, C.J., where you should've been. Marietta, you hear that Tambourine Chorus shaking, don't you?"

"Yes, Aunt Laura," said Marietta getting her robe from the closet.

"Tell them musicianers, C.J., to give me and Essie a lot of noise when we appear on the stage—rostrum, I mean. I want plenty of *Thank Gods* tonight, honey, bass chords, drum rolls, tambourines, and hallelujahs from all of you-all."

"Yes, ma'am!" answered C.J., as he and Marietta ran up the stairs to the rostrum.

"The Spirit don't need all that ballyhoo and theatre kind of build-up," murmured Essie.

"No, baby, but Laura Reed does. Are you all set to ascend the pulpit?"

"I'm set to ascend."

"Now, I wonder how come them drums upstairs stop playing just when I'm ready to appear?" growled Laura.

"You know Sister Birdie Lee's weakness," Essie said. "I bet she's heading down here."

"That little old hussy we picked up in the gutter can really beat some drums," admitted Laura, "even if she is kinder hateful."

Essie was right. Birdie Lee came scooting down the stairs. "Excuse me, you-all, but I drunk so much beer when I was a sinner that I'm still going to the Ladies' Room. Excuse me!"

"Hurry up, sister, and pee," said Laura, "so you can roll them drums when I step on the stage. Come on, Essie, we'll wait upstairs for Birdie to return. I like plenty of noise when I mount the rostrum. You can sneak in the pulpit quiet if you want to, but I want the world to know when Sister Laura Reed arrives. Let's we ascend."

25

One Lost Lamb

To make his conversion believable, Laura felt, it would have to be worked out carefully, and fortunately she had a flair for such things. The hymn she chose for Buddy's cue to salvation was "The Ninety and Nine." With her pianists, Laura rehearsed it several times.

"You're around the church so much these days, officiating and helping me," said Laura to Buddy as they drove through Central Park one afternoon, "that lots of saints are wondering how come you don't belong to our church—how come you're not converted?"

"So it would be good business then if I came into the fold, huh?"

"It would cover little Mama," said Laura, "and I wouldn't have to answer so many questions."

"Since nothing exciting ever happens in the middle of the week, suppose I get converted Wednesday," said Buddy, curving past the Tavern on the Green.

"Fine!" cried Laura. "That might cool Essie down a little. But listen, Daddy, after you get converted, don't go getting *too* holy. Just learn to melt a little more. Be a little nicer to me, and don't be so hard."

"Don't *don't* me, sugar," barked Buddy, stopping for a red light, then playfully ramming a fist under Laura's chin. "I know how far to go, up or down, right, left, or in between."

"Which is what I like about you," murmured Laura. "Baby, you dig the angles."

"All the angles." Buddy flashed his lighthouse smile as their car purred away.

"There were ninety and nine that safely lay
In the shelter of the fold . . ."

Laura never looked prettier nor sang better than she did that Wednesday night as the services drew near the close. Her tambourine lay silent on the altar. Only the two pianos played softly, very softly, behind her. Laura had expressly commanded Birdie Lee *not* to hit a tap as she sang. "And *don't* sing with me!" The orchestra was not to play, only the soft, soft, sad, sweet pianos. There were almost a thousand people in the church, but Laura was singing to Buddy. The congregation knew only that she had asked for converts, requesting all who wanted to come to God to walk down the aisle and accept salvation.

Laura had not intended to cry on the rostrum. But as she sang, somehow in spite of herself, tears came. She found herself suddenly wishing that she, too, were like Essie seated in the red chair behind her—truly a Christian.

"One lamb was out in the hills away
Far from the gates of gold . . ."

Lamb! Buddy! Buddy! Tower-tall Buddy! Unsaved Buddy!

"Away on the mountain wild and bare,
Away from the tender Shepherd's care."

How lonely the song, how lost and lonely, as Laura turned and walked toward the rostrum where the Bernstein Bible shone.

Sobs broke out in the old rat-trap of a theatre-church and Deacon Crow-For-Day cried, "I once stood in the wilderness, too. I were lost! I were lost!" Laura pointed to the massed choir on the platform in their singing robes.

"Lord, Thou hast here Thy ninety and nine:
Are they not enough for Thee?
But the Shepherd made answer,
One of mine has wandered away from me.
Although the road be rough and steep,
I go to the desert to find my sheep,
I go to the desert to find my sheep."

A piercing cry rent the auditorium and a woman fainted. Laura looked down at the long aisle that ran through the auditorium to the vestibule and out to the hard road of the Harlem pavements and she saw the park where the taxis sped up from Penn Station where the trains came in from the South where the roads were unpaved and the shacks had no windowpanes and the money for the ticket North had been purchased with sweat, maybe blood, and sin, and surely sorrow:

"Lord, whose are those blood drops all the way
That mark out the mountain's track?

They were shed for one who had gone astray
Ere the Shepherd could bring him back.
Lord, whence are Thy hands so rent and torn?"

How could Laura's hands be the Lord's uplifted there? But somehow they were His hands when she lifted them up. Nobody doubted that those hands were the Lord's hands.

"They are pierced tonight by many a thorn,
Yes, pierced tonight by many a thorn."

Look! Look! My hands! My dark hands! Shaking the brooms and mops of a nation, scrubbing and cleaning the floors of a nation, mining the coal of a nation, carting the slag of a nation, cleaning the outhouses of a nation.

"But none of the ransomed ever knew
How deep were the waters crossed,
How dark was the night
That the Lord passed through
Ere He found His sheep that was lost."

So lone! So lost!

"Out in the desert He heard its cry,
So lone, so helpless, ready to die."

"Save me! Lord save me," cried Buddy.

Buddy was not sure himself then that he did not mean his cry. Suddenly he got up and stumbled to the altar. Then the drums rolled—for Birdie Lee forgot what she had been told. The old man played on his flute, the trumpet blew a golden note, C.J.'s guitar sounded like a thousand strings, the tempo changed and Laura's voice hit each word hard like a trip hammer:

"All through the mountains thunder-riven
And up from the rocky steep,
Oh, there arose a glad cry to the gates of heaven,
Rejoice! I have found my sheep!"

Then the chorus picked up the words and a hundred voices proclaimed:

"God has found, God has found His sheep."

So it was that Big-Eyed Buddy became a member of Tambourine Temple. And at that moment nobody doubted Buddy's conversion except Essie, who seldom in all her life had taken the Lord's name in vain. But when she saw Buddy bow at Laura's feet to beat his head upon the floor crying, "I'm saved! I'm saved! Thank God, I'm saved!" Essie said, "This is the God-damndest shame yet!"

She then went into a pause from which nothing could move her until everybody had gone home. Then she put out the lights in the empty theatre and locked the door.

26

Moon over Harlem

Big moon, golden moon, sifting its rays down through the trees in the park.

"You asked me to tell you about my mother, C.J.," said Marietta, "so, even if you have got something else on your mind, *I'm going to tell you about my mother.* Listen!"

C.J. held her close, very close in his arms on the park bench.

"I know Sister Essie's a good woman, Marietta, so there's not much more to tell, is there?"

"She *is* a good woman. Like I told you, Mama wanted me to be with her for years, but she couldn't manage it. She didn't just want me to be with her under any kind of circumstances. I wanted to be, though, but she didn't. Mama wanted things nice for me—a big apartment and all—and she waited until they were nice."

"Nice," C.J. said, his hand following the warm curve of her breast.

"C.J., I know you're the same way—I can tell you're good. And, listen! If you want to make love to me now—the way you want to right now, here in this park in the dark—if you was to have me now, then you wouldn't want me maybe when things got right for us."

"I would, I would want you," whispered C.J., "I would."

"Maybe you'd want me, but you'd think you shouldn't."

"I'd want you! I want you *now,* and I'd want you any time, all the time."

"You might disrespect me, C.J., if I gave in to you *quick* like this. We've only known each other a little short while. I love you, C.J., but I want you to love me, too, not just—be with me."

"I got to be with you, Marietta, I got to, I need to."

"You will, sweetest boy in the world, you will—but please, not tonight."

"Suntanned, honey-brown, honey-gold, you're sweet, you're sweet! You're so sweet!"

"No, C.J."

Suddenly he was angry. "Aw, you ain't all that pure." He took his arms away and put his hands into his pockets. Silence. Moonlight. Leaves.

"I'm not pretending to anything, C.J.—except I love you, that's all."

"You love me?" said C.J., as if he'd never heard the word before. "You really love me?"

"I love you."

"I love you, too, Marietta. I'll be damned if I (pardon me, I'm a saint) I'll be *dogged* if I don't! Come on! I'll walk you home."

He didn't touch her any more. He just looked at her in the soft drift of moonlight that came through the trees. Then C.J. stood up. Obediently, Marietta rose from the park bench and took his hand.

"If that Buddy guy, or anybody else, tries to touch you in New York City, or anywhere else, I'll beat the living be-Jesus out of 'em."

"Kiss me."

"Marietta!"

27

Shower

The nights when Buddy stayed with Laura, in the morning he would take a shower and when he took a shower, to Laura Buddy was like iron walking through the room naked to the shower, as clean and hard before the water fell as afterwards, glistening clean.

When Laura took a shower and walked around the room naked, to Buddy she was like chocolate in summer on the verge of going soft, yal, about to become sticky, melt, before or after the water fell the same.

About Buddy nothing at all sweet-sticky to Laura. Nothing about Laura firm and unsticky to Buddy, body soft and gooey like chocolate over almonds in a summer almond bar. A too-sweet taste in the mind's mouth, yal, too much.

To Laura no taste at all—the hard clean iron of tall brown glistening Buddy. Cool smooth nothing-to-rub-off, to skin like fruit, nothing to bite off, keep, dry like a flower in a book, smell, taste about Buddy, nothing.

Everything melting, to need-to-wipe-your-fingers-clean, sweet sticky softness about Laura, even after a cold shower. The smell of woman, even after a shower. Like it? Sure, yal! Love it? Naw! I get sick to my stomach.

"I need ten dollars for a couple of Scotches, baby, on my way to church. I said ten dollars, Laura!"

Buddy, don't you ever, Buddy, Buddy, ever need to just hold, need to hold me, Buddy, hold me still and quiet still-like, do nothing but hold me? I am Laura! How can you be so big, organ-sounding words, brown, strong, straight, clean, big—and nothing gives at all, bends, melts to me, warms me in my heart at all? So damned-looking clean—iron legs, thighs, iron chest, iron arms, hard, hard iron lips, teeth, iron tongue—nothing gives. In the end nothing. I try to imagine, Buddy, I try.

"Throw me a towel—two towels—two big towels, baby."

"I can't hear you, Buddy, with the water running."

"You *better* hear me, Laura, and throw me a towel!"

"Buddy. . . ."

28

Cross to Bear

Meanwhile, that summer Essie moved to Mount Vernon, made the down payment on a little frame house there—a house with a front porch and a back porch and in the yard an old-fashioned rocking two-seated wooden swing that the former tenant left behind. She and Marietta loved it. They could sit outdoors all the afternoon in the back yard rocking, have a dog, a cat, canary birds, and Essie could go barefooted around the house again as she used to do down South, and fill the icebox with soft drinks and watermelon and forget the smell of wine and whiskey. Somehow she didn't miss Laura. They saw each other every night but Saturday at the church. Essie became a commuter, up and down the steps of the 125th Street Station, from Harlem to the suburbs and back by train.

What He's done for me!
What He's done for me!
I never shall forget
What He's done for me!

Now Laura had the fine apartment all to herself, which was just what Laura wished—except that she did miss Essie. And Buddy—whose birthday present had been the red car—didn't stay there as much any more, now that he could stay freely. Just like a tomcat of a man! To Laura's ears in the beauty shop came rumors, and the rumors turned out to be true. One day on Seventh Avenue Laura saw her with her own eyes sitting in the sleek new Cadillac with the top down and Buddy at the wheel. She had the kind of hair that blew in her eyes—this other woman—and was as young as Marietta.

"Jesus had a cross to bear, so has everyone," quoted the beauty shop operator who served Laura, of course to another customer. "But that pretty little model's a glamorous cross for Laura Reed to have to put up with—after all that money she's spent on that Negro Buddy. A no-good dog!"

"Them handsome dogs is the worst kind," said the customer. "I would not have no handsome man for mine, with all the women in town eying him. No, sir, not Claybelle Jones."

"Miss Jones, nor would I," said the beauty shop operator. "And if I did, I wouldn't give him a thing but my money, not my heart. But that sanctified Reed sister loves that devil. I can feel the fever in her brow since he's started acting up. I see her temples throbbing whilst I am fixing her hair. Laura's going to have nervous prostitution if she don't watch out. And all over Buddy Lomax, who everybody knows is a mother-fouler."

"A good-looking rounder!"

"The Bible says, 'As an eagle fouleth his nest!' Miss Jones, how wide do you want this blond streak I'm putting in your hair?"

"Same width as from the left eyebrow to my right," said Claybelle Jones. "Just a little blond ripple to tease the men."

"Sister Essie's got sense. She's buying herself a home in the country."

"So I heard."

"And educating her daughter."

"Pretty as Dorothy Dandridge."

"They tell me that's what started it all—Buddy tried to make Marietta."

"Which is why Essie picked up her bed and walked to Westchester. I wish Buddy would try to make me. I'd give him at least a jigger of a break."

"Buddy's a keen-looking stud."

"Heartbreaker! That Big-Eyed Buddy!"

"A cross for any woman to bear."

"Yes, Jesus, Lord!"

"Now, girl, look in the mirror. How do you like your new hair style?"

"Solid, honey, solid! That's boss!"

29

Apple of Evil

When in the dusk-dark of evening Laura's big black Cadillac drew up to the stage door of the Temple and her new little old black chauffeur jumped spryly out to open the door for her, Laura could hear inside the Tambourine Chorus:

"Listen to the lambs all a-cryin' . . ."

It sounded beautiful indeed. But since Laura did not see Buddy's car parked anywhere in the street, there was a frown on her face as she went inside and down the corridor to the big room under the stage. Upstairs the evening song service had started.

"Listen to the lambs all a-cryin'—
I want to go to heaven when I die."

The big room was empty save for Sister Mattie Morningside, the Mistress of the Robes, a title lately given that large and amiable woman who was Laura's personal saint, attendant, and caretaker of her churchly garments. She was always downstairs faithfully awaiting Laura's arrival every night.

"Evening, Sister Morningside! Ain't Sister Essie here yet?"

"No, Sister Laura. You know, since she's moved, it takes her a right smart time to get down here from the country."

"Seems so. And Brother Buddy?"

"Not yet, neither. But the chorus is all upstairs, singing wonderful. That's Sister Birdie Lee now."

"Set down! Well, I can't set down!
I just got to heaven and I can't set down!"

"I hear her," muttered Laura, "attracting attention to herself. Hang my coat up carefully on a hanger in the closet—and *lock* the closet. Minks don't grow on trees, Sister Mattie."

"Sure don't—and you got a *fine* piece of skin here for a lady minister."

"Since prostitutes dress good, and call girls and madams, there's no reason why saints shouldn't."

"Saints should look the best," said Sister Mattie as she disappeared into the anteroom. While Laura was taking the heavy costume jewelry off her arms, Buddy came in and threw his camel's hair coat over the table.

"So you beat me here tonight, heh, babes? My little red convertible can't purr like your big old car, I guess."

"You're kinder late."

"I started from the apartment just after you did."

"No stops on the way?"

"Just a nip at the Shalimar."

"Well, nip yourself on up the steps with some cases of that Holy Water for the congregation tonight."

"Hell, Laura, why didn't you let your driver pack them cases up?"

"He's a chauffeur, not a saint—paid to *drive*. But you're a part of this church now since your conversion."

"You can't say good ain't happening. Marty's grinning like a chesscat over the way his number writers have been picking up business since you been giving out them Lucky Texts—eighteen thousand dollars in this neighborhood last week."

"That ofay gangster ought to be happy."

"Laura, if you don't tell nobody, I'll let you in on a secret. Marty's gonna give you a diamond wrist watch for Christmas."

"I can sport it, too, baby."

"Marty asked me what should he give Sister Essie, but I told him to leave her be, *period*! Just don't give her nothing—and start that old hassle over right and wrong again. Seems like Essie even yet don't think *I'm* converted."

"You ain't—and I'm glad she moved that daughter of hers out of your path."

"Marietta's squab for C.J., I guess. But *you're* pigmeat for me." And he ran one hand down the neck of Laura's dress. But Laura drew back.

"Sometimes, Buddy, I'm disgusted with everything about you—but you."

He laughed. "Cut the kidding, Laura! It's hot down here. I'm gonna pack a case of Jordan Water upstairs and stand in the wings and listen to your rock and roll. Are you coming up?"

"I'll be up directly. Looks like a big crowd, so I got to robe myself sweet tonight. Believe I'll wear the scarlet with the gold stole."

"Gild your lily," said Buddy. "Decorate your righteous hide!" He disappeared into the corridor and up the iron steps to the stage with a case of Jordan Water on his shoulder, so Sister Mattie knew it was time for her to come back with the robes. She brought three of various colors for Laura's selection.

"The scarlet one tonight," said Laura, "Maybe the Nile green tomorrow."

Upstairs the music mounted and Laura knew that soon the congregation would be ready to give her a shouting welcome. The way that chorus built up the spirit, it was worth the money—even if the director had asked for a salary Laura never dreamed any church would pay a gospel musicianer. But the tambourines collected it all back, and more sometimes, in a single night.

> *"Back to the fold,*
> *How safe, how warm I feel!*
> *Back to the fold,*
> *His love alone is real!"*

Essie came in and paused at the foot of the iron stairs to drink in the music. "Sounds so good this evening."

"Long as I don't hear Birdie Lee croaking," said Laura. "I believe I'm gonna have to get rid of that old woman."

"Why, the way she hits them drums, the congregation loves her."

"That's just it. I want them to love me—and you—without Birdie's competition. Besides, she just naturally grates on my nerves."

Following Essie by a kiss or two in the hall came Marietta and C.J., bounding lightly into the room.

"Mama, we're going upstairs."

"You and C.J. both should've been up there making music at eight o'clock like the others." Laura was cross tonight.

"It's my fault, Aunt Laura," apologized Marietta. "C.J. came up to Mount Vernon to spend the afternoon with us, and I made a cake that was late getting out of the oven."

"But it was good—ummm-mmm-m!" said C.J.

"Cooking for him already, and you're not married yet. Women are fools," said Laura, looking around for her purse.

"We will be married in the spring, soon's I graduate from high school. Come on, C.J." Marietta pulled him and his guitar toward the stairs.

"He's a nice boy, Laura, and I'm so glad for my child," said Essie.

"I'm glad you got Marietta in the country. Harlem's a den o' sin," growled Laura, rummaging in her pocketbook.

"But don't you reckon our church has made it a little better? Still, I hear some peoples is taking this temple for a numbers center. Them white gangsters . . ."

"Marty and them 'gangsters' as you call 'em, squared the violations on this church. It's still a firetrap, you know."

"But we're gradually getting it repaired. And some of the money we're spending like water could . . ."

"If you're talking about my new coat, Essie, you know I always said I was going to have a real *fine* fur some day. You keep on wearing your old rags if you want to, with that same old Lenox Avenue knife of yours in that ragged pocket. What are you protecting?"

Essie laughed, "Nothing. You sure got yourself a pretty beaded purse. But why you dumping everything out on the table?"

"I'm looking for something," said Laura, as she turned the contents of her pocketbook inside out. "I thought I had some of the apple of evil in here—money. You know, I always try to carry a few greenbacks with me. But you, you put all your money except what you live on, back into this church, like a fool. At least, I finally got you to buy yourself a new white velvet robe for the pulpit—up there looking like a scrubwoman, and you the chief saint! Just being robed in goodness, you know, is not enough for the type of folks we attract. They like color, glitter, something to look at along with these fine rhythms we're putting down. I told you that Ed Sullivan mentioned our Tambourine Chorus in his column, didn't I? This church is headed for big money, girl. We're doing all right."

"I ain't for so much publicity," said Essie.

Laura was carefully putting comb, mirror, lipstick, powder, kerchiefs, and odds and ends one by one, back in her purse as the frown on her face deepened.

"Go on, Essie, get upstairs there and make your presence known, before we start an argument. Anyhow, I want to be the *last* to enter tonight. Sister Mattie, come here!"

Essie got to her knees in one corner and prayed briefly before she panted up the narrow stairs, and the Mistress of the Robes came in to see what Laura wanted.

"Sister Mattie, go up and tell Brother Buddy to come down here a minute—*now*! Suppose you set in with the chorus and sing a little. I want to speak to him *private*."

30

Rascal of God

Alone, Laura looked at herself in the mirror, carefully inspecting the flow of her scarlet robe before she flung the golden stole about her neck. Upstairs she heard the congregation shouting and clapping and she knew that Essie must have walked onto the rostrum. Suddenly there was a bitter taste in Laura's mouth and a swimming in her head.

I wish Essie would get holy enough or lazy enough or something to quit my Temple, thought Laura, but she won't. The stronger Essie gets in faith, the louder that woman sings and the stouter she sits on the rostrum—and folks just love Essie for *just sitting*. All they have to do is see her up there, and they feel happy. But look at the money I would make without her—and I wouldn't have to split it with no woman, just Buddy. Sometimes, though, I believe Buddy would cheat even me—in fact, I know it. Buddy and Essie! One's *too* honest, and the other one ain't honest enough. Jesus, I got two crosses to bear, and both of 'em's galling my back.

Laura loosened the golden strip of velvet about her neck and softened its folds as a frame for her face. Then she heard his footsteps.

"What wantest thou, Sister Laura?" Buddy mocked, head down, eyes teasing as he came in.

Laura wheeled accusingly, and there were no preliminaries. "Did you take that hundred-dollar bill out of my purse?"

"I *sure* did," smiled Buddy.

"The dough you're getting from this church is not enough?"

"It *sure* ain't," grinned Buddy.

"You're not satisfied?"

"No," smiled Buddy.

It was the sight of his big nonchalant teasing lips with the white teeth between them that infuriated Laura. "So you're planning to spend some more of my dough on that bitch, heh?"

"Watch your language, sister! What bitch?"

"You think I don't know? I mean that cheap little model you've been riding around in that convertible I gave you."

"She's no cheap little model—she can sing. She's got a contract at the

Vanguard, moving on up to the Blue Angel. Next thing you know she'll be in the Copa. Marty's underwriting her."

"Somebody'll be *undertaking* her if she don't stay out of that car I bought you. She'll be singing in the Devil's Graveyard with an everlasting contract."

"Ha-ha! Says you!"

"Says I, baby. Brazen as she is with you, it's a wonder it ain't all written up in *Jet*. It will be next week, I expect. *Lorna*—why, even her name sounds like my name!"

"She don't look like you, baby."

"No?"

"Don't kid yourself. I'm a young man, Laura. You're old enough to be my mama."

Laura stood for a moment in silence. Upstairs the choir was singing:

"God gave the people the rainbow sign—
No more water, but fire next time . . ."

"Buddy, you don't have to say things to hurt me," Laura said. "I just wondered who took my money, that's all."

"You knew who took your money," Buddy said. "I can have it, can't I?"

"Yes, Buddy, I guess you can have anything I got," she answered quietly. "But now my pocketbook's empty after you made your raid—so I might as well leave it downstairs here. I believe I'll stash it in Essie's old coat pocket."

Laura went toward the hook on the wall where Essie had hung her heavy black coat, and into Essie's pocket she put the beaded purse. For a moment her hand lingered in the pocket there. As she turned to Buddy, the long sleeves of her velvet robe covered both her hands like drooping wings.

"Maybe you can tell me," Laura said, "why it looks like, no matter what a woman does, a man can't never seem to act right? You try to treat a man nice, and looks like he has to turn around and drop the boom on you. Ain't a woman suppose to be nothing but dirt under a man's feet?"

"Just about all, in my opinion," said Buddy. "You feel so good under my feet."

"You don't try to hide *your* ways, do you?"

"Why try? You can't hide nothing from God, can you? Nor the police. So why worry? The police I can pay off—God you *pray* off."

"And me?" asked Laura.

Suddenly Buddy leaned savagely across the table. "You? I'll slap the hell out of you, if you fool with me! A woman like you is supposed to put out some dough—if you want to keep a guy like me around. I don't mean peanuts. Believe me, baby, now that you've got me, *you're gonna keep me.* I ain't gonna give you up. Besides, I'm a partner in this deal—from the Holy Water and the Lucky Texts to the tambourines. You told me, I'm a saint also. What did I go to all that trouble of getting converted for? Since I been functioning in this church, look how many more young girl members you got—just on account of me and my presence. Two beat-up old women saints like you and Essie maybe can pull in those wrecks out of the gutter like Crow-For-Day and Birdie Lee—but me, I bring in the young girls. There's something about me, Laura, that the chicks go for." He looked at her a long time, then smiled. "You admit I'm a m-a-n—*man,* don't you, kid?"

"God gave the people the rainbow sign—
No more water but fire next time. . . ."

Playful again, Buddy from behind put an arm around Laura's neck, pulled her head backward toward him, tall, and kissed her from above, "Hummm-mm-m!"

Laura suddenly thrust her tongue between his teeth. "There *is* . . . something about you, Buddy—doggone it!"

"I know, baby—so the women tell me. There's something about you, too, Laura, now that you're close. . . ."

Suddenly Laura cried, "You sweet rascal of God!"

She turned and, as she found herself in his arms, she let his lips find hers. Swiftly the wide sleeves of her scarlet robe swept upward like velvet wings and suddenly her right hand descended between his shoulder blades—and something in that hand went deeper into Buddy's body than the thrust of her tongue in his warm moist mouth.

Hurrying through the open door at that moment came Sister Birdie Lee who, at the sight of the lovers, paused politely on the threshold before crossing the room. "I'm sorry, you-all, but my kidneys is bad."

Rushing, Birdie cut across the basement toward the sign that said TOILET as Laura stepped back. Suddenly, before Birdie got where she was going, Buddy fell straight forward at Laura's feet and the startled Birdie saw him sprawled face downward on the floor with the blade of a gleaming white switchblade knife stuck in his back. The spreading ooze of blood stained his jacket.

"Oh!" said Birdie Lee. "Lemme get to the bathroom."

Birdie rushed in and closed the door. Laura stood where she was over Buddy's body, but her eyes followed the woman. "You had better not come out—you hear me, Birdie Lee? Unless you are struck dumb. Speechless! I say, struck dumb!" When Birdie pulled the chain and emerged, Laura repeated, "Did you hear what I said?"

"Yes, Sister Laura," the little black woman trembled, "I heard."

"You'd better be speechless, Birdie! If you so much as open your mouth anywhere to anybody, with my own hands I'll . . ."

As the scarlet sleeves fell back from her brown arms, Laura's fists went up into the air and their fingers opened like two frightening claws. The words choked in her throat. When she got her voice back, Laura shooed the petrified Birdie to the door. "Get back upstairs to your drums, you evil hussy! Give me a *big* drum roll when I make my entrance to the pulpit. You hear me—a *big* drum roll!"

Birdie tumbled up the stairs. From the pocket of Essie's coat Laura took her purse, looked down at Buddy motionless on the floor, then ascended to the altar where the music swirled.

31

Everlasting Arm

"Oh, this world is just my dressing room,
But now, at last, dear Lord, I'm coming home.
Down in the mire too long my feet have trod.
Now, at last, I'll make my home in God."

Walking in rhythm out from the wings, her scarlet robes swaying, Laura advanced toward the congregation as a thousand hands clapped in time to the music, the tambourines trilled, the drums rolled, and the trumpet gleamed, its notes round and full.

"Thank God!" said Laura. "Thank Him for His son, for the Holy Ghost, for Sister Essie, for the Tambourine Chorus, the Gloriettas, and for this great church here tonight. Also for this Holy Water, precious fluid from the Jordan, imported just for you. Blessed water to purify your home, one dollar a bottle, friends, just one dollar! While I sing, ushers, pass amongst the people with these bottles. If they run low, there's more here beside me on the rostrum. While Sister Essie goes into the wings for meditation, pass amongst the people with the water."

Essie, who never stayed on the platform for this performance, rose, bowed her head, and walked off while Laura sang:

"I'm going to lay down my soul
At the foot of the cross,
Yes, and tell my Jesus
Just what sin has cost . . ."

The Tambourine Choir joined with her in the singing, so loud and strong that no one heard the startled scream that suddenly echoed from the room below the stage.

"Now, comes the time for testimonials," said Laura, "for one and all to declare his determination. And I ask you with a song:

"Who will be a witness for my Lord?
For my Lord? For my Lord?
Who will be a witness for my Lord
On the day of jubilee?"

It had not occurred to Laura that a cracked old voice would sing out behind her without missing a beat on the drums:

"I will be a witness for my Lord!
For my Lord! Yes, for my Lord!
I will be a witness for my Lord
On the day of jubilee!"

And at that moment the spotlight of the spirit fell on Birdie Lee who took the song away from the star. Birdie Lee could sing louder than Laura.

This just is *not* my night, Laura thought, wheeling to stare at the little old drummer in the corner above the chorus. "Well, since Birdie Lee seems to want to take over," she said to Marietta seated in the front row of the singers, "you go downstairs and tell your mother she can return from her meditations and be a witness, too."

Birdie Lee ceased her drumming and stood up defiantly to testify. Laura, thinking fast, took a seat in her big red chair behind the rostrum and said "Amen!" Suddenly, a serpent with a diamond in its head whispered to Laura as Birdie Lee talked.

"I want to tell you-all what it means to be a witness, a witness for God, and a witness for men and women, too," cried Birdie. "I were in a trial once, a court trial and I lied. I let an innocent man go to jail for a crime he didn't do, to protect some old Negro I thought I loved. Another man, innocent as a lamb, served time. But that old Negro I lied for lived to beat up, and cut up and shoot up two or three more people. In fact, that man did not appreciate what I did for him by not telling. Fact is, he lived to kick my—excuse me, I meant to say, to mistreat me, too. That man were so mean he wouldn't let me do a damn, excuse me, I mean not a blessed thing. I'm just excited tonight, folks. But I tries always to keep bad words out of my mouth, now that I'm a Christian woman. What I'm trying to say to everybody this evening is, that when the time comes, in God's name, I got a determination, and my determination is *I'm gonna testify!*" And her speech blended into song, the old song that Birdie liked to sing as she picked up her drumsticks and started to drum.

"I'm gonna testify!
Yes, I'm gonna testify!
I'm gonna testify till the day I die—
Gonna tell the truth
For the truth don't lie.
Folks, I'm gonna testify!"

She fixed her gaze on Laura and sent her voice darting down from her corner across the rostrum and out to the people.

"I did not know such strength I'd find.
Thank God A-Mighty, I'm a gospel lion!
Things I've seen, I cannot keep.
Thank God A-Mighty, God does not sleep!
I'm gonna testify! Yes, testify—
Tell the truth—For the truth don't lie.
Yes, I'm gonna testify!"

"Aunt Laura! Laura! Aunt Laura!" It was Marietta's voice calling shrill and frightened from the wings.

Laura rose and addressed the church. "Excuse me, saints, let me go see what little Sister Marietta wants so urgent. She's calling. Till I resume my seat on the rostrum, we'll turn the services over to our beloved deacon known in love to all of us as Brother Crow-For-Day. Deacon, come forward, and raise a song."

"Leaning, leaning . . .
Leaning, leaning,
On the everlasting arm . . ."

As the massed chorus raised its hardy voices behind her, Laura walked in her scarlet robe with long sleeves flowing toward the steps that led below.

If the Tambourine Chorus had not been singing so lustily behind Crow-For-Day, those on the rostrum might have heard a piercing wail of pretended anguish beneath the stage, and Laura's voice crying, "Essie, you've killed Buddy! Essie, you done killed Buddy! Oh-ooo-oo-o! I know you never did like him, now you've killed him! You killed my Buddy!"

32

Judas in Scarlet

Laura groveled on the basement floor, careful never to touch Buddy's blood, nor put her hands near the body. "Buddy! Buddy, baby, darling! What she done to you? What's Essie done to you?"

Sensing something wrong, from her place in the chorus, Sister Mattie Morningside came bustling down the iron steps in the room beneath the stage. What she saw caused her to stop in her tracks and shake like jelly on a plate.

"Police! Sister Mattie, get the police," screamed Laura. "Look what Essie Johnson's done done to Buddy Lomax."

"Jesus, help us, Jesus!" Sister Mattie moaned on her way to the street in search of the Law.

When the three were alone, Laura turned on the silent Essie who stood as if in a trance with Marietta weeping beside her. "So this is the way you even scores, heh, Essie? It's *your* knife stuck in his back!"

"Laura, you know I didn't do it."

"There's blood on your robe."

"When I bent over him to see if I could help him, I got blood all on me."

"Why didn't you help Buddy when he was living? No, you wouldn't do that! You wouldn't help us then. You're too good, too sanctified. But he was smart. Buddy had ideas, the Holy Water, them Lucky Texts, ideas for making you and me both rich and happy, but you hated him! So holy, you! Now you've up and committed murder! How could you do this to me, Essie? How could you do it?"

"You know I didn't, Laura."

"Mama wouldn't do anything like that," cried Marietta. "She couldn't! You know she couldn't."

"That's what you think, Little Miss Holier-Than-Thou. I've known your mother longer than you have, and she's always carried a knife."

"Don't worry, honey," said Essie gently to her daughter, "God will straighten this out."

Two policemen, one white and one colored, rushed in followed by the panting Sister Momingside and Laura's wizened little chauffeur. The scarlet sleeves of Sister Laura's robe waved wildly toward Buddy, then toward Essie.

"Look, officers! Her knife in his back and nobody down here but her. Blood on her robe! Essie Johnson killed Buddy. Brother Buddy! Oh-ooo-oo-o! and he just got converted last month!"

Laura buried her head on Sister Mattie Morningside's ample bosom and sobbed for the benefit of the Law.

"Don't nobody touch the body," said the white officer. "We'll send for the coroner." To the colored officer he said, "Put that woman in the squad car." The woman his thumb indicated was Essie.

Upstairs the church was singing "Get on Board, Little Children" while tambourines shook ecstatically.

33

Watch with Me

By and by, when the morning comes,
Saints and sinners all are gathered home.
I'll tell the story how we overcome,
And I'll understand it better by and by . . .

"If they send me to the electric chair," mused Essie, "I'll understand it better after I get to Beulah. But I don't want to die, nor be put away in the penitentiary for life. I got my child to live for, I got my daughter, and I got my church."

Watch with me one hour
While I go yonder and pray.
Just watch with me one hour
While I go yonder and pray . . .

There were exactly twenty-four bars to her cell and Essie sat behind all twenty-four. She had never been in jail before. It was like being in hell. That night cold sweat popped out on her brow—as she figured sweat must have popped out on the brow of Christ when He was praying in the Garden.

Were you there when they crucified my Lord?
Were you there when they nailed Him to the Cross?
Oh, sometimes it causes me to tremble, tremble!
Were you there when they crucified my Lord?

In the dark of the garden, alone, Jesus, who had said, "Before the cock crow, thou shalt deny me thrice," said also, "Friend, wherefore art thou come?" And Judas kissed Jesus on the cheek and betrayed Him. Peter said, "I do not know the man." And the cock crowed.

I must walk this lonesome valley,
Got to walk it for myself.
Nobody else can walk it for me.
I got to walk it for myself.

The old melodies came back to Essie in a flood of song as she sat alone in her cell.

The blood came tricklin' down
And He never said a mumblin' word.
Not a word, not a word, not a word . . .

They plaited a crown of thorns and they put it on His head.

And they pierced Him in the side
And He never said a mumblin' word . . .

If Jesus could stand what they done to Him, I reckon I can stand what's done to me. Only if I just had my Bible to read! After all, I reckon

It's nobody's fault but mine,
If I die and my soul gets lost
It's nobody's fault but mine.

I should have riz in my wrath and cleaned house, Essie thought staring at the walls—which is what I guess is the matter with me all these years, setting—just setting doing nothing but accepting what comes, receiving the Lord's blessing whilst the eagle foulest His nest, till the sinner gets struck down by somebody else with my own knife in his back. I let Buddy fill the house of God with sin, and vanities of vanities take over, and Laura parade her fur coat and purr in her fine car before them poor people what brought us their hard-earned money for God's work—to which only such a little miteful did go. Religion has got no business being made into a gyp game. Whatever part of God is in anybody *is not to be played with*—and everybody has got a part of God in them.

I let Laura play with God—me, Essie Belle Johnson—when I should have riz in my wrath and cleaned house.

34

One of the Least

The next morning Essie stood with her hands on the bars and looked at Marietta. "Daughter, I did not mean to ever let you see your mama in a place like this."

"But, Mama, I got news, news, good news! They found fingerprints on that knife—just like Aunt Laura's. And, Mama, Birdie Lee, Sister Birdie Lee went to the police and told them last night how some hoodlums had already threatened to kill her. But this morning she girded herself in the strength of the Lord, and got herself a lawyer, and went to the Precinct House and told them that when she ran downstairs to the toilet Sunday night she saw Aunt Laura with her hand at Buddy's back, and that knife was there, too—*in his back*. Then Buddy fell flat on his face in front of her before she could get to the bathroom, and he bled. Birdie Lee swears Aunt Laura killed Buddy herself just before Laura came upstairs for services. And Mama, your lawyer says you'll be out soon, maybe by afternoon, quick as he gets down here with the papers. And Sister Birdie Lee, she's outside in the Reception Room waiting to see you now, but they wouldn't let her in being she's not a relative, unless you say you want to see her. She's brought you a Bible. You'd like to see her, wouldn't you, Mama?"

"Birdie Lee and the Bible *both* your mama wants to see, Marietta."

"Then I'll tell them to let her in. And I'll be back to get you with the lawyer."

When the turnkey brought Birdie Lee down through the aisle of cells she began to shout *Hallelujahs* even before she saw Essie, and *Bless Gods* and *Amens*. She cried as she stood before the cell, "I have brought the Book. But before I give it to you, Essie, I want to read thereout and therefrom and I want you to listen—Matthew 25—for Sister Essie: 'I was an hungered, and ye gave me meat. I was thirsty, and ye gave me drink. I was a stranger, and ye took me in.' In spite of Laura Reed! Sister Essie, the light is the truth, and the truth don't lie. 'Naked, and ye clothed me. I was sick, and ye visited me. I was in prison,' yes, the prison of my sins, 'and ye came unto me.'"

Birdie slapped her hand down on the Bible.

"It's right here in His holy Word, Essie, how you took me out of the gutter of Lenox Avenue, raised me up to the curbstone of redemption, brought me into your gospel band, and let me shake my tambourine to the glory of God and drum my way to jubilation. Sister Essie, you did that for me! Gangsters or no gangsters, Laura or no Laura, it's my determination to testify exactly who stuck that knife in Big-Eyed Buddy's carcass—to take the stand and tell the truth—for the truth don't lie! And listen to this text through your bars of sorrow, Sister Essie, for it appears as if these words was writ for you—Matthew 25:40—'Verily,' it says here, 'Verily I say unto you, inasmuch as ye have done it unto one of the *least* of these'—and I was the least—'ye have done it unto me!' Hallelujah! Oh, if I had just brought my tambourine, I would shake it here in jail to God's glory, to you, Sister Essie, who by your goodness lifted me up out of the muck and mire of Harlem and put my feet on the rock of grace where I, Birdie Lee, can stand and redeem myself of the lies I once told and the souls sent to hell—this time to testify the truth! Praise God, your Honor, Judge Almighty, I'm gonna testify!"

35

As in a Dream

When the jailers brought her lunch, Essie was reading in her Book the verses Birdie had found for her. She saw in her mind's eye Laura who had clothed herself in a scarlet robe and had made her buy a white one, and she remembered white being for purity. And she thought, Laura brought me to God, but I was too slothful to save my friend from sin. I did not try hard enough in God's ways. But I pray now in my heart for Laura.

It seemed almost like a dream, or a scene in a movie, that now a key should turn in the door at the end of the cell block, and the door should open, and clank, and close, and a warden should lead down the aisle a fine frame of a woman with her head down, not looking to the right or the left as she passed, until Essie cried, "Laura!"

There with her hands on the bars, with the bars between them, stood her partner in song. A long pause, then, "Essie, I'm sorry," Laura whispered hoarsely, "sorry as hell for what I did to you—and with your knife, too. The Law knows now that I did it. I confessed. I might as well. That little rat of a Birdie Lee put the finger on me. I never did like Birdie. But I would have told, anyhow. Believe me or not, Essie, I got down on my knees last night and prayed. I couldn't sleep for thinking about you in jail, and Buddy dead. The two people I loved most in my life! And the fault mine! I would have told the police anyhow I did it. Essie, can you find it in your heart to just, maybe, pray for me?"

"You're my friend, Laura. In spite of all, you been my friend. In my heart eternal, I pray for you—and I'll see that you get a lawyer, too."

"A dozen lawyers phoned me already this morning. They think I got money. But I took all the hundred-dollar bills I had stashed away in drawers and car pockets and handkerchief boxes, and places, and put them in the bank early this morning when it opened, in the church's name before the police came to question me. Essie, I'll come before the bar of justice as poor as I was that night when we left out of that tenement and took our stand for the first time to raise a song on Lenox Avenue. My car, the dealers can take back. It's not paid for. I have nothing now, Essie, but Jesus—since He comes free." Laura smiled a wry smile. "Maybe somebody'll buy me a drink."

It was a long cell block and they locked Laura in a cell far down at the end of the corridor, so far away that Laura did not hear Essie sobbing. Essie sobbed as quietly as she could, but it was hard for a big woman like Essie to weep so bitterly without a sound.

36

Jubilation

"What He's done for me!
What He's done for me!
I never shall forget
What He's done for me!
He took my feet out of the mirey clay.
He set them on a rock to stay. . . ."

"I never shall forget," cried Essie, "what He's done for me."

A thousand people in the temple, and a hundred in the chorus behind her sang.

"He put a song in my soul today.
What He's done for me!"

"Done for all of us," cried Essie. "Praise His name! All you who helped to make this church, to raise its walls from the curbstone to this rostrum, helped me to buy the first tambourine I ever had in my hand! Tambourine Temple, I want to tell you what, with His help, we're gonna do. Here on this very corner, I visions me a Rock. Today I seen the contractor. We're gonna turn that big room downstairs into a pretty day nursery where you mothers that goes to work can leave your children. Oh, Rock of Comfort, free from worry! I seen the real estate man. We're gonna buy that old building next door and turn it into a clubhouse where you can meet to have your anniversaries and parties and such. Oh, joyful Rock! That empty vacant lot three doors down, we're gonna turn into an outdoor playground so our teen-agers can play basketball in summer and flood it with ice so they can skate in winter. Happy Rock! Oh, friends, so many nice things we're gonna do for this Harlem of ours with His help! And now, folks, another announcement, my earthly aid from this day on, my staff of youth in this church and in this pulpit, is my daughter, Marietta! She's going to study next fall at the Lincoln Hospital to be a nurse so she can help me take care of the sick in this church. While I pray with the sick, Marietta can tend them and relieve their pain. Come forward, daughter."

"Jehovah God!" cried Birdie Lee. "Jehovah God!"

Marietta stepped down shyly from the choir. Essie beamed.

"This is Marietta Johnson. But there's more I want to tell you about her. She won't be Johnson long. She will have a helper or he will have his helper, both will help each other, the son of this temple, our son, C.J., to be my son-in-law."

"Amen!" affirmed the crowd. "God bless them both." Then silence that Marietta might speak.

"It's wonderful to be in love with God," the girl said, "and with this church, with you-all before me, and C.J."

Essie beckoned C.J. forward to join hands with Marietta. "Now, let them praise God together, and all of us praise God with them—Marietta, C.J.—*our children!* Hit your guitar, son! Let my daughter sing."

> *"Rise and shine*
> *And give God the glory!"*

Shake, tambourines, shake! Help 'em, Crow-For-Day, help 'em! Drum it, Birdie Lee! Drum to the Lord God Jehovah! Drum for the least of His servants, me, Essie Belle Johnson! Halleloo! And, folks—

> *"If you've got a tambourine,*
> *Shake it to the glory of God!*
> *Glory! Glory! Glory!*
> *Shake it to the glory of God!*
> *Tambourines! Tambourines!*
> *Tambourines to glory!*
> *Tambourines!*
> *Tambourines*
> *To glory!"*